Sep 17

REAPING THE AURORA

DAW Books proudly presents
the fantasy novels of
Joshua Palmatier:

SHATTERING THE LEY
THREADING THE NEEDLE
REAPING THE AURORA

The Throne of Amenkor:
THE SKEWED THRONE
THE CRACKED THRONE
THE VACANT THRONE

REAPING THE AURORA

JOSHUA PALMATIER

DAW BOOKS, INC.

DONALD A. WOLLHEIM, FOUNDER

375 Hudson Street, New York, NY 10014

ELIZABETH R. WOLLHEIM
SHEILA E. GILBERT
PUBLISHERS
www.dawbooks.com

DAW TRADEMARK REGISTERED
U.S. PAT. AND TM. OFF. AND FOREIGN COUNTRIES
—MARCA REGISTRADA
HECHO EN U.S.A.

PRINTED IN THE U.S.A.

This book is dedicated to my agent, Joshua Bilmes, who took me on mid-series. May all of our hopes and dreams for my career come true.

PART I:

Tumbor

One

"KARA WAS RIGHT. Erenthrall *has* completely changed."

Allan didn't react to Bryce's words. They were standing on the edge of a cliff looking down onto the city they'd once called home, although the majority of that city had sunk a thousand feet into the plains.

Allan could pick out pieces he recognized: the shattered stubs of the towers of Grass in the center of the city, the districts that surrounded them, including Hedge where he'd lived with Moira and Morrell, and the glittering waters of the rivers threading through the destruction. If he shaded his eyes, he could see the twin waterfalls cascading down into the new depression, hazed by distance. After that, the rivers had mostly returned to their natural beds below, although he didn't know what paths they were following once they converged and reached this side of the city. Based on the lack of water flowing through the river's original bed south of here, he'd guess it had found an outlet underground. Or through the depths of the massive cracks that riddled the plains in all directions from where Erenthrall had once sat.

But he wasn't here to determine what had happened to the river.

"What do you see?" he asked, cutting across the low conversations that had broken out behind him. He faced the rest of the scouting party sent by Kara, Marcus, and Commander Ty from the Needle. There were twenty of them, including Bryce, the Wolf pack leader Grant, three of Grant's Wolves, nine fighters—a mixture of Bryce's Dogs from the Hollow and Ty's enforcers, although they all wore the enforcer uniforms now—the Wielder Dylan, and four of the common folk from the Needle led by Gaven. They'd brought four wagons with them.

They were arrayed on a street that had once led straight toward the heart of the city, the remains of collapsed buildings of one of the outermost districts surrounding them.

"I see a giant pit in the earth where Erenthrall used to be," Grant growled. He stood a few paces behind Allan, arms crossed over his broad chest, his half-altered wolfish face twisted into a frown. His nostrils flared as he scented the air, one ear twitching. "This was caused by the ley?"

"According to Kara, yes," Dylan said. "The instability of the ley caused the quakes. Then, when the distortion over Erenthrall began to collapse, it destroyed a significant section of the earth. You can see it." He climbed down from his seat on the wagon next to Gaven and stepped forward, limping only slightly from the knee injury he'd received during his last visit to Erenthrall. A few of those scattered around the broken lip moved forward as well. "See the ring that surrounds the city, where the buildings and streets appear to be churned up? That's where the edge of the distortion was. It shredded everything in its path as it closed. The entire central part of the city would have been nothing but rubble, like that ring, if Kara hadn't managed to heal the distortion."

"That doesn't explain why the city sank a thousand feet below the level of the plains," Bryce pointed out.

"Kara said there were massive caverns underneath the city. The land was stable until the quakes, and then it was weakened further when the distortion began to close. After that, it was only a matter of time before the caverns collapsed, taking the city with them."

"I'd say the city survived the collapse rather well," Gaven added.

"There's been additional damage—from the quakes and the collapse." Allan gestured with one hand. "It looks like the southern part of the city suffered the worst. I don't see many buildings left intact there. And the western sections had already been decimated by the fires immediately after the Shattering. But the northern and eastern districts appear to have been mostly unaffected."

Bryce swore.

"What?" one of the enforcers asked. "What does that mean?"

"It means that there's a good chance that the Rats, Tunnelers, and Temerites survived the collapse largely unscathed. They may still be out there, although I don't see any obvious movement from here."

"We wouldn't," Allan said. "The towers in Grass are blocking our view of those districts. And they'd be too distant, regardless. Even the towers are hazy from here."

"I don't even see movement in the nearest streets below."

Allan dragged his gaze from the far towers of Grass to the districts beneath them. He stepped forward, a chunk of stone cobble at the jagged road's edge dislodged by the movement, plummeting toward the city below. It was like looking down onto an eerily detailed map, the streets laid out in a grid, the blocks in between filled with debris. A few mostly intact buildings remained—a tenement here and there with a façade missing, a stone arch over a street, a toppled statue in a park or stone fountain in the center of a plaza. The sun was almost directly overhead, so there were few shadows. If there had been someone out in the open, close by, they would have seen them.

But that meant little. There were still plenty of places inside of buildings for the survivors of Erenthrall's second cataclysm to remain hidden.

"I don't trust it," Allan said. "Not after what happened the last time we came to Erenthrall. I want everyone on alert. We're here to figure out who's survived and what shape they're in, nothing more. If we can avoid meeting anyone, that would be best."

"Who lived in this section before the distortion's collapse?" Gaven asked.

"The Gorrani."

Nearly everyone stilled. It had only been a month since the Gorrani who had lived near Tumbor had attacked the Needle and been nearly wiped out by Prime Wielder Lecrucius' white wall of ley. Four thousand had died almost instantly, only a thousand escaping. They had retreated to the south, toward the Gorrani homeland, but it was possible that those who remained in Erenthrall knew. If so, they wouldn't welcome anyone who wasn't Gorrani, especially those from the Needle.

Bryce stepped up to Allan's side. "We have a more pressing issue than the Gorrani."

"What's that?"

The former Dog motioned toward where the roadway they'd been following through the outskirts of Erenthrall broke off a few feet from where they stood. "How in hells are we going to get down there?"

It took them the rest of the day to backtrack far enough through what little remained of Erenthrall on top of the cliff to one of the cracks in the earth that was wide enough and with a shallow enough grade to accommodate the wagons. They camped at the edge of the crack, on the open plains, while Grant sent his Wolves down into the depths to scout out a safe path for the wagons. Once they descended into the depths, they wouldn't be able to see whether they were headed toward Erenthrall or traveling toward a dead end.

The next day, an hour after sunrise, they slid into the shadows, the walls of the crevasse rising up on either side as Gaven heighed the horses carefully over the rough scree. Allan couldn't suppress a chill across his shoulders as they descended, shadows engulfing them, with only a thin band of blue sky overhead that narrowed the farther they went. Torches were lit and passed along the length of the small caravan, the Wolves leading them forward, bypassing larger chasms and off-shoots in the maze of cracked earth. Without them, Allan would have been lost within an hour. Occasionally, clumps of dirt and dust cascaded down from above, showering them with grit, the earth still settling even after a month. At one point, they hit a section where the side wall of the chasm had collapsed and they were forced to wait while the Wolves found another way around it.

By the time the crevasse widened and they finally emerged onto a rough slope of rock and earth that ended on a street filled with debris from the collapsed buildings on either side, Allan's skin was prickling with apprehension brought on by the suffocating, confined space. He breathed in deeply as he stepped out into the open and rolled his shoulders free of the tension he'd felt escalating all day. The sun hovered above the western lip of the sunken city, still hours from true sunset but casting a long shadow across Erenthrall's remains. Over half of the city was cloaked in an early dusk, only the jagged tops of the towers in Grass and the easternmost cliffs and districts still lit by sunlight. The edge of the crevasse was high enough they could see out over the rooftops of the nearest buildings, which were two or three stories high at most in this district.

The first thing Allan noticed was—

"Fire!" Dylan barked, then winced as his voice carried out over the nearest buildings and echoed in the chasm behind them. Bryce glared at him, along with at least five of the other Dogs and enforcers as they emerged from the chasm.

"So much for remaining cautious," someone muttered.

Allan ignored the comment. "It looks like signal fires, clustered in an area to the northwest of Grass. It could be the Temerites, it's hard to tell. Too distant for us to worry about now. I don't see anything closer."

"The Wolves report no one in the immediate area," Grant said.

"Then we should set up camp here for the night. Bryce, see if any of these buildings are safe enough for us to shelter in. Find one easy to defend, if you can. Gaven—"

"I know the routine," the older member of the Hollow grumbled, already reaching behind him into the stash of supplies they'd brought with them. "Are we going to need a fire, or will we have access to the ley?"

Dylan closed his eyes, brow creased in concentration, as the rest of those with them broke into action. Bryce was already ordering the enforcers and Dogs out into the surrounding area. Those there to help Gaven were digging into the supplies as well, even before Dylan opened his eyes and answered.

"Like Kara predicted, now that the nodes that were locked within Erenthrall are open, the ley in the immediate area has mostly stabilized. I can tap into it and create a heating stone without any trouble."

"Then there's no threat of a quake or any ley geysers?" Allan asked.

Dylan shrugged. "The system isn't completely stable. A few of the nodes were destroyed by the collapse of the distortion, but I don't think we'll have any quakes. Kara managed to secure most of the ley lines in the city from the Needle before we left. Anything we feel will be minor adjustments made by the lines themselves locally. It's the distortion over Tumbor we'll have to worry about. Any shifts in the ley there may be felt here as aftershocks."

"So it's uncertainty as usual," Gaven grumbled under his breath as he walked past Allan. Then, louder: "Dylan, get down here. I'm going to want that heating stone."

The ex-Dog spared one last glance toward the cluster of fires to the north before descending to the rubble-strewn street. The quakes had lessened since Kara had healed the distortion over Erenthrall and restored some of the ley lines, compensating for the sinking of the city,

which had lowered nearly all the nodes. He didn't understand how the
ley structure worked, but Kara had obviously repaired a significant section of it. There was concern about the distortion over Tumbor, much
larger than the one that had encompassed Erenthrall, but she and the
other Wielders at the Needle were already considering how to heal that
one. Once they freed Tumbor using the new Nexus they'd created at
the Needle, they could repair the distortions over the rest of the major
cities that hadn't yet quickened and then bring the entire system back
into some semblance of order.

But that was the Wielders' problem. Allan was more concerned with
the dangers presented by the various groups who threatened the Needle and, to a lesser extent, the Hollow. Most of those groups resided
here in Erenthrall—or they had before the city had sunk into the plains.
But there were still the Gorrani and the group at Haven who had attacked the Hollow a few months before. Baron Aurek, the Haven's
leader, had been killed at the Needle, but his second-in-command,
Devin, was still unaccounted for. Allan wanted to find out who now
controlled Erenthrall and whether they were a danger to the Needle,
and also what had happened to Haven, if possible.

He halted in the center of the street and scanned the activity, Bryce's
men calling out to one another as they picked their way through the
buildings, their attention mostly on the tallest—a three-story apartment building with only minimal damage along one wall and one corner of the roof collapsed. Gaven was already setting up a fire pit before
it, Dylan concentrating on the flat stone he'd placed in its center, one
hand splayed over its surface. A spit was being erected, others breaking
into their food stock, pots in hand. The Wolves were pacing restlessly
around Grant, who stood to one side, observing everything with his
usual intensity. Since the Gorrani attack on the walls of the Needle,
Allan had grown used to the pack leader's brooding presence. He spoke
little, yet noted everything.

Allan headed toward him, satisfied everyone was busy. He raised a
hand and called out, "Bryce!" motioning the Dog toward him for a
small conference.

The Wolves eyed them both warily as they approached their pack
leader, one of them settling down by Grant's side. The others continued pacing behind him.

"Report."

"It looks like that three-story building will serve our purposes for now," Bryce said. "The enforcers are searching it, looking for any signs of recent tenants. I've set the Dogs up on patrol, about a block out from here. They're checking the surrounding buildings just in case."

Grant rumbled, an impatient sound coming from deep in his chest. "What do you need from the Wolves?"

"I know you're here to find and recruit any Wolves remaining in the city," Allan said, "and to find your wife, but I'm concerned about the Gorrani who held these southern districts. We haven't seen any sign of them since we arrived. I'd like to know where they've hidden themselves."

"If they survived the quakes," Bryce added.

"I can search the southern part of the city with my pack tonight. We'll look for our brethren and the Gorrani. We can cover more area without the rest of you slowing us down." Grant hesitated, then added, "You haven't forgotten the Wolves still trapped in the shard Kara mentioned?"

"No, I haven't forgotten. We're going to see if Dylan can free the Wolves and the people still trapped there as soon as we know that the area is safe."

"Then we'll be back before sunrise."

Grant spun on his heel, emitting a low growl, the three Wolves halting and listening intently before loping out ahead of him, vanishing into the shadows of the crumbling city without a sound. Allan and Bryce watched Grant's back until he turned a corner.

"Do you think he'll find any other Wolves?" Bryce asked.

"Yes. We know there were some trapped in the distortion—those who were following Hagger, for one. And I'm certain the auroral lights have transformed others since the Shattering."

"I'm surprised he didn't have Morrell change him back to being fully human as soon as she arrived at the Needle."

Allan tensed. He still wasn't comfortable with the idea that his daughter could heal others simply by touching them. Watching her change Drayden from Wolf form back to human had been disturbing, but he'd been able to ignore it by focusing on rescuing Kara and the others from the Needle. Morrell had only been at the Needle for a few days before Kara approached him about returning to Erenthrall with this group, providing him with another distraction.

"He'll have better luck convincing any Wolves he finds to join him if he's partially transformed," he said curtly, then faced Bryce and changed the subject. "What did Kara tell you before we left?"

"That we were to scout out Erenthrall, determine the lay of the land, and return. If we ran across any food or supplies, bring them with us, but that wasn't the main goal."

"That's the gist of it. But there's something more. Besides rescuing that family from the shard that was left behind, and seeing what groups have survived and how they've changed without the distortion blocking the center of the city, we're also supposed to see if we can find some allies."

"Allies? Here? Everyone has either tried to kill us or has traded us away for food."

"Not everyone. The Temerites left our scavenging parties alone."

"That's because we stayed clear of their enclave when we were here. You know they clashed with the Rats and some of the other groups to the east."

"Kara's got it in her head that we should be trying to work with the groups here in Erenthrall, rather than fight with them over the resources released from the distortion. Before we left the Needle, she told me to try to contact the Temerites to see if they'd be interested in some type of arrangement."

"What kind of arrangement?"

"Mutual trade between the Needle and Erenthrall. Help establishing a more solid presence here in the city. A coalition against the less desirable groups here, like the Rats." Allan shrugged. "Whatever I can work out."

"And you think that's possible?"

Allan didn't want to admit that he'd given Kara the idea while they'd been captured by the Tunnelers, so he simply raised his eyebrows. "Why not? As you said, we steered clear of the Temerites when we were here before. Now that we have the resources of the Needle, maybe we can use them to regain some control of the chaos here."

Bryce broke into mumbled curses, then planted his hands on his hips in resignation. The tension in Allan's shoulders relaxed slightly; he hadn't looked forward to arguing with Bryce if he'd taken exception to the idea. "How are you going to approach the Temerites? Just walk up to their wall—if they still have one—and knock on their door?"

"If necessary. But if another opportunity arises, I'll take it. I wanted you to know, so that the Dogs and enforcers would be prepared." He began to walk toward where Gaven and the others were now stirring the contents of a pot resting on the heating stone, two hares rotating on the spit to one side. Bryce hung back a moment, then followed. The scent of roasting meat struck and Allan's nostrils flared as he involuntarily sucked in a deep breath. He picked up his pace, even though he knew the meal wasn't ready yet.

Bryce caught up to him and asked, "What's the plan for tomorrow, then?"

"Unless Grant reports something unusual after his excursion tonight, we'll cut across Erenthrall, through some of the districts that were trapped in the distortion, and try to free those Wolves and that family from the shard. After that . . . we'll see."

"What did you find?"

Grant had barely emerged from the gray shadows of dawn, but Allan had been watching for him. The large man huffed as he stalked forward, his furred face creased with a scowl of worry. Allan's eyebrows rose when five Wolves emerged from the darkness behind him. "Two more of our brethren. There were others, but they fled like prey." His lip curled in disdain. "We will find them."

"What about the Gorrani?"

"We hunted their old territory, but they were not there. Their scent is strong in that area, though, and in the part of the old city that used to be trapped in the distortion nearby." His gaze shifted toward where the rest of the camp had begun to rouse, Gaven already cooking by the heating stone, Bryce's men donning swords as they ate. "Are we moving?"

"Any idea where the Gorrani went?" Allan countered.

Grant returned his attention to the ex-Dog. "To the cliffs to the south. We could see their fires."

"Will they be a problem?"

"Not if we skirt their territory. They are foraging, like rabbits."

"Then, yes, we're moving." Allan spun back to the camp, giving Bryce a signal, the Dog calling out orders. The activity in the camp picked up, everyone scarfing down what they could, while Gaven scrambled to collect everything and load the wagons.

"We aren't staying here?" Grant asked.

"I don't know if we'll be able to make it back, so we're taking every-thing with us. I don't trust Erenthrall anymore."

Within twenty minutes, they left the three-story building behind, dawn's light pulling the ruins of Erenthrall from the shadows. Grant's Wolves vanished, although their pack leader stayed with Allan. Bryce sent out scouts. They headed straight toward where Kara had described the shard she'd left behind, even though it would take them through part of the released section of the city.

They reached the churned-up edge of the circle where the distor-tion had been by noon without encountering anyone. The demarca-tion between the earthquake-cracked roadway and the utter destruction caused by the distortion's collapse was dramatic. The road simply cut off, the ground inside the collapse splintered and broken, granite sliced into random blocks and thrown into a haphazard pile. The rub-ble had been dragged toward the center of the distortion—toward Grass—churned into a heap a hundred feet wide before Kara had managed to heal the distortion from within. Gaven groaned when he saw the pile of stone, but a quick glance to either side revealed that there would be no going around it. The residue of debris arced off in either direction, nearly uniform in height. The only option was to climb over.

They cleared the worst of the shattered stone, creating a narrow path for the horses and wagons, then continued onward, losing an hour of time. But once they'd passed inside the ring, spirits improved. This part of Erenthrall had been caught inside the distortion and hadn't been affected by the quakes. Buildings were more intact, the damage caused by the Shattering. Bryce sent out his enforcers to scour the closest buildings as they moved, most reporting back that many of the homes and businesses hadn't been looted yet.

Then they crossed a threshold and the tenor of the buildings changed. Allan thought at first that they'd passed into a new district, the stone of the cobbles and the surrounding buildings suddenly ancient, his skin prickling with age. He drew in a deep breath of unease, the air tainted with dust and decay, the scent thickening.

"What happened here?" Bryce asked, drifting closer to Allan as they progressed.

They passed a reddish-brown building, the stone façade sliced diagonally across two floors. The stone below the slice was a vibrant color, that above faded as if bleached by sunlight.

Allan grunted in sudden understanding. "This section was in one of the shards where time ran faster. The bleached stone feels older because it is."

Bryce shuddered and unconsciously picked up his pace.

They slipped from the decaying stone into a new section.

A few hours later, they neared an area where all the buildings were shrouded in a fine layer of spider's silk. The enforcers clustered about the wagons as they slid past, the horses snorting and stamping their feet, eyes wide in fear. Holes penetrated the layered silk, boring through doorways and windows into darkness. Staring into those depths, Allan's skin crawled, his palms suddenly clammy. Something deep in the darkness shifted with the scrape of skittering feet, and a section of the webbing trembled, although Allan saw nothing.

Beside him, Grant bared his teeth and growled, the sound a low and dangerous rumble in his chest. "Don't go any closer," he said, his voice quiet. "It's watching us."

They edged beyond, Allan not relaxing until they'd turned a corner and the eerie tenements were left behind. "What was it?"

"Men were transformed into more than Wolves after the Shattering."

They never entered Grass, passing by the truncated towers a few districts away. But dusk began to fall before they were near the ring of destruction on the far side of Erenthrall. Allan ordered a halt, and they camped in the gardens of what was once a lord's manse, behind its walls. Once again, they could see firelight to the northeast, closer now. To the south, fires lined the walls of the cliffs that surrounded the city, Allan marking the Gorrani's location. Overnight, howls broke the quiet, Grant and the other Wolves perking up, the two newest members pacing near the wrought iron gates of the wall and whining. Ley light also punctuated the darkness, some sections near Grass glowing with a low steady pulse, others throughout the city sputtering fitfully. Most were mere pinpricks, like stars.

"We didn't see any of those ley lights last night," Allan commented.

Dylan pointed toward the steady section. "Those were likely blocked from view by Grass."

"They're near where the Temerites were camped before the distortion was healed."

"The Temerites might have Wielders. They could have stabilized the ley once the nodes were freed. They might be actively using the ley again."

"What about the other lights?"

"Ley lines that were left open at the Shattering are now active again because their connections to the inner nodes have been restored. The ley runs where it can. If ley globes were attached to its flow and left on, they'd light up again, assuming they survived the surge. They won't be glowing as strongly now because the Nexus isn't there to augment the strength of the ley."

Allan thought about all the lights that had once lit the city, recalling the web of ley lines he'd seen from the hills over a year before, how the city had glowed in the darkness of the plains with a strange brilliant beauty.

The glow of ley he saw now was nothing compared to that.

The next morning, they followed the edge of the river, crossing it eventually on a cracked but still standing stone bridge. The waters flowed dark beneath them.

Then they climbed the distortion's ring of debris and entered the territory near where Allan, Kara, and their previous group had run into the Tunnelers and the Rats. Bryce stepped forward, taking the lead, and Allan let him, knowing the Dog knew how to handle his men. With Dylan's help, they angled toward where the shard containing the trapped Wolves and the family they had been chasing stood, moving slowly, everyone on edge. But they saw no one and heard nothing.

They entered the square where the shard glowed with a faint orange-pink light, even beneath the sunlight. Bryce barked out orders, and the enforcers spread out around the square as Allan, Grant, Dylan, and the wagons pulled up alongside the shard. Stepping up to its edge, Allan could see the cart trapped inside, the man who drove it tensed in grim determination, the horses lathered with sweat, eyes wide in terror. Another man, a woman, and two children cowered in the cart behind him, three Wolves hounding the cart from behind, caught in mid-snarl. When they'd been here last, Kara, Dylan, Artras, and Carter had healed the shards that surrounded this section. But they'd been unable to free the people trapped here, because it would also free the Wolves.

And because this shard was really composed of multiple pieces, some of which sliced through the woman, the small boy she clutched to her chest, the driver's legs, and the horses.

"Can you release them?" Allan asked as he felt Dylan halt beside him.

The Wielder sucked in a deep breath. "I'll have to heal the breaks inside the shard first; otherwise, it will cut those poor people in half. Then I'll release the shard. Which means the Wolves will be freed at the same time."

From behind, Grant said, "I'll handle the Wolves." He whistled, the sound sharp, and all five Wolves loped out of the shadows of the surrounding buildings, trotting toward them. Allan hadn't even realized they were that close.

Grant turned back to Allan. "Tell us when you're ready."

Allan signaled Bryce, the enforcers drawing in closer around the shard, Gaven and his crew stepping down from the wagons as well. Bryce's men focused their attention outward, while Gaven and the Wolves focused on the trapped people and Wolves.

"Whenever you're ready, Dylan."

The Wielder licked his lips, then closed his eyes. Allan stepped back, keeping his distance. He knew he could affect the ley in odd ways and didn't want anything to interfere with the release of the shard. But he tensed, ready to charge forward as soon as the shard released.

Nothing happened at first, until Allan noticed that the fractures inside the shard were slowly fading. The face that cut through the people and the horses dissolved, sinking back on itself, toward a focal point to the right of the cart. Sweat broke out on Dylan's forehead as he worked, a droplet trickling down to drip from his nose. He raised a trembling hand—

And then the entire shard collapsed. Screams, snarls, and the desperate shouts from the driver slammed into the silent square as the cart leaped forward. The Wolves in pursuit lurched forward as with a splintering crack one of the cart's wheels faltered. The cart sagged sideways, spilling the woman and the boy she clutched to the cobbles, her scream cut off. The man in the bed clutched at the headboard with one arm, roaring in defiance as he snatched for the girl and missed. She tumbled out a breath after her mother as the bed's corner struck stone and jerked sideways. The horses screamed as they fought the suddenly cumbersome weight, the entire rear axle cracking, the second wheel spinning off to the side.

Allan darted forward, heading toward the girl. Out of the corner of his eye, he saw Gaven and the others doing the same. They'd known they'd only have seconds before the Wolves would be on them, even before the wheel gave in.

Even those few seconds wouldn't have been enough if it hadn't been for Grant and his own Wolves.

Before Allan had made it halfway to the girl, a blur of gray fur sped before him and launched itself at the snarling Wolves in pursuit. Eyes fixed on the girl, Allan heard two heavy bodies slam into each other, a vicious snarl cut off with a sharp, startled yip, which instantly devolved into a mess of thrashing growls. He snatched the girl—no more than six—from the street, dragging her to his chest in a protective huddle, then shouted "I've got her!" before sprinting across the space toward where some of Bryce's enforcers waited on the far side. As soon as he passed their line, he spun, breath heaving.

Behind, Bryce was dragging the woman and her son, younger than the girl, back from the edge of a snarling mass of Wolf teeth and claws. Grant's pack had attacked the three Wolves that had been in pursuit of the cart and blood now slicked the cobbles. Grant had stayed back, although he stepped forward as soon as Bryce, the woman and child, and the rest of their men retreated from the fray.

A low growl churned up from his chest, building in intensity until it cracked and broke into a shouted, "Enough!"

Grant's pack broke free of the fight, twisting and rolling out of their attackers' reach, pulling back in a rough circle. Some of them were bloody, bites and claw marks on their sides. One of them limped slightly. All of them had teeth bared and were growling.

The three Wolves left rolled into defensive stances, fur bristled across shoulders, lips drawn back. Their feral eyes glared at their fellow Wolves before latching onto Grant.

One of them stepped forward, head lowered, body bracing for a leap.

Grant barked out a command, mostly snarls, and the two Wolves behind their leader flinched. The leader didn't.

The girl in Allan's arms began to struggle. He loosened his hold and shot a glance toward where the cart had headed, glad to see Gaven and a few of the others had the panicked horses under control but were keeping their distance. The two men in their midst looked confused, but he trusted Gaven to handle it and turned back to the Wolves.

Grant stepped forward, to within arm's reach of the lead Wolf, and knelt. The Wolf's growl deepened and one paw stepped forward.

Without warning, Grant's hand moved forward and cuffed the Wolf hard enough to shove him to the side.

Those watching gasped. The Wolf's head snapped back, teeth flashing. But Grant's hand wasn't there anymore. The Wolf's jaws closed on air, and Grant cuffed him again from the other side. He yelped this time, rounding on Grant again. The two stared at each other, until the Wolf leader's rumbling growl of defiance broke off, and he dropped his head with a plaintive whine and attempted to lick Grant's hand.

Tension leeched out of the square as Grant stood and gave Allan a curt nod. Allan sighed, then glanced down toward the girl in his arms.

She looked up at him with wide-eyed curiosity, her eyes a penetrating green, her hair a silky yellow, like corn tassels. Blood had beaded along a scrape on one cheek where she'd struck the cobbles while falling from the cart, another more serious scrape along one forearm, but she didn't appear to notice either one.

"Are you here to save us from the ley?" she asked.

Allan strode toward the girl's mother, who stood next to Bryce, her face frozen in shock. That transformed as soon as she saw Allan and her daughter.

"Ellie!"

She stumbled forward, snatching the girl from Allan's arms and bending down to set both the boy and girl on the ground as she kissed their foreheads and checked them over for injuries.

Bryce had come up behind her. "Looks like we managed that. Now what?"

"Now we regroup and find a place to settle in for the night."

He glanced warily at the Wolves, Grant and the others still surrounding the three new additions, although they weren't bristling at each other anymore. "We should probably keep them separate, don't you think? Until we know if the newest ones are going to follow Grant's lead?"

"Not a bad idea."

He raised his fingers to his lips. A piercing whistle and hand wave called Gaven and the two men released from the shard toward them, one of the men crouching down beside what Allan assumed was his wife, hugging her and the two children close as he broke into tears.

The other man—the driver of the cart—stood over them, arms crossed, eyeing Bryce, Gaven, and the rest as they converged back on their own wagons.

His gaze finally settled on Allan, mouth downturned with unease, tainted with suspicion. "Who are you people?"

"Survivors of the Shattering . . . and the healing of the distortion." Allan could tell the words meant little to him.

"That man, Gaven, said we were trapped in the distortion. That you freed us."

"Yes. We would have freed you sooner, but we couldn't with the Wolves attacking you. They were caught in the distortion as well. It's taken us a few months to get back to you."

"Months." The man fidgeted uncertainly, glancing around at the surrounding buildings, the cliffs, the ring of debris caused by the distortion not that far away, broken only by the section where Kara and the others had healed shards before it had started to collapse. "He said we were trapped in the distortion for over a year."

"Yes. A lot has happened since the distortion quickened."

"So it would seem."

The second man finally released his wife, although the woman still held both children close to her side.

"Forgive my brother," the man said, extending his hand. Allan hesitated, then shook it. "He's always been untrusting. I want to thank you all for saving us from the Wolves." He laughed, the sound shaky, as if he were barely holding on to sanity. "From our perspective, you simply appeared out of thin air. One moment we were alone, running for our lives, the next—there you were!"

"Charles, hush," the woman said, grabbing his arm to calm him. But she turned to Allan with a thin smile. "We are grateful, whatever has happened."

Charles' brother suddenly tensed. He nodded toward one side of the square and said, "You have company."

Before Allan could turn, one of the enforcers cried out in alarm. Bryce's men formed up around the wagons as a dozen men emerged from one of the streets on the far side of the square, creating a short wall between the buildings to either side. Archers trained arrows on them, but no one fired. Three men passed between the archers' ranks, stepping out before them, then halted. Allan couldn't tell who they were at this distance. The Tunnelers? Temerites? Another group?

The fact that they hadn't already attacked told him they weren't Rats.

"Get your family to the wagons," Allan said, not bothering to look back to see if Charles and the rest were complying as he stalked toward where Bryce and the enforcers stood. Grant and his Wolves remained clustered to one side, their attention fixed on the newcomers.

"That didn't take long," Bryce said as he approached.

"Can you see who they are?"

"Not at this distance."

"Stay here. It looks like they want to talk."

Bryce sucked in a breath to protest, but Allan was already walking across the square. He flicked orders to Grant with one hand, the pack leader nodding once in acknowledgment.

Then he focused on the group ahead. As he drew closer, he relaxed slightly. The lead figure was obviously Temerite, the thin face and neatly trimmed beard a dead giveaway. Most of the others sported the same beards. They were dressed in the armor he'd seen the guards of the Temerite nobles who'd visited Erenthrall using, although then it had gleamed. Now the polish had worn off, the uniforms obviously blemished from hard use. Pieces had been replaced with whatever could be found at hand. Even the leader's uniform—slightly more embellished but still practical—showed wear.

Allan halted ten paces away from the leader, acutely aware that at least four of the arrows were trained on him.

He and the Temerite eyed each other for a tense moment. Then the Temerite's eyes flicked toward the rest of Allan's group in the square. "That was impressive. We've been trying to figure out a way to release the family for months now." His attention returned to Allan, his gaze hardening. "What group are you with and what are you doing here in our district?"

Two

ALLAN HESITATED, not letting his gaze waver from that of the Temerite's. He knew that whatever he said next would determine the Temerite's reaction. But he also knew that the Temerites must have an idea of who they were and where they came from, even if he did sense confusion in the Temerite leader.

He cleared his throat and said carefully, "We're from the Needle."

"The White Cloaks," one of the betas behind the leader hissed, his hand snapping up, the archers behind him tensing, pulling back to fire with a creak of straining wood.

But the leader shouted, "Halt! Don't fire!"

The beta glared at his back, but kept his arm raised. The archers remained ready.

The leader lifted his chin. Allan noted a small scar along his cheek, nearly hidden by the cut of his beard. His hair was salted with gray as well and Allan adjusted his age upward, placing him closer to forty. "You claim you come from the Needle, yet I see no White Cloaks with you, although obviously you have a Wielder."

"There's been a change in power at the Needle."

"A change in power," the Temerite said. "The Father and his White Cloaks are no longer in control? Who succeeded them?"

"Father Dalton still leads the people, but he is only a figurehead. The Wielders—led by Kara Tremain—have seized the node. She's the one who healed the distortion here and stopped the quakes. She and Commander Ty run the Needle now."

This caused a few of the archers to stir.

"He's lying," the beta behind him muttered. "No one person could have healed the distortion, let alone stopped the quakes."

"She didn't do it alone," Allan said. "She had the help of the other Wielders. And the node."

"Why are you here then, in Erenthrall, in our territory?"

"The last time we were here, this wasn't your territory, it was the Tunnelers'. What happened to them?"

"You mean the Underearthers? The ley returned to most of the ley lines after the quakes. They were forced above ground. They've taken over the University. Those that survived."

"And the Rats?"

The beta grinned, the expression unpleasant. "We drove them out."

"You still haven't answered my question," the leader said. Then, deliberately: "Why are you here?"

Allan sighed. "We came to free the family from the shard and to see how Erenthrall has changed since the healing of the distortion. We also came to see if we could find any allies in the city."

All the Temerites stilled, even the beta.

"Allies?" The leader's voice was tentative.

Allan spread his arms, palms out. "Why are we fighting? We've been watching you since the Shattering. We have the same enemies, the same goals. We both need food and supplies, all of which is harder to find when we have to watch our backs constantly." Allan switched his attention to the beta. "My guess is that you may have pushed the Rats out, but they aren't gone. They're still here, somewhere, causing problems. And then there are the Gorrani, who've retreated to the southern cliffs. They're still foraging in the city, aren't they? Still a danger? There must be other groups as well, to the east, to the north." He watched the leader carefully, saw the man shift his weight at mention of the north, confirming Allan's suspicions that Haven hadn't been eliminated as a threat. He hid his disappointment, even though he wasn't surprised, and returned to his original point. "So why should we fight each other? Why not pool our resources and help each other survive?"

The Temerite leader's head lifted as he considered. Behind him, his beta said, "We don't need them, Captain. We've been doing fine without them."

"That's not for us to decide, Lieutenant."

The leader focused his attention on Allan, a muscle near the scar twitching. "You've shown good intentions by releasing the family from the shard. For that, I will grant you an audience with our Matriarch. She will decide whether we will risk an alliance with the Needle. I will escort you to her, along with your men. But your Wolves"—his gaze shifted toward Grant and the pack—"must stay behind. We will not let them inside our walls."

"Understood."

"Lieutenant Boskell, if you please."

The beta slowly lowered his arm, the archers lowering their bows at the same time. He bellowed an order in Temerese and the archers relaxed, stepping to either side as another group of Temerites poured forth from the buildings behind, these men bearing swords. They spread out across the buildings facing the square and Allan's group, forming disciplined ranks. There were at least forty infantry, along with the archers. They made no threatening moves toward Allan's group, but they eyed them and the Wolves warily.

The captain stepped forward, right arm extended at shoulder height, a traditional Temerite greeting in place of a handshake, where men of equal rank grasped each other's shoulders. Allan had seen it done at Baronial events, but had never participated.

Aware that Lieutenant Boskell and the captain's men were watching—as well as his own group—he reached out and gripped the captain's shoulder, the gesture only slightly awkward.

The captain smiled slightly. "Captain Lienta, seconded by Lieutenant Boskell, of the Temerite enclave that remains here in Erenthrall."

"Allan Garrett."

Lienta squeezed Allan's shoulder, then let his hand drop. Allan did the same. "Why don't you introduce me to your party." Over his shoulder, he said, "Lieutenant, send someone to warn the enclave and the Matriarch, then remain here with the unit."

"Very well, Captain."

He motioned Allan forward, falling into step beside him as they crossed the square toward Bryce and the others. The Dog watched them approach, the enforcers behind tensing in uncertainty, everyone else huddled by the four wagons except for the Wolves near Grant off to one side.

As they drew closer, Lienta said quietly, "You have an interesting collection of individuals, Allan Garrett. Wolves, Wielders, enforcers, and Dogs. I look forward to hearing how such a varied group came about. Assuming our Matriarch doesn't order your deaths."

The casualness of the statement sent a shiver through Allan's shoulders. He didn't have a chance to respond, though, as Bryce stepped forward and asked, "What's happening?" his voice guarded.

"Bryce, Captain Lienta. He's going to escort us to the Temerite wall so that we can speak to the Matriarch."

Lienta had stiffened formally at the introduction and nodded minutely. "We won't require that you discard any weapons, although we will keep most of you in the outer yard. Only three of you may see the Matriarch."

Bryce asked, "Are you certain you want to do this?"

"It's what Kara wanted."

Bryce's look of annoyance spoke volumes, but he ordered the enforcers and the rest into position around the others. Allan waved Grant closer.

"We're going into the Temerite enclave, but they don't want the Wolves inside."

"Nothing personal," Lienta said, although his discomfort at having the half-transformed man this close was obvious. His gaze never left Grant's face, his entire body rigid.

Grant's lips peeled back to expose a few too many teeth. His nostrils flared. "We will hunt in Grass and search for the Wolves who attacked you before the quickening. We will find you afterward, once the Temerites free you. And if they do no"—his eyes flared a feral yellow—"then we will hunt inside the Temerite enclave."

The broad-shouldered pack leader turned away, uttering a low growl to his Wolves, all of whom loped off into the side streets of the square, vanishing into the falling shadows of dusk.

Lienta watched them silently, then looked up toward the darkening sky. "We'll need to hurry if we're going to reach the walls before nightfall."

"We're ready," Bryce said.

"Then follow me."

They rolled across the square, the Temerites falling into ordered positions around them, cutting them off from a quick escape. As the shadows deepened, night descending, lights flickered on in the city around them—both firelight and ley light. The most prominent came from the Temerite walls where they were headed, but there were ley lights over the old University walls, one globe steady, the others flickering or completely out. Pockets of light dotted the landscape in all directions, few concentrated. Noises erupted from the darkness. Howls broke off to the south, startling everyone, and Allan wondered if they came from Grant and his pack, or from others. A short time before they reached the Temerite walls, frenetic ululations came from the northwest, obviously human, although wild and animalistic. At a questioning glance from Allan, Lienta said curtly, "Rats."

Then they were at the walls, multiple fires blazing on the rooftops overhead, the broad thoroughfare in front of the buildings that the Temerites had boarded up to create the main structure of the wall cleared of all debris. Anyone who tried to approach the Temerites would be exposed and within range of the archers lined up along the roofs' edges. Men shouted down a question as they approached, Boskell shouting back, and a moment later the heavy wooden doors that had been built across a narrow street, connected to the buildings on either side, groaned outward. They'd obviously been pulled from a trading house or mercantile and moved to form the barricade, the wood reinforced with piecemeal sheets of metal. A few of the exposed wood sections were charred, as if someone had tried to burn their way through the doors at some point, and only after that did Allan notice that the buildings the Temerites had chosen for their walls were all made of stone.

They passed into a courtyard crowded with people, nearly all of them Temerites, although there were a few others mixed in. On one side, a large group was engaged in training, men and women being drilled in swordsmanship, some practicing with shields. All were being directed by sharp commands from a score of Temerite military, in uniforms like those Lienta and his unit wore, with the bearing to match. Allan had not known there were that many Temerites of military standing in Erenthrall, but then he hadn't paid attention that closely before the Shattering. The Temerites had never factored into his goals when he'd come before.

The rest of those around the courtyard were busy working at more mundane tasks, such as repairing broken harness and cart wheels, patching clothes, or tanning hides. Across from the makeshift gate, at the opposite side of what had once been one of Erenthrall's marketplaces, two carts loaded with stone debris trundled down the cross street, headed south. The entire plaza and the street beyond were lit with torches and fires; Allan saw no ley globes or any sign of the ley at all.

"Your carts and the rest of your group can wait there," Lienta said, motioning toward a corner of the square opposite those training but still near the front gate. He'd already dismissed Boskell and the rest of the unit, all of them moving off toward the training yard and the buildings beyond. "You and two others can accompany me to the Matriarch."

"Bryce and Dylan, come with me," Allan said, the two stepping forward as he turned to Gaven and Bryce's beta. "You two, keep watch and make certain everyone stays here and out of trouble. I don't want anyone leaving this square."

"We'll be fine," Gaven said, as he eyed the work the Temerites were doing.

Bryce's beta kept his eyes on those training. "We'll be waiting here," the beta said, a cool gaze falling on Lienta, "when you return."

Lienta ignored the underlying threat. "This way, then."

They crossed the square, another cart loaded with stone passing by in front of them. Allan followed it with his eyes, but said nothing as Lienta led them down a side street, past an old warehouse, an immaculate church to Bastion scarred by quake damage, and a walled park, before cutting through a section of tenements to another plaza. This one contained a fountain, its basin studded with four obelisks, one cracked and toppled, with a central stone statue of a hand thrust up out of the ground, clutching a giant ley globe. Moonlight cast the entire plaza in a silvery sheen.

As they crossed the plaza, Dylan raised one hand as if to brush the surface of the ley globe as they passed. "Why is it not lit?" he asked, hand falling as they headed toward a series of three-story homes filling the block to one side, their windows glowing with candlelight. Allan hid a flicker of surprise. He'd thought the Matriarch would have housed herself in the much larger and grander mercantile house that reared up dark and foreboding behind the fountain. It had a palatial feel to it, far surpassing the less ornate architecture of the other homes.

"After the Shattering, the ley no longer worked in this section of the city. That's one of the reasons the Matriarch had us seize control of it.

It helped that our embassy was already here, and that it was deemed a strategic location that, with some modifications, would be easy to defend."

"Modifications like using the buildings as a wall and blocking off the streets with gates?" Allan asked.

"Yes. There was also the distortion to consider. We used it to our south as part of our wall. It proved extremely effective . . . until it collapsed."

"Buildings do not make structurally sound walls," Bryce interjected. "They have a tendency to collapse as well."

"They don't when they are filled with stone."

They'd reached the row of houses, the steps leading up to the brownstone near the center guarded by four Temerite watchmen. They said nothing as Lienta ascended, one of them reaching to open the door for them, warm light spilling out onto the steps.

Allan halted abruptly within three steps of entering the massive foyer inside, and Dylan gasped. The room took up the entire front half of the brownstone, a grand staircase curving up one side to a second level. Doors led off to left and right, another straight ahead, watchmen posted to either side of them all, but it was obvious that the houses they'd seen from the street were an illusion. The entire block was really one large building, the doors to either side entrances to what, from the outside, would be the houses to the left and right. Allan guessed that the building was deeper than most would suspect as well, possibly even extending all the way to the next street.

"What is this place?" Bryce asked sharply, tension bleeding from him in waves.

"Welcome to what used to be Erenthrall's Temerite embassy," Lienta said.

He led them to the left. None of the watchmen acknowledged them; they didn't move at all. Allan scanned the sparse furnishings of the foyer, noting the patched cracks in the walls caused by the recent quakes. It may have been cleaned up, but the Temerites weren't as unaffected by the recent disasters as they'd like to pretend.

The room beyond contained a large desk stacked with disheveled papers, cloth sacks, and small boxes. A sizable crack traced its way diagonally across the wall behind the desk. In front of the windows that looked out onto the plaza, behind where the fake front door of the exterior house would have opened into the room, sat an array of chairs, a Temerite woman of at least fifty years ensconced in the center. She held a sheaf of papers in one hand, an attendant to her left, a small table to her right containing quill and ink and a tray with a carafe and short glass. She was clothed in a tan-and-dun shirt blocked in the usual Temerite style worn by nobility, with a shawl over her shoulders and a blanket spread across her legs. Rings adorned nearly every one of her fingers, and a fine but understated necklace surrounded her neck. Her skin was lined with age, but her gaze when she glanced up at their approach was sharp.

She set the papers aside and rested her hands on the sides of the chair, her back rigid with formality. "I see that Lieutenant Boskell's note was correct," she said, her voice cracking slightly but with steel beneath it. "You have found others. From the Needle, no less. And you thought it appropriate to bring them here."

Lienta's steps faltered for only a second, but the Matriarch wasn't paying attention to him. Her gaze had raked through all three of those behind him and after that single pass had settled on Allan. He had been the subject of such penetrating gazes before; the most memorable had been Baron Arent before the Shattering. The Matriarch exuded the same sense of power and intelligence and control.

"Did Lieutenant Boskell also mention that they claim the White Cloaks are no longer in control of the Needle?" Lienta asked, coming to a halt directly before the Matriarch and executing a stiff bow.

"No, he did not." The Matriarch sniffed her irritation, one eyebrow rising slightly. "Is this true?"

Lienta stepped to one side, since the question was obviously not directed at him. Allan moved forward, Bryce coming up on one side, Dylan on the other. The Wielder was nervous, his hands in constant motion.

Allan resisted the urge to bow. "There has been a shift in power at the Needle, yes."

"I hope you saw fit to toss that Kormanley pretender who called himself Father off the Needle itself."

"No," Allan answered. "He's still alive and still speaking to the people, giving his . . . religious services."

"Pity. But if that's the case, then how has the Needle changed? If this Father is still preaching his hatred of Erenthrall to the people—"

"He isn't. Commander Ty of the Needle's enforcers has him under control. He and the Wielders have forced Father Dalton to accept certain rules and restrictions. He is escorted to his sermons and allowed to speak by Commander Ty himself, then escorted back to his rooms. He isn't allowed to roam free alone. All of the decisions regarding the Needle are handled by Commander Ty and Prime Wielder Kara Tremain."

Dylan shot Allan a look at the use of the title Prime Wielder, but Allan knew that nearly every Wielder at the Needle considered her a Prime after her healing of the distortion. And he knew that the title would carry weight with the Matriarch.

"What happened to Prime Wielder Lecrucius?"

Allan was surprised she knew the previous Prime Wielder's name. "He's dead. He was killed during the Gorrani attack on the Needle and the collapse of the distortion, annihilated by a surge in the ley."

"How fortunate," the Matriarch said dryly. "And what about the Father's Son, Marcus? He was a White Cloak. Why did he not seize control?"

Allan hesitated. The Temerites knew more about the Needle than he'd expected. Much more. He wondered how much of what he was telling her now was information she already knew. "Marcus still lives, but he follows Kara Tremain now. There is no more Son, and there are no more White Cloaks. Not like before."

"Hmm." The Matriarch reached to pick up the glass and sip at the dark brown liquid it contained. Allan caught a whiff of what smelled like brandy. She swirled the drink before setting it aside again. "Assuming what you say is true, why are you here now? From all our reports, the Needle has no need of Erenthrall. It has already ransacked it dry."

"The White Cloaks may have traded or stolen whatever they could before the collapse of the distortion, but circumstances have changed. Tumbor is lost to us, along with all its resources. That leaves only Erenthrall and the supplies that were released when the distortion was healed."

"The Needle has no rightful claim to those resources."

"No claim stronger than anyone else's, no," Allan agreed.

"The White Cloaks before you would have brought in their enforcers and seized control of the inner city, at least until it was empty of anything useful. They tried that before."

"Again, the White Cloaks no longer command the enforcers."

The Matriarch leaned slightly forward. "So then, what do you propose?"

"An alliance. The Temerites are already established in Erenthrall. You have access to the supplies that we need."

"And in exchange? What would we receive for this alliance?"

"Protection."

The Matriarch and Lienta exchanged looks, Lienta shifting uncomfortably.

The Matriarch settled back into her chair. "Protection? We have our own Temerite soldiers here to protect us. Why would we need your help?"

Unease prickled across Allan's shoulders. "I'll admit that you have more guardsmen here than I expected. I didn't realize the Temerite contingent in Erenthrall before the Shattering was that large."

"It wasn't," the Matriarch said flatly. "Before the Shattering, the trade agreements between the Baronial plains and the Temerites were set to expire. My husband and I had traveled here with our household, including its guard, to renegotiate the terms and sign a new agreement. We had almost finished when the ley shattered. My husband—" Her voice caught, the only sign of emotion she allowed before her expression hardened. "My husband was in Grass at the time, in the Amber Tower. He did not survive."

An awkward silence fell, broken by Dylan. "Why did you stay in Erenthrall, then? Why didn't you return home?"

The Matriarch sucked in a sharp breath, expression tightening for a scathing retort, but Lienta leaped in. "It was considered. But we saw the pulse that headed toward Temerite lands down the ley line, and we could see what had happened to Erenthrall and the surrounding cities. Rather than risk traveling back to a capitol that had been destroyed, we sent messengers asking for information and orders, then set about fortifying our embassy here."

"Needless to say, our messengers never returned," the Matriarch added. "And now here we are."

"So you've been cut off from Temer," Bryce said. "You're isolated here in Erenthrall. I don't care how many of your household guards you brought with you, you must feel alone, surrounded by unknown and violent forces. I would think you'd welcome an ally or two, especially one who can control the ley."

The Matriarch frowned at the last statement. Allan mentally sighed. Coming from Bryce, it sounded more like a threat than an offer of help.

"What Bryce meant—" Allan began, but the Matriarch cut him off.

"I know what he meant. As you likely noticed, we no longer trust the ley. But he raises a valid, if antagonistic, point. The ability to manipulate the ley, even if it isn't completely stable yet, would be a distinct advantage against the groups that are amassing here in Erenthrall."

Something seized hold of Allan's gut and squeezed. "What do you mean? What groups?"

Outside, they heard a shout, muffled by the walls. Someone raced across the plaza bearing a torch, headed straight for the outer door. The Matriarch craned her neck to see, then motioned toward Lienta, who darted out of the room with a grim expression.

The Matriarch met Allan's questioning look with a thin, humorless smile. "We may have need of your help sooner than you expect."

In the awkward silence that followed, they heard the front door to the embassy open and the tread of panicked feet. Gasps were punctuated by a report that Allan couldn't make out, but he did hear Lienta's response clearly.

"Are you certain?" He swore at the answer. Then: "Spread the word. And bring back a report from each of the walls."

The messenger charged out of the embassy, his torch cutting to the left outside as he raced away. Inside, Lienta snapped out orders, the guardsmen at the entrance and in the doorways running off in various directions, their heavy boots echoing against the embassy's floorboards.

Then Lienta reappeared. "They're coming."

"Who's coming?" Bryce demanded, but Lienta and the Matriarch ignored him.

"Which direction?"

"The main force is coming from the north, but there are groups converging on us from the east and west as well."

"Then they didn't manage to coerce the Underearthers into their little pact. Or the Gorrani."

"And they must not know how weak our southern defenses are, or they would be targeting us there." One of the guards reappeared and muttered something to Lienta, who turned back with a short bow. "I need to report to the walls, Matriarch."

She waved a hand in dismissal. "Go. And take our potential allies with you. It seems they chose a particularly bad time to approach us. Now our fates are intertwined, regardless."

Lienta spun on his heel with a curt, "Come with me."

Allan started forward, Bryce on his heels with a low mutter of, "What have we just stepped in?" as Dylan fell in behind.

In the foyer, Lienta gave a few last orders about securing the embassy and the Matriarch to the men waiting there, then stepped out onto the plaza, two of the guards joining him. Without a word, he broke into a run, headed north. There wasn't any time for questions, even if they hadn't been running. They reached the Temerite wall within three blocks of the embassy, the street once again closed off with a gate made of doors pilfered from some other building. Temerite soldiers were gathering outside, arriving in groups of five to ten, while others shouted down at them from the rooftops. Lienta cut immediately toward the building on the right, entering and sprinting up the stairs. As they ascended to the roof, Allan noted that stone debris spilled out of the doors to what had once been apartments on the side of the buildings facing out toward the city. He suddenly remembered the carts of stone headed toward the south, and Lienta's comment that the wall to the south wasn't as secure. They must still be fortifying the buildings they'd chosen to replace the distortion after it collapsed.

He motioned toward the stone, but Bryce merely frowned, not understanding. Then they burst out onto the roof, a gust of smoke-tainted wind catching Allan full in the face. He, Bryce, and Dylan paused on the threshold of the roof's access, shoved aside a moment later by more Temerites, these men carrying satchels of arrows. They spread out across the rooftop, dropping the satchels every few dozen paces, scrambling over to the next roof and proceeding down the block.

"What are they doing here?" someone demanded.

Allan turned to see Lienta approaching Boskell, the beta glaring at them.

"The Matriarch wanted them here," Lienta answered.

"Are they allies now?"

"Only by circumstance. Now tell me what you know."

Boskell dismissed them as he edged up to the lip of the building. "Our scouts report that the largest group entered the outer districts about an hour ago. But unlike their previous excursions, this group is at least three times the size and they aren't separating and scouring the city for food. They're staying together, headed straight for us. They also report that the Rats are riled up, more so than usual, and recently left their lair to the west. We aren't certain where they're headed yet, but it seems too much of a coincidence they're on the move at the same time as the other group, especially in such great numbers. We haven't heard from our scouts to the east, but we can see the glow of torchlight headed this way. It's safe to assume the Butcher and his crew are out as well."

"But no movement from the Underearthers?"

Boskell shook his head. "No movement yet. They're still holed up at the University. And we haven't seen the Gorrani north of Grass since the sinking of the city."

"The Gorrani won't be working with anyone except their own," Allan interjected from behind.

Boskell and Lienta turned back. "Why not?"

"Because five thousand of them attacked the Needle, and only a thousand walked away. The White Cloaks unleashed the ley on them, burned them from the walls. They aren't going to trust anyone who isn't Gorrani for a while."

Boskell's look of horror was almost comical. "You immolated them with the ley?"

"*We* didn't," Dylan snapped defensively. "The White Cloaks did. *We* stopped them as soon as we could. It just . . . wasn't soon enough."

"As long as they don't band together with these other groups, it doesn't matter." Lienta's voice cut across Boskell's retort, and Allan stepped in before Boskell could recover.

"About these other groups: I've never heard of the Butcher; and what group is coming from the north?"

"The Butcher leads a group to the east, dominating a few districts there. Initially, they were simply scavengers, but when resources ran low, they turned to cannibalism. We thought they'd given that up once the distortion fell, since they had new areas to raid, but rumors are they still feed on whoever they can catch."

Swallowing back the taste of bile, Allan asked, "And those from the north?"

"They came once before, but we hadn't heard from them in a while. Once the city sank, they reappeared. They come from a place called Haven."

Allan's head dropped in resignation. When he raised his eyes, he found Lienta watching him. "Who's their leader?"

Lienta shrugged. "They only call him Baron."

It couldn't be Aurek. They'd killed him before the walls of the Needle.

"What do you know about him?" Lienta asked.

"We've run into the group before. We killed their previous Baron. I don't know who his replacement is. But if his beta survived the attack on the Needle and the quakes . . ."

Someone shouted, and everyone turned to see one of the archers pointing out toward the city with his bow. Crowding up to the lip of the building, a stone edge not quite waist-high, Allan strained to see what had caught the archer's attention. He didn't see anything . . .

But then the nearby streets across the wide thoroughfare that separated the Temerite wall from the rest of the city began to fill with people. They emerged from side streets, alleys, and doorways, and dropped from windows with a steadily increasing roar, brandishing swords, axes, and clubs. A few even held spears and shields. Allan's grip on the edge of the stone tightened as he recognized the makeshift armor, grizzled faces, and twisted, unkempt beards that marked them as coming from Haven. Except the closer he looked, more and more of them appearing below, it became obvious that these men weren't as disciplined as Baron Aurek's had been.

They began surging up onto the rooftops opposite the wall, screaming and hollering without any purpose, almost within bowshot.

"They're wilder than they were before," Bryce commented from over Allan's shoulder. "More dangerous."

Allan didn't answer. Below, those on the street were parting, making way for someone. For two people, he realized, although his eyes kept slipping away from the second figure, as if he weren't really there. It felt as if he had an itch on the back of his eyeballs, the sensation odd and yet familiar. He had to concentrate to keep the second man in focus.

But the first man he recognized instantly when he stepped from the edge of the raiders, hands on hips, and contemplated the closed gates. As his gaze drifted up to the rooftops, face exposed to the torchlight that lined the Temerite walls, Allan muttered, "Devin."

And then he suddenly remembered where he'd felt that odd itching sensation.

rned toward Bryce and Lienta in shock.

und. Devin has a Hound."

Lienta frowned in confusion, but Bryce surged forward to take Allan's place at the wall. His curse split the air a second later. "It's difficult to pick him out, but he's there." His eyes scanned the rest of the raiders intently. "I don't see any others. Maybe it's just the one."

"One is enough."

"Where is this Hound?" Lienta asked, next to Bryce.

"He's standing next to Devin, their Baron." Bryce's voice was laced with contempt. "You have to concentrate. Your eyes will slide right off him. Focus on the strange empty space to the Baron's right."

Lienta squinted, then he gasped. "How did he find a Hound?" His voice trembled, a hint of panic underneath, tightly controlled.

"I see you've heard of them."

"Of course I have! Baron Arent threatened the Temerites with them repeatedly, and we saw what damage they did to the Baronies during his rise."

"Then you know that this changes everything. No matter how secure you thought you were behind these walls, you aren't."

"There's only one of them," Boskell scoffed. "And we've held this Baron off before."

"One is all Devin will need, if he's foolhardy enough to unleash him." Allan rested his hands on the parapet, watching the Hound closely. "I wonder how he's managing to control him. Is it because he calls himself the Baron?"

Lienta stared at Allan. A moment later, his eyes narrowed with a decision. "This isn't your fight," he said. "Boskell, escort them back to their wagons and let them go. Then send word to the Matriarch. Tell her to prepare to abandon the embassy. Spread the word along the wall. We'll hold the wall as long as possible, but if there's a breach, we'll fall back to the embassy and get the Matriarch out of here."

"We can help—" Allan began.

"Don't argue," Lienta snapped, then caught himself. He took a deep breath, then reached out and clutched Allan's shoulder, looked him in the eye. "If you waste any more time, you won't be able to escape before the Rats close in on the western wall. So go. Now."

Allan gripped Lienta's shoulder and nodded.

Then Boskell gestured impatiently. "Follow me, and don't slow me down."

They raced down the stairs, Boskell shouting orders as he went, men sidestepping or flattening themselves up against the walls until they broke out onto the street beyond. Boskell's pace increased after that, Allan huffing before they'd gone two blocks. He heard a shout from behind and glanced over his shoulder to see Dylan flagging, his limp from the crippled knee slowing him, but Bryce shouted and waved Allan onward, falling back to help the Wielder. They followed the wall, Boskell pausing only to pass on Lienta's orders, cutting across a few blocks only when they neared the corner.

The western gate was a roil of activity, Boskell charging into the center of it, leaving Allan to plow through a square packed with at least fifty Temerite soldiers hastily preparing for a fight. Gaven and the enforcers were watching nervously from the edge of the wagons, the enforcers in a loose, protective circle.

"Gaven!" Allan shouted as soon as he caught sight of them. "Get the wagons ready to roll! We need to move fast!"

Gaven began to scramble into the driver's seat, shouting to the others.

"Where are Bryce and Dylan?" Bryce's beta demanded.

"Right behind me. The Temerites are going to open the gates and let us out, but we don't have much time. The Rats are coming to attack the wall."

The beta nodded sharply, the rest of the enforcers ranging themselves in front and alongside the wagons. Gaven slapped the reins, the horses lurching forward, picking up on the tension.

Ahead, Boskell gestured toward the men operating the gates and they began to swing open. Allan glanced back and caught Bryce dragging Dylan through the last of the Temerites and tossing him into the seat beside Gaven before charging toward Allan.

"We'll only open the gates wide enough to let your wagons through," Boskell said, coming up on Allan's other side.

"Right. Gaven!" Allan motioned to the gates, already wide enough. Bryce's beta and two other enforcers ran through the gates—

And then a spear sprouted from the beta's throat. He reached up to clutch at it as he staggered backward, blood coating his hands and sheeting down his neck. He fell, another spear clanging against the half-open gates. The two other enforcers retreated with a bellow of warning, and then a familiar ululating roar rose into the air, sending a shudder down Allan's spine. Rats began pouring from the buildings beyond the gate, heading toward the opening in a wave. Boskell screamed for the gates to be closed. Temerites rushed toward the opening as Gaven yanked the wagons to a halt and the two enforcers outside rejoined them, turning just inside to help the Temerites. Ten Rats made it through the gates before they thudded closed, the Temerites converging and dispatching them without mercy.

Boskell ordered those on the walls above to fire into the Rats as they pounded on the doors, men already moving to add braces and bar them closed. Then the Temerite beta turned back to Allan, a grim look on his face.

"*Now* we are allies. How is your Needle going to help you now?"

He stalked away, barking orders as he headed toward the roof and top of the wall.

Three

KARA APPROACHED FROM BEHIND the slew of enforcers standing guard over Father Dalton and his retainers, but halted a few paces back from where Commander Ty stood watch. They were arrayed along the length of one of the temple's tiers, oil burning harshly in the two urns set to either side of the ledge where Dalton stood above the crowd of worshippers gathered in the plaza below. Kara didn't understand the significance of the two fires, although she admitted that the flames thrashing in the breeze and the thick black smoke that rose from them—thicker than it should be—added a dramatic flair to the sermon, even at midday.

"Korma has blessed us all, for *we* were the ones chosen to destroy the tangled web of ley Baron Arent Pallentor and Prime Wielder Augustus used to ensnare and enthrall us and bind us to the city of Erenthrall. *We* were the ones chosen to break their hold on us, and their insidious hold on the ley, and return the world to its natural order. *We* were the ones chosen to pick up the strands of that destruction and repair the damage the Baron and Prime Wielder did to nature."

Kara suppressed an urge to roll her eyes at Father Dalton's proclamations. But the followers shouted in response as he paused, half of them kneeling, most with arms raised up toward the edge of the tier and the thin black spire of the Needle beyond. Dalton stood at the edge of the platform of stone that jutted out toward the crowd. He was dressed in loose white robes that flapped in the stiff breeze coming from the northwest, the sun almost blinding as it hit the cloth. The symbol of the Kormanley—a thick black vertical line with a thinner diagonal cutting down from the upper left, merging with the first line, symbolizing convergence and a return to the natural order—was emblazoned on the front of his robe, although Kara couldn't see it.

She must have made some noise—a snort of derision or annoyance, perhaps—for Commander Ty glanced back, his frown falling away as he recognized her and turned, positioning himself to her right.

"Come to see the show?" he asked.

"I didn't realize he would be here," she said. "I don't remember a request for a sermon today."

"It wasn't planned much in advance. He asked for it this morning. I didn't see any reason not to allow it. He's been remarkably compliant with our demands, more so than I expected."

"He has," Kara said, crossing her arms over her chest and staring at Dalton's back. "So why the sudden request this morning?"

Ty cocked an eyebrow. "Suspicious?"

"Always, when it comes to the Kormanley. And especially Dalton."

"I've heard you have reasons."

"Many."

"So far, it's been disappointing. He's stuck to his usual script. 'We are the chosen. Korma will protect us if we trust in the ley and steer clear of the path taken by Baron Arent and Prime Augustus.'" He halted. "I would have expected a few snide comments about how we've seized control and have kept him more or less imprisoned since the attack by the Gorrani, but he's kept his sermons focused on Korma and the ley."

"He knows that you're watching and listening, and he was never stupid. If he tries anything, he knows you'll drag him from his perch and lock him in his rooms. He'd have no contact with the people then."

"You don't honestly believe we could do that, do you?"

Kara sighed. "No. His followers would scream bloody murder and we'd be worse off than we are right now."

"Glad to see you haven't lost touch with reality." He changed the subject. "So why did you come up here, if not to hear Dalton preaching?"

Kara turned to stare out over the small city that surrounded the Needle and its temple. The first tier was high enough she could see out over most of the nearest stone buildings—only two or three stories high—to the surrounding stone wall. Between the buildings, where streets ran directly from the temple to the outer perimeter, she could see the tents that filled the area between the buildings and the wall. The temple had been built hundreds of years ago; no one was certain exactly when. Before the rise of the Barons on the plains, certainly. It bore the markings of pagan religions in the myriad sculptures of birds and animals that alternated with the stone urns around the edge of each tier. This first tier also contained a massive mosaic of colored stone, centered around a circular sun. Hernande surmised that it was built before the Barons seized control of the caravan routes here, when the tribes of the plains roamed back and forth with the seasons, migrating with the game herds. This site must have been sacred to them, because of the ley node at the center of the temple. It had certainly been a place of worship; based on his investigation of the writings and the sculpture, the nomadic people had stopped here to pray to the gods of nature, sensing the power of the ley that was concentrated here, even if they didn't actively use the ley itself. The University mentor thought that the node they'd discovered in the caves near the Hollow a few months before was older—the drawings on the cave walls appeared far more archaic in nature and design, possibly even from before written history—but the stellae surrounding the Needle itself contained the same Amanskrit writing as those in the caves. For some reason, the node here had become a central focus of the nomads' worship, while the other node had been lost.

Kara breathed in deeply, let it out in a long sigh.

"I came up here to relax," she said, scanning the horizon beyond the city. The plains stretched off into the distance in all directions beyond the walls and the low slope of earth that ringed the shallow depression that the Needle sat in. Only the large jagged crevice that had opened during the massive quake that had struck during the Gorrani siege marred the view, slicing through the city from the southeast, south of the temple, to the northwest. It had breached the walls on both sides and swallowed a section of the buildings of the outer city, but left the temple intact, with only minor cracks in the foundation. It stretched at least a hundred yards out from the city to the northwest, twice as far as to the southeast, and was so deep no one had yet reached its bottom. Not that many had tried. Smaller cracks had appeared in the surrounding plains, but nothing as wide or as long as the one here at the Needle. "The openness of the plains and the sky overhead is soothing."

Ty surveyed the same view as Kara, hands on his hips. "I suppose."

They stood in silence for a moment, Kara mentally blocking out Dalton and the echoing roars of approval from the crowd below. She'd become fairly adept at ignoring him and his Kormanley followers in the last month.

"I take it that the progress with the new Nexus and the healing of the distortion over Tumbor isn't going well," Ty finally ventured.

Kara's shoulders slumped as she turned away from the view, the gaping wound in the earth that split the city suddenly too much of a reminder of what they risked if she and the other Wielders failed.

"We're still working on stabilizing the ley as much as possible."

"We've certainly had fewer quakes recently, especially in the last several weeks."

Kara nodded, now facing the two upper tiers of the temple and the thin black spire of the Needle reaching toward the thin clouds drifting above. The sun blazed overhead as well, the summer heat faintly sheening Kara's skin with sweat. "We haven't needed to make many adjustments to the ley lines bypassing Tumbor. Most of our corrections have been to the crystal panes in the Nexus here as we attempt to maximize and balance the ley lines coming from the north, south, and east. Correcting the crystals doesn't seem to produce quakes, only shifts in the ley lines themselves."

"Then you are making progress."

"Yes. We can't do anything about Tumbor until the ley is as stable as possible." She tried not to let any of her uncertainty seep into her voice. She and the other Wielders were working blindly, reacting solely on instinct and whatever Marcus had learned from Prime Lecrucius before he'd been forced to kill the Prime in order to halt the wall of ley that had annihilated the Gorrani forces surrounding the city.

"And you'll be able to heal Tumbor as you did Erenthrall?"

Kara faced Ty, fighting back the stone of self-doubt that had lodged in her chest. "We have to. The ley structure we've cobbled together right now won't hold forever."

Commander Ty's brow creased, as if he could hear the self-doubt in the roughness of her voice. "What about the mentors from the University? I thought they were going to work with the Wielders, as they did in Erenthrall before the Shattering?"

"We've been meaning to, but we haven't quite found the time. Besides, we have only three experienced mentors, and none of them worked actively with the Primes before the Shattering. They were all teachers at the University, theorists. They never applied their theories to the real world. That was someone else's job. So, like the Wielders adjusting the crystal panes, we'd be learning as we go."

Ty would have responded, but Father Dalton's voice suddenly rose in pitch, catching their attention.

"But we cannot be complacent," he shouted down at the crowd below. "Our work here is not done. The ley is not yet settled. The land is still angry at the abuse it has suffered. The wounds we see from our walls—these rents in the earth that we have grown used to over the past month—they are but warnings! They foretell what will happen if we do not continue to repent of Baron Arent's sins, of Prime Wielder Augustus' transgressions."

Commander Ty took an uncertain step forward. "This is new."

The roar from the crowd below swelled, men and women proclaiming they would not be complacent, that they had not forgotten the quake that had nearly destroyed them a month before. Most of them believed that Father Dalton had saved them all. He'd predicted how the Gorrani would be defeated and had been visibly calling upon Korma to protect them when the quake struck, even though it was Kara and the Wielders hidden in the depths of the Nexus who had truly ended it by healing the distortion over Erenthrall.

But none of that mattered to them. As far as the masses were concerned, it was Father who had saved them.

And now their Father held his hands up and said, "I have had a vision."

The crowd below quieted and Commander Ty swore, hand falling to his sword as he stepped forward. But Kara caught his arm, held him back.

"We have to stop him," he snapped.

"You can't. It's what he wants."

She jutted her chin in Dalton's direction, and Ty spun to see the Kormanley priest looking back over his shoulder to see what Ty would do. The enforcers were asking for direction as well, fidgeting where they stood.

Ty fumed, but allowed Kara to restrain him.

Dalton smiled, the expression turning Kara's stomach, then returned his attention to the crowd below. She let her hand drop from Ty's arm.

"I have had a vision!" Dalton repeated in triumph. "I have seen a black stone, cracked near its center, sitting in the sand. To the south of the stone, the world shimmers with auroral lights. To the north, it roils with black clouds lit from within by three piercing lights. From the aurora slithers a giant snake. From the clouds, a feral dog. And above the black stone, the two meet, serpent striking with poisonous venom, canine snapping its jaws closed on scales with a snarl. The two struggle as the black stone trembles in the sand beneath and blood rains down over all, until the stone cracks completely in two and is washed away in a flood and the three piercing lights wink out, casting everything in darkness."

The crowd below gasped in horror, a few wailing and falling to the ground. But then someone from below shouted, "What does it mean?" someone else picking up the cry with, "Yes, Father, what does it mean?"

Father raised both arms again and waited until the crowd had quieted.

"Unless the ley is healed and the land restored, the three piercing lights—the Three Sisters"—here he pointed toward where the three piercing lights of the distortions over Ikanth, Severen, and Dunmara to the north rested above the horizon like stars—"will quicken and destroy us all."

"Do you believe him?" Cory asked.

"About the Three Sisters?" Kara snapped as she paced back and forth along the length of the massive table that Father Dalton had had set up in the orrery. The ley-powered globes of the planets orbiting the sun hovered overhead, their colors casting the room in vibrant hues, but the table had been set to one side, lit mostly by the sunlight coming through the windows. Marcus had wanted to abandon the room after they'd seized control, but it had proved too convenient for their occasional meetings. Instead, Kara had enlisted the help of the servants and the enforcers and had cleaned the room, removing the detritus that had piled up in the corners and at the base of the walls as the paint had peeled and flaked away. The walls had been scrubbed and the wood paneling had been treated with oils. The room still appeared faded with age, but it was an improvement. "No, I don't believe him. I don't even believe he had a vision. I think he's finally realized how he can attack us without being blatant about it."

"How is this an attack?"

Kara halted abruptly. "Don't you see? He's been stewing in his room since the Gorrani attack, for all intents and purposes imprisoned there."

"You've let him out to give his sermons."

"That doesn't count. He knows he can't do anything blatant during his sermons. Commander Ty is always there, ready to shut him down if he begins preaching against the Wielders or the enforcers. He'd be shoved back into his rooms and never let out again, no matter how much his followers might protest. He knows that.

"But by mentioning this . . . this *vision* of his today, he's gone on the offensive again. He's trying to undermine us indirectly, the Wielders in particular."

Cory's hand traced patterns on the tabletop from where he sat. Numerous blocks of wood and various stones were scattered across the table, signifying the last known locations of certain larger groups such as the Gorrani, along with Ty's own enforcers and scouts. "How?"

"He focused the thrust of his vision on the Wielders, on us being unable to heal the ley! His parting shot essentially claimed that if we couldn't heal the ley, the Three Sisters would quicken and destroy us all! It was a challenge."

Cory met her gaze over the length of the table at the outburst, eyebrows raised, and she suddenly realized he wasn't being obtuse. He already understood the implications of Dalton's supposed prophecy. He was baiting her, trying to get her to work out the anger and aggression seething just beneath her skin.

She wanted to reach out and strangle Dalton. Instead, she sucked in a deep breath, shoulders raised, then released it in a single harsh huff. Raising a hand to the bridge of her nose, she said, "It's been a month, Cory." She heard him stand and round the table toward her. "Dalton knows we should have been able to do something about Tumbor by now. He's going to use his prophecy"—the word tasted bitter in her mouth—"to convince the people that the Wielders—that *I*—won't be able to heal the ley. Not without him, at least."

Cory's arms wrapped around her waist, and he pulled her into him, letting her head nestle in the space beneath his neck. He rested his chin on top of her head. "You don't know that for certain." Cory's voice vibrated from his chest into her, soothing away some of her prickling anger. "All he did today, from what you said, was claim that the Three Sisters would quicken. We all know that's a possibility. It could happen at any time, just like Tumbor. It could happen to any of the cities with distortions hanging over them."

He pulled back, catching her face with both hands. "He's trying to rile you up, and he's succeeded. Don't let him throw you." He kissed her, and she allowed some of the tension to seep from her shoulders before breaking the contact and nestling back into his chest.

"It's all lies," she muttered, staring at the makeshift map spread across the tabletop, the pulsing glow of the planets of the orrery reflected in the polished wood.

"Are you certain?"

Kara jerked back from Cory at Marcus' voice, and Cory grunted in frustration, shooting a dark look at the Wielder. Kara suddenly wished she hadn't summoned Marcus and Hernande to the meeting hall immediately after Dalton's little spectacle.

"Of course they're lies," Kara said curtly. "They're all lies."

Dierdre entered behind Marcus with a snort. "You expect her to believe, Marcus?" The black-haired Kormanley supporter—now dressed in the white clothing of a White Cloak even though she'd never been a Wielder—settled a contemptuous gaze on Kara. "She's done nothing but denigrate and demoralize Father's followers since she arrived here and seized control."

"She didn't seize control," Marcus said in a long-suffering voice, as if he'd argued with Dierdre about this particular point before. "The Wielders follow her because she proved she can control the ley better than anyone else here when she healed the distortion over Erenthrall."

"She didn't do that alone," Dierdre countered.

Marcus rounded on her. "For all intents and purposes, she did."

"Then why hasn't she healed the distortion over Tumbor yet?"

"You know why. If you weren't so full of jealous fury, you'd acknowledge that."

Cory had stepped closer to Kara when Dierdre entered and now entwined his fingers in hers between them, squeezing slightly in encouragement. The tangled threads of the friendships, loves, and betrayals woven among the four of them hung in the air, centered mostly on Marcus and Kara. Before the Shattering, Dierdre had lured Marcus away, seducing him with the promises of the Kormanley. Kara had thought Marcus had died during the Shattering. Discovering he was still alive had been a shock, reopening old wounds.

Discovering Dierdre had survived as well, and that she and the Kormanley still held him in thrall, had only ground salt into those wounds.

But she had Cory now, even though Marcus had redeemed himself somewhat when he'd rebelled against Dalton and Prime Wielder Lecrucius during the Gorrani attack.

She squeezed Cory's hand in reassurance.

Dierdre might have responded to Marcus, but Commander Ty entered the room and halted, taking in the situation with one glance. Hernande entered behind him, along with a servant carrying a tray with a decanter of wine and an array of glasses. The servant set the tray on the table and left.

"I see we're all here," the University mentor said, tactfully not acknowledging the tension in the air. "I apologize for the delay. I was working with the University students."

"I only just arrived myself," Ty said.

"Is Dalton secure in his rooms?" Kara asked, releasing Cory's hand and moving forward to select a chair at the table. After a moment's hesitation, the rest of them did the same, all except Dierdre, who stood in stiff disapproval to one side.

"He is. He cooperated without incident, although the urge to smack the insolent smirk from his face was strong."

"What happened?" Hernande asked. "Did he finally rail against his imprisonment to his followers?"

"Nothing so obvious." Ty reached to pour himself a glass of wine, offering it to the others before setting the decanter back down and settling back into his seat.

Kara controlled another surge of anger. "He ended his sermon today by announcing he's had another vision."

Hernande's eyebrows rose, but it was Dierdre's gasp that drew everyone's attention. The Kormanley follower swallowed and straightened under the scrutiny, then said defensively, "I thought you were talking about what Dalton said in general earlier. I didn't realize he'd announced a new prophecy." Her eyes hardened and grew distracted. "Neither he nor Darius said anything to me." Then she realized they were all still watching her. "What was this prophecy?"

Kara related what Dalton had said—about the black stone, the snake, and the feral dog, ending with the Three Sisters flaring and destroying the world. "But it's all lies. Dalton is obviously making it up to put pressure on the Wielders."

"What kind of pressure?" Ty asked.

"Political pressure. He's using the vision to suggest we aren't going to be able to heal the ley network. Now, every time there's a quake or shift in the ley, he can use it to attack us. He's going to keep pushing until the people believe him, and then he'll take back control with promises he can fix it himself."

Ty grunted. "You got all of that from his little display out there today? All I heard was a warning that the Three Sisters were going to quicken and the results would be disastrous."

"You're reading much into his words, Kara," Hernande said. "From what you say, he never even mentioned the Wielders."

"He mentioned healing the ley. That's enough." Kara bristled at the skeptical look shared between Hernande and Ty. "You can't honestly say you believe in his vision, can you? You know Dalton, Ty. You've dealt with him since the Shattering. You know how he thinks. This is just the beginning."

Ty shifted uncomfortably in his seat.

"She's right."

Everyone turned to Marcus, Dierdre muttering something under her breath before spinning on her heel and stalking from the room.

Marcus hung his head a moment before continuing. "This is how Dalton operates. He doesn't do anything overtly. Now, it's a suggestion. People will begin talking, he'll let it simmer for a while, and then he'll nudge it a little further, maybe mention the Wielders, even indirectly. His followers will make the connection themselves and the next thing you know, they'll all believe the Wielders are refusing to heal the ley because they don't want to lose control of the Needle and Dalton will have said nothing you can use against him to refute it."

"All because of a damned vision he made up," Kara added for emphasis.

"Are you so certain he lied about the vision?"

"You believe him, Hernande? Since when did you become a member of the Kormanley?"

Hernande leaned forward in his seat. "I'm not Kormanley, nor do I necessarily believe that Dalton is having visions of the future. But *he* believes he has visions of the future. And consider this vision. It's more complicated than it needs to be. If all he wanted to do was plant the seed that the Wielders would not be able to heal the ley and that disaster is coming, why mention the snake? Why bring in this feral dog? He could have simply talked about the Three Sisters—if that's what those piercing lights really represent—and left the rest of it out."

"That's true," Ty said. "Why did he mention the snake and the dog?"

"Don't forget that he predicted the attack by the Gorrani and how we'd survive," Marcus threw in.

"As I've said before, I've always questioned that vision. He didn't reveal it until after he found out the Gorrani were coming and after Prime Lecrucius told us he could use the ley offensively."

"But it was rather precise," Marcus countered. "The Gorrani attack and our response fit his prophecy perfectly. He couldn't have known exactly how Lecrucius meant to use the ley. Not at that point."

Ty drew breath to argue, but Hernande cut him off with a gesture. "Let's assume for a moment that Dalton has had a vision—whether it was simply a dream he's chosen to interpret in a particular way, or some kind of divine intervention. What does it mean? In his interpretation, he ignored nearly all its particulars, focusing exclusively on how it ended."

They all sat in silence for a moment, mulling over the details of the vision. Kara crossed her arms over her chest and sagged back into the chair, refusing to participate. Her mind returned to the new Nexus they had managed to stabilize beneath the Needle and the nagging worry of the distortion over Tumbor.

"Based on the previous vision," Marcus began, "I think the black stone is obvious—the Needle. The crack probably represents the chasm caused by the quake that's split the city."

"And, like before, the snake represents the Gorrani. It was coming from the south, and our scouts report that is where the Gorrani retreated after being routed here by Lecrucius and the ley. It's not much of a stretch to think they'd come back again after regrouping, even though we haven't seen any signs of such activity. But who or what does the dog represent?"

"It came from the north," Cory interjected, "from black clouds roiling beneath three piercing lights. Any of us who've traveled on the plains know that there are constant storm clouds covering the Steppe and the Reaches. Could it be a group coming from there?"

Kara rolled her eyes. "You can't trust the vision that much. The Gorrani snake came out of the auroral lights, and we haven't seen any of them as far south as the Gorrani Flats recently. The clouds Dalton supposedly saw could mean nothing. The dog could mean nothing. It could all be nothing but the ravings of a madman."

"A madman who swore he saw the destruction of Erenthrall before the Shattering," Marcus said quietly, "who claims that if he'd had more faith—in himself and his visions—he could have stopped it. That's why he created the Kormanley—not the terrorist organization bombing the city, but the peaceful sect, the one Ischua belonged to, the one Dierdre drew me into. If he'd believed in himself more, the Kormanley might have succeeded. That's why he gathered us all here at the Needle, why he created the White Cloaks. Since he didn't stop the Shattering, he was intent on saving those who had survived."

"He wasn't trying to save everyone. What about the Temerites in Erenthrall? Or the Rats and the Tunnelers? What about the Gorrani and the rest of the groups in Tumbor?"

"He couldn't save them all individually. He was trying to save them by repairing the ley."

Kara opened her mouth to respond, then clamped it shut. She couldn't argue that. She'd seen what the Wielders had created here at the node, knew that if they'd been given more resources and more time, they might have succeeded.

Even if she did think that Dalton—along with Prime Wielder Lecrucius—had grown used to their power and would be loath to give it up.

The group remained quiet for a long moment. Then Cory ventured, "So . . . what should we do about him?"

"Dalton?" Ty took a sip of his wine. "We keep him locked up."

"We can't," Marcus countered. "It will only make the rumors about his vision and the connection to the Wielders spread faster." At the suspicious looks leveled at him from Cory and Ty, he added, "You know it's true."

"I agree," Hernande said. He was chewing on the end of his beard, a habit that Kara found particularly disgusting. "We can't keep Dalton away from the people. It will only further his cause."

"Then what? We can't let him continue to undermine us. He can't be allowed to speak. At least not for a few weeks. He's gone that long without speaking before."

Hernande's gaze fell on her. He spat out his beard and smoothed it down with one hand. "We need to counter him somehow. If you're right, he's trying to attack the Wielders, specifically their ability to heal the ley. If you want to convince the people that you are right and Dalton is wrong, then you need to prove that you *can* heal the ley."

"We have been healing it. We've stabilized all of the ley lines in Erenthrall and we've been working on those bypassing Tumbor through Farrade."

"No one can see those changes," Ty said. "As far as the populace is concerned, the Wielders have been sitting idly in the Needle since the healing of the distortion in Erenthrall."

Kara felt a hard, hot stone settle in the pit of stomach. "So what are you saying?"

"We need to do something more dramatic," Marcus said.

Kara looked at him, then at each expectant face around the room, ending with Hernande.

She drew in a deep, steadying breath and said, "You want me to heal Tumbor now, rather than later." When no one responded, she shook her head. "I refuse to do that. We aren't ready yet. The Nexus isn't ready yet. We don't have the power we need to be successful."

"Then you're going to have to accept that Dalton's little ploy today will work," Hernande said. "He's issued an ultimatum. Eventually, his followers will force you to act—either to heal the ley and prove yourself right, or to release him so that he can do it himself."

⟞⟝

Dierdre stalked through the corridors of the temple, only vaguely aware of the servants and enforcers who stepped swiftly out of her way.

"How could he?" she snarled, noting the undertone of hurt in the words and hating it. "How could he agree with her? He's Kormanley. He's Father's Son. He should have argued to let Father speak!"

But she couldn't ignore the pain in her chest brought on by the doubt and fear and jealousy that had settled over her the moment Marcus had returned to the Needle with Kara in tow. She'd hoped, even prayed, that Kara had died in the Shattering. Or if she'd survived the Shattering, perhaps she'd been caught in the quickening of the distortion.

But when Marcus had actually found her . . .

She halted in the middle of a corridor and leaned heavily against the canted wall, head bowed. Then she straightened, shoulders back, and brushed the moisture from the tightened skin around her eyes. She'd once seduced him away from Kara and the Wielders with the promises of the Kormanley. She'd done it for Dalton, for the cause. It had taken the Shattering for her realize how deeply she'd fallen for him in the process.

Now, with Kara alive and well and apparently staying here at the Needle, she realized she'd need to seduce Marcus once again. Not for Dalton and the Kormanley. For herself.

But in the meantime, she needed to find out more about Father and this new prophecy.

She wiped at her face again and adjusted the white clothing Dalton and the rest of those loyal to the Kormanley had adopted after the Wielders abandoned it. Settled, she headed toward Father's chambers.

Her brow creased when she rounded the corner in the uppermost tier of the temple and saw the doubled guard outside Father's door. Of the six, only two of them were loyal to her brother Darius, Commander Ty's second, but after a moment's hesitation she strode forward as if she belonged there.

She halted before the two men standing directly in front of the double doors into the inner chamber. "I've come to speak to Father."

"Commander Ty left explicit instructions that he was to be isolated," an enforcer blocking the door said. He was not one of those loyal to her brother.

One of the other men spoke up. "He did say those in the inner circle could enter, so that they could question him if necessary."

Dierdre glared at the first enforcer. "I just came from our meeting. You can verify this with Marcus or Commander Ty. I'm certain they're still in the orrery."

The man held her gaze steadily, then nodded, the gesture minute. He opened the door for her and let her slide past. Before he closed it fully, she caught him motioning to one of the others, the enforcer heading off in the direction she'd come from.

She swore beneath her breath. Technically, she wasn't part of the inner circle. Only her association with Marcus gave her some leeway to attend the meetings. Often, when they were discussing more important issues, she was asked to leave. She wasn't certain how much time she'd have with Father now.

Searching the inner chamber, shrouded in shadows and reeking of incense, Dierdre picked out Father in the far corner, staring out the window, his back turned to her. Sunlight poured in the open windows, that section of the room almost too bright. Through the window, Dierdre could see a black section of the Needle, framed on either side by the cloud-scudded western sky. Soon, the sun would sink low enough that it would reach even the deepest recesses of the room.

"I'm surprised they let you in to see me after this afternoon's sermon."

Dierdre huffed and joined Father at the window. "They may change their minds. They sent someone to ask Commander Ty if I should be allowed in or not."

Father turned toward her, gazing directly at her, as if he could see her, even though his eyes were completely clouded over with a thick white film. His dark hair was streaked with gray, only that above his ears turned completely white. "Then we should talk quickly. Why have you come?"

"They said you announced another vision."

"Yes." He turned away, gazing out the window again. "It began the night Commander Ty and the others seized control of the Needle. A snake, a dog, and the Three Sisters." He drew out the last syllable; the hissing sent a shiver down Dierdre's spine.

"Then it's a true vision. You didn't make it up."

"Is that what they are saying?"

"Even Marcus believes it." She couldn't hide her disgust.

"Ah, Dierdre." He reached over and stroked her long black hair, then rested his hand on her opposite shoulder, drawing her closer to his side. It was a comforting gesture, and she leaned into him. "Don't you remember doubting me? Before the Shattering, you questioned my vision of the end of Erenthrall." She tensed, but he patted her shoulder. "Oh, you never said anything out loud. To me, at least. But you doubted. I could see the uncertainty in your eyes."

"I never doubted the philosophy of the Kormanley. The Baron and the Prime Wielder were abusing the ley. That was obvious. It needed to be stopped."

"And it was, just not in the way I'd planned. Or imagined." Outside, the sun lowered enough that the clouds began to change from white-gray to shades of pink, darkening to orange. "Doubt is always part of faith. If you do not question sometimes, then how can your faith be real? How can it have meaning? You stayed by my side, even though you doubted, and your faith was restored by the Shattering and what followed afterward. Now you believe. Marcus will become a believer again as well."

Dierdre thought of Kara and her influence, of all the other unbelievers that surrounded them now, but kept quiet. Instead, she focused on the new prophecy. "Your vision . . . what does it mean?"

Father let her go to step forward toward the light. He turned his face toward the sun, his skin washed with the coming sunset. "I'm uncertain. Like all my visions, it isn't clear. But the vision . . ." He shuddered. "It is a portent. And it involves the Three Sisters. Of that, I am certain."

Behind, the double doors were flung open and the enforcer who'd confronted her stepped inside. Dierdre jumped, startled.

Father merely said, "It appears our time is up."

❧

The informal meeting broke up as soon as the enforcer arrived to ask whether Dierdre was allowed access to Father Dalton. After Commander Ty rose to deal with the situation, the others had merely shared unsettled glances. There hadn't been anything left to discuss. Marcus stood first, muttering something about finding Dierdre and calming her down, since she'd likely be furious. Cory and Hernande shifted closer to Kara.

"Do you think she'll present a problem?" Kara asked, thinking about Marcus.

"Potentially," Hernande said. "She is certainly one of Dalton's more faithful followers, before and after the Shattering, if what you and Marcus have said is true. It will depend on whether she believes in his visions enough to act on them."

"She can't be trusted," Cory said forcefully. "She and her brother Darius are too close to Dalton. Both of them have visited Dalton on a regular basis before today's incident."

Hernande tugged on his beard. "I would certainly suggest that she be watched more closely from now on. And I'd recommend not allowing her into any of our future meetings."

"I think that's a good idea," Kara said. "I'll talk to Ty about it."

"And what about Marcus?" Cory asked.

"What about him?"

Cory stared at her, incredulous. "Dierdre has her fingers wrapped around him. Even if she doesn't attend the meetings, Marcus is probably telling her about everything you discuss. It isn't enough to kick her out, you need to deal with Marcus as well."

"He isn't like that. He wouldn't reveal information he knows is supposed to be confidential."

"Really? Kara, he joined a subversive group potentially linked to terrorist acts in Erenthrall. You know he told them secrets about the nodes, about the ley structure. He manipulated the damned Nexus for them!"

"He's changed since then. He helped us seize control of the Needle, even killed Lecrucius, our only Prime. And he didn't support Dierdre today. He agreed that Dalton's visions were likely fake and that Dierdre shouldn't have access to Dalton after what happened."

Cory's mouth opened, then clamped shut. He threw up his hands in disgust. "I don't understand you. He betrayed us all once before, he'll do it again if it suits him." He turned toward Hernande, but not before Kara saw the flicker of hurt that crossed his face. "You talk to her. Maybe she'll listen to you."

A pang of guilt burrowed into Kara's stomach as she watched his retreating back. She held her breath until he'd vanished, then exhaled, gripping the back of one of the chairs. "What am I doing, Hernande? What's happening here?"

He said nothing for a long moment, eyeing her with such intensity that she finally met his gaze. "You still have feelings for Marcus."

It wasn't a question, but she protested anyway. "Impossible. He betrayed me for Dierdre, for the Kormanley!"

"It doesn't matter. At one point, you loved him. There will always be a part of you that loves him. Cory knows this. Like you, he thought Marcus was dead, that these feelings you had for Marcus were no longer a threat. But now, here, at the Needle, you both discovered that Marcus is alive. And, more than that, he betrayed the Kormanley in order to destroy Lecrucius and save us all. The part of you that once loved him sees hope in that act. Cory recognizes this."

Kara couldn't move. What Hernande had said was too close to a truth she didn't want to acknowledge. "So what . . . do we exclude Marcus from the meetings because of what he might say to Dierdre?"

"I think the more relevant question is, do we continue to invite him simply because you are uncertain of your feelings for him?"

Kara winced and looked away, staring at the sun and planets and moons as they shifted in their orbits in the orrery overhead.

"We can't exclude him. He helped us take control of the Needle. We owe him for that, regardless of how I feel about him."

"Then someone needs to speak to him about Dierdre and the potential risk she represents."

"You don't think he already knows?"

"Of course he does. It's one of the reasons there's so much tension between them. But it should still be done."

Kara's shoulders slumped. "I'll take care of it. But not right now."

She pushed away from the chair and headed for the door. She stifled a surge of annoyance when Hernande fell into step beside her. "Was there something else?"

"Yes, actually. I'm concerned."

"About what?"

"About you."

Taken aback, Kara halted. "Me? Why are you concerned about me?"

Hernande motioned her forward again. He let her lead the way and without thought she guided them toward the Needle and the new Nexus Marcus and Lecrucius had created there.

"Since you healed the distortion over Erenthrall—and allowed Morrell to heal your wounds—you've been working yourself hard on stabilizing the ley lines and learning to use the Nexus. I know you've been studying the distortion around Tumbor as well. But in the last week or so you've become . . . prickly."

"Prickly?"

He waved a dismissive hand. "Short-tempered, curt, easy to rile. I've never known you to be so tense. The others believe it is simply stress caused by overwork."

"The others?"

"Ty, Marcus, Allan and Bryce before they departed for Erenthrall . . . and Cory."

Kara thought back to earlier that evening, when Cory had been goading her with questions, prodding her, like a cook disturbing the coals of a fire, keeping his distance. He'd only come close after she'd caught on to what he was doing.

"I suppose I have been a little . . . *prickly* lately." She couldn't help a wry, twisted grin at the word.

"It's more than overwork, though, isn't it?"

They'd reached the lower level of the temple and now stood before the doors leading out to the small stone garden filled with stellae and the black base of the Needle. She shoved through the doors, halting a step beyond, squinting as her eyes adjusted to the light of the sunset, its fiery orange in stark contrast to the thin black spire of the Needle.

"What do you mean?" she asked.

"It's Tumbor."

Her heart clenched, although she tried not to let the reaction show.

When she didn't answer, he continued. "You've been working to repair the ley lines, but I think you've done what you can, except for general upkeep. We haven't had a quake—even a minor one—in two weeks, and yet, instead of relaxing, you've grown more tense." He turned to look at her. She could feel his eyes on her, like an itch against her skin. "The only pressing issue remaining is Tumbor."

She let her gaze drop from the lurid sky overhead to the base of the Needle, to the entrance that led down to the pit beneath. "It's . . . huge. Larger than the distortion over Erenthrall. It's . . . daunting."

"Are you saying it can't be healed?"

"No, it can be done. But the ley system isn't ready to handle it yet. The Wielders aren't ready." *She* wasn't ready.

Hernande reached forward and gripped her upper arm, squeezing in reassurance. "There is still time. And don't forget the mentors. We haven't yet figured out how we and the other University students can best be used to help heal it, but I know it can be done. You are not alone. But Dalton will not wait. Now that he has begun, he will not stop."

Kara bit her lower lip, thinking about all that they'd done with the new Nexus, all that needed to be done if they were going to be able to handle the distortion over Tumbor, all that they had not yet figured out.

Then she sighed and said, "I know," stepping forward into the depths of the Needle.

Four

"LOOK. To the southeast. I see smoke."

Cutter shifted his attention away from the band of wagons headed south along the deep cut—more a ravine now—of the river where it had been diverted by the distortion over Tumbor. With the quickening, the river had formed a small lake at the distortion's edge, the water eventually carving out a new path southeast around the obstruction. But, unlike the rivers in Erenthrall, it hadn't found its way back to its former path. Instead, over the last month it had eaten a new course into the plains, diverted into a southeasterly flow.

The small communities that had survived the quickening of the distortion had adapted. Those north of the city had entrenched themselves into their already established holdings, building up their defenses in the form of wooden stockades and the use of the natural landscape around them. Cutter and the four enforcer scouts that formed his party had spent the last two weeks gathering information about those groups. But as soon as they'd discovered the divergent river, they'd begun following it.

They were now two days beyond Tumbor, its distortion still glowing a rose-orange tinged with purple behind them. They were keeping a discreet distance from the river, traveling parallel to its course so they wouldn't run into the occasional small groups of two or three wagons like the one below. Groups of wagons of this size were rare now, having been thinned out after the Shattering by larger groups like the one he and the others from the Hollow had encountered from Haven, intent on theft if not all-out slaughter.

"Where's the smoke?" he asked Larrin, who lay in the grass on his right. Larrin was the youngest of their group, nineteen, with unruly brown hair and a gangly body, although he wasn't especially tall. The other three enforcers were behind them, keeping their horses quiet and out of sight.

Larrin carefully pointed. "On the horizon. I'd say at least another half day's ride. Looks to be on the river, though."

"Can you see what's causing it?" Cutter scanned the southeastern horizon, picking out the faint trace of smoke angling up from the plains. His arm throbbed with pain where he'd been shot by the White Cloaks in Erenthrall before Kara and the others had been captured. Morrell had healed it after she'd arrived at the Needle, but Cutter still felt it throb at odd moments.

He wondered if it were one of the enforcers he now worked with who had shot him.

Larrin squinted, eyes barely slits, then shrugged. "We're too far. Could be a bonfire or a campfire."

"It's no campfire." The smoke was black, the column thick. That's the only reason they'd been able to pick it out against the blue sky. "It could be another settlement like the one we've already passed. Maybe that's where this group is headed."

He glanced back down to the wagons trundling along, a shout from one of the men drifting up toward them. The wagons began to slow, drawing to a stop near a shallow section of the new riverbed.

"Do you think they've seen us?" Larrin asked, voice tense.

"No." He glanced toward the smoke. "And they couldn't have seen the smoke yet either, not from the river. They're likely stopping to rest the horses."

As he spoke, the men—and one woman carrying a sword and crossbow, he realized—called out an all clear, and everyone began spilling from the wagons.

Cutter waited long enough he was certain they were simply halting at a convenient location, then pulled Larrin back from the low ridge. They rejoined the other three enforcers, Cutter taking the reins of his own horse back and immediately mounting.

"Find something?" Marc asked as they all followed suit. He was the oldest of the group and resented the fact that Cutter, a mere woodsman from the hills, had been given leadership of the scouting party. Broad-shouldered, he towered nearly a foot over Cutter, but could be surprisingly silent and unobtrusive when he wanted to stay hidden.

"Smoke in the distance south of here."

"How far?"

"Another hour at most."

"We're already two days out of range," Marc said, not quite a protest.

"Another hour or two won't hurt. I want to see what's causing that smoke."

Marc shrugged. "It's your lead."

The others glanced between the two, fidgeting, picking up on the tension. Cutter ignored them, kicking his mount into motion. They cut away from the river, swinging out and around in a low arch, moving slowly enough they could spot potential threats with time to hide. But they saw nothing, and an hour and a half later they halted, having angled back toward the river again. Larrin—who Cutter had sent out slightly ahead of the group—returned at a light gallop, face grim.

"There's a small copse of trees ahead," he said. "We can use it as cover."

"Marc, come with me. The rest of you stay with the horses."

They followed Larrin to the copse, skirting between the trees and the underbrush before hunkering down at its edge.

Ahead, the column of black smoke rose from the burning remains of what had once been a fortified village nestled in a curve of the river. Sharpened logs had been erected in a rough circular stockade around a cluster of a half dozen buildings. But the defenses had proven worthless. One section of the wall had been pulled down—Cutter couldn't see how—and the buildings inside were only charred remains, three of them still burning furiously, flames shooting toward the sky. Carrion crows circled the destruction, and Cutter picked out over two dozen bodies inside the enclosure, left where they'd fallen, distorted by heat shimmer.

"What's that?" Marc asked, nodding toward a dark stain on the grassland a short distance from the walls. The enforcer's tone had changed. The derogatory hint of disrespect that had colored all his comments since they'd left the Needle had died. "Did the grass catch fire?"

Cutter frowned. "No, it's not scorching. It's not dark enough." Then it hit him, and his stomach turned. "It's the rest of the villagers. What's left of them."

Larrin gulped, then bent over and retched into the underbrush to one side. When he stood back up, his face was white and he still looked sick. His hand trembled as he wiped a string of bile from his mouth. "I didn't notice it before," he said weakly. "I only saw the fire."

Marc sniffed in disdain and returned his attention to the village. "I don't see any movement at all. Whoever did this has already left."

Cutter took a closer look at the land surrounding the village, noting the rough markings of a dirt road winding close to the river, heading north and south. It faded the farther it got from the village, but it was obviously worn into the earth by wagons like the ones they'd seen earlier. The texture of the plains changed to the east, where scattered trees dotted the grassland, a verge of darker forest beginning not too far from the village, the likely source of the wood used in the stockade.

But what caught his attention was the trampled earth that angled into the village from the southwest. He didn't see another path leading away, which meant whoever had attacked had retreated along the same route. He wouldn't be able to verify it unless they took a closer look.

"Larrin, go get the others."

The youngest enforcer nodded reluctantly and retreated.

The smell of charred flesh struck them first as the wind shifted and blew the smoke toward them. The other two enforcers gagged, one falling to his knees and vomiting into the dirt road. The horses grew skittish and backed away, nostrils flaring. The smoke burned Cutter's eyes, and he coughed and pulled the collar of his shirt up over the lower part of his face to filter out some of the ash, but he continued forward, dragging his horse with him. Sweat broke out on his forehead as he rounded the edge of the pine-scented wall where it had been pulled down and the heat from the fire hit him. Wood hissed and spat as it burned, reeking of boiling sap. It hadn't been cut that long ago. He squinted and shaded his face with one hand, but the fire was too intense. He backed away to where the others had halted.

"We won't be able to get any closer," he said. "Not until it dies down, and I don't want to wait that long. But the stockade is relatively new. It hasn't been here long. Let's check out that trail."

They circled away from the blistering heat, around the remains of the collapsed wall, and halted, stunned into silence as they stared out at the slaughtered villagers. Cutter had thought they'd simply been gathered up by whoever had attacked and then cut down, but it was far worse.

Far worse.

The bodies had been mutilated, eviscerated and hacked apart, arms and legs chopped off, heads severed and thrown aside, to the point where there would be no way to identify individual body parts to piece them back together again if they tried. The grass was soaked with blood and entrails and gore, all of it cloaked with the glistening bodies of the feasting carrion birds.

Marc swore, then clamped his jaw shut, his muscles rigid with outrage. Larrin had hung back, but the stench was overwhelming and he succumbed to another bout of retching. Cutter's own stomach rebelled, and he was forced to crouch down, head bowed, sucking in deep breaths through his mouth to keep control. Tears not caused by the smoke pricked his eyes, then coursed down his cheeks.

Behind him, one of the other enforcers muttered, "They didn't even spare the women or children."

Cutter's fingers dug into his own flesh where his hand rested on one knee. With effort, he controlled himself and stood, turning his back on the carnage. "Let's go." His voice cracked. He didn't bother wiping the tears as he stalked away.

"Who did this?" Marc asked through clenched teeth as Cutter passed him.

"Someone filled with rage. With hate."

"But who?"

Cutter could think of only one group that would have cause for such hatred, but he simply said, "Let's find out."

The attackers had left a clear path, the earth churned and trampled into thick mud. Cutter knelt at the edge and examined the tracks before edging out further. The others followed, spreading out. Marc stayed close to Cutter, watching intently as he shifted from one set of footprints to a section closer to the splintered, fallen wall, where the mud had been gouged with deep grooves. Here, clear imprints from horse hooves littered the area. He grunted and stepped to the remains of the wall, partially embedded in the mud. The heat from the fires within the stockade boiled outward, already baking the mud solid, but it was the top of the collapsed wall that drew him. He knelt again and traced out freshly clawed gouges in the tree bark beneath the sharpened points of the ends of each log.

"What is it?" Marc asked.

"Something bit into the wood here, like a claw."

Marc scanned what remained standing of the stockade. Something inside the enclosure cracked and part of a building collapsed in a shower of sparks, striking and knocking over another section of the wall. "Grappling hook," he said, then motioned to the deeper trenches dug into the earth beside him. "They hooked the wall, then pulled it down with their horses."

"From the tracks, I'd say the force was small. No more than fifty."

The muscles in Marc's jaw twitched. "Fifty. And they did all of this." He waved toward the slaughtered villagers.

Larrin suddenly shouted, causing both of them to turn. He stood a hundred yards away, off to one side of the trampled path, waving frantically.

"We'd better see what he's found," Marc said.

They headed toward the young enforcer, the two others moving to join them, abandoning their own search.

Larrin stood over a body stretched out on the grass. He rested about ten feet from the edge of the main set of tracks, nestled inside a natural depression in the earth. He wore familiar armor, the mail gleaming in the sun where it wasn't splattered with dried blood. His hand still clutched a distinctive curved sword.

Cutter grabbed a shoulder and rolled the body onto its back. Thin darkened features stared back at them, the thick beard braided in a complicated knot, tied with colored string. More dirt and gore caked the front of his armor and face, some of it from a wound he still clutched at his left side, beneath his armor. His entire left leg was sheathed in blood, still damp, having been trapped between his body and the grass where he'd collapsed.

"Gorrani," Marc spat, kneeling at the man's side. He pulled the man's hand away from his side with a jerk and examined the wound. "Knife wound. Deep. Not that wide. It could have come from a kitchen knife rather than a dagger. He bled out. Probably didn't think it was that serious." He did a quick search of the rest of the body. "No other significant wounds, only scratches and nicks."

"At least someone fought back," one of the enforcers muttered.

"There had to have been other casualties," Marc said, standing again and gesturing toward the stockade. "A wall like that doesn't come down quickly. They would have had time to pelt them with arrows and form a line of defense inside."

"You're assuming there were more than simple villagers here," Cutter said. Marc bristled as Cutter continued. "But you're right. There must have been other wounded, if not dead. They must have taken them with them, gathered them up before setting the fire and butchering the villagers still alive."

"How'd they miss him?" Larrin asked.

"He stumbled off the main path and fell in this ditch, probably when they were retreating."

"Thank Korma," Marc muttered, genuflecting. "Otherwise we might not have found out who did this."

"But why?" Larrin asked. "They didn't take anything. They just destroyed everything and left."

"Revenge." All the enforcers looked at Cutter. "We killed four thousand of their warriors at the Needle with the ley. Four thousand dead in the space of a breath, not even their bodies left behind." He let that sink in before adding, "Look at how we reacted with a few hundred villagers slaughtered here. Now, how do you think the Gorrani feel?"

He saw the realization dawn in each of their faces, confusion slowly seeping away to fear. All except for Marc. His expression settled into grim determination edged with anticipation.

"They're going to attack everyone who isn't Gorrani," he said.

Cutter didn't know how to respond to the look in Marc's eyes, so he turned and headed toward his horse.

"Are we going to follow them?" Marc called out from behind.

"No! We're going back to the Needle. We need to warn them about the Gorrani threat."

"It's not that deep," Morrell said, folding the fabric of the man's shirt back from the wound. He hissed as it pulled at the already coagulating blood matted to the cloth.

"It hurts like hell," he grumbled.

Morrell grabbed a clean cloth, wet it, and began to dab at the wound, trying to get most the blood clear. "I'm certain it does. How did it happen?"

The man—in his early twenties with a three-day beard and dark bruises under his eyes, smelling faintly of alcohol—shifted nervously on his cot. "Stupid enforcer sliced me with his knife."

Morrell frowned, only half of her attention on what the man said. The wound had been exposed, a slash across the man's bicep, no more than two inches long. It looked clean, but she poured water from a small pitcher next to her over it, the man gasping at the sudden pain. Her fingers unconsciously dug in deeper to keep him from jerking away from her. It was certainly a blade wound of some type. No jagged edges. No ragged skin. Although she doubted it had come from an enforcer.

As she touched the flesh around the wound, her own skin prickled with a now familiar sensation, like an itch, only somehow more pleasant. A wisp of colored light, like the auroral lights that drifted across the plains, wrapped around her fingers, but she held it in check. She'd learned some nominal control of it since leaving the Hollow and coming to the Needle to join her father. And she'd learned that she didn't need to heal every patient.

Sitting back, letting the prickling sensation fade, she said, "It's deep enough that it will require a few stitches. I'll be right back with a needle and some thread."

As she rose, the man grabbed her arm and halted her, his grip too tight. "I thought you were that girl . . . the one who heals people. Aren't you going to"—he lifted his wounded arm with a wince and wriggled his fingers—"you know, heal it?"

She pulled out of his grip in disgust. "I don't heal everyone that way. Only the more serious cases."

She walked stiffly to the side of the long room lined with beds for the wounded, although most of them were currently empty. Four other patients waited to be seen, two of them with obvious flus or colds from their haggard expressions, one with some type of rash, and another with what might be a broken wrist. They were being seen to by healer Freesia—a thickset woman in her mid-forties with a mild manner but a steel spine when riled and wild hair that would not be tamed no matter how much she tried—and two other assistant healers. Morrell had been afraid of how she'd be received when she arrived, knowing how Logan in the Hollow had initially balked at accepting her mystical talents, but Freesia had been awed rather than fearful. When one of her assistants had made some disparaging remark under his breath, Freesia had slapped him and told him he could leave her hospital at once if he truly felt that way. The young man, Cerrin, only a few years older than Morrell, had rubbed his already reddening cheek and shook his head. Only Morrell had seen the resentful glare when Freesia had turned away.

As she snatched up a needle and some thread from the supply cabinets along one wall, movement from the far side of the room caught her eye. Drayden—the Wolf she'd transformed back at the Hollow and now her self-proclaimed bodyguard—had shifted forward in concern, but she waved him back and returned to the man with the knife wound, plopping down into the chair by the bed without looking the man in the eyes. Most of her initial disgust had died while fetching the materials, but as she pulled his arm toward her, he said, "But won't stitching leave a scar? I've heard that when you do it—you know, without the thread—that there's not even a blemish."

She met his gaze, saw the look of hope and excitement there, and her disgust flared back full force.

She smiled sweetly. "That depends on how much you struggle when I'm stitching this up."

His look of shock sent a warm thrill of satisfaction through her. She grabbed his arm and said, "Now hold still. This will only hurt a little."

He groaned and writhed slightly as she jabbed him and pulled. She'd intended to make it hurt, but the innate healer inside her refused to cooperate and she stitched the wound closed with precise efficiency, tugging the thread taut and biting it off the way Logan had taught her. Then she wrapped a bandage around the man's arm and led him to the door. She may have shoved him a little harder than necessary to get him moving when he initially resisted, a protest half formed on his lips.

As soon as he was out the door, she sighed. But then Freesia called her over to the woman with the hurt wrist.

"I can't tell if this is simply sprained or actually broken," Freesia said in exasperation. "Could you take a look?"

Morrell nodded, taking Freesia's place beside the dark-haired woman, who glanced back and forth between the two of them with a slightly fearful look before settling on Morrell.

"I tripped and fell down the stairs inside the temple," she said, extending her arm.

"Can you move it?"

"A little. It doesn't hurt at all."

"But if she turns it in just the right way," Freesia supplied, "she says she gets light-headed."

"That's why I came in to have it looked at."

Morrell had already touched the woman's skin, the prickling sensation returning, along with the wisps of light. The woman gasped as those lights strengthened, Morrell reaching out with her senses. The woman's blood rushed through Morrell's ears as she sank beneath the skin, through muscle and tendon and tissue to the bone. The flesh was bruised in places, both here at the wrist and in the woman's hip and shoulder. There were a few minor scrapes as well. But Morrell focused on the many tiny rounded bones at the wrist.

"Two of the bones here are fractured," she said, her words sounding loud in her ears. Her senses were heightened when she worked with the aurora—sights, sounds, smells, tastes, and textures sharper. "When you turn your wrist the wrong way, they grind against each other."

The woman shuddered. "Can you fix it?"

Morrell hesitated. It wasn't that significant or life-threatening. If the woman bound the wrist and kept from using it for a few weeks, it would heal on its own. She didn't need to heal it herself.

But she was already wrapped deeply into the woman's body, their breath synchronized, their pulses thudding in tandem. She'd wound herself into the intricate and delicate balance of her body, could sense her heartbeat, the contraction of her lungs, the minute shifts in muscle as she fidgeted on the cot. All it would take would be a little nudge—

The auroral lights surged brighter for a moment, and heat washed from Morrell into the woman's wrist. The woman gasped as a tingle ran up her arm and into her chest, a tingle Morrell experienced through her. At the same time, a wave of weariness washed through Morrell's own body. Nothing too significant, but as she pulled her hands away from the woman's wrist, the auroral light dying out, the weariness didn't completely fade.

"You should be fine now," Morrell said. Her voice had a faint tremor in it, but she steadied it. "Go ahead, move your wrist around."

The woman's brow creased in consternation, but she tentatively began rotating her hand. When there was no dizziness, her eyes widened. "You've . . . you've fixed it. I don't understand how, but . . ." She laughed, a short, sharp, disbelieving sound, then stood. "Thank you! Thank you!"

Morrell suddenly realized the woman hadn't known about her healing powers. Unlike the man before her, she'd simply wanted Morrell to reassure her, bandage it up, and send her on her way.

Morrell smiled and sank back in her chair, unaccountably grateful. She hadn't even realized her shoulders had been tensed up . . . or that she hadn't smiled when she'd finished healing the woman.

"This way," Freesia said, bustling the woman toward the front of the chamber. Morrell could hear the woman speaking to the healer as they went, but she didn't listen in. The incredulous tone told her enough.

"It's a nice feeling, isn't it?"

Morrell jerked in her seat and spun around, her heart thudding once painfully in her chest before she recognized the voice. "Hernande!" she exclaimed, jumping out of the chair and hugging him tightly. He oomphed as she squeezed him, but chuckled, giving her a tight hug himself before she pulled back.

"How are you feeling? It didn't take that much out of you, did it?"

"No. I'm being careful."

"She still shouldn't have done it," Freesia scolded, coming up from behind Hernande. Her expression was stern, but it didn't quite touch her eyes. She waved her other assistants toward three new arrivals. "That woman's wrist would have healed fine on its own. There was no need for you to bother with it."

"I know. But it was easy."

"And what would you have done if someone with a shattered arm or a crushed leg had come in and we'd needed you for that? If you burn yourself out on these unnecessary, petty things, you won't have the reserves for anything more significant. Just because you can heal, doesn't mean you should."

"I didn't heal the man before her." It came out more petulant and defensive than she'd intended.

"And what was his problem?" Hernande asked.

"A knife wound on his arm that only required stitches."

"And why didn't you heal him?"

"Because he was being an ass," Freesia said before Morrell could answer. "Don't think I didn't overhear." Then, to Hernande: "He wanted her to heal him, like she did the woman. I wouldn't be surprised if he cut his own arm, just to see her do it."

Morrell gasped. "Why would he do that?"

"Because some people have no common sense," Freesia said. "When he came in, he specifically asked for you. I sent him to see what you would do. And you handled him perfectly. Better than I would have. He'd probably have a scar if I'd stitched him up."

She caught Morrell's shocked expression and laughed, cupping the back of Morrell's head briefly with one hand. "Oh, don't look so surprised. I vowed not to harm. I never said anything about leaving behind reminders of stupidity. Now, I believe someone is here to speak with you. We're not too busy right now, so go. We can handle it for a while. But come back when you're done. We still have work to do."

She moved off after a warning look at Hernande. He raised a questioning eyebrow at Morrell.

"She's teaching me new techniques," she sighed. "Things Logan hadn't gotten around to yet, or that Logan didn't know."

"I see." He led her down the row of cots, out into the outer rooms, and into the street. Drayden followed them at a discreet distance. Morrell had gotten used to him trailing her around, his presence more obvious when her father was away. She blinked up at the mild sunlight, half blocked by clouds. The large bank of a storm loomed off to the northeast, bearing down on them, flashes of lightning occasionally brightening it from within. The gusting wind pushing through the streets of the outer city smelled of rain, and the people in the tent city that began at the far end of the street were rushing to drag possessions inside and tie down loose flaps. Those on their own street were sprinting for shelter.

"That's moving in faster than I thought," Hernande said in irritation. "We'd better head to the temple."

They didn't make it, a crack of thunder rumbling through the city a moment before the deluge began. They dashed down the last section of street and plowed through the lowest tier's door with a gasp, dripping cold water onto the stone floor, Drayden shaking himself like a wet dog. Shivering, Hernande led her and Drayden to the temple's kitchens, setting her down before one of the ley heating stones to dry off and warm up as he went to harass the cook into handing over some

fresh bread. The kitchen staff worked around them, the noise of rat-
tling pots and pans, barked orders, and thudding cleavers almost overriding the growls of thunder from overhead.

Morrell bit into her slice of bread with abandon, relishing its warmth
as she continued to shiver from being drenched. It must have just come
from the ovens. The only thing that would have made it better was if
Hernande had stopped to find some butter or honey.

"Not where I'd expected to have this conversation, but it will do,"
Hernande said between his own more conservative bites.

Morrell paused, suddenly wary. "Conversation about what?"

"About what happened months ago with Cory."

Morrell couldn't hide her surprise. "Cory?"

"Yes, Cory. Remember the quake that caused the partial collapse of
the ceiling in the node chamber in the caves near the Hollow?"

"Cory's leg was trapped under the boulder. The Wielders managed
to move the boulder, and I healed his leg."

"I don't think they moved the boulder. I think *you* dealt with it."

Morrell stopped chewing. The bread suddenly tasted like a mouthful
of dried bitterbane herb. She swallowed it with a painful grimace and
said quietly, "That's impossible. The boulder was huge."

"I agree. Far too large for the Wielders to handle, even though there
were half a dozen of them trying. It's been nagging me since I first
walked into that chamber and saw where Cory had been caught."

"If you don't think they could move it, then how could I have—"

"I didn't say you'd *moved* it. I think you . . . reshaped it, so that the
indentation Cory's leg was caught in was large enough he could be
pulled free."

She grew still, Hernande remaining silent. She recalled that moment, an echo of the fear and desperation to help Cory washing through
her again with a shudder. She'd touched Cory's leg to see how badly
damaged it was, had felt the stone around it that held it trapped. She
remembered pushing at the stone with her mind as the others strained
to shove it aside.

"Is it that far of a stretch?" Hernande said softly. "We know the auroral lights are transformative. Look at what they did to the Wolves.
And we know your talent is associated with the auroral lights. We can
see them when you're working. If the lights can warp buildings and
humans alike, why couldn't you?"

"But I don't feel the stone," Morrell protested, "not like I can feel what's wrong with my patients or the Wolves when I heal them." Which wasn't exactly true. She *could* feel the stone around her, just not in the same way she felt people when she touched them.

"I wouldn't expect you to feel the stone," Hernande said. "It's stone. It doesn't have blood or tissue or tendons. It doesn't have a specific base state, a 'healthy' norm. But that doesn't mean it can't be molded. Even the Wielders learned to reshape stone for their own purposes. They used it to build many of the buildings in Erenthrall in some of the inner districts, like the Amber Tower." His brow creased in sudden thought and his hand drifted up to his beard. "I wonder if they were using some form of the auroral lights and didn't realize it? Maybe there's a connection between the ley and the aurora, just as there's a connection between the ley and the Tapestry . . ."

Morrell took another bite of her bread, aware of Hernande's tendency to drift off onto tangents. She stared into the soft glow of the heating stone. Had she saved Cory by reshaping the stone? She didn't know. It had been too chaotic. And afterward, the exhaustion from healing him had claimed her.

But now that Hernande had forced her to think about it . . . was "healing" a stone any different than healing a fractured or broken bone?

"Here," Hernande said, startling her out of her thoughts.

She held out her free hand, and he dropped a stone into it. It was smooth, like a river stone, a speckled gray in color, but it had been cracked, the seam of the crack not quite stretching from one side to the other.

"See if you can heal it."

She popped the last of her bread into her mouth and cradled the stone in both hands as she chewed. Once she swallowed, she said hesitantly, "I'm not certain I'll be able to call up the aurora. It doesn't usually come unless I'm touching someone's skin."

"Try."

Concentrating, she willed the aurora to appear, picturing it threading around her fingers as it had earlier that day, but nothing happened. No wisps of color weaving across her hand. No prickling in her skin. Her shoulders tensed with the effort, her jaw clenched.

She exhaled sharply, unaware she'd been holding her breath, and shook her head. "It's no use. It's not coming."

"Hmm." Hernande eyed her critically, the end of his beard stuck in his mouth. "Perhaps you're trying too hard."

"What do you mean?"

He shifted, so that they were facing each other, and reached down to cup her hands in his.

"I mean you're *trying* to call it forth. But is that what you do when you're healing someone?"

"Not exactly. I don't really think about it. The aurora usually just appears when I'm examining the wound or infection or whatever."

"Then that is what you must do here."

"I don't understand."

He tapped her hands with his fingers. "Look at the stone."

She glanced down at it.

"Don't think of it as a stone," Hernande said, his voice soft and soothing. "Think of it as you would a patient. Look at the fissure in the stone like you would a wound. Think of how the stone should appear, smoothed by the waters of the river, its surface unblemished. The crack is a flaw. It shouldn't be there. It needs to be healed."

Morrell felt herself sinking into his voice as it washed over her, and a moment later felt herself sinking into the stone as well. It wasn't the same as with patients. There, the flow of blood, of life, grabbed her and pulled her down into itself, like a river current dragging her into its embrace. Here there was no flow, no current. But she sank into the stone's surface nonetheless. It was more difficult—there was more resistance—but the texture of the stone became rougher and she could sense subtle differences in the composition of the stone, flecks of block-ier crystals that gave it its mottled appearance, a vein of something softer threaded through one side—

And the crack. She could trace out its depth, could feel the weak-nesses in the stone around it. If she tapped the stone right *there* with a small hammer, it would shatter into a hundred pieces.

As soon as she felt the fissure and realized it was a flaw, her fingers began prickling. She gasped as the aurora appeared, shimmering around both her and Hernande's clasped hands and the stone. Hernande stilled.

"Good," he said. If he were concerned about the aurora that flickered around his hands, it didn't color his voice. "Now, see if you can fix the crack."

Before he'd finished speaking, she felt the warmth rush from her hands into the stone as it had earlier with the woman's hand and her fractured bones. As it heated in her palm, she gasped, jerking back, the stone dropping to the floor. It rattled around the kitchen's flagstones as Hernande reached out to steady her, and Drayden lurched forward with a warning growl.

"Are you all right?" Hernande asked.

She sucked in a steadying breath, then exhaled heavily. "It grew warm."

"Did it burn you?"

"It wasn't that hot. It just startled me."

Drayden backed down, and Hernande searched the floor until he found the stone again. He picked it up and held it a long moment before looking at Morrell with a curious expression on his face.

He handed the stone to her without a word.

The crack was gone, the surface returned to its original smoothness. An unexpected thrill of satisfaction tickled through her, and she smiled even as a wave of exhaustion hit. It was heavier than before, when she'd healed the woman's wrist, but it wasn't enough to smother her excitement. "I did it."

Hernande smiled. "I knew you could." Then his smile faltered. "But we should probably keep this between ourselves for now. No need to draw further attention to yourself."

Morrell thought of Freesia's assistant Cerrin, who already resented her, and those like the man who'd cut himself simply so he could have her heal him. "I won't say anything."

Hernande retrieved the stone. "I've kept you long enough. Freesia will be furious if I don't get you back soon."

With a guilty start, Morrell suddenly realized she didn't know how long she'd been away from the hospital. She leaped up out of her seat. "She was going to go over the medicinal herbs used for fevers, to compare with what I'd learned from Logan!"

She dashed for the kitchen door, not waiting for Hernande to rise. Drayden trotted at her heels. The University mentor shouted after her, "We'll talk about this more later!"

Then the kitchen fell behind as she raced through the temple toward the outer city . . . and whatever punishment Freesia decided was appropriate for returning so late.

Hernande watched her and Drayden's hasty retreat, then stared down at the stone in his hand.

Closing his fingers around it in a fist, he left the kitchens and began searching for Kara. He found her where he expected to find her: in the pit of the node.

Enforcers halted him inside the entrance to the Needle after his mad dash through the rain across the stellae garden. They sent a runner down into the node as he shook himself off, a Wielder—Artras—returning to escort him down. The elderly Wielder smiled when she saw him and ushered him forward, brushing the wisps of her hair away from her face.

"I don't know why they don't simply decree that you and Cory and the other University students and mentors have access to the node," she exclaimed, shaking her head. "It seems like the logical thing to do."

As they descended the steps, the black stone of the Needle pulsing with threads of ley around them, Hernande answered, "It has little to do with logic. There's always been animosity between the Wielders and the University, if not outright suspicion and hatred."

"That was in Erenthrall. And between the Primes and the University, not the Wielders. Both of them had their secrets and guarded them closely. We can't afford secrets anymore."

"No, I suppose not." But then Hernande halted.

They'd descended into the pit, the black stone of the outer Needle dropping away, replaced by much older river stones as the stairwell opened up. The chamber was far larger than Hernande remembered from the last time he'd been here. The stairs circled around the outer wall to the floor of the chamber, which stretched from the wall toward a large opening in the center of the room. White ley light washed up from the opening, tendrils of ley stretching up from below and cascading down in an elegant dance. A half dozen Wielders surrounded the pit, Kara among them, most with their arms stretched forward as they manipulated the ley, or so Hernande assumed. He couldn't feel the ley itself—those at the University studied the Tapestry—but he could see the looks of concentration on the Wielders' faces. Kara gave out orders, directing their efforts, her voice echoing through the chamber.

Artras gave him a moment, then tugged on his sleeve, drawing him downward. He picked out six crystal panes hovering over the pit, all canted at odd but precise angles. As he watched, one of those panes shifted, swinging on an unseen axis, Kara muttering, "Careful . . . careful . . . good. Now hold it there. Steady. Everyone, get ready. Marcus, I want you to release it."

"It's not going to remain in place," Marcus said, his forehead beaded with sweat. "There's too much ley coming down the Farrade line."

"Then be ready to catch it. We don't need another cascade effect like the last time. It would take us days to reset everything."

Marcus grimaced, but nodded. "I'm ready."

"On my mark, then. Everyone, control your own crystals; don't worry about the others. One, two, three, mark."

Marcus stepped back, arms lowering, as everyone else tensed. Hernande kept his eyes locked on the pane that had shifted. It remained where it floated for one breath, two—

And then it began to tilt. Kara swore and one of the other Wielders cried out as Marcus' arms snapped back up, as if he were attempting to catch the crystal. And he did, somehow, for the pane slowed and halted.

Kara shook her head in disgust, glancing to the side and catching sight of Hernande and Artras. "That's enough for today. Return the prisms to their previous configuration and take a break. We'll regroup tomorrow."

Many of the Wielders exhaled in relief, a tension in the room dissipating as Kara turned her back on the ley and approached them, her expression taut with worry.

It appeared his little talk with her had not allowed her to relax.

"Progress?" he asked.

She waved a hand dismissively. "Not much. We've been trying different configurations for days now. None of them are stable enough to hold on their own, and I don't want to have Wielders down here constantly keeping them in place. Monitoring them and making subtle adjustments when they drift out of place is one thing. Constant control of their placement is entirely different. If we're going to attempt healing the distortion over Tumbor, I want this Nexus to be stable and channeling more ley than it is now."

"Perhaps the mentors could be of help? We've been meaning to work more closely together, now that we think there's a connection between the ley and the Tapestry."

"I know, and I've been meaning to sit down with you and Jerrain and discuss it. I've just been too focused on repairing the ley network."

"Maybe we can find a way to keep the crystals in place without active help from a Wielder. In Erenthrall, the mentors created constructs to help channel the ley. I'm certain something similar can be done here with those prisms."

"We'll find the time—"

"It's been a month, Kara."

She bowed her head, then looked back up with a weary grin. "Tomorrow, then. I'll meet with you tomorrow. But I doubt that's why you dragged yourself all the way down here. What do you need?"

"Actually, I have something to show you." He glanced meaningfully at Artras, who caught the look with a small start and raised eyebrows.

"I'll see if Marcus and the others need any help," she said.

After she'd wandered toward the pit, Hernande produced the stone he'd given to Morrell to "heal" and dropped it into Kara's hands.

"What's this?" she asked.

"A stone."

Kara gave him a dry look. "I realize that. Why is it important?"

"Because less than an hour ago, it had a crack running through it. I gave it to Morrell. She fixed it."

Kara's eyes widened in disbelief. "She fixed it?"

"She called on the aurora, as we've seen her do when she heals someone, and she sealed up the crack. I can't even tell where it was anymore."

Kara examined the stone carefully, rolling it around in her hands before shaking her head. "Neither can I."

"And there's more. Not only did she fix the crack, she changed the shape of the stone as well. It's more rounded than it was before. I don't even think she realizes she did it. She was too focused on the crack itself."

Kara stared at him a long moment, then tossed the stone upward, catching it, and then handing it back to him. "What does it mean?"

Hernande shrugged. "I'm not entirely certain yet. But she's more powerful than she realizes. More powerful than any of us realize."

Five

"WHY HAVEN'T THEY ATTACKED the walls yet?" Bryce muttered, slapping his hands down on the lip of the rooftop that overlooked the eastern section of Erenthrall outside the Temerite enclosure. In the midmorning sunlit streets below, the Butcher's rabble were visible, mingling with some of Baron Devin's forces from Haven. They'd set up a line far enough away they couldn't be targeted by the Temerite archers, but close enough and with enough men that if Lienta tried to open the gates, they'd be attacked almost instantly.

Much farther east, still outside the city's edge, an auroral storm washed across the horizon. Allan couldn't determine where it was headed— it was too distant and had too many coruscating colors—but it was one of the largest storms he'd seen to date.

"You sound as if you want them to attack," Boskell said.

"It's been two days. They should have done something by now."

Allan and Lienta shared a long-suffering look. The two betas had been nipping at each other's throats since the night they'd been forced to retreat behind the Temerite walls.

But Bryce was right. Something should have happened by now.

Allan crossed his arms over his chest, fingers tapping lightly at his upper arm. They'd completed a full circuit of the Temerite walls and found that they were all essentially the same. The Rats had settled into the west, the Butcher's men to the east, with Baron Devin's men covering the north and spread out to either side. He never would have expected the Rats to follow anyone else's orders, let alone remain focused enough to cover a wall for two days without acting. Their perusal of the western walls showed that the Rats were becoming impatient, but Devin's men were keeping them in line. The Butcher's group below appeared content to sit and wait, most of them sharpening weapons as they sat around makeshift fires, roasting meat over the flames, or tossing dice for entertainment. At least, Allan assumed they were dice. He hadn't taken the time for a closer look at the meat or the dice, afraid he'd find they were body parts and bones, after Lienta's description of the Butcher. Devin's contingent certainly kept their distance, huddling in their own little groups and keeping a wary eye on their supposed allies.

There were no forces guarding the southern wall. Allan hadn't understood why at first, until Lienta had explained that there were no gates in the southern wall; they hadn't had time to incorporate any into it. It hadn't even been a wall initially; the distortion had kept anyone from approaching from that direction. After its sudden collapse, the Temerites had scrambled to block the breach in their defenses, hastily filling in the exposed gaps in the streets with debris from what the distortion had destroyed near at hand, then working on filling in the buildings they'd chosen for their wall. They would have been overrun immediately if the other groups in the city hadn't been reeling from the shock of the quakes, the collapse of the distortion, and the subsequent sinking of the city.

However, Allan had to agree that the Temerites had chosen the placement of their fourth wall wisely, given how quickly they'd been forced to act. They'd pulled back from the edge of where the distortion had been, using the blocks with the largest buildings and the fewest cross streets. That meant they had the fewest gaps to fill in with debris. And the process still hadn't been completed. Even now they were filling the interiors of the buildings with stone, carts running from some of the collapsed buildings inside the enclosure to the southern wall day and night.

"They're obviously waiting for something," Allan said.

"But what?" Lienta countered.

"If I knew, I would have said something by now."

Bryce pushed away from the wall and turned toward them. "They haven't used their Hound yet either. He's still skulking around the northern gates, accompanying Devin."

"Hounds aren't that useful in full-frontal assaults," Allan said. "Unless you unleash them simply to cause wholesale chaos in the middle of the fight. They're mostly useful for assassinations or infiltrations. They're essentially spies."

"But Devin hasn't even unleashed him for that," Lienta muttered. "We can still see him at Devin's side at the northern walls."

"We did see a contingent break off from the main group the afternoon after they appeared," Boskell said, "heading south. They haven't appeared at the southern walls yet. Maybe they went to the Underearthers or the Gorrani, to see if they were willing to join them. They might be waiting on a response."

"It's possible. We agree they have barely enough men to overrun the walls if they went for a frontal assault now."

After a long silence, Lienta sighed. "It's unlikely we'll figure out what they're up to simply standing here. Boskell, head back to the northern gate and keep an eye on this Baron Devin and his Hound. If they make any move at all, especially if that Hound of his disappears, inform me immediately."

"Of course."

"Bryce, go ahead and accompany him."

Bryce shot Allan a bitter, betrayed look, but followed Boskell, the two keeping a short distance apart, both refusing to speak to each other.

"They're like children," Allan muttered.

"Boskell has always been difficult. He's still the best second I've ever had, both here in Erenthrall or back in Temer."

The two turned toward the stairs leading down to the interior street below, Lienta angling toward the Temerite embassy.

"You don't think they're waiting for support from the Underearthers or Gorrani, do you?" Allan asked.

"No. The Underearthers aren't numerous enough to give them any kind of advantage over the forces they have now, and from what you said, the Gorrani who've taken up residence in the cliffs to the south won't cooperate with them no matter what they offer."

"I agree. There's something else going on here." He rolled his shoulders with unease. "You mentioned plans to abandon the embassy. How do you intend to get beyond the walls and Devin's forces?"

Lienta didn't answer at first, walking in silence. Then, abruptly: "The ley barge lines."

Allan halted in consternation. "There isn't a ley station inside your walls."

"No, but one of the quakes immediately after the Shattering and the quickening of the distortion caused a collapse into the barge line that runs beneath the embassy. It wasn't safe to use at first, since the ley was so erratic. Sometimes the line would be free and other times it would be flooded with ley. Since the distortion collapsed, it has remained free of ley. It runs from the Valor district to the northeast to the ley station in Eld."

A dagger of apprehension sank into Allan's gut and he closed his eyes. "So you're saying there's a tunnel beneath the walls of your enclosure."

"A narrow tunnel, yes. It isn't wide enough to admit a significant enough force, not with the guards we have placed on it."

Allan opened his eyes and grabbed Lienta's arm, hauling him back into motion toward the embassy. "It might not be large enough for a decent-sized force, but you forgot about the Hound."

Lienta pulled out of Allan's grip, but didn't stop moving, Allan's tension and anxiety seeping into his own step. "But we've kept an eye on the Hound. He's still with Devin."

"What if there's more than one Hound?"

Lienta's eyes widened at the possibility, and he increased his pace, almost breaking into a run. "I have over a dozen men stationed down there, on either side of the line."

"That *may* be enough."

Lienta swore.

They raced toward the embassy, Allan suddenly wishing he hadn't sent Bryce to the northern gate with Boskell. As they turned the corner into the square, Lienta shouted toward the guards placed outside the embassy's door. They drew to attention.

"When was the last report from the men in the tunnel?" Lienta asked as they trotted up the stairs.

"Two hours ago," one of the guards reported. "We're expecting another check-in shortly."

Lienta relaxed slightly as they entered the main foyer. "I've had them reporting in every two hours," he explained. "Two guards from each entrance, who rotate out their shifts when they return."

"Then maybe we're overreacting."

"I'd still like to verify it."

"So would I. But if we're going down into the ley tunnels, I'll want my Wielder with me, and a few others."

"I'll gather a small force of guards to accompany us."

Allan left the Temerite captain in the foyer, heading deeper into the embassy toward the guest rooms where he and the others in his group had been placed. He jogged up the stairs to the second floor, walking briskly down the hall, feeling slightly out of place as he passed artwork hung on the walls and side tables with fine sculptures and urns in niches to either side. The luxuries were at odds with the destruction and desperation of the city outside.

But then he ran into Gaven, the wagon master, carrying a pitcher of water and a cloth in one hand. He startled as Allan grabbed his forearm and pulled him down the hall, but didn't cry out.

"What's happening?" he asked without preamble, setting the cloth and pitcher on a stand next to a statue as they passed.

"Maybe nothing," Allan said. "Go rouse our enforcers. Tell the rest of our group to be ready to move, just in case. I'll fetch Dylan."

Gaven nodded and ran ahead of Allan, who halted outside one of the rooms. He knocked—a quick rap—then opened the door. Dylan had already swung his legs over the edge of the bed where he'd been resting.

"Come with me."

Dylan stood. "Have they attacked the walls?"

"No, not yet. There's another issue."

Dylan didn't ask for clarification, merely followed him out into the hall, where Gaven had returned with the eight surviving enforcers, some of them still belting on swords or uniforms. One of them was gnawing on a piece of meat. Behind them, one of Gaven's men tossed a satchel into the hall before ducking back into the room. Farther down, Charles' suspicious brother—from the family group they'd rescued from the shard—came out into the hallway from their own room to watch, but didn't approach.

"What's happening?" the enforcer gnawing on the bone asked.

"Lienta told me how he intended to escape if Devin attacked. We need to make certain the route is still secure."

The new beta—or so Allan assumed—eyed him as if trying to decide whether he should wait for orders from Bryce, then tore a last chunk of meat off the bone and tossed it to the floor. "Then let's go."

Allan frowned, not liking this new beta's attitude—it reminded him forcibly of the Dogs who'd aligned with Hagger before the Shattering—but he didn't have time to deal with it.

To Gaven, he said, "Stay here, but keep your eyes open."

Gaven nodded.

Allan motioned the rest of the enforcers and Dylan to follow him. Dylan stepped up to his side as they moved down the hall.

"Why do you need me?"

"Because Lienta's proposed escape route is through the ley barge tunnels. He claims the line beneath their embassy has been free of ley since the collapse of the distortion, but I'd like you there to verify it."

They reached the stair, Lienta already waiting below in the foyer with a group of ten guardsmen. He glanced up as they appeared. "The two guardsmen from the northern end of the ley line have checked in with no sign of activity. We haven't heard from those at the southern end of the line yet."

"We should head there first, then."

"I thought the same. Follow me."

He led them deeper into the embassy, into a section that none of those from the Needle had been allowed to roam over the last few days, passing rooms that had been emptied or abandoned. There was no pretense of normality here. Walls were cracked from the quakes, with dust, paint, and brick and mortar littering the floors. Tables and stands had toppled, urns and statues left broken where they fell. No attempts had been made to clean up the debris or to repair the damage. There weren't even footprints in the dust in any of the rooms, only in the main corridors they traversed.

They reached a back staircase, the stone steps leading down into the depths. Lienta grabbed torches stacked in a side alcove and lit them, handing off two of them as he descended into the lower level. These rooms had been used for storage and showed signs of more recent activity, numerous footprints and tracks in the dust leading up to the barrels and crates stacked inside. A few servants stepped aside as their contingent passed, turning down another corridor into a slightly wider central hallway. At its end, they found another set of steps, narrower than the first.

Below, the rooms were more like vaults, the stone older, with low ceilings and shallow arches serving as entrances. Allan guessed they had once been used as wine cellars and further storage, although now they were empty. The ceilings had collapsed in many of the chambers, the walls crazed with cracks. He shuddered at the signs of instability and the realization that the embassy rested on top of these crumbling structures.

Then, ahead, Lienta halted, holding his torch over a gaping crevice in the floor, the top of a ladder jutting up out of it. Coming up to the Temerite captain's side, Allan stared down into the fissure, a torch below illuminating the familiar contours of a ley barge tunnel. The channel was lined with stone, arched at the top but square at the bottom. It appeared empty.

"Dylan."

The Wielder stepped through the guards, halting between Allan and Lienta before going still, a sign Allan knew meant he was reaching for the ley.

A moment later, he shook his head. "There's no ley in the channel below. I followed it to the northern end. It's been blocked there by someone. I didn't sense any ley or a block in the southern direction."

"Ley did occasionally pass through here while the distortion covered the city," Lienta said. "It flooded this lower level at least twice during that time."

"Then the block is new. Kara must have put it in place, to control the flow of the ley to the proper nodes."

"As long as it's blocked and there's no ley down there now," Allan said. He shifted toward the ladder, but Lienta stopped him with a hand on his chest.

"Allow me," the Temerite captain said, then whistled sharply.

The Temerite guardsmen slipped forward and down the ladder, spreading out and disappearing down both sides of the channel below. Allan heard commands echoing back and forth, then one of the guards reappeared at the base of the ladder.

"All clear."

Lienta descended first, then Allan, Dylan, and the eight enforcers from the Needle. Below, the Temerites had spread out, guarding the channel in each direction. Lienta waited until they'd all reached the floor of the channel before saying, "We should have run into the two guards sent to report by now." He turned to one of his men. "Lieutenant, take four men and check in with our group in the northern tunnel."

The Temerite man nodded, selecting four others with gestures and departing up the northern channel, their torchlight receding with distance.

The rest of them proceeded southward, Lienta and his guards taking the lead, Allan and Dylan behind, with the enforcers at the rear. They moved swiftly, fanning out across the channel, some of the men drawing weapons. Allan suppressed a shudder as memories of being captured and dragged through the more complicated ley line system by the Tunnelers surfaced. But this was different. There were no junctions or branches that led deeper into the ley system here. This was simply a channel used by the barges to transport people from one section of the city to another.

After what felt like an hour but had to have been less than half that, Lienta's men called out from ahead. Allan pushed forward, but they'd only reached a section where the ceiling had collapsed into the channel, the walls of either side broken and shattered for a long stretch.

"We're outside the compound now," Lienta explained, waving toward the torn-up earth and the collapse. "This is where the distortion stood. And the damage it caused when it started to collapse. Our unit should be waiting a little farther ahead."

Allan knew something was wrong before the first body came into view; they should have seen the guards' torchlight by now. When their own light fell across the crumpled corpse, a Temerite guard swearing and rushing forward, illuminating the remains of the five other guards stationed here, an odd calm settled over him. He held Dylan and the others back as Lienta and the rest of his guard verified that the watchers were all dead. Lienta rolled the nearest over onto his back, staring at the man's face, his own jaw clenched. The man's throat had been cut, the pale uniform stained nearly black with blood.

Lienta reached down and dabbed his fingers in the pool that had gathered beneath the body, rubbed his fingers together, then glanced up at Allan. "It's still damp, but has started to turn tacky. He's been dead for at least an hour, possibly two."

"They were likely killed as soon as the two replacement guards arrived after the last report," Allan said.

Lienta stood, glancing over the rest of the dead before motioning toward a sword lying on the stone nearby. "A few of them managed to draw blades, but it appears they were taken by surprise."

"A Hound."

Lienta stiffened. "We passed no one on our way here."

"Which means the Hound is already inside your enclosure."

"But why? As you said, the Hounds are assassins. There's—" His eyes shot wide. "The Matriarch!"

He spun toward his guardsmen. "Remain here and secure the exit. Make certain it's free from here to the ley station. Reinforcements will be sent immediately." Then he turned on Allan, already moving as he spoke. "We must find the Matriarch. If she's alive, we'll put her under guard and begin a search of the embassy."

He didn't give Allan time to respond, snatching at one of the torches and breaking into a run down the channel. Allan ordered everyone else into a light jog to keep up, grateful Lienta hadn't gone for an all-out sprint.

As they raced for the embassy, cracked stone flying by, the enforcer beta paced him and managed between breaths, "Is he . . . not concerned with . . . the gates?" At Allan's questioning look, he added, "The Hound . . . could open . . . the gates . . . from within."

Allan swore, a pit opening in his stomach. "Lienta!" he shouted, his voice echoing down the length of the tunnel. But the Temerite captain didn't slow, too caught up in his fear for the Matriarch to heed him. Cursing again, Allan picked up his pace, the beta following suit.

"What's your name?" Allan barked as they reached the ladder, Lienta already gone. He heaved himself up the rungs as the beta answered, "Kurtch."

The beta ascended in a scramble that belied his bulk.

"Hand me the torch," Allan called down. Dylan passed it up. "Stay with me, Kurtch. The rest of you, catch up when you can."

Dylan nodded, being shoved up the ladder by the other enforcers, who looked pissed at being left behind. Allan and Kurtch bolted after Lienta, shadows flaring around them, the mouths of the vaults gaping wide and empty as they sped past. When they reached the first set of stairs and came out on the next level, they could see Lienta at the end of the corridor ahead. Allan called out again, but he ignored them, turning the corner. Allan charged after him, putting on more speed. In the hallway beyond, Lienta had been slowed down by the servants who hadn't seen him coming and didn't get out of the way in time. They'd nearly caught up to him by the time he reached the main floor of the embassy and burst out into the foyer.

"You three," the Temerite captain snapped at the startled guards at the entrance, "with me. Where is the Matriarch?"

"H-her rooms," one of the men stuttered.

"Send another twenty guards into the ley tunnel below. It's been breached. Then begin scouring this building. There may be a Hound present."

As the guard stammered out an acknowledgment, Lienta and his new escort sprinted up the stair opposite to those where Allan and the others had been given rooms, Allan and Kurtch hard on his escort's heels.

Lienta slammed through the large double doors at the end of the extended hall, coming to a halt in the receiving chamber beyond, where between Lienta's and the guards' bodies Allan saw the Matriarch look up from the papers she was examining at the desk, a disgruntled look crossing her face at the disturbance.

She sat back in her chair, setting the papers aside. "What is the meaning of this?"

Lienta stepped forward, a gesture sending the three guards with him into a search of the two adjoining rooms. Allan noticed three others in the room—two guards and the attendant that had been with the Matriarch when Allan and Bryce had been brought before her the first time. He and Kurtch were still in the hall outside.

The Matriarch's gaze followed the guards, then flicked toward Allan and Kurtch before returning to Lienta, one eyebrow raised.

"Excuse our sudden appearance, Matriarch. I have recently discovered a breach. Someone killed our guards on the southern ley tunnel beneath our walls. It is believed that a Hound has made it inside our enclave."

The Matriarch's eyebrows shot up. "I thought you've been keeping an eye on the Hound who follows this Baron Devin around outside the walls."

"We have, Matriarch. He is still at Devin's side. We believe there is another Hound."

"But you have no proof."

The guards returned from their scrutiny of the other two rooms and shook their heads. "Empty," one of them reported.

Lienta did not relax, Allan noted. "Someone killed those guards and entered our walls. Whoever it was is here now. We need to move you to a safer location."

"And where exactly would that be?"

"A room that's easier to defend, Matriarch."

She considered him at length. "Very well. Janote, if you would get my chair."

The assistant stepped into one of the side rooms and pulled in a chair with two large wheels attached to its sides. Janote maneuvered the chair close to the Matriarch's side, then—with the help of one of the guards—lifted the Matriarch up from behind the desk and into the seat. Her legs dragged limply behind her, but after being seated, the Matriarch settled them into position, her feet resting on a small ledge that had been built into the base of the chair. Janote had gathered up the papers and placed them in a satchel, handing it over to the Matriarch when he was done.

"I'm ready, Captain Lienta."

Allan shared a shocked look with Kurtch. He'd only run across the Matriarch a few times over the course of the last few days, but he had never suspected. From Kurtch's stunned gaze, neither had the beta.

He suddenly had a greater appreciation for Lienta's concern over any kind of evacuation. Moving the Matriarch through the embassy and down to the tunnels, then through the devastated streets of Eren-thrall, would present considerable challenges.

Lienta merely nodded. "Take the Matriarch to the first floor receiving room for now, while I arrange a better escort."

Janote and the guards nodded and began rolling her toward the hall. Lienta exited before them, pulling Allan and Kurtch along with him, his expression troubled.

"If the Hound wasn't after the Matriarch," he said, "then where would he have gone?"

"My guess would be—"

A horn suddenly sounded, plaintive and desperate, the low, drawn out note suddenly breaking with a ragged splutter.

"—the gates," Allan finished.

Lienta grabbed his shoulder and sprinted down the hall, footsteps pounding up the stairs from below. They met more of the Temerite guardsmen at the landing overlooking the foyer.

"The northern gate—" the lead lieutenant shouted.

"I heard," Lienta snapped, cutting him off. "Take someone to the roof with a spyglass. Have them report immediately." The man snatched at another guardsman behind him, both of them running down the hall in the direction of the rooms Allan and the others had been given. Allan saw Gaven and the others from the Needle heading toward them, the family they'd rescued from the shard trailing behind. He motioned them forward as Lienta descended to the foyer below, shouting more orders about the Matriarch's escort and rousing the rest of the guard and the populace housed inside the walls. Dylan and the rest of Kurtch's enforcers stood to one side of the foyer below, keeping out of the way.

"What's going on?" Gaven asked.

"We think there's a Hound loose in the enclave. He may be at the northern gates."

Janote arrived with the Matriarch; with an efficiency that indicated they'd done this a hundred times, the guards of her escort lifted her out of the chair in a seated position and descended, Janote coming behind with the chair, the wheels thumping down step by step. Gaven watched with mild surprise, turning to Allan with a questioning look.

"I didn't know either," Allan said.

The main doors flew open below and more Temerite guards poured in, some of them immediately surrounding the Matriarch. Lienta sent some of them down the passage leading to the tunnel, others back out into the square and the streets beyond. The door remained open, and Allan could hear an escalation of activity out on the square and, further distant, the sound of fighting.

He turned to Gaven and the others. "Go get our packs. I have a strong feeling we aren't going to be staying here much longer."

Gaven and his four helpers scrambled back down the hall where the satchels were stacked outside their rooms. They began throwing them over their shoulders, two or three packs per person. Charles' family ducked into their own room, Charles' brother urging them to hurry, the wife speaking softly to the two children.

Allan descended the stairs into the chaos of the foyer, winding his way toward Lienta. Kurtch followed him, signaling the rest of the enforcers and Dylan to wait.

"Lienta!" Allan called out, the captain turning, although he didn't stop listening to reports and handing out orders in return. He motioned Allan closer. Allan shoved through the crush of guardsmen surrounding him and said over the noise, "If the gate has fallen to the Hound, you need to send everyone through the tunnel!"

"We could still push them back. But I haven't heard about the northern gate yet. All I know is that there's a fight going on somewhere. It could be on the top of the wall."

"Or Devin and his men could already be in the streets. If they are, then the Hound is likely on his way to one of the other gates, to let in the Rats or the Butcher."

Lienta didn't answer, stalling as he issued a few more orders. To a young man, no more than fourteen, although he was dressed in an ill-fitting Temerite guardsman's uniform, he said, "Tell the lieutenant in charge of the commoners to hold for now," then patted the youth on the shoulder as he darted away. Then he turned to face Allan.

"Think of the Matriarch," Allan said.

Lienta flinched, gaze flicking toward where the Matriarch sat in her wheeled chair to one side, watching without comment, although her sharp gaze followed every movement in the room. She held his eyes a moment, then nodded slightly.

Allan didn't understand what had passed between them, but Lienta suddenly pointed toward the youth he'd just spoken to, nearly at the door, and said loudly, "Belay that order!"

Someone snatched at the young man, catching him before he could run out the door. The room quieted for a moment, all eyes on Lienta.

He bowed his head, then raised his chin and spoke to the youth, although his voice was directed toward the entire room. "There's been a change of plans. Tell the lieutenant to send the commoners here. We're abandoning the enclave."

The youth nodded and fled out the door. Allan caught a glimpse of him threading through the guardsmen milling around outside before he vanished.

Inside, the tenor of the room had changed. Lienta was issuing new orders, a contingent already converging on the Matriarch. They led her into the hallway leading to the back stairs and the vaults and ley tunnel. Servants left, returning with packs not unlike those Gaven and the others carried, loaded with supplies. They'd obviously been readied ahead of time. More and more people began funneling down the hall-way toward the stairs.

Lienta suddenly appeared at Allan's side. "Your group should head down to the tunnel, since you're already here. The rest of our people will be arriving shortly. Have them follow the Matriarch's guard to the ley station in Eld. After that, we'll have to ascend back to the city streets."

"What about you?"

"I'll stay here to see that our people make it into the tunnels."

"How many people do you have here?"

"Not as many as you might think. Close to three hundred, half of those Temerite guards or those that took up the uniform since the Shattering."

Lienta was right. Based on what he and the others from the Hollow had seen on their excursions to Erenthrall before the distortion collapsed, he'd have guessed there were maybe twice that many people in the Temerite enclave. He wondered if there had been at one point and they'd simply been whittled away by the events since the Shattering, but he didn't ask.

"That's still a good number of people to move."

"We've had this plan in place from before the sinking of the city," Lienta said, "even when ley did flow through the tunnel. Everyone knows what they must do."

Before Allan could answer, the two guardsmen Lienta had sent to the roof suddenly reappeared, their pounding tread announcing their approach moments before they burst onto the landing above the foyer, the lieutenant gasping, "The northern gates have been opened! The Baron's men there are already in the streets, working their way here. Lieutenant Boskell is doing his best to hold them back, but there are too many of them. The western gates also opened a short time ago, letting the Rats in. The two forces are converging on the main living quarters northwest of the square."

"Are the people retreating from that area yet?"

"Not yet, although we saw increased movement on the streets."

"Very well."

"Captain," the lieutenant added, still breathing hard from his dash down from the roof, "there's also a large auroral storm headed into the city, coming from the northeast."

"Is it going to hit us?"

"Hard to say."

Lienta grimaced. "Return to the roof. Report any change in either the storm or the Baron's forces immediately."

The two vanished again, Lienta staring at the floor in grim thought.

Allan wondered what had happened to Bryce, but called Kurtch and Gaven forward.

"Take your men and the family we rescued from the shard down to the tunnels and follow the Matriarch's escort to the ley station in Eld."

"What about you?" Gaven asked.

"And Bryce?" Kurtch added.

"I'll stay here with Lienta to wait for Bryce and help out where I can."

Kurtch nodded, already turning toward the enforcers.

Gaven hesitated. "Don't wait too long. I don't want to have to tell Morrell or Kara that I lost you. They both made me promise I'd bring you back alive."

Allan grinned to hide the flinch of guilt he felt over leaving his daughter yet again to come to Erenthrall. She'd protested when he'd brought it up, but not as forcefully as she had before, a sign she was growing up far faster than Allan liked. "I'd hate for you to feel my daughter's wrath, let alone Kara's. I won't stay long."

Then Allan returned his attention to Lienta. "The western gate fell too soon after the northern one. Not even a Hound could have covered that distance in that short a time."

"I thought the same. Which means either someone else came in with the Hound and took care of the second gate—"

"Or there's more than one Hound," Allan finished. He thought for a moment, recalling what he knew of the Hounds from his time as a Dog. "Hounds follow the orders of their alpha—who's either Devin or the Hound with Devin. They don't often extrapolate from those orders, unless given leeway to do so. But if I were Devin, I'd have given them secondary targets once they were inside the walls."

"The eastern gate. And possibly the Matriarch."

"Or at least the embassy, if they're aware of it."

"There's not much more we can do about either of those possibilities that we haven't already done."

Unfortunately, Allan agreed.

Gaven and the others left, Kurtch bringing up the rear. Allan was forced to revise his opinion of the enforcer—who had obviously been a Dog before the Shattering. He still reminded Allan uncomfortably of Hagger and his cohorts, but he tried to shrug that aside. So far, Kurtch had done nothing to warrant Allan's apprehensions.

The first of the Temerite enclave's commoners not already in the embassy appeared, filtering through the doorway and hastily being herded down the embassy's hall toward the tunnel by the guards. Allan and Lienta stood to one side of the foyer as the men, women, and children were urged to move faster. A few of them were sobbing in terror, or clutching at loved ones being dragged along, but most were surprisingly resolute and determined, faces hardened. Many of them were Temerite, with the thin faces and lanky bodies common to the easterners, but there were others scattered amongst them.

A short time later, Bryce appeared with a contingent of Temerite guardsmen. The Dog caught sight of Allan from outside and forced his way through the crowd, expression twisted in annoyance.

He was cursing beneath his breath when he finally made it to Allan's side. Allan noted his clothes were dirtier than that morning, with a few stains that looked suspiciously like blood. A rent appeared across his shoulder, obviously made with a blade.

"What happened at the gates?" Lienta demanded. "Where's Lieutenant Boskell?"

"The bastard stayed behind," Bryce said, voice a mixture of contempt and respect that Allan had heard only from fellow Dogs before the Shattering. "He ordered me to warn the men protecting the rabble once it became obvious that we weren't going to be able to hold the gates. Then he stayed behind to keep the Baron and his men at bay for as long as possible."

"How did the gates fall?" Allan prodded.

"It was another Hound—not the one who's been at Devin's side since they arrived, a different one. No one saw him until at least three of those guarding the gates were dead, and then no one could get close to him. He held everyone off until he managed to get the gates opened, and then he began an indiscriminate slaughter as the Baron and his forces poured in. He must have taken out a dozen men in those first few minutes, and no one managed to get a single hit on him. I lost track of him once Devin attacked. Then Boskell sent me away."

He turned to Lienta. "He's retreating street by street, but he's not going to be able to hold them off long."

"He likely has even less time than he thinks," Lienta said. "The western gates were breached, and we think the Hounds are headed to the eastern ones as well."

"Hounds?"

"We think there's more than one already inside the walls," Allan said. "The western gates fell too quickly after the northern ones for it to have been the same Hound, especially after what you've told us."

"How did they get in?"

"Through the same tunnel we're using to escape," Lienta said tightly. His attention had shifted, and as he stepped forward, Allan glanced up to the second-floor landing to see the men who'd been watching the roof return. "Report, Lieutenant."

"The eastern gate is open. Our forces to the north and west have been pushed back from the walls nearly five blocks in both directions. They've hit the residential buildings. Most of our people are already here, but there are a few stragglers. They're being overrun."

Lienta grimaced, tension pulling the corners of his eyes taut. "We don't have the men to spare to save them. They're on their own. Signal Boskell and the rest of our forces. Let them know they can fall back to the embassy."

"Captain, there's also movement to the south."

Everyone tensed.

"The Gorrani?"

"It would appear so. They've left their cliff and appear to be heading in this direction."

Lienta swore, then waved a hand in dismissal.

As the lieutenant vanished, returning to the roof, Lienta scanned the room. The press of people had subsided, the Temerite guards pushing the last of the commoners outside toward the embassy doors. A horn sounded, muted by the building. Allan could hear the fighting more clearly now, and through the large windows to either side of the door could see a dark, thick plume of smoke rising over the buildings on the far side of the square.

"Something is on fire," he said.

Lienta barely reacted. "The Rats are inordinately fond of setting our buildings aflame. Perhaps it will keep them distracted long enough for us to escape."

He didn't sound particularly hopeful.

Outside, the last of the Temerite refugees were shoved inside the embassy and the lieutenant in charge of them called out, "That's it! That's the last of those who were with us."

"Very well. Send your men down to the tunnel. Make certain everyone heads toward the Eld ley station. Move them along as quickly as possible."

The man motioned his men into action, the entire group withdrawing into the building as Lienta shifted forward, stepping out onto the short steps of the embassy, facing the square. Allan, Bryce, and two Temerites who had obviously been given orders to stay with Lienta followed.

The clash of the fighting doubled as soon as they left the shelter of the building, along with a crackling roar as the fire started toward the west began to spread, the black plume widening against the early evening horizon. Allan's stomach growled as he suddenly realized that hours had passed since they'd done the rounds of the walls that morning and that none of them had eaten. Except Kurtch. He'd forgotten one of the cardinal rules of the Dogs—eat and sleep whenever and wherever you can.

They stood silently, the fighting getting closer, Lienta taut with unexpressed emotions, like the strings of a fiddle. Allan could feel him vibrating. The square before them was oddly vacant and peaceful.

When the Temerite captain finally spoke, the conflict now no more than a few blocks distant, Allan suppressed a startled flinch.

"We carved this place out of the remains of Erenthrall after the Shattering," he said, his voice raw. "Temer . . . Temer is likely gone. At least, we've heard no word from them. Perhaps they are simply too preoccupied with their own troubles to be concerned with us. This was home." He drew in a ragged breath. "Where shall we go from here?"

"The Needle."

Lienta faced him. "The new overseers of the Needle would take us in?"

"Yes."

The captain considered this, returning his gaze to the square. Finally, he said, "We will have to escape Erenthrall first."

As he spoke, the first of the retreating Temerite guard spilled out onto the square from the north, followed a moment later by others from the west. Lienta straightened, and one of the guards left behind cleared his throat.

"Captain, we should retreat into the tunnels."

Lienta's hand fell to the sword at his waist, still sheathed. His grip tightened on the handle, but then he let it fall, with a sharp nod.

They fell back through the hallway, down the stairs, through to the lower vaults at a trot. As they descended the ladder into the tunnel, numerous Temerite guards waiting both above and below, the unmistakable sound of swords echoed down from the far corridor. The retreat had reached the embassy. Then they were in the tunnel, Lienta's men pulling back with him as they ran down the ley channel, climbing the collapsed ceiling where the distortion had been, past where the guards had been killed by the Hounds.

The tunnel beyond felt as if it went on forever, lit by the occasional torch jammed into cracks in the wall, some of them already threatening to gutter out. A wave of exhaustion hit Allan as the day's activities and lack of food caught up with him, but he fought it back. They could hear fighting in the tunnel now, edging closer.

Then the ley station appeared ahead, men on the edge of the barge platform shouting as they caught sight of them, urging them toward the edge where ladders had been erected. Guards began climbing, a few of them jumping, arms outstretched as they were caught and hauled up by those on the platform. Allan followed Lienta up a ladder, the captain ushered immediately toward the far end where a corridor led up to the station proper above.

Allan moved to follow when Bryce grabbed his arm and pointed toward Dylan, the Wielder rushing toward them.

"They're close," Allan snapped, even as he heard Lienta shouting orders, the Temerite guardsmen forming up at the end of the platform, swords drawn, ready to hold the Baron's men back. "We don't have much time."

"I know, but I can stop them all, at least from attacking through the tunnel."

"What do you mean?"

"I can release the block at the northern end. Once I do that, the entire channel will flood with ley. It's strong enough that anyone in the channel will be killed."

Allan halted, the implications obvious. "You'd be able to do that?"

Dylan swallowed, a stricken look crossing his face. He knew Allan wasn't asking about whether it was possible. But then he stiffened defiantly. "It's similar to what was done to the Gorrani at the Needle, yes. But I don't see that we have any other choice."

"It's not exactly the same," Bryce muttered. "At the Needle, Commander Ty could have held the Gorrani at bay. We don't have a chance of keeping the Baron's men contained. That hope died the moment they breached the enclave's walls."

Beneath the platform, more of Lienta's men began pouring out of the ley channel, the rear of Boskell's force, Allan assumed. Men began hauling them up, making room for others, the platform becoming crowded.

Allan drew in a deep breath, then exhaled heavily. "We'll let Lienta decide." He spun and shouted, then began shoving his way through the Temerites to Lienta's side. The captain ordered them to be let through and a moment later Allan explained Dylan's plan to release the ley into the channel.

"It won't flood this chamber?" Lienta asked doubtfully.

"The channel isn't blocked south of here. It will run through as it did before the Shattering, to whatever the next junction is, and flow from there. I've already checked."

Lienta considered, brow creased in furious concentration. "We'll have to risk it. As soon as my men are clear, release the ley."

He began pressing toward the edge of the platform, Allan, Dylan, and Bryce a few steps behind. Orders were passed to get everyone up and out of the channel, to hold the line at its edge, met with consternation and confusion, but the Temerites reorganized swiftly as men continued to emerge from the opening to the north.

Then the clash of swords grew, the Baron's forces suddenly surging from the opening, the battle echoing in the domed ceiling overhead with the clatter of metal, with shouts and curses, with screams and groans as bodies fell to the side. Caught in the crush of guards near the edge, Allan saw Boskell swinging with grim determination, his sword and Temerite uniform already coated with blood, his face smeared with it. His line fell back to the wall of the channel beneath the platform, still fighting, the attackers pushing outward down the length of the opening. The Temerites hauled them up while keeping the attackers at bay.

Allan turned to Dylan. "Release the ley."

Dylan's face was sheened with sweat, yet pale. "Already done."

Allan spun around in time to see Lienta reach down and grasp Boskell by the back of his uniform. He heaved, but the Temerite watchman was too heavy. Lienta lost his balance and fell into the barge line.

Without thought, Allan ran and leaped in after him. He crashed into the crowd of bodies, grasping at Boskell's shoulder. The Temerite watchman caught him and shouted, "What in bloody hells are you doing?" as they both reached for Lienta.

A breath later, ley light flashed through the mouth of the channel, slamming through the conduit with a blinding flare. The ley globes still intact around the platform sizzled, lighting briefly before exploding. Everyone on the platform ducked, arms thrown upward to ward off the bright lights, crying out.

In the channel, Allan staggered as the ley shoved him from one side, surging around him, its current nearly ripping him from his feet. Both he and Boskell thrust Lienta up over the lip of the channel. Then they both turned.

The ley coursed through the channel fifteen feet away in every direction, parting around Allan's position as if he were a stone in a river. All the men within those fifteen feet, both Temerite and those of Devin's men close enough, were protected from its killing white light. Those outside had already been consumed. Parts of those who'd been caught at the edge lay inside the sphere of protection—an arm, a foot— blood seeping from the severed stumps.

"Stop staring and get the hells up here!" Lienta bellowed, his voice shaky.

The men still in the channel backed away from the ley, Lienta's men reaching down to haul them to safety. Neither Boskell nor Allan moved.

"What's happening?" Boskell asked.

"It's me," Allan said. "I somehow counteract the ley. Although it's never been tested like this before." He considered the distance to the ley. "Normally, I start affecting it at about thirty feet. It must be shorter here because of the concentration of the ley."

Boskell didn't respond, stunned into silence.

Lienta tapped them both on the shoulder. "Everyone else is out."

Allan motioned to Boskell. "You'd better go first."

"Right." He grabbed hold of Lienta's offered arm and climbed out.

Then it was Allan's turn. Bryce and Dylan hauled him up. As he was lifted free of the channel, the sphere of protection shifted and the ley filled it completely, smooth and undisturbed. All of those who'd been in the channel aside from those near Allan—Devin's men and a few of Lienta's—were gone, burned by the ley from existence. The only sounds on the platform were the gasping of the men who'd a moment before been fighting for their lives and the crackling of the destroyed ley globes.

"Well," Dylan said into the strained silence, "that was interesting."

The alpha Hound stood back from the fissure beneath the Temerite embassy, watching Baron Devin stare down into the harsh white light of the ley as it coursed through the tunnel beneath. His two fellow Hounds waited a short distance down the corridor near one of the wine cellars, with some of Devin's men. When they'd emerged from their den beneath the Amber Tower into this altered world, they'd been lost, confused and uncertain. A Hound needed a master, someone who gave orders and dealt out punishment, like the captain of the Dogs or the Baron himself, someone in control, powerful, confident. When they'd run across Devin and his men within the decimated streets of Erenthrall, the alpha had thought they'd found their master. After all, he was a Baron. He controlled men who acted like Dogs: hard, dangerous, vicious.

But as he watched Devin glaring down into the tunnel filled with ley, he felt a niggling worm of doubt. He drew in a deep breath through his nose in unease, scented the Baron's fear sweat, tainted with rage, with weakness.

Devin faced him, the muscles in his jaw clenching. Through gritted teeth, he asked, "Why didn't you tell me there were tunnels beneath their enclave? We could have used them to gain access to the embassy. We could have cut off their only retreat!"

The alpha frowned in consternation. "You ordered us to find a way to open the gates. Nothing more."

Devin took a single step forward and punched him, the blow driving him to his knees. He could have side-stepped with ease, could have drawn his dagger and stabbed the Baron in at least three fatal places before his fist landed, but he merely spat out blood and stood, his entire face throbbing. He'd committed some transgression. He didn't understand what—he'd followed his orders precisely—but his master was obviously displeased.

Devin shook his hand, glancing back toward the crack in the stone floor. "We'll have to cut them off from above ground now. Where does the tunnel emerge?"

"Eld station."

Devin swore. "Right where the Gorrani are headed."

He stalked toward his men, calling out orders, everyone scrambling back down the hall and into the building above.

The alpha hesitated, then trailed after.

"What did we do wrong?" the youngest of his brethren asked, falling into step behind him.

"I don't know."

"We did nothing wrong," his beta said. "He should not have punished you."

"He is the Baron. He is our master."

"He reeks of weakness. Not like the captain of the Dogs before. Not like the previous Baron."

The alpha didn't respond, the scent of his own blood overpowering even the rankness drifting back from Devin and his men ahead. He touched his lip where it had split, let the pain drive away his doubts.

"He is the Baron," he repeated, nostrils flaring. "That is all that matters."

Although he was beginning to ask himself, the Baron of what?

Six

"THEY WON'T BE FOLLOWING US through the tunnel," Boskell muttered. He was still trembling, the aftereffects of his close call with the resurgence of the ley and the exhausting retreat from the breached gates.

Allan felt a little shaken himself. He hadn't known he'd be protected from the ley. When he'd seen Lienta fall into the channel, he'd reacted on instinct. "Not unless they manage to find some ley barges."

The irritable Temerite lieutenant halted a vain attempt to brush off his uniform to stare at Allan. "Could they find them somewhere?"

"It's unlikely," Dylan said. The Wielder looked as ragged as Boskell. He'd just killed an untold number of people with the ley.

"Why?" Boskell asked.

"Because the ley barges were in the ley channels when the pulse that caused the Shattering hit. They were made mostly of wood. The surge would have annihilated them, as it did anyone and anything organic too close to the center of the explosion."

Boskell merely grunted. He didn't look completely recovered yet, but he turned to search for Lienta. The Temerite captain had ordered his guards up into the mezzanine above, now that the ley channel was secure. "We still haven't escaped the city yet."

"We haven't even escaped this attack," Bryce said. "They can come at us through the city, and there's still the Gorrani to contend with."

"The Gorrani?"

"Just before abandoning the embassy, we noticed they'd left their southern cliffs and were headed in this direction," Allan explained.

Boskell visibly gathered together the shreds of his strength and will and headed toward Lienta.

The others followed, Allan falling back to walk next to Dylan. He reached up and gripped the Wielder's shoulder, squeezing in reassurance. "You did what you had to do. They would have overrun us."

Dylan made a strangled noise. "It was so . . . so easy. All I had to do was unlock the block at the northern junction. Just reach out and twist." He mimicked the action, as if he were turning a key. He shook his head. "It's *too* easy. I don't think the Wielders understand what kind of power they actually wield. It's not like before the Shattering. Then, we simply worked with the ley. There was no need to use it to harm . . . to kill. We never even considered it. The ley was simply there. Now . . . now, after what happened to the Gorrani at the Needle, after this." He waved back toward the platform. "We're too powerful. We need to be controlled."

Allan raised an eyebrow. "And how do you propose we do that?"

"I don't know."

Troubled, Allan let his hand drop from the Wielder's shoulder. They'd reached the back of the group funneling up through the corridor to the mezzanine, Lienta, Boskell, and Bryce a few paces ahead of them. Others closed in behind as they jostled up through the narrow passage and spilled out onto the grand floor of the main ley station. The columns interspersed around the wide-open floor arched out overhead, carved in the shape of branches, the ceiling like a canopy of leaves. Much of the glass in the windows looking out onto the streets was broken, fading sunlight lancing in at a sharp angle as the sun neared sunset. A large group of Temerites were clustered around the Matriarch, who'd been loaded into the front of a cart, her wheeled chair in the bed behind her surrounded by many of the packs the servants had carried from the embassy. A half dozen other carts were loaded down as well. Lienta and Boskell immediately moved toward the Matriarch with an entourage of guards. Gaven, Kurtch, and the others stood uncertainly around one of the tree-like columns to one side.

"Bryce, go check in with the others."

The Dog trotted off. Allan headed toward Lienta.

"Look," Dylan said and gestured toward the northeastern edge of the building.

Allan halted, squinting through the streams of sunlight.

Tendrils of aurora flickered over the tops of the buildings outside the station, drifting slowly southward.

Allan resumed his trek toward Lienta. He waited until Lienta noticed him and paused in the report he had been giving the Matriarch. After leaning forward for a quick word with her, he motioned Allan forward.

"We'd like to accept your offer of sanctuary at the Needle," the Matriarch said, her tone formal, "presuming the offer still stands once we reach it."

"It will, unless Kara and Commander Ty are no longer in control."

The Matriarch smiled grimly. "One thing I have learned since the Shattering is how to adjust to new and changing situations." Allan didn't comment; she appeared to be taking the loss of their enclave and embassy rather well, unperturbed by the fact that she currently sat in the driver's seat of a cart in the middle of a cracked and crumbling ley station. "We cannot stay here," she said, shifting her attention partially toward Lienta. "This Baron will soon discover the ley tunnel's destination and he's certain to come here to find us."

"Agreed," Lienta said. Allan noted that none of them presumed that Baron Devin had died in the ley tunnel. "What do you propose?"

She gave her captain a droll look. "From what you've told me, we have little choice. The Baron is to the north, the Gorrani to the south, and this auroral storm presses in from the east. We must head southwest, cross the Urate River, and find passage up to the upper plains."

"We know of a way up to the plains," Allan offered. "It can accommodate the carts as well."

"Good. Lienta?"

The captain nodded toward Allan. "It appears you are to have that alliance after all, although not precisely as you expected. If your men could lead the way?"

Allan bowed tightly toward the Matriarch. "Of course."

As he turned away, Dylan trailing him as he made his way toward Gaven and the others, Lienta began passing on orders to Boskell and his other lieutenants.

"Are you going to be able to find the same chasm we came down to get here?" Dylan asked.

"Let's hope so."

A half hour later, he, Bryce, Dylan, and Gaven led the Temerite caravan, such as it was, from the steps of the Eld ley station and through the streets of Eld toward the bridge over the Urate. They crossed into what had once been East Forks as darkness fell, the ley globes on the walls of the University shining on the waters of the river beneath them. Allan caught the silhouettes of a few watchers on the walls and wondered what Cason, Sorelle, and her band of Tunnelers thought of the activities of the last few days. She must have seen what had happened at the Temerite enclave, even if she didn't know the details. He wondered if she still felt secure at the ancient University, behind what had once been defensive walls for Erenthrall's founding Baron. Perhaps she did.

But she didn't know that Devin now controlled Hounds.

They trekked another two hours through the city, winding through the streets in the darkness, using as few torches as possible, halting only when exhaustion finally forced the issue. The Temerites—both commoners and guardsmen—camped out in the middle of the street, most simply collapsing where they'd halted.

As food was passed around—overseen by the Matriarch and Janote—Allan, Lienta, and Bryce found the nearest tall building and ascended to the rooftop, Lienta with a spyglass.

They scanned the northeastern sections of the city in silence. Fire still raged inside a section of the Temerite enclave. The auroral storm bore down on the city, rippling along a line east of the enclave with sheets of vibrant green, yellow, and deep purple. Allan shivered at the sight. Directly in its path, the streets were lined with torches: the Gorrani closing in on Devin's men. More torches surrounded the Eld station. And on all sides, sporadic ley lights and firelight glowed or flickered—the University, the broken towers of Grass, and various other minor camps strewn through the streets.

"The Gorrani are going to run right into it," Lienta said, his spyglass focused on the auroral storm.

"What will it do to them?" Bryce asked.

"Who knows." Allan leaned forward onto the wall, a deep-seated weariness settling into his bones. "What about Devin? Is he following us?"

Lienta shifted the spyglass toward the Eld station and the activity there. "No. Not yet. I'll have watchers posted."

Shouts suddenly rose from the street below. All three of them shifted their attention downward, Lienta lowering his spyglass.

Temerite guards were scrambling to form a line across the street, facing southward. None of them could see what had roused them, though, until a figure stepped into the edge of their camp's torchlight, followed by at least ten loping Wolves.

They halted twenty paces away from the edge of the guards.

"Grant," Bryce muttered. "And it looks like he's found a few new recruits."

"But not his wife."

Below, a few of the Wolves lifted their snouts to the sky and howled.

They'd find the passage out of the sunken city now for certain.

⬎

"How much longer until they finish repairing the wall?" Kara asked.

Commander Ty gestured toward where the breach that Hernande and Jerrain had created to get into the Needle marred the uniformity of the outer wall below them. "Still weeks away. And it will never be as sound as it was before. Your mentors managed significant damage during their little rescue."

Scaffolding had been erected both inside and out, workers busy shoring up and rebuilding the outer sections. The University mentors hadn't been subtle, blowing a gap in the wall that they could use for an entrance, then collapsing the wall above to fill it in. Kara and Ty stood at the edge of the indentation in the walkway at the top. Rather than remove all the broken stone from the mentor's handiwork, the engineers had elected to simply wall in the collapse. They were within ten feet of the walkway now.

But the damage done here was nothing compared to that of the quake.

"What about that?" Kara asked, turning from her perusal of the wall to jut her chin out at the massive chasm that cut through the wall and the city beyond. "Have we come up with any way to repair that damage?"

"Repair it? No. I don't think we can. Is it a breach? Yes. But it's not as significant a flaw in our defenses as what was left by your mentors . . . or even the main gates, for that matter. The chasm itself is deep enough that we don't need to worry about men approaching from that direction, although we've obviously kept up a watch. An army would have to scale the rather unstable walls of the chasm, and we'd notice any army of decent size doing so before they arrived. What we do have to worry about there is a smaller force intent on sneaking in. But again, I've placed watchers along both walls."

"What about extending our walls along both sides of the chasm?"

"It's possible. But erecting a wall of that size and length would be a significant endeavor, requiring massive manpower and hours of labor, not to mention a ton of stone."

Kara eyed the dark mouth of the fissure, like a scar from the battle against nature that had played out here, a scar caused by the ley. Baron Arent and Prime Wielder Augustus had sought to enslave the ley, and the earth had fought back. This was only one such manifestation of that battle. According to their scouts, sent out in all directions in an ever-widening circle, there were fissures and chasms of various sizes like this everywhere.

But the earth had settled . . . for the moment. She knew the calm was only temporary. As Father Dalton claimed, they still hadn't repaired the ley. In that respect, the Kormanley priest was correct, which was one reason Kara despised him so much.

"We have plenty of stone," she said, pointing toward the buildings near the chasm that had collapsed during the quake. "We need to clear that stone away anyway. Why not use it for a wall?"

Ty planted his hands on his hips as he contemplated the ruins of the streets. "I suppose we could take those not dealing with what little farming Father Dalton had the residents doing and have them start work on that. The engineers will be ecstatic with a new project. And it may keep some of the followers of Father Dalton occupied as well. They're becoming more agitated the longer we keep Dalton isolated in his rooms."

"Are they causing problems?"

"Not yet, but it's only a matter of time. We haven't allowed him to talk to them in five days."

"He's gone longer than that without speaking to them before."

"But he hadn't revealed a new vision then. They're anxious about what it means and unhappy that Dalton isn't there to calm their fears."

Kara lowered her gaze to the wall's parapet, kicking a loose rock over the edge. "Let them stew in their fears for a while longer. Maybe some of them will realize that his prophecies are nothing but words."

"Perhaps."

"Do you think we should let him talk to them?" she demanded sharply. "You didn't think so at that first meeting."

Ty didn't flinch at her tone. "He might quell their fears."

"And he might goad them into doing something more drastic than simply gathering in the square to hear him preach. No." She shook her head vehemently. "We already allow him too much leeway. He can speak when we're ready to let him speak, not before. Let them wait."

"We won't be able to wait too much longer. A few days at most." Then, as if he were broaching a new topic, even though Kara knew he wasn't: "How goes the work with the new Nexus?"

"I don't want to talk about it."

"That well, huh?"

She waved a dismissive hand toward the thin spire of the Needle and turned toward the nearest stairwell down off the wall, Ty following. "What are the latest reports from our scouts?"

Ty let her change the subject. "We're still running across random groups of people to the northwest and west, survivors who hunkered down in the hills and mountains that separate us from the Demesnes. Some have returned with our scouts here to the Needle, others choose to remain where they are. Those we've questioned who recently come from across the mountains claim that the Demesne Houses have sunk into tribal warfare. Our best guess is that the Shattering destabilized their already precarious political structure. Hernande agrees. Before the Shattering, the Houses vied with each other constantly, but the politics were always handled covertly, with spies and assassinations. Now, they have armies marching on each other. Entire Houses have been wiped out."

"What about to the south?"

"The Gorrani." They'd reached the base of the wall and headed toward the temple, winding their way through the crowded tents between the wall and the ring of stone buildings near the temple. The mingled scents of roasted meat and corn, spices, and the stench of too many people living too close together assaulted them. "They appear to have withdrawn from their original encampment to the south, since the river dried up. They may have returned to their homeland in the Flats."

"Let's hope so." Kara worried about the Gorrani, even though she worked with Okata, a Gorrani Wielder, on a daily basis. They could be reasonable, even if they were easy to anger and violent in their reactions. But Okata knew what had happened in the pit of the node during the Gorrani attack; those outside the walls—those who had survived the fiery white surge of ley that Lecrucius had released—didn't. "And to the north and east?"

"We've heard nothing from Allan's group, and our scouts have seen nothing of the raiders from Haven between Erenthrall and the Hollow. No significant activity east either. Still no contact with anyone from Temer. There were few people living on the plains between Erenthrall and Temer to begin with, except along the ley barge lines, and most of them appear to have withdrawn either east or west, leaving the plains in that direction empty."

"Then I'd better return to the node and find Hernande and the other mentors. I agreed to meet with them days ago." She scrubbed her face with her hands. "There's just not enough time for everything. I never realized how much was involved in leading a city. I wasn't cut out for this."

Ty halted. "That's why you aren't doing it alone. I'll return to the barracks, check up on Darius and the rest of the enforcers. After your meeting with Hernande, you should get some rest."

Kara waved him off, then proceeded to trudge toward the temple, her shoulders already tensed in frustration. She knew Cory and Hernande felt the ley and the Tapestry were connected somehow, but she still didn't see how that was going to help her heal the distortion over Tumbor. It wasn't a matter of control, but of size. The distortion was huge, ten times the size of the one that had engulfed Erenthrall, maybe more. The Nexus Father Dalton and Lecrucius had created here at the Needle had barely managed to repair the one in Erenthrall; she didn't think it was powerful enough to heal Tumbor.

But she owed it to Cory and Hernande to at least listen.

She found them on one of the tiers of the temple, the students standing in a circle around Jerrain, Hernande, and Cory. She didn't see Sovaan anywhere, but that didn't surprise her. The pompous administrator felt working with the students was beneath him.

As she approached, Jerrain said in a professorial tone, "See how the folds of the Tapestry are woven together? Not broken—you should never tear the fabric of reality—but if they are twisted and layered one atop the other, over and over again, and then pulled taut, you can create substance from thin air. This is what the mentors who worked with the Prime Wielders did to create the conduits for whatever construct the Primes needed in their work. Some of the conduits were permanent, like those that direct the ley lines through the junctions in the city, creating channels in midair so that the ley would run along the appropriate path. We'll show you how to tie this weave off to make it permanent once we figure that out ourselves. Most of the constructs were only temporary, channeling the ley to a specific location so that the Wielders could use it to sow the great towers of Grass or imbue the cloth used in the sails of the flying ley barges with ley, something like that. This block I've created before you, with the help of Hernande, will dissolve the moment we shift our focus elsewhere. But for now, it should be solid enough to hold a person's weight. Cory?"

Jerrain waved toward the air before him, in the center of the circle of students. Kara noted that they'd placed themselves in the middle of the sun emblem of the stone mosaic on this tier. As Cory stepped forward, she reached out with her senses, the ley in the node pulsing intensely behind her, but could feel nothing in the area where the mentors and students were concentrating. However, Cory set one foot on what appeared to be empty space, then pushed off with his other foot, until he stood hovering a foot above the stone sun. The students gasped in surprise, edging forward for a closer look. Cory settled his weight onto both feet, while sweat began to bead on Hernande's and Jerrain's foreheads.

A moment later, Jerrain said through clenched teeth, "Get . . . down."

Cory immediately stepped back, but Hernande and Jerrain obviously lost their hold on the Tapestry because he stumbled, the foot still on whatever they'd created giving way suddenly. Hernande caught him, noticing Kara standing behind the students at the same time.

"As you can see," he said, voice cracking, "it's difficult to hold something as solid as a person for any length of time. We assume that it's much easier to channel the ley, although we have yet to try."

Kara winced at the mild reprimand as Hernande caught Jerrain's attention and pointed toward Kara. The elder mentor looked relieved to see her and immediately began shooing the students away.

"That's enough for today," he said, "we have a visitor. Go harass the kitchen staff or whatever it is you students do in your spare time."

The seven students, of varied age, turned toward Kara before heading off toward the tier's main door. Kara approached Cory and the two mentors, aware of a few of the students staring at her back and whispering amongst themselves as they departed.

"Was that for my benefit?" she asked. Cory wrapped the fingers of one hand through hers in greeting.

"We didn't know you were coming," Jerrain said curtly.

"We've shifted our lectures and studies toward whatever we think might help you and the Wielders and what might shed some light on the connection between the ley and the Tapestry," Hernande explained. "Have you come to talk about that, or is it something else?"

"Mentor—" Cory began defensively, but Kara him off.

"No, I deserved that. I meant to come a few days ago. I didn't. I apologize. But I'm here now."

Jerrain huffed, still disgruntled, but relented, motioning toward a stone bench abutting the wall of the next tier. "I need to sit. That demonstration was exhausting."

Jerrain and Hernande settled onto the bench, while Cory and Kara stood.

"You wanted to talk about working together, the Wielders and the mages?" Kara prompted.

"Yes, I think we can help."

"How?"

"We know the Primes worked with the mentors in Erenthrall," Hernande began.

"Unfortunately," Cory interjected, "we don't know exactly what they did. Neither Hernande, Jerrain, nor Sovaan took part in that. None of those at the University did."

"We were not always aware of what happened beyond the University walls. Only now do I realize how isolated we really were. But we do know the principles behind what those mentors did for the Primes. They used the Tapestry to create the support systems for their workings. If they needed the ley directed toward a particular location, the mentors would provide the channel. The Primes would manipulate the ley itself. We think we can do the same for you and the Wielders here at the Needle. In particular, we think we can help keep the ley in check when you attempt to heal the distortion over Tumbor, so that the other Wielders will be free to help in other ways."

"Again, how?"

Jerrain gestured toward the sun mosaic impatiently. "As I'm certain you heard earlier, we can use the Tapestry to create channels for the ley to follow."

"We already have ley lines leading directly to Tumbor."

"Ah, but you don't have reservoirs in Tumbor anymore, do you? All the nodes and junctions and pits are locked away inside the distortion now. We can create reservoirs here at the Needle where you can store the ley until you need it. We can connect the reservoirs with channels, so that your Wielders can shift it to where it would be most useful. Otherwise, you're taking ley from Erenthrall, directing it to the Needle, then immediately directing it to Tumbor. That's a complex system, requiring the undivided attention of Wielders here at the Needle to redirect the flow. Reservoirs here would help regulate it. It's all about control and ease of movement, so your Wielders can focus on healing, not holding the ley in check."

Kara considered in silence, the two mentors and Cory watching her with various degrees of anticipation and eagerness.

"It could work," she said finally, "but not if you can't control your channels better than the single block I saw here today."

Jerrain waved a hand dismissively. "We'll figure out how to set the weave permanently. Not a problem."

"And as Jerrain mentioned, the ley is much lighter than a person," Hernande added. "The strain on us and our students should be significantly less."

"You think," Kara said pointedly. "We'll have to test that out to see if it's true."

All three of the men nodded. "Of course." They seemed inordinately pleased with themselves. She hated to disappoint them.

"That doesn't help solve the real problem, however."

They all stilled.

"And what is that?" Hernande asked.

"Power." She began pacing before them. "I don't think the amount of ley we have here at the Needle—or waiting beneath Erenthrall—is enough to heal the distortion over Tumbor. It's not a matter of the amount of ley we have, it's a matter of how concentrated it is. The original Nexus in Erenthrall and the one here at the Needle were designed to augment the power of the ley. The crystals reflect and refract the ley back and forth upon itself, honing it, refining it into a purer form. It's less diffuse when it leaves the Nexus, more concentrated. We have six panes here at the Needle. From what Marcus tells me, in Er-enthrall there were hundreds. After stabilizing the ley lines, I've spent all my time attempting to find a better configuration of these six panes, one that will somehow generate more power. We've succeeded, to an extent. But it's still not enough to heal Tumbor. At least, not enough for me to take the risk of collapsing the distortion and losing Tumbor al-together. What you're suggesting will free up Wielders . . . but that doesn't help produce more power."

She halted. No one spoke. Cory had hung his head. He, at least, al-ready knew what had been keeping her awake at night and driving her into exhaustion.

"Are you saying that the distortion can't be healed?" Jerrain asked.

"No. It can be healed. We simply need to find a way to configure the crystals to generate more power."

"And now Dalton has issued his challenge with this vision." Her-nande had begun chewing on the end of his beard. "He's forced you into a time constraint. His followers won't wait forever."

"Exactly."

Hernande bowed his head. "When I was at the Nexus last time, you were attempting to hold the panes without Wielder intervention be-cause the strain of keeping them in place was too much for the Wield-ers to handle on a constant basis."

"If the configuration is natural, then the crystals will mostly stay in position. They only need to be adjusted occasionally due to drift. But if we want them in an unnatural position, they must be constantly held in place or they begin to rotate out of control."

"Do some of these 'unnatural' configurations yield more power?"

"Yes."

Hernande turned to Jerrain. "We should be able to hold the panes in place using the same technique we use to create the channels."

"We'd *have* to figure out how to set them permanently, then."

Hernande straightened and focused on Kara. "You figure out what configuration you want for the crystals. We'll figure out how to hold it in place."

⌁

"I need to speak to Father," Dierdre stated for the third time, her arms now crossed over her chest, her back ramrod straight. "It's important."

The enforcers guarding Father Dalton's rooms—his *prison*, Dierdre thought—remained unmoved. "We have strict orders not to let anyone in to see him, not you or our Second, Darius."

Dierdre's eyes narrowed, but she could tell that none of the enforcers were going to contradict their orders. Obviously, none of them were sympathetic to the Kormanley.

Disgusted, she spun on her heel and stamped down the hall, turning the corner with a swirl of her skirt.

By the time she'd reached the rooms she shared with Marcus, she'd calmed down somewhat. Moving to the sideboard where they kept some small essentials, she tapped the ley heating stone and set about making a cup of tea, her mind mulling over Father's prophecy and its potential ramifications, circling constantly back to her worries over Father and the fact that she couldn't speak to him. Had he had any additional visions to clarify the prophecy? Was he being treated well, given food and drink?

Was he even still alive?

The knife she was using to cut a few slices of bread from a loaf halted mid-motion as she stilled and looked up, staring unseeing at the stone wall before her. But then she shook off the sudden horror of the thought. "They wouldn't have killed him," she muttered to herself as she buttered the bread and bit into it. "Kara would never allow it."

"Kara would never allow what?" Marcus asked as he came through the open door.

Dierdre jumped, choking on her bread. "What are you doing here?" she spat as she covered her mouth with one hand and coughed, bread crumbs flying.

Marcus crossed the room instantly, beating her on the back to help with the choking. "Are you all right?"

Dierdre sucked in a deep breath and straightened, pushing aside Marcus' concerned attempts to help. "I'm fine," she managed, her voice weak, her eyes watery.

Marcus grabbed a glass and poured her some water, handing it over. She drank it down in one long gulp, wiping her mouth with the back of her hand. Her chest still hurt, and she was certain she'd breathed a chunk of bread into her lungs. "You startled me."

"I didn't mean to."

She bit back a sharp retort, remembering her intent to seduce him back to her side.

She tested the kettle on the stove and began spooning tea leaves into an infuser. "Why *are* you here?" she asked again as she poured herself a cup and dipped the rounded infuser into the hot water to steep. "I thought you'd be down in the node." She tried to keep the accusatory note out of her voice, but failed.

If Marcus noticed, he didn't react.

"Kara was away this morning. She went to the wall with Ty to review the repairs on the breach, among other things. Without her there, we can't do much more than maintain the crystals in their current positions."

Dierdre leaned back against the sideboard, tea in one hand. "Why not?"

Marcus settled into a chair at the small table for two against the opposite wall. Their bed rested beneath the window overlooking the stellae garden and Needle at the center of the temple, the sheets still rumpled from the night before.

"No one dares mess with the configuration unless Kara is there to restore it if something goes wrong," he explained, dropping his head onto the table with a weary sigh. "It's one of the reasons she's constantly at the node."

Dierdre set her cup aside and drifted across the room, settling in behind him, her hands finding his shoulders, digging into the tensed muscles there. He groaned as she massaged the knots out. "She isn't the only one being driven to exhaustion," she muttered. "You've been there as much as she has."

Marcus mumbled something noncommittal she didn't catch.

"But why can't you adjust the crystals on your own?" she prodded. "Won't she allow it?"

Marcus lifted his head and leaned back into her, head resting beneath her breasts, his eyes closed. Her fingers shifted slightly forward, digging into the tops of his shoulders.

"She hasn't said anything about it one way or the other."

"So everyone is simply afraid."

"Of course we're afraid. Don't you remember what happened during the Gorrani attack? Or the Shattering, for that matter. One mistake and the crystals could collapse. The resulting quakes as the ley shifts could destroy us. Not to mention potentially trigger another Shattering."

She slapped him lightly on the cheek with one hand, leaning in close. "I didn't mean afraid of the ley. I meant they're afraid of her. Of Kara."

Marcus stiffened beneath her hands, but when she continued the massage without further comment, the new tension slowly eased.

"I suppose they are. She did save us all during the attack. And healed the distortion over Erenthrall. They know that none of us could have done it alone."

Dierdre frowned, knowing Marcus couldn't see her. She wanted to point out—again—that Kara hadn't done it alone, that the others had supported her, but she knew that argument wouldn't sway Marcus at all.

Instead, she asked, "So why doesn't she heal the distortion over Tumbor as well?"

"Kara claims that the Nexus isn't strong enough to support the power needed. Not in its current configuration. She's trying to find a stronger arrangement of the crystals."

Dierdre stilled. "So she's not ready yet." Or she's afraid.

Marcus stirred beneath her and she realized she'd halted the massage. She dug her fingers in deeper and he settled back down.

"*We're* not ready yet," he said, exhaling as he let his entire body relax. "She keeps trying new orientations, new placements, but the crystals either won't hold position or the new configuration reduces the augmentation of the ley's flow. She's tried everything. I think she's even repeating orientations now, almost stubbornly."

Dierdre considered his words carefully, aware that if she pushed him too hard, he'd become defensive. But still . . .

"Perhaps," she muttered, as if merely thinking out loud, "perhaps she's run out of ideas. She was never a true Prime, after all. She didn't receive their training. Maybe . . . maybe someone else has thought of something new, something different, but they're too afraid to come forward. What about Iscivius? Or Irmona?"

Marcus barked out a bitter laugh. "You think she'd listen to anything either one of them said? She barely trusts them in the pit working with the node under strict supervision."

Dierdre retreated. "True, true. But what about you? You must have thought of something she hasn't tried yet."

"I have a few ideas."

"I knew you would. Tell her."

He shifted uncomfortably beneath her. "I doubt she'd listen to me. Not after what happened between us in Erenthrall."

"Not even after you supported her takeover from Lecrucius?"

"Not even then." He sounded wounded.

Dierdre leaned forward again and whispered, "Then perhaps you should try these configurations when she isn't there."

Before he could respond, she kissed him, her hands shifting down toward his chest. He resisted at first, as if he wanted to protest, but then he gasped and twisted in the chair, one hand rising to cup the back of her head, to pull her in closer, the kiss becoming rougher, more passionate.

Moments later the chair clattered to the floor and they were stumbling toward the bed, clothes being shed along the way, each grappling the other. They fell into bed, Dierdre uttering a startled cry that ended in a laugh as Marcus reared above her, her wrists caught in his hands. His breath came in ragged gasps of need and want, his thick blond-brown hair tousled, his face flushed, his startlingly blue, intense eyes staring down at her. Her own breath caught in her chest with a sharp, painful ache of triumph and possession and loss.

Then he fell on her, mouth roaming her neck, the hollow of her throat, her breasts, her skin hot and sweaty, burning from the inside. She arched into his hunger, moaning, but when he shifted lower she growled low in her throat and twisted beneath him, rolling him forcefully onto his back so that she straddled him, his wrists now caught by her hands. He struggled briefly, trying to reach for her, to seize control again, but she clamped her thighs tight around his chest and refused to let go.

Only when he stopped writhing beneath her did she loosen her hold. They were both gasping, flushed, sheened with sweat. She caught and held his gaze, each staring deeply into the other's eyes. Something crackled between then, unseen, only felt in the core of her chest, in the tingling of her fingers and toes.

His breath hitched and caught.

Only then did she smile, leaning down to kiss him, her long black hair falling to trail across his chest. The kiss held, long and lingering, shivering deep into her body. Marcus trembled beneath her, gasping again, desperately, when she released it, as if he'd been submerged beneath water for too long. He fought to catch his breath.

After that, he didn't struggle against her at all.

Hours later, after Marcus had returned to the node, Dierdre dressed in a dark shift, a length of cloth pulled up over her head to obscure her black hair and shadow her face, and slipped from the room into the halls of the temple. She skirted the rest of the living quarters used by the Wielders, avoiding even the passages used only by the servants. The temple was vast, with numerous corridors and rooms that hadn't yet been explored by the enforcers or those that lived within it. Most of the rooms that were used were centered around the stellae garden and Needle and the functional rooms such as the orrery and storage vaults.

She wound her way up to the third tier, coming up on the corridor outside Father's room far from the last torch, so that she'd be hidden in shadow. She'd hoped that the guards would have changed, that the replacements would be those aligned with her brother Darius, but she didn't recognize any of them, so she withdrew with a silent curse.

If she couldn't speak to Father herself, perhaps her brother had been able to gain access and would have news.

Retreating through the empty halls, she waited at a servants' corridor until the passage was clear and reentered the main living area of the temple. Removing the shawl from her head, she walked purposefully toward the barracks for the officers, crossing one of the wide main corridors that ran directly from the outside of the temple to the Needle. Its length was illuminated completely with ley globes scavenged from both Erenthrall and Tumbor.

The residences on the far side of the corridor were more austere, the atmosphere more regimented and ordered. She passed a few enforcers in the halls, all of them nodding to her briefly. Some were working on polishing their armor or boots in their rooms, glancing out at her as she went by. Many were in the central gathering room, playing cards or dice or simply eating.

Darius' room was slightly larger than the others, befitting his place as Second, but when she rapped lightly at the door, no one answered.

She bit back another curse.

"He's at the wall."

Dierdre looked up to find a red-haired female enforcer watching her from a doorway farther down the corridor. When she saw who it was, she frowned and stepped out into the hall, her face pale in the torchlight. She was dressed informally, in shirt, breeches, and boots, although Dierdre noted the blade at her side and the knife thrust through her belt.

"You're his sister Dierdre, right?" she asked.

"Yes."

The woman's gaze flicked to check the hall beyond Dierdre, then back behind herself. She licked her lips nervously and shifted forward. "His shift ends soon," she said, her voice lowered, "but he won't be returning here. There's a meeting." She gave a sign with one hand, one Dierdre recognized from before the Shattering, one the more violently-minded Kormanley sect had used.

Dierdre raised an eyebrow and gave the return signal, the woman nodding curtly in response, relief flashing briefly in her eyes.

"The meeting is in the outer city," she said, her tone more confident now. "I'm headed there now, if you wanted to join me."

"Of course. But I don't know the way. Darius hadn't given me the location yet."

"I'll show you."

She led Dierdre out of the temple using the main corridors, speaking only to greet other enforcers or servants as they passed. Her pace was brisk, leaving little room for talk. Dierdre followed, wondering who the woman was and how she knew the old Kormanley signal. And this meeting . . .

What had Darius done? And why had he not included her if it related to the Kormanley?

Annoyed, she followed the woman into the outer city, built of more recent stone than the temple, but still ancient, from before the rise of Baron Arent and the creation of the Nexus. They passed through the street containing the general barracks and kitchens for the enforcers, then out into the more common areas. As they moved through the streets and alleys, Dierdre noted how much more active they'd become since Kara and Ty took over. She knew they'd been bringing in more and more refugees, but these streets felt crowded, almost like the streets of Erenthrall before the Shattering. It was late afternoon, the sun already slanting between the buildings in thick shafts of dust-strewn light. Men, women, and children were lining up at the communal kitchens for their allotment of bread, meat, and vegetables. Most of the staples were doled out by workers guarded by enforcers, a system originally set up by Father Dalton and then expanded upon by Ty and Kara once they began taking in others. Many of the workers wore white shirts, although Dierdre doubted many knew why. They had once had the Kormanley symbol of convergence stitched onto their arms.

But not everyone relied on the food provided for them. Many of them had arrived at the Needle with their own supplies and had set up camp in the tent city outside the circle of stone buildings, either bartering what they had or plying their own trade, such as weaving baskets or working with stone or clay or leather. A small market system had arisen, not unlike the marketplaces of Erenthrall from before, growing as more people arrived. Dierdre wasn't certain how long it would last—there were only so many resources within easy reach of the Needle—but for now it survived. She had heard of excursions into the hills to the north and west, groups of ten or twenty men and women heading off in hopes of finding something worthwhile to bring back like fresh meat, hides, or supplies left in abandoned farms or villages. Others headed south, although they risked running into the Gorrani there. Few headed east, since the riches of Tumbor were now encased inside the distortion.

Dierdre's enforcer led her through the throngs of tents, not pausing to take in the variety of odd wares being offered at most. The stalls were mixed in with the tents used as homes, with only a few central locations for trading. Many had simply set their offerings out before their tent flaps. They passed a man bartering little hand-molded clay bowls, another showing carved wooden utensils, and a woman with little dolls made of tied and twisted straw.

Then her red-haired guide cut back through the tents and into the stone city again, except these streets weren't as well traveled. She couldn't shake images of the Eastend and West Forks districts in Erenthrall, where no one could be trusted and few respectable people moved around outside of midday. Certainly not this close to dusk. Dalton had used such districts to the Kormanley's advantage, recruiting to the violent sect from them and keeping himself hidden there once he'd been connected by the Hounds to the attacks on the city during the Purge.

Dierdre hadn't realized the Needle contained such areas. But she supposed that every gathering of a significant amount of people developed an underbelly. And the Needle had grown over the last month, nearly doubled now.

The woman halted in front of a three-story building with yellow lantern light showing in three of the twelve windows. There were still a few hours before sunset, but the narrow street was already sunk in shadow. Dierdre picked out a few architectural motifs above windows and the front door, lintels and sills with geometric designs, but she didn't know their significance. They entered the building after a short pause, the red-haired enforcer glancing back at her once.

Inside, she moved immediately to the back of the building, avoiding the stairs that led to the upper floors. She tapped on the far door on the left, a muffled voice coming from within. When she opened the door, lantern light spilled out into the hall. She grabbed Dierdre's arm and tugged her inside, closing the door behind her.

Four others sat around a rough wooden table, three men and another woman, none of them Darius. All of them stared at Dierdre, a few of them trading the hand signals with the red-haired enforcer. She recognized three of them as other enforcers, out of uniform. Two of them were playing cards.

One of them grunted. "I didn't realize she would be coming." He was older, closing on fifty, and he had a pipe resting to one side, smoke curling up from its bowl. He stuck it between his teeth and pulled on it, eyeing her as he exhaled. The slightly sweet scent of arruga leaf permeated the room.

"She was looking for Darius," the red-haired enforcer said as she moved forward to take a seat at the table. "And she knew the signal."

The elder enforcer's eyes narrowed as he blew another plume of smoke into the air. "Darius wasn't certain of her."

Dierdre hid the clench of her gut at her brother's betrayal with a scowl, crossing her arms over her chest.

"She's here now," one of the others said—younger, with a black mustache that needed trimming and long shaggy dark hair. He played a card. "Your turn."

The elderly man shrugged and turned back to his cards, setting the pipe aside. "We'll let Darius decide. He should be here shortly."

That appeared to settle things, the others relaxing as a few low-murmured conversations broke out and the card game continued. Dierdre remained by the door, watching carefully, trying to eavesdrop. But the discussions were trivial, gossip among guardsmen, complaints about their watches and duties along the wall or with the cooks and servants providing food.

She flinched when another tap came at the door, the elderly enforcer barking out, "Come!" as everyone shifted their hands unobtrusively closer to weapons. Dierdre hadn't noticed this when she'd entered.

But it was her brother Darius, entering with two other enforcers at his side.

"Who brought her?" he demanded as soon as he caught sight of her, the tension in the room instantly escalating. The two men with Darius closed in on either side of her.

She stiffened in affront. "You aren't *certain* of me?" she spat in accusation before anyone could answer. "What's going on here? Why are you meeting in secret? And why are you using Kormanley signals? Does Father know of this?"

"Because this is the Kormanley . . . or at least the start of it. And no, Father doesn't know about this."

Dierdre glanced around at all of them. Those at the table watched with a casual, dangerous intensity, the cards and conversation discarded. The two new men who flanked her appeared to be twins. Mussed brown hair, thin faces, hard eyes.

They were all waiting for a decision from Darius.

She returned her gaze to him, met his brown eyes flecked with yellow, mirrors to her own. "What do you mean the start of the Kormanley?"

Darius didn't answer immediately, his expression fixed, judgmental.

Then he spun and took two steps to the table, leaning on it with both hands. "Is this everyone?"

The twins relaxed, pulling back from her sides and drifting toward the table as well. The others shifted forward, hands withdrawing from knives and daggers. The cards and conversations lay forgotten.

"All of those who could make it," the red-haired woman said, her fingers drumming on the table in annoyance. "A few were placed on guard duty at the wall or are otherwise occupied by Ty in the temple or outer city."

"There are others I don't quite trust enough yet to bring to the meetings," the elder enforcer added. He sucked on his pipe, his eyes shifting toward Dierdre. She hadn't moved from her position, but at his look she stepped forward, taking a place to one side of her brother. She'd never liked living in his shadow. In Erenthrall, Dalton had always sent him out to the drop-off points, coordinating the cells of the violent sect of the Kormanley, occasionally attending the small and secretive meetings. She'd been used mostly as a courier and recruiter.

"What is it that we're here to discuss?" she asked bluntly.

"Father," Darius said curtly. "The way they are treating him is intolerable."

"Have you seen him recently?"

"Not since his revelation of a new vision. Ty has managed to keep the guard on Father's door using enforcers mostly loyal to himself." He nodded toward the older enforcer and the red-haired woman. "Trenton and Cerena—we've been seen too often together at the wall. He knows about you both, or at least strongly suspects. Javers and Jonnas, I'm not as certain about."

The twins shrugged, one of them saying, "He hasn't paid undue attention to us."

Darius shifted toward the other three. "I'm fairly certain he's unaware of the rest of you, including you, Armone."

The mustached younger man grinned. "I've been careful to stay clear of you lot when on duty."

Trenton blew smoke toward the rafters. "He's suspicious of everyone not in his own inner circle or part of that group from the Hollow. That's how he's been able to keep you from Father. One of his own or someone from the Hollow is always in charge of the guards at the door." He pointed toward Dierdre with the end of his pipe. "And I assume you've had no luck gaining an audience either."

"No. I managed to see him immediately after his last sermon, when he told of his vision. Marcus, Kara, and the others were in council then and hadn't yet decided to cut him off completely. But they came and dragged me out before we were finished talking."

Darius shoved back from the table. "Which is why we're meeting. It was an outrage when Ty seized control after the Gorrani attack and imprisoned him, then handed the Needle over to the Wielder Kara, but Father ordered me to wait, to be patient, to bide our time. He said he needed to see what visions would come." He shot them all a penetrating look. "Well, he's had his vision. Only now we can't find out what it means and plan accordingly, because we can't speak to him."

"They can't keep him locked in those rooms forever," Cerena said. "He's only been held for a little over a week. He's gone longer than that without giving a sermon. They'll let him speak eventually."

"Will they?" Darius asked the room, and everyone shifted uncomfortably. "I don't think they will. They know how much power he can wield with a simple vision. They won't hand that power to him."

"Why didn't they pull him from the tier's wall when he first mentioned the vision?" Armone asked. "They must have known how much damage it would do."

"They couldn't," Dierdre said, with an unpleasant smile. "It was too late. Think of the outrage of those listening if he'd been cut off in the middle of explaining what he'd seen. They would have had a riot on the plaza right then."

"Maybe there should have been a riot," Javers said. Or Jonnas. Dierdre didn't yet know which twin was which.

"We may have been able to free Father in the chaos," the other twin finished.

"Or Father may have been killed instead," Darius countered. "A convenient accident."

Dierdre frowned, recalling her own earlier thoughts about Father dying. "They wouldn't."

The doubt from the others was palpable.

"They may have a riot yet," Armone said, slouching back into his chair, one hand raised to his chin, finger stroking his mustache. "Father's followers are restless. They have questions about this new vision. They want answers."

"Which is why we're here," Darius muttered sharply, stepping back to the table and rapping his knuckles against it to capture their attention again. "We need to use this unrest to our advantage."

"How?"

"We need to break Ty's hold on the enforcers. We've already started recruiting our fellow enforcers to our cause, but it won't be enough without some other force putting the pressure on Ty as well. If we can get Father's followers to protest his imprisonment, cause a few riots, perhaps create a few of our own, then Ty's hold on many of the enforcers will weaken."

"Cause a few . . ." Dierdre trailed off, her gaze darting toward the others' faces, their own eyes studiously lowered.

The start of the Kormanley.

She turned on her brother. "You want to return to the tactics we used in Erenthrall. The bombings, the threats—"

"The preaching," he interrupted. "It doesn't have to start with bombings. But consider what Commander Ty and this Wielder Kara Tremain are doing. Is it any different than what Baron Arent and Prime Wielder Augustus did in Erenthrall? They are controlling the people using the supplies scavenged from the surrounding communities and they have seized the node at the Needle. They don't have the same level of power that Arent and Augustus did, but their power is growing. Do we want to let them create another Erenthrall here? Another society controlled by an abuse of the ley?"

Dierdre drew breath to protest—she knew Kara wasn't using the ley to control anyone, that she was using it to heal the ley system.

But Darius stepped close to her, face-to-face. She forced herself not to step back, although one hand fell to the table to steady herself.

"Can we trust you? Or has Marcus blinded you to what Kara and the others are truly doing?"

Her jaw snapped shut as anger boiled up in her chest.

"Kara's afraid," she blurted, the betrayal of what Marcus had confided to her slicing down through the anger. But she ignored it, turning to face the others, one by one, as she spoke. "It's not enough to break Ty's control, you'll have to break Kara's grip on the Wielders as well. You can do it by forcing her to use the ley when she isn't ready, isn't prepared, perhaps even cause an accident within the node itself."

In sudden inspiration, she grabbed Darius' shoulder and smiled. "And I know exactly who we can ask to help us."

"Marcus?"

"No, not Marcus. He isn't ready yet. Someone who already hates Kara. Two people, actually. The Wielders, Iscivius and Irmona."

Seven

"WHAT'S GOING ON HERE?" Commander Ty roared as he and the twenty-four enforcers he'd gathered as he charged through the corridors of the temple toward the open plaza came upon the enforcers already clogging up the exit. There were six of them, holding the doorway against the surging crowd outside. The noise from the plaza was deafening in the narrowed corridor, an amalgam of furious shouting, angry retorts, and the distinct sound of a brawl.

When no one responded, Ty's own fury edged up another notch. Ty grabbed the shoulder of one of the enforcers before him and jerked the man around. He had shaggy dark hair and a limp mustache. His eyes narrowed when he saw Ty, then shifted toward the enforcers behind him with relief.

"What's going on?" Ty demanded again.

"The Father's worshippers are rioting," the man said. "We tried to calm them, but when we refused to bring out Father Dalton, they became agitated. We've managed to keep them out of the temple, but they're attacking our men in the barracks and kitchens."

Ty swore, craning his neck so he could see out through the opening the enforcers held and onto the plaza beyond. Commoners from the outer city and the tents thronged the area, some clothed in the white shirts they'd taken to wearing in support of Dalton and the Kormanley. A few even had the Kormanley convergence symbol stitched or painted onto their shirts with ash.

For a moment, a sense of sickening dislocation swept over Ty and he found himself back in Erenthrall, at the edge of a crowd gathered in a marketplace to witness the judgment of a suspected Kormanley man, part of the Dogs intent on keeping the crowd under control. Nervous sweat slicked his skin beneath his uniform as the tensions and unease within the citizens grew, until it boiled over and the entire marketplace erupted in chaos. Ty's alpha had ordered his unit into the crowd, their swords wounding and killing indiscriminately. Men, women, children—it hadn't mattered.

It had been the beginning of the Purge . . . and the riots had only gotten worse.

A bitter taste in his mouth, Ty glanced down at the enforcer he still held by the shoulder. "What's your name?"

"Armone."

"Find Second Darius, Armone. Tell him to bring as many men from the wall as he can spare. We need to quell this riot now, before it escalates and expands into the streets of the outer city. Tell him to use whatever force necessary."

Armone nodded and pushed past Ty and the others in the hall as Ty turned toward them.

"We're going to push out into the plaza," Ty said, voice raised to reach the men at the back. "Draw swords or blades if necessary, but try to only wound if you can."

With that, he shouldered through those holding the door, coming face-to-face with a man, maybe thirty, screaming in outrage and grappling with the last enforcer at the edge of the plaza. Ty punched him in the face over the enforcer's shoulder, then shoved out into the plaza, instantly surrounded by people crying out at the blasphemy of holding Father hostage, hands snatching at his red shirt, dragging at his arms. He tried to move through them, protecting himself with hunched shoulders—

And then a woman spit in his face.

Ty grabbed the woman by the throat, lifted her, and flung her into the crowd behind, three other people falling to the ground under her weight. He wiped the spittle from his cheek, then clenched his jaw and waded into the fray, stepping on one of the fallen bodies. He punched at faces, kidneys, lower backs—hauling his victims aside as they screamed in pain or moaned and folded over his fists. All the brawling techniques that the Dogs had trained for in the den beneath the Amber Tower resurged with a vengeance. He sank into the moment, breath heaved in through his mouth, exhaled out through his nose with a low grunting sound, but he never lost control. The riot eddied around him, a background of shouts and cries of pain, but his focus remained on the men and women immediately before him. Some of them dove at him, faces looming from the tangle of arms and legs and bodies as they attacked. He grabbed their arms, jerked them into range as they grasped at him or scratched, then drove them to their knees with a head butt or fist to the gut. Or he twisted their arms behind them and shoved them to the flagstone. Some of the leering faces spouting hatred wrenched back from him in fear. A few were weeping, attempting to flee but trapped by the press of bodies.

He'd made it twenty paces out into the plaza, a string of groaning bodies behind him, when he sensed a commotion from the other side of the square and realized Darius had arrived. He continued forward, catching anyone within reach, but the tenor of the crowd had changed. Instead of shouting "Let him speak!" or "Usurpers!" as they pushed forward toward the temple, they were now attempting to escape, the tidal flow receding.

For a moment, the desperation escalated, the crowd knotted as the intent shifted, and then, like a dam that suddenly breached, the rioters poured out of the square, scattering out into the tent city partially blocked by Darius and his men and into the side streets and alleys of the buildings to either side. Ty's men chased after them briefly, until he called them back. Darius harassed the followers as they fled, although he left them a wide opening for the tents and Ty didn't see any of his men landing a single solid blow.

His eyes narrowed at his second, but then he tasted blood in his mouth. His lip throbbed and he touched it lightly with one hand. Someone had hit him hard enough to split his lip and he'd hardly felt it during the fight. He spat blood to one side, fresh bruises beginning to throb on his side, along one cheek. His knuckles throbbed as well, and there were multiple scratches across his arms and neck. He grunted and glanced around at the two dozen bodies littering the nearly empty plaza as Darius headed toward him with his own men. All of them were rocking back and forth, cradling wounds or curled into fetal positions, except for two, who weren't moving at all. He stepped up to the nearest, rolled the man onto his back, then sighed in relief when he realized the man was simply unconscious, not dead.

"Check the others," he ordered, the scent of blood and sweat and vomit—the scents of violence—beginning to permeate his nostrils. "Take the wounded to the hospital. Inform me if any of them are dead." He prayed to Korma that none of them were.

"What happened?" Darius demanded, voice angry and accusing. "Why did you attack Father's followers?"

Ty turned on Darius slowly. "We didn't attack them. They tried to break into the temple."

"And you couldn't hold them off? A bunch of commoners with no weapons except words?"

Ty bristled at the audacity of his second, confronting him here, in the plaza, in front of their enforcers. He should have waited until they were alone, back in the barracks or the orrery. "You will not speak to your alpha with that tone," he said, low and dangerous. Anyone who'd been part of the Dogs would have recognized the warning for what it meant.

Darius straightened in challenge. "Or what?"

Ty's hands clenched back into fists, but before he could call his beta out—the challenge was too blatant to go unremarked—one of the enforcers shouted, "Commander, look at this!"

"What is it?" he snapped.

"Someone's defaced the temple wall. It's some kind of . . . symbol."

He dipped his head toward Darius, his second not reacting, then spun on his heel. "Where?"

"Here."

A cluster of enforcers stood beneath the jut of stone that Father Dalton used to deliver his sermons. The enforcers parted before him, revealing a section of gray temple stone where someone had used a piece of white chalk to scrawl a circular icon. He had expected the convergence symbol of the Kormanley, but this was completely different, more complicated and detailed, although it was still rudimentary. A simple circle sat in the center, surrounded by a serpent head and neck above, forked tongue obvious, and a dog-like figure beneath, both curled about the circle. The snake appeared to be biting the dog's tail, the dog the serpent's.

The reference to Father's vision was obvious. It sent a cramp through Ty's gut and he tasted bile in the back of his throat.

He turned to the enforcers hovering behind him. "Wash it off, before anyone else sees it. And I thought I ordered you to take care of those wounded in the scuffle!"

At the sharp tone, the enforcers scrambled toward those who still remained in the plaza, a couple rushing toward the barracks where those off duty had been caught in the riot. Many of them were nursing bruises and scrapes as well, although none seemed inclined to report to the hospital. He surveyed the activity, before his gaze fell on Darius again.

The second watched him a moment, then turned and gestured for his own men to return to the wall.

Ty glanced back at the graphic symbol on the wall as three enforcers arrived with a bucket of water and some rags. He swore as they began to wash it off.

"Where's Kara?" he muttered to himself, heading back into the temple. "She needs to know about this."

⚊

"Help!" someone cried from the front of the hospital ward.

Morrell glanced up from her current patient—a woman who'd accidentally stabbed herself with a spinning wheel's spindle—to see two men entering the hospital, one of them supported by the other, both covered in blood. Behind them were others, some cradling arms, others limping or holding shirts or cloth to head wounds.

"Bastion's bloody hells," Freesia said from three beds away, already rising and wiping her hands on a clean cloth. "Cerrin, Morrell, help me with the newcomers!"

Morrell clutched the woman's arm, the spindle still jutting from the palm of her hand, and said, "I'll be back in a moment. Try not to move your hand."

The woman merely nodded, her face streaked with tears. There'd been surprisingly little blood and the spindle had slid between the bones. She'd be fine as long as no one tried to remove the wooden needle.

Drayden stepped forward in concern as she stood, but she waved him back, then hustled to catch up to Freesia and Cerrin, already leading the walking wounded to new beds. She took one man by the arm and escorted him to a cot. He groaned as he sat down, clutching his side, but she'd already checked and the bruising wasn't life threatening.

She told him to wait, then grabbed someone else. As she, Freesia, and Cerrin sorted through the new arrivals, the men and women moaning or cursing or sobbing, Morrell pieced together what had happened, her stomach churning with fear and dismay as she realized that everyone present was a supporter of Father Dalton and that they'd been attacked in the plaza.

"They attacked us!" one woman cried out in disbelief as Morrell lowered her to a bed. "They clubbed my husband to the ground and then began kicking him! When I tried to pull him away to safety, they began beating me!"

Her cheek was covered in blood and multiple bruises were beginning to form on her face. Morrell quickly pulled back a length of hair and checked the scalp wound, but it wasn't serious, merely bleeding profusely. Nothing was broken, and the bruises weren't deep, although they'd be ugly by the time they finished darkening and swelling.

"You'll be fine," Morrell said, pushing up from the side of the bed. But the woman grabbed her with trembling hands.

"Have you seen my husband? He's tall, with a dark, full beard. Is he all right?"

Morrell pried the clawing fingers from her shoulder. "I haven't seen him, but I'll watch for him. Stay here. Someone will be by shortly to help you."

She pulled away and ran into a burly man, twice her width at the shoulders and at least a foot taller than her.

"How could they do this?" he shouted in her face, then latched onto her upper arms and began shaking her. "We only want to see Father! We only want to speak to him!"

"You're hurting me," Morrell gasped as pain shot up her arm and into her shoulder. She tried to wrench out of his grip, her head snapping back and forth, but she couldn't gain any leverage, her feet practically lifted off the floor. "Stop it!" she shouted, panic crowding outward from her chest. It began to tingle in her arms and she realized her fingers were bathed in the auroral light, that she'd already woven herself into the man's body. He'd only suffered a few scrapes and bruises, nothing significant, but his skin was flushed with a feverish fear and a growing hatred. But she couldn't break free—

"Why won't they let us see him?" the man shouted, blood-flecked spittle flying from his lips.

From the corner of her eye, she caught Drayden heading toward her, but when another sharp jolt of pain pierced through her shoulder, she reached forward with her power, frantic, and seized on his heart, squeezing. The man gasped and went rigid. At the same time Cerrin flew blindly out of nowhere, crying out, "Let her go!" in a fierce snarl as he tackled the man from the side.

All three of them crashed to the stone floor, Morrell wrenched out of the man's grip. She rolled onto her hands and knees, wincing as numbness shot down the arm he'd held the tightest, and then Drayden was there, crouched at her side protectively, teeth bared. He helped her up. Before them, Cerrin and the man were grappling between two cots, the woman and man on either side clutching tight to the beds' rails as they were jounced by an occasional hit. Cerrin pounded at the man with his fists, the blows ineffective. With Morrell's connection to him broken, the man heaved Cerrin's much lighter body aside and began crawling to his feet.

"Enough!" Freesia bellowed through the escalating turmoil as others began to get riled up by the fight. The healer's voice cut through the complaints like a heated knife, slicing and cauterizing at the same time. The burly man halted, half standing, using the two beds on either side for support. His breath came in heaves and he glared at Freesia. She didn't flinch. Cerrin scrambled up from where he'd landed, ready to attack again, his motions lithe and quick, like a feral cat. Morrell wouldn't have been surprised if he'd hissed in warning.

The man's gaze shifted to Cerrin, and he lurched fully upright. Cerrin took two steps forward, placing himself between Morrell, Drayden, and the man, but Freesia's voice brought them both up short again.

"I said enough!" She stalked forward, facing off against the man, making certain she stepped in front of Cerrin. "You brought the first few wounded in here, didn't you?"

The man dropped his gaze from Cerrin to Freesia. "Yes."

"Good. We'll take care of them now. You should go see if there are any others that need help."

The man drew back from her as if she'd slapped him, then glared around at everyone, his anger fading, replaced by bewilderment. He rubbed at his chest and Morrell shuddered. "I suppose I could do that."

He hesitated, but then he turned and headed toward the door. As he passed by the last few cots, three enforcers stepped inside. For a moment, the man and the enforcers stared at each other. Then the man pushed past them, vanishing into the outer room and the street beyond.

The enforcers watched him go, tense, then turned back toward the room. Morrell recognized the leader: the second, Darius. She didn't know the mousy man with the mustache or the red-haired woman.

"Is everything in order here?" Darius asked.

Many of those on cots shifted forward, a restless, unsettled sound, but Freesia stepped toward the enforcers purposefully. "Everything is fine. Should we expect any more wounded? We are already over capacity." Morrell scanned the room and realized that many had been seated on the floor between beds or were standing off to one side.

Darius' eyes narrowed, but he nodded respectfully. "The riot in the plaza has been halted. There should be no more wounded from that incident."

"Good. I would hope that next time the enforcers could be so kind as to temper their reactions to such gatherings. We much prefer our hospital be inactive."

The enforcer with the mustache snorted and the red-haired woman grinned.

"We'll take that into account. Next time."

Darius waved the other two out as he cast one last look around. The tight smile of satisfaction as he turned to leave sent a stab of unease into Morrell's gut.

"I think he was marking faces," Morrell muttered.

"Probably taking note of the troublemakers," Cerrin said, "so they can catch them more easily next time. Or beat them more soundly."

Morrell stared at him, his face in profile as he watched the doorway. His hair was mussed from the scuffle and his cheek reddened and dirty from an abrasion, probably received when he was thrown to the floor. His hands were still closed into fists. He huffed and turned toward her, their eyes catching. His were a tawny brown. She hadn't noticed before.

"Thanks," she said. "For trying to help me." She didn't mention that Drayden would have stopped the man cold in another moment. Or that she could have saved herself. The thought of what she'd done—or nearly done—already sickened her. She didn't need to add to her guilt with whatever Cerrin's reaction would be. Although the way he was looking at her now . . . could all his venom be a front? Why had he rushed to help her? He hadn't needed to do that, not with Drayden always so close. Unless . . . he actually liked her?

"Are you healers or are you gawkers?" Freesia snapped from a few paces away, causing both her and Cerrin to jump. Morrell placed a hand over her racing heart; Cerrin scowled.

"Why don't we let Morrell heal them all?" he asked in an ugly tone. "She's the one with the magical powers."

Morrell's gut curdled at derision in his tone and she stiffened, tears pricking the corners of her eyes. How could she have thought, even for a second, that he cared for her? She was a Hollower. And she was different.

Freesia cuffed him upside the head. "I thought we'd discussed that particular sentiment of yours already. Do I need to repeat myself?"

Cerrin ducked his head. "No."

"Then go take care of the wounded. Start at the far end on the left and work your way forward. Morrell, take the right. Treat only what needs to be treated and send them on their way, except for any serious cases, of course."

Cerrin shot Morrell a dark look, as if it were her fault, then trudged to the back of the hall.

"Are you all right?" Drayden asked, his voice rumbling up from his chest. The hair on the nape of his neck still bristled.

She patted his arm in reassurance. "I'm fine. Just . . . shaken."

Morrell sank into the work, bandaging a scrape, stitching up lacerated skin and muscle, prodding bruises and testing arms and legs for broken bones. She used the aurora only to make certain she wasn't missing any internal bleeding from those who'd been kicked in the gut or back or chest, or to verify bones weren't fractured. Most who caught the faint flickers of auroral lights around her fingers merely gasped, staring at her with an awe like that they showed for Father Dalton; a few flinched or ground their teeth together until the lights faded. Only one refused to let her examine him, shifting from her side of the room to Cerrin's.

Drayden kept a sharp eye on them all from the nearest wall.

The entire time she worked, her patients grumbled about what had happened in the plaza. A few compared it to the riots in Erenthrall during the Purge. Others were silent, seething with an intense anger. The majority simply wanted Morrell to stop their pain and let them go, more wearied or shocked than anything. Morrell remained silent as they spoke. She hadn't grown up in Erenthrall, hadn't been there for the Purge. Her father had only taken her to the city once, right before the Shattering, and that had been a disaster. They'd been captured by the Dogs and locked into the cells beneath the Amber Tower. Of course, if they hadn't been in the cells when the Shattering hit, they likely would have died in the explosion. They *would* have died afterward, if not for Kara.

She grimaced, her thoughts circling around and around, refusing to settle or focus on what was truly bothering her: what she'd done to the man shaking her using the auroral lights. She'd squeezed his heart. If Cerrin hadn't intervened, what would she have done? What *could* she have done? Twisted him, as the auroral lights had twisted the Dogs from Erenthrall, making them into Wolves? She'd spent days transforming the Wolves who'd wished it back into humans, or as close to what they'd been before as she could manage. Some of the Wolves had chosen to remain transformed, although most of those had gone with Grant and her father to Erenthrall.

Sudden tears leaked from her eyes, but she scrubbed them away angrily. She wanted to speak to her father, to tell him what she'd done, but of course he wasn't here. He was never here, not when she needed him. Which she knew wasn't fair, but she felt that way anyway. She couldn't help it.

"It's all right, poppet."

Morrell lurched back with a gasp, dropping the old woman's wrinkled and callused hand she'd been checking.

The old woman's eyes widened slightly. "Are you all right?"

"I'm . . ." Morrell swallowed, leaning forward and taking up her hand again, flustered. "I'm fine. It's just . . . you called me poppet. My father always calls me that. I hate it."

The old woman chuckled as Morrell turned her hand over. "It doesn't mean anything. I'm old. Everyone is a 'poppet' to me. You were crying. I thought it would make you feel better."

She brushed at her eyes again with the back of her hand. "It's nothing. I was just thinking about him, that's all. He's . . . away. He's always away."

"Ah, I thought you were upset because of what happened at the plaza."

"No," Morrell said, then realized how that sounded. "I mean, yes! I am upset about that, but . . ."

The old woman eyed her. "But that wasn't why you were crying."

"No, that wasn't why I was crying." She turned back to the woman's hand. "It's only an abrasion. I don't think anything's broken. Keep it clean and it should heal like new."

"Nothing heals like new at my age," the woman said, but she sighed and shifted, as if getting ready to stand, before catching Morrell's gaze. "Does he leave on purpose? Does he want to go?"

It took Morrell a moment to realize she meant her father. "Yes. No." She sucked in a deep breath, then exhaled sharply. "I don't know. I don't think so."

"Then he's leaving out of a sense of duty and you can't fault him for that. No more than you can fault us for wanting to hear from Father, or the enforcers for wanting us to remain peaceful. That doesn't mean you—or any of us—have to like it. You do what you can with the abilities you have."

Then she stood, using Morrell's shoulder for support, and walked steadily out of the hospital hall.

Morrell watched her silently. To one side, she noticed the woman who'd caught her arm earlier hugging a man Morrell presumed was her husband; he was tall with a dark, full beard anyway.

She shifted to her next patient, the woman with the spindle stuck through her palm.

"It hardly hurts anymore," the woman said. "I think I've grown numb to the pain."

"Why didn't Freesia see to this?" Morrell said in exasperation. "It's certainly more serious than many of these other wounds we've looked at in the last hour."

"I don't think she noticed me."

Morrell sank into a crouch at the woman's side. "If I yank the spindle out, it will hurt."

"That's what I assumed."

Morrell examined the wound again, turning her hand this way and that. She didn't want to yank it out. The woman had already suffered enough after being forced to wait so long.

You do what you can with the abilities you have.

She glanced up at the woman. "Don't move, no matter what happens."

Before the woman could respond, she called on the aurora, clasping the woman's hand between both of her own, the length of the spindle laced through her fingers on either side. Then, sinking herself into the rhythm of the woman's body and at the same time into the wood of the spindle, she severed the spike near the entry wound. The top portion fell away with a clatter, the bottom sliding from the wound cleanly. The woman tried to jerk back in surprise, but Morrell held on tightly, already working on the gaping hole. Blood started to flow immediately, but warmth enfolded her hands as she knit flesh and tendon and muscle back together again.

The energy drain wasn't as high as she'd expected, but she still slumped backward as she let the woman's hand go. When she dragged her head up, the woman was holding her hand in front of her in awe. The hole was gone, visible only as a slightly pink circle of new flesh.

She turned to Morrell. "Thank you," she whispered, then stood unsteadily—the healing drained the patient as much as it did Morrell—and drifted toward the door, running her fingers over her palm in wonder.

"Good job," Freesia said, coming up to rub Morrell's shoulders from behind. "I knew you'd handle it. If we'd tried, it would have been . . . messy. We're almost done here. Why don't you go rest in your rooms?"

She rose to her feet, Freesia stepping back. "I think I will, thanks. If you're certain you don't need me here?"

"Cerrin and I can handle everyone else."

She caught Cerrin's scowl from across the room but decided to ignore it.

"Then I'll go."

Picking up her things stowed in the small room stocked with jars and pots and bottles of medicinal herbs and unguents and oils, she stepped out onto the streets of the outer city, Drayden shadowing her. She turned toward the temple, but not to return to her room.

Her father might be away, and Janis may have decided to stay in the Hollow, but she still had others she could talk to, such as Cory and Hernande. And she needed to talk to someone.

"It's slipping again!" Marcus shouted from across the open space of the pit.

Kara growled in frustration, sensing the crystal Marcus held wavering. The others connected to the Nexus—Iscivius, Irmona, Okata, and Carter—tensed. She didn't need to see their faces, she could feel the tightening of muscles and the gritting of teeth through her connection to the ley. It had grown since the Shattering, since she'd been forced to submerge herself in the ley on a daily basis. She'd grown attuned to it, and to those who were connected to it.

Drawing in a ragged breath, she called out, "Let it go," her voice calm, revealing nothing of the turmoil she felt in her chest, in her gut. For a moment, a nearly uncontrollable urge to cry washed through her from head to toe. She shuddered with it, then suppressed it as Marcus let the crystal pane swing back into its original stable position.

Before her, white ley light fountained up from the well beneath. She let the motion of the ley—like water, even though it wasn't liquid—soothe her. The others began to gather, returning from their positions around the well. The crystals had been reset and wouldn't waver unless there was a surge from the ley lines.

"It's simply not holding," Marcus said with a shake of his head. "It should—I can see why that configuration would be stable—but it isn't. I don't know why."

"Isn't it obvious?" Iscivius asked.

Kara stiffened. She wasn't certain why Iscivius and Irmona's attitudes had suddenly shifted a week ago, but she didn't trust it. They were still abrasive and cold to both Kara and Marcus and a few of the others, like Okata, but they'd begun offering up suggestions during their brief stints in the pit.

It galled Kara that many of their thoughts and comments were useful.

"What's obvious?"

"The configuration isn't holding because part of it is missing. We need another crystal, one that could be inserted into the Nexus beneath the others, to act as . . . as an anchor for the rest."

"But we don't have another crystal," Okata objected, "and only the Primes knew how to make them."

Iscivius began to sneer but caught himself. "Lecrucius made these six, true," he said, "but he needed our help. Both Marcus and I worked with him extensively."

"You more so than I," Marcus muttered.

Iscivius bowed his head in acknowledgment. "True. As Father's Son, you had other duties."

A hidden barb of resentment laced the words, but from what Marcus had told her, Kara knew it was true. Marcus had often been sent to Tumbor or Erenthrall; Iscivius had stayed behind. And he'd ingratiated himself into Lecrucius' favor while he was here, undermining Marcus' power at every opportunity.

"Could you recreate them based on what you saw?" Kara asked, her voice cracking with exhaustion.

"I can try."

"You have to try," Irmona said sharply, her gaze falling on Kara. "You've been playing with the crystals for weeks now and you've gotten nowhere. We spent the last two days repeating positions that you tried the week before! At some point you must admit defeat, Kara."

Marcus, Okata, and the younger Carter all bristled at her tone, but Kara raised a hand to halt them.

"She's right. We have been repeating configurations." She turned to stare at the sheets of ley and the hovering crystals. "We've maximized the crystals we have. And there are no more known ley lines to tap into to augment their power. That means we either need to expand the crystals in the Nexus . . . or we need to accept that we've reached our threshold and hope it's enough to bring down the distortion over Tumbor." She didn't want to mention the option of having the mentors from the University hold the crystal in an unnatural state yet, not when they hadn't figured out how to keep their folds of the Tapestry fixed without a mentor continually maintaining it.

Iscivius and Irmona shared a hooded glance. The others stirred, although Kara noted no one disagreed with her. They were more nervous about her reaction than an attempt to bring down the distortion.

She bowed her head. "What do you need?"

"Sand," Iscivius said instantly. "The finest sand we can find. And a barrel of cold water. It will have to be done here, in the pit, since we'll use the ley itself as a forge. Lecrucius handled most of the forging himself, with either myself or Marcus as backup, but I won't have enough strength to do what needs to be done alone. I'll need at least two other Wielders, perhaps three."

"You'll have all of us," Kara said, indicating everyone currently in the pit. "Gather what you need."

Iscivius' eyebrows rose. "Right now?"

"Why not?"

He glanced around at the others. "Okata and Carter, get a barrel down here and fill it with water. Irmona and I will find the sand."

All four of them moved toward the stairs, Okata and Carter first, Iscivius and Irmona behind. Irmona said something to Iscivius, her glance toward Marcus and Kara scathing, but whatever Iscivius said in response, it placated her.

"You know we can't trust them," Marcus said, "no matter how helpful they've been recently."

"That's why we're staying. You'll need to make certain he's doing what he says he's doing, based on what you know."

"I don't know much. As Iscivius said, I was there mostly as backup. Lecrucius didn't allow me to see much of what he was doing."

"How much more would he have shown Iscivius?"

Marcus shrugged. "He'd maneuvered himself close to Lecrucius, with the intent to gain more power. He helped him with four of the six crystals. I was only here for two of them. I certainly don't know enough to even try on my own."

Okata had returned, hauling a huge empty half-barrel over one shoulder, his muscles standing out with the strain. Kara often forgot that he was Gorrani, that he trained with his sword on a regular basis. Carter came behind, two pails of water sloshing as he descended the stairs.

"Where does he want the barrel?" Okata asked.

"Over here," Marcus said, shifting away to show Okata where to place it. "This is where Lecrucius put it anyway."

Okata hefted it off from his shoulder with a grunt and set it down with a solid thud, wiping sweat from his forehead. Carter waited until he stepped back before dumping the two buckets into it. The young Wielder stared into the barrel glumly. "It's going to be many more trips to the well."

Okata gripped him by the shoulder and tugged him back toward the stairs.

As they continued to fill the barrel—and wait for Iscivius and Irmona to return with the sand—Kara focused on the Nexus. She sensed Marcus on the ley, watching her as he supervised Okata and Carter, but she didn't reach out to touch the crystals. Instead, she considered how the Nexus would have to change if another crystal were introduced. The pulses of ley arching up from below, where the ley lines merged before being manipulated and sent back out along different lines, were rhythmic, drawing her into their flows. She allowed herself to be absorbed by them, coasting on their eddies. In her mind, she placed the crystal where Iscivius had suggested, beneath the other six, to serve as an anchor, each crystal pushing against the others, seeking a balance determined by the pressures of the ley. She could see how the seventh could work as Iscivius described, could see how the flow would shift into a new pattern. But would it augment the strength of the ley, or diminish it? Would it allow her to push the crystals into the configuration she wanted?

She couldn't tell. They would have to try it and see.

But was that the only possibility for the seventh crystal? What if she placed it there, adjusted the others slightly . . .

Marcus touched her lightly on the arm. "They're back."

Behind, Iscivius stood over a sack with a frown, sand cupped in one hand, seeping through his fingers in a stream. A second sack sat next to his feet. The others hovered around him, Okata and Carter near the barrel of water, Irmona off to one side with her own frown of disapproval. But Iscivius' was focused on the sand; Irmona's was on Iscivius himself.

"Is it fine enough?" Okata asked.

"It will have to do." Iscivius dumped what remained in his hand into the sack.

"What do you need us to do?" Kara let none of her apprehension over giving control to Iscivius leak into her voice.

Iscivius glanced around at the others, then straightened. "Okata and Irmona, stand there and there. You'll be removed from the creation of the crystal. If anything happens, you're to make certain the Nexus remains stable. Carter, stay by the barrel. Help Okata and Irmona if necessary. You two," he said, facing Kara and Marcus. "You'll be my support. Stand behind me. Watch me, both with your eyes and using the ley. Bolster me if I falter."

No one responded, everyone merely shifting into their new positions. Iscivius edged closer to the pit, carrying the two sacks he and Irmona had brought with them, one in each hand. Kara reached for the ley, felt Iscivius and Marcus do the same. Iscivius began folding the ley inside the pit into layers, pulling the edges up and over into the center, circling around the sides, as if he were kneading and punching down bread dough. Kara had never seen anyone in any of the nodes in Erenthrall working the ley in such a way, had never even considered it. She glanced toward Marcus with a tight-lipped question, but he gave a curt nod. This was what Lecrucius had done.

She turned back just in time to see Iscivius throw the two sacks of sand into the pit, into the center of the bowl of ley he continued to knead.

The fiber sacks were instantly incinerated, the sand falling free, organic impurities caught in the grains incinerated as well. Heavier grains fell through the bowl—Iscivius still feverishly folding layer upon layer from the sides to the center—the lighter, finer pieces caught up in the motion and carried along with the ley. Kara gasped as she realized why the sand needed to be so fine; any coarser and it would all simply fall away into the bottom of the pit.

But then her attention caught on what was happening inside the ley bowl, unconsciously taking a step forward for a better view, Marcus' hand holding her back. Iscivius began accelerating the kneading motion, ley leaping from the edges of the bowl outward and up, then driving down toward the center, carrying grains of sand with it. As it accelerated, it grew hotter. Or rather, the grains of sand grew hotter, agitated by the quickening motion. Fascinated, Kara shoved Marcus' warning hand aside and stepped forward, next to Iscivius. The Wielder's attention didn't break, his concentration as focused and intense as the flaring ley. The sheets were rising and falling so swiftly now they were beginning to blur, but Kara could sense the sand beginning to solidify at the center, where the force and pressure of the motion was greatest. Like sand being heated to form glass in a kiln, the grains were beginning to cling to one another, merging into a new structure.

The ley flared, not with instability but with blinding light. Iscivius' hand shot out and latched onto Kara's lower arm, and through the contact she felt him shuddering. Sweat beaded his brow, began to trickle down his face. It already stained his clothes beneath his armpits, across his chest. He uttered an inarticulate growl, his hand tightening into a claw, fingers digging painfully into Kara's muscles.

"He's struggling to hold the flow!" Marcus shouted, suddenly at Iscivius' other side. "We need to help him! If the process falters now, it will fail!"

Without thought, Kara stretched out and connected with Iscivius, pouring her own strength into him, using herself as a conduit for the energy of the ley. A second flow joined hers from Marcus' direction and together the two of them steadied him. His shuddering eased, but his attention never left the pit, never left the blazing white inferno of the ley, now a pyre in the shape of a teardrop that reached toward the obsidian roof overhead. Kara couldn't see the individual folds any longer, but she could sense them as the entire structure spun and shifted in upon itself a hundred times per breath. And still the crystal at its center continued to grow, to smooth out, a specific shape forming, with defined edges, clear planar surfaces.

Iscivius began to tremble again, even with Kara and Marcus bracing him. His jaw clenched, muscles tightening, but the tremble escalated into a shudder that traveled through his entire body. His arms began to flail, Marcus catching his arm on the right to steady him. He began to heave, his breath a ragged, wet rasp. Irmona shrieked something behind them, but Kara ignored it as Iscivius began shifting the intense construct toward the edge of the pit, toward the barrel of water. Okata and Carter, both on that side, drew back and away, arms raised to shield their eyes.

Kara had begun to clutch at Iscivius' arm to hold him upright when his strength finally gave out. With a cry, he collapsed, Kara and Marcus barely catching his dead weight before letting him slip to the floor. The teardrop shape flared once and then the ley, freed from Iscivius' manipulations, cascaded down in a sheet, like water suddenly released from an upended bucket. The crystal Kara couldn't see dropped with it.

The ley struck the barrel, dissolving its wooden frame at the same instant the white-hot crystal hit the cold water within. A hissing thunderclap reverberated throughout the chamber, jolting Kara back in surprise. Ears echoing, she heard the others crying out in shock as well, the sound muted.

Then Irmona shoved her aside, screaming something about intentionally killing Iscivius while he was trying to help them, as the ley from the construct flowed across the pit's stone floor and back into the well. Marcus scrambled up from where he'd fallen, moving toward where a damp section of stone, round metal braces, and a towering column of steam marked where the barrel had been. Irmona rolled Iscivius onto his back and leaned over him, still cursing and screeching. Then she slapped him.

The Wielder didn't rouse.

Irmona turned on her, eyes filled with hatred. "You killed him."

Ignoring Marcus and the others, Kara lurched forward, kneeling at Iscivius' side, her heart a hard stone in her throat. She snatched Iscivius by the chin and turned him toward her, before exhaling sharply.

"He's not dead. He's still breathing. He's simply unconscious."

Before Irmona could respond, she stood and stalked toward Marcus, Okata, and Carter, all three of them kneeling or standing over the same section of stone. As she approached, Marcus leaned forward and gathered something up off the floor, his motions careful and precise. He rose to his feet and spun, holding a thick, flat pane of glass before him. Except it wasn't glass. It was too clear, too smooth, without a ripple or bubble in its surface or a single fleck of impurity. Held at the right angle, Kara would never even know it was there.

"What do we do with it now?" Okata asked, voice gruff with grudging respect.

Marcus' gaze didn't waver, although Kara noticed beads of sweat on his brow. "We take it to the pit." He began to move, cautiously, one foot before the other. As he passed Kara, he said, "Everyone should be ready to hold the other crystals. I don't know how they'll react when we introduce the new one."

Kara gestured to Okata and Carter, the two slipping around to either side of the pit. Her gaze fell on Irmona, Iscivius still unconscious beside her, but the Wielder merely glared at her, one hand resting protectively on Iscivius' chest. Kara stepped up behind Marcus as he neared the edge, the ley and the other six crystals before him.

"Ready?"

"Yes," she said. "What are you going to d—"

Without warning, he tossed the crystal into the ley fountaining up from below.

Kara gasped. Okata cursed.

As soon as the crystal hit the ley it was caught in its flows, carried upward toward the rest of the crystals. The ley interacted with it instantly, refracted, and bent into new pathways. The repercussions of the new flows struck the old crystals within a few breaths, setting most of them spinning. Okata swore again, one hand rising unconsciously as he tried to control those nearest to him. Kara struggled with her own as Marcus muttered, "I've got the new crystal, you take care of the rest."

"I'm trying," Kara answered through gritted teeth. The entire Nexus shuddered as all four of them attempted to bring the seven crystals into a new alignment. But none of them had ever dealt with seven crystals at once. Every subtle movement caused a cascading effect, jolting the other six crystals into new gyrations. As soon as one crystal steadied, another moved, pushing the first out of place. It was a delicate dance, every moment on the cusp of collapse. Kara's muscles pulled taut, even though she wasn't moving, her body bracing for an explosion that she would have no hope of surviving. She sensed Marcus shifting the seventh crystal into place beneath the other six where Iscivius had said it should be placed, and as soon as it was centered, the chaos of the entire system halved.

She exhaled sharply, drew in a still tense but more relaxed breath, and said, "Hold it there, Marcus. Don't let it move. Okata, steady those two, then shift the one on the right upward. Now tilt it toward the pit. Yes, like that."

"I've got it," he said, voice tight with effort.

"Carter, position the one on your right downward. Mirror Okata's positions." She wanted to reach out and help the younger Wielder, but she didn't. He was touchy about receiving help, especially from her, still harboring some resentment of her position, elevated even more here at the Needle than it had been before at the Hollow. "Good."

Then she focused on her own crystals, bringing one up and the other down to the same heights as Okata's and Carter's, so that the panes alternated up and down around a rough circle, with the seventh centered below.

As soon as her last crystal slid into place, tilted just so, the entire diamond-shaped structure stabilized and all four of the Wielders exhaled in relief. Kara's shoulders slumped, head bowed, tension flowing off her in waves. Her body felt clammy with sweat, her knees weak.

But she dragged her head up when she heard someone tearing down the steps of the pit behind her. "Artras."

The elder Wielder, followed by two others, reached the base of the steps and headed straight for Kara, her eyes wide and wild, fixed on the Nexus. "What happened? I felt the ley shuddering. I came directly here."

"Was there a quake?"

"No. No quake. But we could still feel it from within the temple."

The two Wielders behind her nodded in agreement, spreading out to either side to survey the Nexus. One of them gasped. "You created another crystal!"

"I didn't," Kara corrected. "Iscivius did."

Everyone turned to where the Wielder lay unconscious on the stone of the pit.

"I can't wake him," Irmona said accusingly.

Now that the Nexus was stable again, concern bubbled up in Kara's chest. "You can't?" She moved forward, Artras walking next to her, while Marcus was already kneeling at Iscivius' side. He checked the Wielder over, leaning forward to listen at his mouth and chest, then shook him and patted his cheek, tentatively at first, then harder.

"He's still breathing," he said, "but I'm not getting any other reaction from him."

"Okata and Marcus, gather him up. Irmona—" She'd been about to send her off to find a healer, but the stubborn set of her jaw forced her to change her mind. "Lead them back to Iscivius' room. I'll send Carter for a healer. Artras—"

"I'll take care of the Nexus. Go. Get Morrell, if you can find her. She'll know what to do."

Carter had already raced up the curved steps to the Needle above. Okata and Marcus were shouldering Iscivius into a standing position, his body obviously dead weight. Arms draped over their shoulders, they hauled him toward the steps, Irmona leading the way.

Kara followed.

At the top of the stairs, she glanced back at the new configuration, the power of the ley pulsing through her, and smiled for what felt like the first time in over a month.

They were finally *doing* something.

Eight

"—THEN I REACHED INTO HIS CHEST and squeezed his heart," Morrell said. Her hand drifted forward, as if she'd actually seized the man's heart with her hand and not her power, her fingers curled. "I squeezed it, and he went rigid. I could have killed him. With a little more pressure, I could have ruptured his heart. He would have dropped dead at my feet."

Hernande shifted in his seat beside her and she glanced up in time to see the University mentor raising an eyebrow at Cory, who sat across from him, on Morrell's other side.

But then Hernande turned his attention to Morrell. "But you didn't kill him, did you? You stopped yourself."

Morrell let her hand drop. "Cerrin charged in and knocked me free of him. And then Drayden was there to protect me. I didn't have the chance. I don't know what I'd have done otherwise. The man was hurting me."

Hernande gripped her shoulder—the one the man hadn't wrenched—and met her eyes. "You would have done what was necessary. The fact that you hesitated tells me that. If he hadn't let you go, you would have forced him to. I doubt you would have killed him. You're a healer, after all."

"But I could have."

Hernande squeezed her shoulder, then released her, rising. They sat outside, in the sunlight, in the stellae garden that surrounded the base of the black Needle, Drayden standing behind her. "Yes, you could have. That is one of the dangers of power. Any kind of power. It can be used in a variety of ways—for healing, for protection, to fight, and to kill. Look at the ley. Before the Shattering, it was used to power the ley barges and the flyers, transporting people across Erenthrall or farther, to other Baronial cities or the world beyond. But Lecrucius used it here at the Needle to destroy the Gorrani army." He faced her, a breeze tugging at the sleeves of his shirt. "And then there's the Tapestry."

"What do you mean? I've never heard of any of the University students or mentors doing anything like what Lecrucius did."

Hernande looked at Cory, whose eyes had gone wide. "Tell her," the mentor said. "Based on what she's told us, she deserves to know."

"You remember at the Hollow, before the attack by the fake Baron and his raiders?" When Morrell nodded, Cory drew in a steadying breath. "Before they attacked, we discovered we could use the Tapestry to cause small explosions. You probably remember us practicing the knots on the hills and trees around the caverns where we hid."

"I remember everyone complaining that you were driving away all of the game."

"I'm certain we did." His smile faltered and his gaze fell to his hands, his fingers playing with the hem of his shirt where a few strands of stitching had come loose. He twisted the strands between his fingers as he said, "When they finally attacked, I ran to the village. I ran into one of their guards just outside the cottages. I used one of the knots to kill him." Cory glanced up. "I released it inside his chest, a tiny little knot in his heart."

Morrell recoiled, eyes wide, mouth open. Hernande watched her from behind Cory, nodded quietly to her when she shot him a questioning look.

She never would have thought Cory could do such a thing.

And when she turned back, Cory was once again looking down, head bowed. "I tried it again when one of the raiders attacked me in the village, but it didn't work. At least, not as cleanly. The knot exploded in the man's arm, nearly tore it from his body. After that . . ." He sucked in a deep breath and met Morrell's gaze again, his expression open and frank. "After that, I couldn't do it. I couldn't release the knots inside anyone else. I can't. I won't."

"Won't and can't are strong terms," Hernande said. "Don't make promises you cannot guarantee you can keep." But even as he said the words, he eyed Morrell. He'd begun stroking his beard. "You made yourself similar promises, didn't you?"

Morrell thought back over what she'd done since she'd seized the man's heart, then shook her head. "No. I healed those at the hospital that I could, and then I came to find you."

"Perhaps you are more like your father than I thought."

Morrell stiffened, but before she could protest, he continued.

"The point is, Morrell, that we all have power, and with that power comes responsibility, because power—no matter what form it takes—can always be used to do good or unspeakable evil, to heal or to harm. Declaring that you will never use your power to harm may be morally correct, but it isn't practical." He motioned to Cory. "Cory found out that the Tapestry could be used to kill, in horrifying ways, but he discovered he disliked it." Cory shuddered, unable to meet Morrell's eyes. "That dislike is laudable, even exemplary, but it shouldn't be taken to its extreme. Sometimes, situations arise in which those horrifying and terrible techniques are required."

Morrell shifted on the stone. "What do you mean?" She agreed with Hernande—she'd been raised by those that lived in the Hollow, where hard choices were sometimes necessary, such as killing the milk cow for her meat in order to survive the winter or cutting off a gangrenous foot before the rot spread—but wasn't certain she understood exactly what Hernande was trying to say.

"He means sometimes doing something horrible is necessary," Cory said. "At one point, I could have killed Baron Aurek. He and his men had already attacked the Hollow, but maybe if I had killed him then, we wouldn't have lost so many when we attacked the Needle."

Hernande placed a hand on Cory's shoulder. "No. At the time, killing Aurek wasn't the only option. Second-guessing events that have already taken place is unproductive. What I mean is that sometimes there are no other options. When we attacked the Needle, our forces were scattered by the quake. Aurek caught your father and me off guard during the chaos. He had his sword pointed at your father's back. Your father would never have been able to draw his own blade in defense before Aurek shoved the sword through his spine. There were no other options, except to let Aurek kill your father. So I released a knot in Aurek's chest and killed him."

Morrell pressed her lips together. Her father hadn't told her—not the part about having a sword at his back. He'd simply said Hernande had killed Aurek during the attack. Perhaps he'd simply forgotten.

Much had happened during the attack on the Needle and the move from the Hollow that followed.

More likely, he'd simply not wanted Morrell to know how close he'd come to dying.

Behind them, the doors into the main part of the temple suddenly opened and the chattering of a half dozen people filtered through the stellae around them, headed in their direction. A moment later, Jerrain, Sovaan, and four University students emerged from between the stones, the younger students stopping short when they saw Morrell. The elderly but spry Jerrain barely blinked an eye, but the administrator Sovaan frowned in disapproval after a moment's hesitation, heading directly toward Hernande.

"I thought we were to have a practice session outside with our students today. What is she doing here?"

Morrell bristled, but Hernande didn't react at all. He simply stared at her, still stroking his beard in thought. "We do have a session, Sovaan. Followed by an hour's lecture afterward inside." A few of the students groaned. "Morrell had come to me with some concerns. We were simply discussing them here, while enjoying the sunlight and stellae gardens."

Morrell drew breath to say she could leave, but Hernande shook his head minutely, turning to face Sovaan for the first time since he'd arrived. "I'm certain you've heard of Morrell's healing abilities?"

"Of course, I have. I can't say that I believe it, but—"

"It appears that her ability extends beyond that of healing the body," Hernande interrupted. Morrell's heart seized in her chest; she didn't want anyone else to know what she'd done to the man at the hospital. "A few weeks ago, at my prodding, she repaired a crack in a small stone. I've been working with her since, off and on, when her duties allow, with Cory's help. But I think . . . yes, I think we should begin training her with the other students. I believe she could use the guidance of mentors . . . and that she should learn the principles expected of University students—the morals and codes that we ascribe to uphold. I believe she would find them beneficial."

Morrell's heart began beating again. Jerrain raised an eyebrow at Hernande and turned his attention in her direction.

Sovaan spluttered. "But we know nothing of her power! How can we be expected to help her?"

Jerrain cackled. "I think that's precisely the point, Sovaan. We know nothing . . . and neither does anyone else. There's no one to guide her." He made his way toward her, cane thudding into the ground. He eyed her up and down, so close she could smell the fried onions and peppers on his breath from his lunch.

"If there's no one else to guide her," Hernande said as she endured Jerrain's inspection, "and no one else who knows the depths of her power, then shouldn't it fall to us to take her in? To learn what we can—for her sake as well as ours?"

"We can't have an unknown power such as hers roaming free," Jerrain said, shaking the end of his cane at her chest. His words were harsh, but there was a humorous glint in his eye. "Who knows what havoc she can wreak?"

Sovaan glanced from Hernande to Jerrain and back again. "Bah!" he muttered, waving a hand in dismissal. "Do what you want with her. I don't teach first years anyway, haven't for at least a decade. She's your responsibility." He motioned toward two of the other students. "Jasom, Tara, come with me. Let's see how well you studied Knudsen's Theorem and its five corollaries."

"Be careful with the use of the ley," Hernande warned. "The Wielders have been extremely active inside the Needle for the last few hours."

Sovaan continued as if he hadn't heard them, already grilling his two students with rapid-fire questions.

Jerrain dropped his cane to the ground. "Something new?" he asked.

Hernande frowned. "Something different, at least. Requiring a significant amount of power."

"Hmm," the elder mentor said, casting curious eyes on the black spire beside them. "I wonder what Kara is up to." But almost as swiftly, he turned back to Morrell. "I believe you have something to show us? You can fuse stone? I'd like to see this in person. Cory, find a stone with a crack in it. Keller, help him."

The two immediately began searching the surrounding area, at which Jerrain sighed in exasperation and said, "No, no, not here. Kara would have us skinned alive if we shifted a single stone in these gardens. Something about the energy lines. You'll have to find one in the temple."

The remaining student—a girl only slightly older than Morrell named Mirra—sidled closer to her and muttered, "Welcome to the University . . . such as it is."

As soon as the thin black spire of the Needle appeared on the horizon of the plains to the west, Cutter kicked his horse into a run. Behind him, he heard Marc bellow an angered question, could imagine the guard's disgust when he was ignored. He glanced quickly over his shoulder and found the four guardsmen a short distance behind, keeping pace.

After that, he kept his eyes on the Needle, watched it steadily draw nearer.

It took another two hours to reach the ridge of earth that surrounded the city beneath the Needle. Only then did Cutter relax, allowing his horse to slow. He'd feared that they would arrive too late to warn Kara and the others, that they would find the Needle a smoking ruin and the grassland surrounding the outer wall drenched in blood like the last settlement they'd seen. The last of many.

Marc and the others caught up to him, their own mounts lathered with sweat. Marc shot him a disgruntled look.

"I was afraid we'd be too late," Cutter said.

"It's still here," Marc said, only slightly mollified. "Let's go see if they have something to eat besides rabbit."

He nudged his horse ahead of Cutter's. The others followed suit.

When they reached the gates, they were halted by the guardsmen, until Marc protested and one of the other enforcers recognized him. Cutter felt a prickling in his shoulders. As the two spoke, he glanced around, eyeing the guards and the men and women who passed in and out of the gates. Carts were being searched, mounds of hay stabbed with swords, crates and barrels opened. The searches were perfunctory, but no one was simply passed through. Everyone was questioned. He overheard two guards asking a couple about the Kormanley and whether they knew anything about the rioters in the plaza. The couple looked confused. Another man denied knowing anything about some type of snake-dog drawing. The enforcer showed him a sketch made on a sheet of parchment, but the man merely shook his head. The guard didn't appear to believe him, but passed the man through the gate along with the pelts he carried in a large heap over one shoulder. There were even a couple of Wolves watching everything on either side of the gates.

None of this had been going on when Cutter had left.

He would have listened further, but Marc motioned their group forward, through the main gates and into the inner tent city.

The prickling unease that had only been an itch outside became a full-on shudder as soon as Cutter stepped into the tent-filled court. The fact that there were many more tents struck him first, along with the density of the people. They nearly filled the entire plaza, from the outer wall to the inner edge of buildings near the center. He'd grown up in the Hollow, knew that his distaste for crowds larger than ten or twenty could account for some of his apprehension, but not all. What he sensed ran deeper than mere distaste. This was a deep-seated undercurrent of discontent.

Marc and the others didn't seem to notice. Larrin—their far-sighted scout—appeared happy to simply be back. The others were chatting about what they intended to do first, hailing an occasional passerby they knew. Cutter trailed in their wake, took note of the facial expressions and body language of the citizens he passed—the eyes that dropped abruptly when a few saw they were guards, the subtle shift in stance, a turned shoulder or narrowed glare. It only happened with a few, perhaps every tenth person, but it was noticeable.

They entered the ring of buildings surrounding the temple, and the closed-in thoroughfare only heightened the sensation. Cutter shouldered forward through the others as they neared the guard barracks and the temple, but he was pulled up short by Marc's hand on his shoulder.

"Where are you headed in such a hurry?"

Cutter pulled out of Marc's grip. "To report what we found to Commander Ty."

"Come on, Marc," one of the others said. "I'm certain Madame Busard has saved us all some ale."

All of the guards except Larrin laughed, nudging and clapping each other on the shoulder.

Marc stared at Cutter suspiciously. "No," he finally said. "Go on ahead. I think I'll go with Cutter, make certain he gives Ty the real story."

A flare of resentment burned up the back of Cutter's throat, and he stiffened as Marc smiled. The others laughed again, one asking if Marc were certain, before cutting off into the barracks. Larrin hesitated, shuffling awkwardly in the crowded street, then gave Cutter an apologetic shrug and followed them.

Marc's smile lasted until they'd left, then dropped like a stone. "Something's wrong. Something other than the Gorrani attacks."

Cutter nodded, and headed toward the temple, where guards surrounded the doorways to either side of the steps that led up to the second tier. "So you did notice the changes?" he asked, then pointed toward the guards. "The number of men guarding the temple has doubled. At the gates, everyone was being stopped and questioned. In the tent city and the inner city, many were apprehensive, touchy, and disgruntled. Can you feel the tension? It wasn't like this when we left."

Marc glanced around as they approached one of the entrances to the temple, eyeing the guards on duty there, but they were too close for him to comment.

Instead, the smile returned and he bellowed, "Wyat! It's good to see a familiar face after being on patrol for so long with this insufferable woodsman as my alpha."

Wyat flinched, startled, hand falling immediately to the handle of his sheathed sword. His eyes flicked from Marc to Cutter, jaw clenched and rough beard bristling, until he recognized Marc. Then he relaxed, Marc slapping him on the back.

"What's been happening here at the Needle?" Marc asked. "I see you've doubled the guard on the temple."

"You haven't heard?"

"I've been on the plains for nearly a month, Wyat. Just got back fifteen minutes ago. Of course I haven't heard."

Wyat nodded in understanding, the rest of the contingent on duty around him remaining at attention, eyes focused on the street. "It's that damn Kormanley priest, Father Dalton. He's got the whole city riled up with some prophecy about the Needle being the center of a coming storm. Something about snakes and dogs. Ever since he spoke about it, Commander Ty and that Wielder, Kara, have kept him locked inside the temple. The citizens have swallowed the prophecy, hook and all, and now they're screaming to let the priest speak. There was a riot in the plaza three days ago, and there's been nothing but grumbling and muttering since. Everyone's on edge."

"Just like the old days back in Erenthrall," Marc muttered, "with the damn Kormanley causing problems. Thank Bastion we have the enforcers to keep things steady, right?"

Wyat said nothing, a troubled expression crossing his face.

Marc caught Cutter's eye. "We've got a report to make. I'll catch you at the barracks, Wyat."

They entered the temple, heading down one of the strange corridors with the walls angled slightly inward, headed toward the orrery that had become the official meeting room and audience chamber.

As soon as they were a discreet distance from the entrance, Marc said, "You were right. A lot has happened while we were gone."

They found guards at the door to the orrery who refused to let them in at first, one of them entering to inform those inside of their arrival while the three others remained outside. A short time later, they were beckoned through the door, the guard stepping back out and closing it behind them.

Commander Ty, Wielder Kara, the mentor Hernande, and Marcus were seated at the large table to the right of the massive room that held the swirling, illuminated globes of the planets and moons in their orbits. Cutter still didn't understand why it awed and fascinated nearly everyone he'd met. Until he'd arrived at the Needle and first entered this room, he hadn't even known about these other planets, content with the knowledge that the sun and moon existed, that they revolved around each other, and that they provided them with plants and sustained the animals that they ate. He needed nothing more than that. The fact that there were other objects hurtling about overhead terrified him.

So he pointedly ignored the fiery orrery and headed directly toward the table. Marc did the same.

Commander Ty stood as they approached. "I assume you have something of importance to report, since you came directly here and didn't report to your own alpha."

"Has Allan returned?" Cutter failed to keep the surprise out of his voice. He hadn't expected Allan and the rest of the party headed to Erenthrall to have returned so quickly.

Ty frowned. "No, they have not, but Allan Garrett is not your immediate alpha. It's Captain Esker. Or if not him, then my second, Darius." He waved his hand in dismissal. "But never mind. You're here now. What did you find to the south and around Tumbor?"

"Gorrani," Marc broke in. "Hundreds of them, raiding from their homelands in the Flats to the south up into the settlements around Tumbor, slaughtering everyone that they find."

All four of those around the table shared looks. Commander Ty sank back down into his seat. "Go on."

Marc deferred to Cutter, who explained what they'd found after investigating the smoke Larrin had seen on the horizon—the wooden stockade with the walls torn down, the massacre of the villagers who'd lived there, man, woman, and child, and the discovery of the dead Gorrani warrior on the path of retreat.

"We turned back immediately," Cutter said, "heading to the Needle, but we decided to cut to the south of Tumbor, to see if there were any signs of other settlements being raided. We skirted a few stockades like the one we found at first, all untouched, but as we headed farther west that changed. In all, we came across three other settlements—not all stockades, some of them simply villages tucked into the plains—that had been razed to the ground. At each, the Gorrani herded the villagers into a central location and then butchered them."

"They're also killing anyone who's not Gorrani that they run across as they raid," Marc added. "We found a small party of Temerites headed east, all dead, their wagons burned, and at least five other groups of ten to twenty, cut down like cattle at the slaughterhouse."

None of the four spoke for a moment. Kara looked sickened, her face pale. Hernande was chewing on the end of his beard, the corners of his eyes creased in thought.

"What did Lecrucius do?" Marcus muttered.

"He angered the snakes," Ty said, abruptly standing again. He gestured toward the table. "Show us where you found these villages, approximately. And where the isolated bands were killed."

Cutter stepped forward with Marc and together they pointed out where the villages were on the impressive map worked into the top of the table. Ty placed black wooden markers at each of the burned-out stockades and villages, green markers at those that remained.

When he was done, it was clear what the Gorrani were doing.

"They're spreading out from the Flats radially," Kara said, her voice quiet, "killing everything in their path."

"Our scouts to the southeast have reported running across isolated bands whose members had been torn apart and left behind, their body parts displayed almost religiously, like a warning, but none of them had seen who'd done it or found any evidence to indicate it was the Gorrani, although that's who we suspected. But those parties were small, no more than thirty members. What you've reported . . . that takes the Gorrani attacks to another level of hatred." He glanced up at both Cutter and Marc. "You've provided us with some essential information. We'll need to discuss it. For now, you should get something to eat and rest up. You both look like hell."

Cutter wanted to bring up what he'd seen in the city—the discontent and disgruntlement—but the dismissal was clear. Marc glared as he hesitated, then tilted his head toward the door.

With a sigh, he followed Marc out into the temple. As they stepped from the room, a wave of exhaustion rushed through him. He rolled his shoulders to fend it off, rubbed at the muscles of his right arm where he'd taken the arrow in Erenthrall, at the phantom pain there.

"We've delivered our report," Marc said, not looking at him. "Now it's out of our hands. One of the advantages of being a beta."

"I should have warned them about what I sensed in the city from the people."

"I'm certain they already know. Now, let's take the commander's advice and get something to eat. I'm famished." He grabbed Cutter by the shoulder, eyebrows raised in expectation. "Madame Busard should have some nice roasted pork, with potatoes and carrots basting in the juice. A far cry better than rabbit blackened over a fire."

❦

Kara stared down at the ragged arc of black-and-green markers on the table's map, her body numb, her arms tingling faintly. "Dalton's right. The Gorrani are coming."

"Simply because they're attacking from the Flats?" Marcus asked. "That's no reason to give credence to Dalton's vision."

Kara slammed her palm down flat on the table, making the markers jump. "I don't want to believe Dalton can see the future any more than you do, Marcus, but look!" She stood and jabbed her fingers at the map. "They've already hit every settlement we know of within twenty miles of the edge of the Flats. If Cutter's report is true, then they've begun edging out from there. That places the Needle less than fifty miles from their nearest attack!"

The chamber echoed with the vehemence of her words, and for a moment no one spoke. Marcus glowered at her, body stiff.

Hernande leaned forward, both hands on the table as he studied the map. "I'm forced to agree with Kara. It appears that Dalton's prophecy that the snakes will come for us from the south are true. Wouldn't you agree, Commander Ty?"

"It would appear so. Although I do not agree that the Gorrani are less than fifty miles from the Needle." He motioned to the map. "The closest markers to us are black, yes, but they only indicate attacks on isolated families or groups, not settlements. It wouldn't take an entire contingent of Gorrani to take a group like that out. I'd say most of those were slaughtered by scouting parties, perhaps of ten Gorrani or less. Based on the information we have now, I'd wager that the bulk of the Gorrani forces are here, near the distortion around Tumbor."

"That's where the resources are. Those less protected, anyway." Hernande caught the commander's eye as he said grimly, "But they will come here, to the Needle. We are the ones who destroyed their army, killed their warriors by the thousands, incinerated their leaders. They will not forget that."

"Even if it wasn't actually us?" Marcus asked sharply.

"Do you think you could convince them it was Lecrucius?" Kara snapped in irritation.

"They would never even give you the chance to speak," Hernande said. "Before you uttered a word, they would chop off your head."

"If they didn't use you for sport first," Ty mumbled. "Or after." He looked to Kara. "We have to prepare. What should I tell the enforcers? If we mention what we know about the Gorrani, it will only feed the tensions about Dalton and the Kormanley."

"Tell them nothing about the Gorrani," Kara said. "Blame the heightened forces on raiders, nothing more."

But Hernande was already shaking his head. "You're too late. Cutter had more than one enforcer in his group. There were at least three others who didn't accompany them to the orrery. They're already in the barracks, if not out in the city. Half of the Needle probably knows about the Gorrani attacks near Tumbor already."

"He's right," Ty agreed. "That secret is already out."

Marcus swore. "Father Dalton's followers are going to have a field day with this. Whatever control we've regained since the riot will be lost."

"Based on the observations of my men," Ty said, "we haven't regained much control at all."

"What do you mean?"

Ty considered for a moment, then pushed back from the table and poured himself a glass of wine from the tray at the far end of the table. "We haven't had another riot, or even much more violence, but the streets of the outer city and the tent city are tense. The chalked snake-dog circles have started appearing everywhere. The enforcers are washing them off as quickly as possible whenever they find one, but it doesn't take long for someone to draw a rough copy, and we've had no luck finding the culprits. Those we ask on the street merely shake their heads and claim they never saw who drew them, although I don't believe that. Someone must have seen something. Someone knows who they are. They're simply not telling us. Protecting them."

His voice had grown hard, and Kara's skin broke out in gooseflesh. She heard the Dog in him, saw it in the tension in his jaw as he stared down into his wineglass, his muscles clenched. With a sickening roil of her stomach, she recalled how the Dogs had manhandled her after capturing her at the University, dragging her up to the Amber Tower and thrusting her into the cell beneath it.

"So what else can we do?" Marcus asked.

Ty drank—one long swallow—then set the glass aside. "We know the names of some of those who were at the riot. We could bring them in, question them, make them talk. Even if they aren't part of the main group, they will know someone who is."

Kara's mouth went dry. "No."

Both Marcus and Ty turned toward her.

"Why not?" Marcus asked. "We need to stop this, before it escalates any further."

"Because the enforcers aren't the Dogs! And we aren't the same as Baron Arent. Can't you see what's happening? We're slipping back into the same situation that existed in Erenthrall before the Shattering. Except now it's *us* against the Kormanley, not Arent. None of us liked what the Baron was doing to the Kormanley and the citizens with his Dogs back then," she said, and then immediately realized she didn't know if that was true—she didn't know how Commander Ty felt about the Baron—but she forged on. "We can't allow that to happen again here. We can't snatch people off the street, make them vanish inside the temple, as Arent did with his Amber Tower. I refuse to be a part of it. There has to be another way."

Marcus and Ty shared a look, but Hernande said, "You could discredit Dalton."

"How?"

"We've discussed it before. Part of his attack is centered on you and the Wielders, that you haven't fixed the ley, healed Tumbor, repaired the white distortions over Farrade and the other major cities to the north and east and we presume elsewhere. The people would be more inclined to listen to you, support you, if you showed them that the Wielders were doing something."

"We have done something," Kara countered. "We created another crystal for the node. We're working on how to use it more effectively. And we've started working with you and the other mentors and University students."

Hernande shook his head. "Again, the people of the Needle can't see that. Unless you plan on escorting those that want to see it into the node, or perhaps doing a public demonstration with my students."

Kara winced, but Ty immediately said, "No. It's too dangerous. It's too great a risk."

"But—"

"What if someone somehow destroys this Nexus?" Marcus countered. "Do you know how to set up another one? We've been working for two days to try to duplicate what Iscivius did and neither you nor I have even come close. Iscivius is still in a coma, one he may never awaken from. We can't risk it."

"We *can* do it without Iscivius. We simply need to practice." Which was true—the process required an extreme level of concentration and a finely tuned skill with manipulating the ley. Both Kara and Marcus had been folding the ley over and over on itself as they'd seen Iscivius do, but neither one of them could manipulate it fast enough yet to create a crystal.

It didn't keep her comment from sounding like a grumbled excuse from a child.

"Even if you allowed the people to see the new crystal or we contrived some demonstration with the University mentors and the Wielders," Hernande said into the silence, "it won't quell Dalton's supporters completely. None of it will come across as a practical solution to Dalton's challenge: the healing of the ley. As we said before, the people need something visual, something for them to remember and hold on to that relates directly to repairing the system."

"We aren't ready to heal the distortion over Tumbor. We've barely even begun to work with the new crystal. We've only tested a few new alignments."

"But you'll be able to heal it soon?" Ty asked.

Kara hesitated. She couldn't tell if the taste of bile at the back of her throat was from Ty's question or because she was already uneasy. "We should be able to heal it once we've settled on the best orientation for the node and figured out how to use the mentors to set up reservoirs of ley here at the Needle."

"So we only need to hold off Dalton and his followers until then." Ty rapped his knuckles on the table as if that had settled everything and turned to go.

But Hernande said quietly, "There is another option."

Ty halted halfway across the room, the orbs of the orrery bright above him. "What?"

"We could let Dalton speak."

Ty barked out laughter. "It you let him speak, it will only make things worse." Then he left.

Marcus turned to the others. "I'm headed to the Nexus."

Kara waved him out. He trailed after Ty.

"Do you really think we should let Dalton speak again? Look at how much damage he did just once."

"Can he do any more damage by speaking than is already being done by keeping him silent? Besides, if he's right about the Gorrani attacking from the south, then perhaps we should hear what more he has to say."

"But we already knew the Gorrani would cause us trouble after what Lecrucius did. It doesn't take much power to predict they'd attack us eventually. And we've heard nothing about these 'dogs' coming from the north. It could all still be nothing."

"Unless we let him speak, how will we know?"

Kara stared down at the table, at the green-and-black markers, and thought of Dalton, of the Kormanley, of what they'd done here and what they'd done to Erenthrall—to her, her parents, Ischua.

Her heart hardened. "No. Unless we find out who these dogs from the north are, we'll keep him silenced. The Wielders *can* heal the distortion over Tumbor. We simply need a little more time to prepare."

Hernande leaned back in his seat, stroking his beard again, gaze distant.

Kara watched him a moment. "What have you thought of?"

He paused, contemplating her. Then said, "The Gorrani will be coming, regardless of whether Dalton's vision of dogs from the north is true. We need to prepare for them. And I've just thought of a way that Morrell might be able to help us with that."

Marcus closed the door to the orrery behind him, nodded to the guards outside, then headed off down the corridor after Ty. He could hear the man's tread ahead of him, so he picked up his pace.

He caught the commander at an intersecting hallway. Ty must have heard him approaching, for he paused and glanced back.

"Marcus."

"What do you intend to do about the Kormanley?"

Ty's eyebrows rose. "Continue doing what we're doing now."

"But you don't agree with that decision."

Ty shifted to face him directly. "It isn't working, and the tensions on the street are only increasing. As I said at the meeting."

Marcus bowed his head. "I know. But I don't think leaving things as they are will solve anything. We need to stop this before it goes any further."

Ty crossed his arms over his chest. "So what do you propose we do?"

Marcus looked up. "I think you should bring in some of those people from the riot and make them talk."

Ty stared at him silently for a long moment. "Dierdre isn't going to like that much," he finally said.

Marcus flushed, the heat rushing from his head to his toes. "I'll deal with Dierdre."

"And what about Kara? And Hernande?"

The guilt intensified the heat, but Marcus stiffened. "They don't need to know, do they?"

Marc groaned as he sank his teeth into a hank of pork loin. Juices burst from the cracked pepper coating on the outside and dribbled into his beard. He took another large bite before he'd even started chewing the first, then tossed the rest back onto the trencher among the roasted carrots and potatoes. The sauce that served as a thin gravy splashed onto the table, some splattering onto Cutter's arm.

"Gods, that's good," Marc muttered through his mouthful. Cutter could barely hear him over the raucous crowd at Madame Busard's. The tavern was packed tight with guardsmen intermingled with random people from the city, serving women twisting and winding their way through the throng with expert ease. Ten other men and women sat at their table alone, crushed onto the benches on either side, but Cutter was thankful for the seat. He would have preferred eating something back at the barracks, bread and a chunk of meat cut from the nearest haunch, but Marc had insisted.

Ignoring the stain on his shirt from the splashed gravy, Cutter cut a slice from his own portion of pork loin, making certain it had a good portion of the cracked pepper coating and some fat, and ate it.

He had to admit it was good. Much better than the overcooked rabbit, scavenged tubers and roots, and dried flatbread they'd been eating for the past few weeks.

Marc reached for his mug of ale and took a hearty swallow, then watched Cutter slice another piece. He snorted. "You really should learn how to enjoy your meals more."

"I'm enjoying this just fine." He stabbed a carrot and ate it. Surprisingly, it was cooked perfectly.

Marc shook his head. "I don't understand you." When Cutter didn't respond, he slammed down his mug, spilling ale on the table. "Where do you get off coming in here from some gods-forsaken village and taking over as alpha of a scouting pack? What happened to training our pups? What happened to earning your way up to alpha?" Some of the guardsmen at the table with them raised a pint in agreement or pounded on its surface in encouragement. Marc grinned at the support and turned on Cutter. "What exactly did you do back in that village?"

Cutter paused with a forkful of potato halfway to his mouth. "I was a tracker. I hunted for game."

Those around the table guffawed or cursed in derision, waving a hand in dismissal.

"A tracker!" Marc said. "That's it? I knew that already. Did you take down a bear? Wrestle a mountain lion? Kill one of those werebeasts we keep hearing about up north?"

"I killed a boar once. Otherwise, mostly deer, squirrel, small game."

Marc stared at him, then swore and turned back to his meal.

They ate in silence for a moment, the others around them already distracted by their own conversations. Marc radiated a slow, simmering disgust, the same low-grade disgust Cutter had felt from him the entire time they were out on the plains.

Except that wasn't quite true. Once they'd discovered the destroyed settlements and the butchered villagers, Marc had changed. Cutter hadn't felt disgust from him at all then. It had been replaced with a mild and grudging respect.

The disgust had only returned here, at this table.

Halfway through cutting another chunk of meat, he sighed, bowed his head, and closed his eyes.

"I never intended to leave the Hollow," he said. "I never expected to. I thought I'd marry, have children, raise them there in the Hollow, and die there."

"Then why did you leave?" Marc asked.

Cutter drew in a sharp breath. He didn't want to talk about it. He never talked about it. It was one of the reasons he'd become a tracker— the isolation. But he'd started this. If he'd wanted to let it go, he could have simply let Marc remain angry.

"When I was fifteen, I was bonded to a young girl. Her name was Laurel. She had the softest curly brown hair I'd ever touched, these pale gray eyes, like thunderclouds, two moles on her chin below her right ear, one slightly larger than the other." He could see her clearly even now. "She was fourteen. We were to be wed when I turned seventeen." He opened his eyes, began cutting into the pork loin again.

"What happened?"

"A year after we were bonded, she got sick. Half the village did. Some kind of flu. Our healer, Logan, did what he could, but Laurel and ten others died. That's when I became a tracker. I started hunting, because it kept me away from everyone else in the village. All I wanted was to be alone. I expected to die alone, in the Hollow.

"And then the ley Shattered. We heard it in the Hollow, felt it. Shortly after that, Allan came with the refugees from Erenthrall, with the Wielders. They talked about the city, and I suddenly realized there was more to the world than the Hollow. So when Allan asked for volunteers to go into the city with him to scavenge for food, I threw in my bow and tracking skills. And after everything that happened in Erenthrall . . ." He shrugged. "There was nothing left in the Hollow for me anymore. So I came here."

He stuck a chunk of pork in his mouth and chewed, not tasting it, thinking of Laurel, of the dark blotches on her skin as she choked to death on her own phlegm. Only when he swallowed, painfully, did he realize that those around him had fallen silent.

He looked up, caught those sitting across from him staring.

One of them chuckled and said, "Well, ain't that a sad story." The rest laughed.

Cutter's grip tightened on the handle of his knife, but Marc said, "Shut up."

Their laughter cut off at the tone of his voice.

But Cutter had had enough. He dropped his fork onto the trencher with a clatter, wiped his knife clean, and sheathed it.

"Where are you going?" Marc asked. It was a casual question, without any of the disgust Cutter had heard earlier.

"Back to the barracks."

"Then I'll see you there."

Cutter stood and stepped away, heading straight for the door. Someone slid into his seat almost immediately, said something to Marc, but he barely noticed. He needed to get out of the tavern, away from its press of people.

He needed to be alone.

"I thought he'd never leave," the man said as he slid into the seat next to Marc.

Marc gave the man a cursory glance—mustache, unkempt hair, a scrawny body frame—then bit another chunk of pork from his portion, intending to ignore the fellow.

But he leaned into Marc's field of view and said, "My name's Armone."

Marc set his pork down and gave the man a closer look. "You're an enforcer," he said as he chewed. "I've seen you around the barracks. You aren't in uniform."

The man grinned. "Neither are you."

"I just returned from a patrol around Tumbor."

"I overheard. Who was the man you were arguing with?"

A prickling sensation ran down Marc's shoulders. He chewed slowly for a moment, giving himself a little time, trying to figure out what it was that Armone wanted. When he'd finished, he grabbed his ale. "That," he said, "was the bastard who was put in charge of our patrol. From that damn Hollow."

Armone's mouth turned down in disgust. "He was given command over you, an enforcer?" He shook his head, taking the mug of ale from the man sitting across from them as his back was turned. "They come into the Needle—blast a hole through our walls!—and then somehow take over with the help of our own commander. Now they're taking away our commands? They haven't even been trained!"

Obviously, Armone hadn't heard Marc's entire conversation with Cutter, only part of it. Enough to think that Marc despised the tracker. But he still didn't understand what Armone wanted, and he clearly wanted something. He was fishing, trying to see if Marc would be tempted by the bait.

Marc hadn't decided what he thought of Cutter, but Armone intrigued him.

He took a long swig of his ale, some of it dribbling down into his beard. "They're taking over the whole damn Needle, not to mention the enforcers."

"Exactly! I think it's a disgrace. I can't believe Commander Ty is allowing it!"

"What else can he do? Their damn mages and those Wielders they have are controlling the ley. Did you see what they did to the Gorrani? They could destroy us all. They've got us all by the balls."

"They do, they do. But Commander Ty's accepted it. He didn't fight them at all, after the Gorrani were dealt with. He practically welcomed that bitch Kara and those Hollowers through an open gate."

"How could he fight them? All they'd have to do is call up a lick of ley, and he'd be nothing but belt buckles and buttons. You can't fight that."

Armone's eyes narrowed and he leaned in close. "Oh, but you can."

Marc screwed his face up in disbelief, then grabbed the stolen mug of ale from Armone and dumped it into his own. "You're drunk. I'm cutting you off."

Armone snorted, unperturbed, suddenly deadly serious. "I'm not drunk."

Marc caught his eyes, mug half raised to his lips. "What do you mean?"

Armone glanced around the tavern, searching the crowd. To Marc, it felt like they were in their own little pocket of space, the attention of the men across the table elsewhere, even the off-duty enforcer brushing against him on his left engaged with one of the servers. Satisfied, Armone shifted and rested an elbow on the table, facing Marc, his body blocking out those seated behind him.

"Are you tired of the Wielders being in control? Of Commander Ty taking their orders like he was a whipped cur?"

Marc set his mug down without taking a drink. "Yes."

"And what about Father Dalton? Did you think the enforcers were stronger when he was in control?"

"We never had any riots when he was in control."

Armone considered for a long moment, then gave a curt nod, as if he'd made a decision. Reaching out with one hand, he gripped Marc's shoulder. "There's a group of people I'd like you to meet, mostly enforcers, but some others throughout the city. We think it's time for Father Dalton and those loyal to the White Cloaks to regain control of the ley and the Needle."

Nine

"I THINK I'M GOING TO TAKE Morrell aside for that little experiment we discussed a few days ago, Jerrain."

Morrell glanced up from where she was watching Mirra practice folding the Tapestry in such a way that the sand they'd spilled onto the stone plaza on the second tier of the temple shifted into different prescribed patterns. Jerrain stood over them both, Keller cross-legged to one side, Hernande approaching from the direction of the temple entrance. Drayden stood in the shadows provided by one of the niches, nearly invisible. He'd attached himself even more firmly to her after the man had attacked her at the hospital. He even slept outside the door of her rooms now.

Over the course of the last few weeks working with Hernande, Cory, and the other mentors from the University, she'd learned that she was neither a mentor nor a Wielder. She could barely sense the Tapestry being used—usually when she was within a few feet of the manipulations, and only then if the person manipulating it was strong. When she did, it felt like a faint breeze. She was more attuned to the ley, could feel it coursing through the ground beneath her, could trace its paths, at least the larger paths, but she couldn't manipulate it like the Wielders. Hernande had wanted her tested, as students had been tested in the schools before the Shattering, but only the Primes had known how to do that, and the last Prime here at the Needle had been killed by the ley during the Gorrani attack. They couldn't even test her abilities as a student at the University, since the orbs used were back in Erenthrall. No one had thought about saving them when they'd fled.

Jerrain placed a hand on Morrell's shoulder, holding her in place as

Hernande drew closer. "Are you certain that's wise? We've barely begun training her."

"We've already determined she can't manipulate the ley or the Tapestry, at least not the same way we do. She's learned the basics, but it isn't going to help her understand her own talents unless we start testing her on those as well. This is as good a test as any."

Jerrain scowled, but released her and shooed her in Hernande's direction. "I still don't agree that she's ready, but as you said earlier, these are trying times. We can't hold too dearly to the old ways when we're living in a new world."

Morrell climbed to her feet as Keller muttered, "Lucky little snit," beneath his breath.

Morrell knew he was merely teasing her, but Jerrain tutted and motioned Keller into Morrell's position. "For that, you'll take over from Mirra now, Keller. And we won't be continuing the basic sand forms. We'll switch to the more complex field shapes that we'll be using to help the Wielders. Let's see how long you can hold them this time. Mirra, get ready to pour the sand into his constructions to see if he can hold them without losing any."

Keller groaned as he clambered into Morrell's spot while Mirra scraped the sand into a heap to one side with a self-satisfied smirk.

Hernande steered Morrell toward the steep stairs that formed most of this side of the temple and led down toward the surrounding city, Drayden slipping into position a few paces behind them. "Any progress?" the mentor asked as, behind, Jerrain said sharply, "Hold it! Hold it!" and Keller gasped in dismay, Mirra's deep-throated chuckle drifting back to them in counterpoint. Then they descended below the tier's level and the sounds of the others dropped away, replaced by the myriad noises of the city beyond—the bleat of sheep, squeal of pigs, and a hundred conversations and shouts from the wide square before the temple entrance. Guardsmen were sparring to one side, before their barracks, others headed toward the kitchens across the way. A few of them, hunched beside the rain barrel they used as a wash basin, glared at her and Hernande as they reached the base of the stairs. Their eyes followed them as they passed into the shadow of the flat stone promontory that jutted out of the center of the stairs toward the square, their interest only waning when Drayden placed himself in their line of sight.

"I still can't really see or feel it when the others work with the Tapestry," Morrell said to distract herself from their stares. "It's like someone has waved a fan in front of my face and then I see the sands move, or I feel a pressure against my skin, as if I'm pressing up against a wall, only there's nothing there."

"Have the sensations grown stronger the more you focus on them?"

"Not really."

"And what about the ley?"

"I think I can sense it better now, especially after Kara took the time to work with me a few days ago. She helped me distinguish between some of the ley lines that are concentrated here at the Needle. I knew of the major ones, of course, but now I can pick out some of the medium ones as well."

"Good. Perhaps we'll be able to figure out how your own talents coincide with those of the Wielders and the mentors eventually."

Morrell didn't comment. She didn't know how much she was learning about herself, but she knew she enjoyed the company of the other students, even if it and her work at the hospital exhausted her.

They passed beyond the large square and mingled with the rest of the residents of the Needle. The crowds were thick, bodies pressed close together as they worked their way down the streets and between the buildings, heading toward the outer tent city. At one point Morrell lost sight of Hernande, her heart beginning to thud hard in her chest as she realized she didn't know where they were headed, but then his distinctive Demesne pointed beard and the yellowish-gold shirt trimmed with red caught her eye as he glanced back toward her.

They'd nearly reached the city when someone lurched into Morrell and bumped her into another man standing close to the corner of a building at the mouth of an alley, back hunched and turned toward the street. The man growled in frustration and spun on her, his dun-colored clothes speckled with white dust that puffed up as he stood up straight.

"You've ruined it, you little bitch," he snarled, hand snapping around to slap her.

Morrell recoiled, but suddenly Hernande was at her back, the mentor's own hand lashing out and snatching the other by the wrist, halting the slap mid-swing. On her other side, Drayden bristled, a low growl rumbling in his chest.

The other man tried to jerk free, but Hernande's grip didn't loosen. In fact, it tightened. Morrell heard bones grinding together in the other's wrist.

"Not a wise decision," Hernande said, his voice with a dark edge that Morrell had never heard there before. Drayden's growl deepened.

The man—he had brown hair and a thin face that didn't match the bedraggled appearance of his clothing—wrenched his hand again, breaking free. Morrell got the impression Hernande had let him go. He rubbed at his wrist and, without thought, Morrell reached out and touched him. He lurched back, coming up hard against the alley wall.

"It's only bruised," Morrell said. "Try not to use it much over the next few days, and it'll be fine."

The man stared at her, bewildered.

Then someone behind them shouted, "What's going on here?" The speaker was headed in their direction.

Hernande nodded toward something scrawled on the wall beside the man—a strange symbol with a snake curled around a circle, what looked like a half-drawn dog beneath. "You'd better leave before the enforcer gets here."

The man's gaze snapped toward the street. Then he spat to one side and scrambled into the depths of the alley. Drayden moved to follow, but Hernande held him back.

"What's the meaning of th—" the enforcer began as he pushed through the last of the crowd behind them, but he drew up short at the symbol chalked onto the wall. "Who drew this?" he shouted, pointing with one hand as he spun toward the crowd. "Did anyone see who drew this symbol? I know at least one of you did! Come forward! Stop defending that damn Kormanley priest! He's filled your head with nonsense since before the Shattering!"

"We saw the man," Hernande said. "In fact, I think we interrupted him."

The enforcer—an elderly man, older than Morrell's father, but broader, with graying hair—turned on them and eyed them suspiciously. He glanced down the alley where the other man had run, but Morrell couldn't even hear the man's footsteps any longer.

"I could find him," Drayden offered, nostrils flaring as he sniffed the air. He looked to Morrell, who shook her head slightly. He huffed in annoyance, but backed down.

"You saw the man?" the enforcer asked. He crossed his arms over his wide chest. "You'd be the first. What did he look like?"

"Brown hair, thin face, and green eyes."

"That describes a quarter of the people here in the Needle. Anything else? Scar? Tattoo? Missing finger?"

Hernande frowned uncertainly. "I'd swear I've seen him before."

The enforcer tensed. "Where?"

"I . . . don't remember."

"Ah, I see. Well, if you do remember, report it to the enforcers, would you?"

He turned to go, but Hernande cleared his throat and he turned back, eyebrow raised.

"What is your name?" Hernande asked. "In case I remember."

The man's eyes narrowed. "Trenton." Then he left, melding into the crowd on the street.

Hernande's hand fell onto Morrell's shoulder protectively. Drayden was still eyeing the alley.

"He didn't want to tell us his name," Morrell said.

"No, he didn't." Hernande steered Morrell back out onto the main street, hustling her along toward the tent city, Drayden on their heels.

"The man chalking the icon wasn't quite right either."

"How so?"

"His clothing didn't match his face."

"You noticed that, did you? You certainly are your father's daughter. We need to speak to Commander Ty about that incident, but later."

They emerged into the edge of the tent city, the density of the people increasing, along with the smells. Roasting meat, sizzling cooking oils, fried onions and peppers, and burnt bread assaulted them within the first few steps, along with a pungent mustard spice and offal as someone passed them with a slop bucket. The rank smell of sweat permeated the tents, along with grease and the faint putridness of sickness. Morrell had noticed the increase in the patients with disease recently, along with infections and even a few cases of gangrene. Now she understood why. The tent city was overcrowded.

"There are so many more people," she muttered as they dodged a small family of goats being herded by two young men, both with long staves and an angry, threatening look in their eyes.

"Yes. Since Kara and Ty took over, they've been allowing anyone who comes to the city entrance to stay. The people need a refuge, and those that can find the Needle are mostly content that there's a place to shelter here, even if it is crowded. Even the city around the temple has become inundated. The Needle won't be able to hold many others. It doesn't help that we lost part of the city to the chasm."

Hernande waved to the left, where the tents had begun to thin out as they neared the huge crevasse that cut through the city to the west. Morrell perked up and angled in that direction. She'd never seen the chasm, had never ventured this far to the west. Drayden followed her instantly. Hernande hesitated, glancing toward the city wall not far distant, then rejoined them.

The tents dropped away over a hundred feet from the wall, the stragglers at the edge eyeing Morrell as she stepped out into the space before the drop-off. Except that there wasn't the edge she expected, or had been led to believe existed from Cerrin's reports at the hospital anyway. Instead, men in the white shirts of the temple workers—like those who distributed food and cooked and cleaned for those housed in the temple itself—were busy building a short wall, blocking the view of the chasm below. Engineers were organizing blocks of stone obviously scavenged from the buildings that had collapsed during the quakes into different piles. Masons were fitting them onto the wall, building it higher and higher, slapping wet mortar in between and filling in crevices. A hundred feet distant, stairs were being built. The wall was rough—not as finely crafted as the outer wall—but it wasn't shoddy. Even Morrell could tell it was solid.

Glancing down its length, she could see that it ran all the way from the outer wall and into the buildings surrounding the temple. Some of the buildings themselves had been incorporated into its construction. She could see the tops of other buildings across the gap, over the wall's lip. It had only been built up to a height of six or seven feet, even lower in some locations.

"Can we go up on top?" Morrell asked, already trotting toward the stairs.

"I don't think—" Hernande began, then sighed in resignation.

When they neared the stairs, the closest engineer headed toward them, but Hernande waved him off and Morrell grinned, racing up the steps to the top.

"Careful!" Hernande shouted from behind.

Morrell gasped, halting at the wall's edge, her stomach rolling with an odd sensation that made her feel both heavy and light-headed at the same time. There was no edge on the far side of the wall—or not much. It simply dropped down into the chasm, a rent that spanned a hundred feet here. The jagged wall cut away almost vertically, striated stone visible in the sunlight, water seeping from the layers, glistening along the multicolored cliff. In one spot, it gushed from the stone, possibly an outlet for an underground stream. Or perhaps it had once been part of the city's sewer system.

The city above on the opposite side hadn't fared well from the quake. Many of the buildings had collapsed, although Morrell could see a few intact farther from the edge. Most of the section of the city that had been cut away was an open area where the tent city had once been, except now it was empty, abandoned as almost everyone who'd lived there had moved to the main temple's side. Yet she could see a few signs of smoke, so some people remained there.

Swallowing back the lump lodged in her throat, Morrell sank down to her knees and placed her hands on the edge of the stone wall. She leaned out and peered down into the gaping chasm below. She heard Drayden scrambling up the steps behind her, then Hernande's more sedate footsteps crunching in the dust and grit. Drayden settled in beside her, straining to sniff the air.

"How deep is it?" she asked.

"Deep enough. Come back from the edge. Your father would kill me if you fell in. Not to mention Kara."

Morrell pulled back slightly, a faint sheen of sweat on her skin, her heart thudding hard in her chest. She shuddered with a perverse thrill. "People are still living over there."

"Yes. They're taking a risk, though. It isn't protected anymore. The wall's compromised, and all of the enforcers have been pulled back here, to the temple. Even this side is compromised. That's why they're building this wall, to provide at least some protection from an approach along the chasm. It's also why I brought you out here."

Morrell looked over her shoulder at him. "What do you mean?"

"When your father and I came here to rescue Kara and the others, we created our own breach." He pointed toward the outer wall, where a jagged vertical shaft of obviously newer stone stood out in contrast to the old wall. It was wider at the top than the bottom and looked significantly rougher and less stable. "The engineers sealed up the breach as best they could, given the fear that the Gorrani would return, but it's a weakness in the wall, a weakness we can't afford."

He faced Morrell. "I thought you might be able to repair it."

Morrell gaped at him. Her stomach rolled again, only this time she felt nauseous.

She climbed unsteadily to her feet. "You want me to . . . fix it?"

"You've repaired cracked stones before."

"But those were stones that fit into my hand! I could hold them! This . . . this . . ." She flapped a hand toward the battered wall, a hot flush coursing through her body from head to toe.

"This is no different than repairing those stones." It was his professorial voice and brooked no argument. "I'm not expecting you to fix the entire wall all at once, but I think you can do it. I *know* you can do it. Jerrain and Sovaan . . . have their doubts. I need you to prove them wrong. Besides, you'd be helping Kara and Ty and every other person residing here at the Needle." He paused, as if considering whether he should say anything more, then added in a softer voice, "The Gorrani will come eventually, Morrell. We can't afford to have them breach the wall because of something your father and I did."

Morrell crossed her arms over her chest, jaw set. She refused to look at Hernande, simply stood fuming, her gaze on the wall, on the section that had been repaired too fast and haphazardly. The longer she looked at it, the more pronounced the discoloration between it and the old wall grew. It had been filled in all the way to the top again, enforcers walking along the parapet without concern, while beneath it a group of men haggled, surrounded by a herd of swine. But Morrell could see how flawed it was. Anyone approaching from outside the walls would be able to see it as well.

She sighed heavily. "I suppose I could try."

Hernande gripped her shoulder. "You'll do fine."

They walked along the new, low wall over the chasm until they neared its end, where it butted up against the outer wall. They had to climb down before they reached it, however, since there was a group of twenty workers busy constructing what appeared to be a new stairwell that would connect the new wall to the upper parapet. Hernande skirted the herd of swine, wrinkling his nose at the smell. Morrell found it somewhat pleasant; it reminded her of the Hollow. For a breath, she felt a pang of homesickness.

They followed the wall, in its shadow here, the air cooler, until they reached the section that had been repaired. Morrell trailed her fingers along the stone as they neared, the change from time-worn smoothness to rough new stone jolting. Almost like seeing an egregious wound for the first time, before her emotions shut down and her clinical detachment took over as she prepared to heal.

That familiarity of emotion steadied her. She took another few steps—the breach here at the base had been about ten feet across—and then halted, tilting her head back so she could stare up the height. The blue sky overhead glowed in contrast to the shadowed gray of the stone. Vertigo tilted the world, even though she still had one hand firmly against the wall for support. She dropped her gaze and searched for Hernande.

He stood behind her, ten paces back, with Drayden, removed but watching her. He gave her a silent nod of encouragement.

She turned back to the wall and placed both hands against the gritty rock. It was a cold, light gray granite, not like the softer stone that had been used to build the temple. That stone had been quarried elsewhere—no one knew where—and carted to this location ages past. This stone came from nearby.

She lowered her head and closed her eyes, leaning slightly forward. Her hands pressed into the granite as she called forth the auroral lights.

She sank into the stone before her, felt its age, its weight. It was easier than she'd expected; her practice with Cory and then the rest of the students had helped. For a moment, the sensations of grinding, scraping rock nearly overwhelmed her, but then she pulled back, distanced herself, and the world settled so that she could pick out individual stones, could feel the gaps in the center where the workers had simply tossed in stone as filler, and the more solidly constructed outer edges to hold those stones in place.

She drew in a breath—noticed the scents around her were stronger: the swine, the sweat of the workers, smoke, and the greasiness of rendered fat—and then extended herself outward, reaching toward the parapet above, where the extent of the damage was wider, then to either side. Even the old wall was flawed. A crack in the wall's core running from the ground to the parapet a hundred feet to their right could be widened and cause a collapse with a steady bombardment from outside. Minor damage through the decades had caused less significant cracks nearly everywhere. Water from rains had hollowed out the core in one location, and here and there animals had found niches and crevices to roost or den in.

But the most significant threat still came from the portion of the wall immediately before Morrell. She pulled back to the stone her hands touched, reached from there deeper into the wall directly before her, until she'd found the outside wall. Drawing on the tingling aurora in her hands, she willed the stones to fuse together, not simply to themselves, but to the old stone of the wall to either side.

She thought she'd have to fight the stone, that there would be resistance. But there wasn't. Almost as soon as she called on the auroral light, it spilled out from her hands, faster and smoother than ever before. She gasped as it flowed from her, draining from deep in her chest, coursing through her arms, her hands burning. Distantly, she heard others cry out in confusion.

In a matter of seconds, she exhausted herself. The flow cut off and she sagged forward into the wall, her forehead pressed against the stone. She couldn't breathe, and her heart skittered erratically in her chest. Heat suffused her, and she turned her head so that her cheek touched the cold wall.

The shock of the cold caused her to inhale harshly and her heart stuttered back into its normal rhythm. At the same time, her legs collapsed beneath her weight. She began to slide down the wall, the skin on her face scraping off, until someone snatched her from behind and pulled her away.

Her eyes fluttered open, the sunlight too bright, blinding. "Hernande," she ground out, her voice cracked and ragged.

"I've got you," the mentor said, clutching at her as he dragged her back a few paces from the wall and settled her down on the ground. Drayden hovered a few feet away.

"Did it work?" she asked. "It felt like it worked."

"Yes, it worked." Hernande's voice was threaded with concern and a thick pride. "You did better than I expected. Look for yourself."

He propped Morrell up from behind. She blinked, trying to clear away the white flashes from the sun, her eyes tearing up.

When her sight cleared, she could see that the entire base of the wall, stretching to a height of at least thirty feet, had been smoothed over, the stone melded so that it appeared to be one solid structure. There were no crevices, no cracks. It looked like some of the buildings she'd seen in Erenthrall before the Shattering, buildings her father had told her were molded from the earth by the Wielders using the ley, before they'd learned how to sow towers instead.

Except she hadn't used the ley.

"I did it," she said, her voice filled with disbelief. A sudden pressure built up inside her chest—an unexpected pride in herself—and she sucked in a deep breath as that pressure threatened to close off her throat. "I really did it!"

Then she broke out in laughter and, inexplicably, tears.

Hernande helped Morrell to the hospital, half carrying her, Drayden keeping the crowds a safe distance away from them. Hernande would have been more concerned for her, except she kept smiling to herself and muttering, "I did it," in a soft, awed voice.

Freesia exclaimed when they staggered into the small receiving room, rushing forward to take Morrell's weight on the other side to help her into the main ward. "What happened? How did she get like this? It's as if she has no muscle strength at all."

Hernande told her what Morrell had done, the hospital warden's eyes widening in surprise even as her mouth tightened in disapproval, her ire squarely centered on Hernande. They settled her on one of the cots. As they spoke, Cerrin cried out and leaped to the bed where Morrell lay. After a quick perusal, he rounded on Hernande in anger.

"Is she all right? What did you do to her?" His hands were balled up into fists.

Hernande's eyebrows rose.

"He didn't do anything to me," Morrell muttered. She struggled up onto her elbows to glare at the young man. "And what do you care? You don't even want me here anyway."

Cerrin swung back to her, mouth opening and closing, a panicked look about his eyes. Then his mouth snapped shut and he stalked away. But Hernande saw the hurt look in his eyes before his back was turned.

Morrell looked stricken, as if she regretted what she'd said, almost calling out to bring him back. But she stopped herself, slumping back onto the cot in confusion.

He shared a glance with Freesia, who rolled her eyes.

Freesia knelt over her and did a quick but thorough check for bruises, breaks, and a fever. "She doesn't appear to be ill, merely exhausted."

"And thirsty," Morrell said.

Freesia stood, touched Hernande's arm. "I'll go fetch some water. Stay with her until I'm back. Don't let her fall asleep."

He stared at Morrell a moment before crouching down at her side; Drayden had settled in at the foot of her cot. Her eyes were closed. "You aren't sleeping, are you?"

"No. Not yet. I heard what Freesia said. Besides, I can't stop thinking about what I did. My hands still feel like they're tingling with the aurora, even though I know they aren't." Her eyes popped open, and she wriggled her fingers before her face, grinning.

"You've done spectacular things before, Morrell. You healed Cory's leg after it was crushed by the boulder. You stitched Harper's bones back together. Then there are all the people you've helped here at the hospital."

Morrell let her arms drop to her sides. "I know, but that's different."

"How is it different?"

Morrell waved her hands. "Those are small things. I'm only helping one person at a time. This was big, and helped everyone, like when Kara kept the distortion in Erenthrall from swallowing the entire city, or like when my father rescued Kara and those other people trapped inside the shards after it quickened."

Hernande shifted forward, into her line of sight. "I seriously doubt that Cory or Harper or any of the others whom you've healed feel what you did was a 'small' thing."

"You brought me back from losing myself to the Wolf," Drayden said from the end of her cot, startling them both. "That was not a small thing. Not for any of the Wolves."

Morrell's brow creased in thought, but before she could come up with a response, Freesia returned with a pitcher of water and a glass. Hernande drew back as she poured and set the pitcher on the stone floor beneath Morrell's bed. Cerrin attended patients, but kept himself within earshot, glancing over every few moments, mouth pinched tight with concern.

"It's as cold as I could get it," Freesia said. "From the spring fountain on Collier Street."

"We've started naming the streets?" Hernande asked as Morrell drank.

"Of course, we have. People like to make wherever they are feel like home, yes? It doesn't look like we'll be returning to Erenthrall any time soon. Not until after we clear out the savages that have taken it over."

Hernande hadn't even considered returning to Erenthrall, not with a perfectly viable community here at the Needle. But he supposed many of the refugees who'd fled here had lived in Erenthrall or Tumbor. They'd want to return to what was familiar, if they could. But he'd also heard the reports from Allan, Bryce, and the others who'd ventured there after the Shattering. He doubted rooting out the enclaves of Temerites and other groups who'd established themselves there would be easy.

Freesia dug some jerked beef from a pocket and handed it over to Morrell, who wrinkled her nose. "Eat it. The salt will do you good."

Hernande stood. "I'd better return to the temple and report what happened to Kara and the other mentors."

"Go," Freesia said. "There's nothing more you can do here for her. I'll let her rest up and keep an eye on her." She sighed without looking as a bowl clattered to the floor a few cots distant. "And I'm certain Cerrin will keep watch as well."

Smiling slightly, Hernande returned to the street, blinking up at the sun that had somehow shifted past midday. A gust of wind tugged at his shirt, smelling of rain, but he headed away from the temple toward the wall.

When he reached the section that Morrell had healed, he found it had already attracted attention. Over thirty people were gathered, staring and pointing, gossiping to each other in low, awed voices. And the crowd was growing. He pushed his way to the front, where the swineherd gestured as he told everyone what had happened—how the young girl had approached the wall, placed her hands on it—

". . . and then shimmering lights appeared, all blues and greens and purples, and they rippled up the wall like water, only running backward, and beneath the lights I could see the stones. They were all melted and runny, like candle wax when it's hot, and then the girl gasped and the lights faded and she collapsed forward."

Hernande ignored the grizzled man, stepping right up into the space between the crowd and the wall, inspecting it up close. It was still granite—it hadn't changed composition—but it was like no granite he'd ever seen before. It wasn't coarse or chipped. He ran his hand over the surface, the texture like smoothed river stone.

Or like the slick black surface of the Needle.

"What happened to her?" a woman asked.

The swineherd latched on to Hernande's arm. "He took her! He caught her and carried her off!"

Those in front surged forward, spouting questions. The swineherd's fingers dug into Hernande's upper arm and with a wince of annoyance, he reached up and pinched the man's wrist in a specific location. The grizzled man yelped and released him, jerking back, shaking numb fingers, but it was too late. The crowd had already shoved Hernande up against the wall.

"Quiet!" he roared, with the volume and sharp command he reserved for his students. They instantly fell silent, those nearest retreating a few paces. He brushed himself off and glared around at them all. "She's fine. I took her to the healers. She was simply exhausted."

"But what about—"

"Will she be back?"

"Can she do something about the chasm?"

"Who is she?"

The questions were overwhelming, rising in volume as everyone tried to yell over one another. Hernande didn't even try to answer the questions, searching for a way out of the crush of bodies as they began to press forward again. A sharp whistle pierced the noise, and he heard Commander Ty bellow, "What in hells is going on here? Clear the way! Let the guard through."

He breathed a sigh of relief as Ty stepped forward. Ty had a group of five other enforcers with him, who began to methodically push everyone back a respectable distance, including the swineherd, who still massaged his hand.

Ty glanced at the eerily smooth wall with a frown, then focused on Hernande. "Did you do this?"

"No, I did not. It was Morrell."

Ty's eyebrows shot upward. "Allan's daughter? I thought she healed people."

"This appears to be an extension of her power. I brought her down here to test it out. I didn't expect it to be so . . . productive."

"Well, it caught the attention of the people." He reached forward and ran a flat palm over the stone, as Hernande had done. "My enforcers report that it's like this on the other side of the wall as well."

"The same size area has been repaired there?"

Ty shrugged. "I haven't seen it myself, and the report wasn't that specific."

"I'd like to take a look."

"Is it safe to let them approach the wall?"

"I don't see why not."

Ty ordered the enforcers to let the people go, then headed out toward the main gates. As soon as they departed, the crowd closed in on the smoothed section of the wall again, touching it reverently. The number of people had nearly tripled in the time Hernande had been there, and he noticed the swineherd front and center again, already spouting out his story.

The closer they came to the gates, the more the tent city that had once been yards from the wall crowded in, until there was only a twenty-foot clearance between the nearest makeshift homes and the stone. As they passed by, the enforcers shoved encroaching baggage and crates and people back from the buffer zone they'd created, a few people lurching up from whatever they were doing with a sharp outcry of disgust or curses, shaking their fists at the guards as they passed on. The smell increased as well, the sweat and rankness of too many bodies pressed too close together for too long, compounded by the grease and stench of hundreds of different types of food being cooked.

"We're not going to be able to continue allowing everyone in," Ty muttered, the gates now within sight. "It's already too crowded."

He kicked a basket of tubers aside, a woman leaping from a nearby tent and snatching it up along with the few that spilled out to the ground. She spat to one side, then shouted, "We have a right to our space, enforcer!" when they were a safe distance away.

"Where do we send them?" Hernande asked.

Ty shook his head. "I'm not saying we need to send them away. But we can't continue to shelter them behind the walls. There isn't enough room. We should send them over to the other part of the city across the chasm or have them set up outside the walls."

"Then they wouldn't have the protection of the walls."

"No, but we don't have an army sitting outside our gates either. They'd be fine."

"Until an army appears."

Ty gave him a sideways look. "The Gorrani are still over the horizon. And if they did appear suddenly, we could bring everyone inside before they got here."

"Kara won't like it."

"Even Kara has to cave to the pressure of reality."

"I'm not certain she'd agree."

At the gates, the flow changed, with handcarts and wagons and people weaving in and out through the entrance, clogged up in the passageway between the thick walls. Even with the enforcers shouting for people to move out of the way, they only edged forward slightly. Most of the people were funneling into the city, returning from scavenging for food or other resources for trade, or simply coming back after an escape from the city itself. This late in the afternoon, few were attempting to leave. There were more mundane dangers on the plains outside after nightfall. Not everyone sought the protection of the enforcers and the walls, preying on whoever attempted to come to the Needle for help. Ty and the enforcers tried to patrol the area and keep such bandits away, but the land was rumpled with many depressions and vales to hide in once you passed beyond the lip of the crater where the Needle resided.

They had finally passed beneath the stone wall with its murder holes and iron portcullis into the sunlight beyond, storm clouds rolling in from the west, when someone on top of the wall cried out.

Hernande and Ty both looked upward, Ty shading his eyes with one hand. Someone was leaning out from the wall, pointing toward the horizon—northeast—gesturing frantically with the other hand. A moment later, a horn sounded, wavering at first before settling into a strident call.

Ty swore, spinning toward the northeast, but there was nothing to see. Not above the crater's lip.

"What is it?" Hernande asked. Those surrounding them glanced around in confusion, but the enforcers were already moving.

"Someone's approaching." He grabbed Hernande by the upper arm and shoved him toward the gates. "A sizable force, possibly an army. Get back inside the walls. Now!"

The tension of the enforcers was spreading, those waiting to be let back in fidgeting, then scrambling toward the gates. Ty kept behind Hernande, urging him forward through the press of people. With a gust of wind from behind, they plowed through the gateway again, Ty cutting to the right as soon as they reached the far side, headed toward the stairs that led up to the wall's height. Hernande hesitated, dragged forward by the momentum of the shouting crowd from behind, then fought his way back toward the stairs and followed Ty to the parapet.

He was gasping by the time he reached the top, forced to halt and lean against the short crenellations. The wall was a flurry of activity, men rushing back and forth carrying sheaves of arrows, spreading them out along the walk. Ty spat out orders, listening to reports, while his second, Darius, stood off to one side. A black look of hatred suffused Darius' face as Ty took over and Hernande jerked upright in surprise. Darius glanced toward him, his expression instantly vanishing into a cold equanimity. He turned away, shifting forward so that Ty and the guards and runners surrounding him blocked Hernande's view.

Heart pounding—in shock now, rather than exertion—Hernande faced northeast, in the direction the enforcers along the wall were pointing. Wind slapped him immediately, chilling his skin with the promise of rain he'd noticed earlier. The storm clouds were rolling in fast. He guessed there would be rain within the hour. But to the northeast he could see a different shadow converging on the Needle. It shifted along the plains, a column of men and horses and carts trundling along the stone road that led from one of the crossroads to the Needle. A large plume of dust angled off to the east, kicked up by the tread of their feet and the wagon wheels. They were too distant to pick out individuals—or even one cart from the next—but the line was too long to contain fewer than a hundred people.

Hernande's concern about Darius and what he'd seen in the second's face in that momentary lapse was superseded by the threat of the approaching army. Hernande leaned out over the wall. Below, the enforcers were frantically attempting to get everyone outside in through the gates, but they were jammed up. Shouts and curses echoed up the wall. At least three carts had been abandoned, causing a blockage. Farther distant, another cart was tearing down the same road the army used, a scattering of people on foot also headed toward the wall. Someone sounded the horn again, Hernande's ears ringing from the noise.

He pulled back from the wall's edge and sought out Ty, who motioned him in closer as soon as he noticed him. The commander sent runners along both sides of the wall, another two to the barracks near the temple to call for reinforcements and to spread more enforcers among the population to keep everyone calm. Then he searched those nearest and swore.

"Where in hells is Darius?"

"He was here a moment ago," Hernande said.

Ty gestured toward the approaching army. "Any idea who they are? Can you see that far?"

"Not well enough to pick out any colors or individuals."

"So no one knows who they are. My scouts haven't reported in from the northeast. I wonder if this is the reason why. Not that we had many scouts posted there. We've been more focused on the south recently."

Hernande caught Ty's eye. "Do you see any dogs with them?"

Ty snorted, then sobered. "You think this is the army Dalton spoke of? The one approaching from the north?"

"It could be."

"If that bastard's vision turns out to be true, I'll have to reconsider my religious beliefs." He suddenly straightened. "I bet Darius is headed to speak to Dalton right now, tell him what's coming, even though he isn't supposed to have access." He stared back at the temple, then snagged a passing runner. "Pass on whatever you were doing to someone else and run to the temple. See if Second Darius is attempting to talk to Father Dalton."

The boy nodded and sprinted toward the stairs.

Ty faced the approaching army again, leaning forward onto the crenellations, the wind blowing his blond hair into ragged tufts. "And now we wait."

To the west, the black-purple clouds moving in lit up with a flare of lightning, although they were still too distant for the thunder to be heard. The initial panic on the parapet calmed down, what defenses they had already prepared. Within the hour, the guard on the gates had doubled; Hernande could see more enforcers lining the walls. The debacle at the gates was unsnagged, and everyone who'd been outside at the first sighting had managed to clear the walls, the gates thundering closed. The three abandoned carts had been left outside, one with a broken wheel. The wind increased, the grasses on the plains shimmering in ripples of green and yellow, like waves on an ocean. The temperature fell dramatically, the sun fading as the clouds converged overhead. Visibility dropped, the approaching army fading into shadow, the men around them cursing. Ley lights flickered on, spilling their white light across the stone at key points along the wall, accompanied by torches in many other locations.

Two hours later, one of the guards shouted and pointed toward something on the ground below, jolting Hernande from a damp reverie. Light rain—more a misty drizzle—had started twenty minutes earlier, but the approaching thunder promised a much heavier downpour shortly. Hernande stepped up to the edge of the wall next to Ty.

"Now what?" Hernande picked out a lone figure running toward the gates, black against the dreary gray landscape.

"One of our scouts." Ty turned as the figure passed out of sight. "Let him in!"

The order was passed down to the gates and ten minutes later a drenched enforcer—a man no more than eighteen, shivering with the cold and damp—came to a halt before them.

"Who's approaching?" Ty demanded.

"It's Allan Garrett, sir, with the Wolves and the Temerites from Erenthrall."

Ten

KARA, TY, HERNANDE, AND MARCUS met Allan and the others outside the walls, rain still pouring down from the skies, lightning flaring and thunder growling all around them. The leading groups of men and wagons emerged from the sheeting rain like wraiths, without even lanterns to guide them. Kara didn't even recognize Allan until he came within twenty steps of the four of them. Until then, nervous tension dripped from her arms and fingers like the rain, even though the scouts had assured them of who approached. They'd closed the gates behind them, in case it was some type of ruse or trap.

When Allan raised his head, hair plastered to his forehead, he looked toward Kara. But it was Ty who stepped forward.

"Welcome back," the commander of the enforcers said, then looked beyond Allan toward the others. His hand rested on the pommel of his sword. "Who are those with you?"

Allan glanced back, the Wolf-lord Grant shifting forward with an escort of two Wolves, along with Bryce and a few of the guards that had been sent along with them. Allan gestured with one hand and the wagon driven by Gaven pulled close enough Kara could see an older Temerite woman sitting in the bed in some type of chair, surrounded by tarp-covered crates and supplies and two other Temerite men, one obviously a protector, the other more like a servant. A smaller group of Temerite guardsmen flanked the cart on both sides. One of these men stepped forward, back rigid with formality, another man a pace behind.

Half-turned, Allan said, "May I present to you Captain Lienta and

Lieutenant Boskell of the Temerite Legion, along with their Matriarch, Isaiella Tunettia."

Lienta and Boskell nodded their heads stiffly in Ty's direction, both of their expressions taut with a grim pride. Boskell's thin lips were downturned with a hint of anger and distrust. The rest of the Temerite guardsmen surrounding the wagon were on edge, fearful but also hopeful. All of them looked haggard and shot longing glances at the wall, lit from above with ley light and torches. Many of them were coughing, the sound thick with phlegm.

"You'll forgive me if I don't stand up to greet you, Commander Ty," the Matriarch said, her voice slicing through the shush of the rain on the grasses. Her gaze flicked from Ty to Kara and Kara drew in a sharp breath. "We are what remain of the Temerite enclave from Erenthrall. It's been a hard and slow journey getting here—a tiring journey—and we would seek sanctuary here at the Needle. Your Lord Allan has told us all about you."

Allan grimaced at the title, but said, "I told them the Needle would take them in. None of us would have returned if not for them." Grant made a soft wuffling noise of protest and Allan rolled his eyes. "Most of us wouldn't have returned."

Ty shot Kara a look. "How many of them are there?"

"Close to five hundred, not all of them Temerites. Some are groups we picked up during our escape from the city."

"Escape?" Kara and Ty said together.

"It's a long story."

Kara heard the understatement in his tone, but said, "We can't hold that many. The city is already too crowded."

"The western district," Hernande said from beside her. "Beyond the chasm."

"Do you have enough guardsmen to protect yourselves?" Ty asked Lienta. "The western district has been mostly abandoned. It does not have defenses along the chasm side."

"We can protect ourselves," Lienta said. The water dripping from his nose ruined his forced dignity. Boskell looked affronted.

"We appreciate any shelter that you can provide," the Matriarch said, as a growl of thunder rolled over them. "We must speak of what has happened in Erenthrall, but first I need to see my people situated." She glanced up toward the ley lights overhead, blinking against the water as it ran down her face. "Where is this western district? This chasm?"

Ty spun and shouted the all-clear signal to the wall, and within moments the gates were clanging ponderously open, the portcullis rising. A ragged cheer came from the Temerites, and Captain Lienta began passing back orders through the wagon train. Allan was already conferring with him, gesturing toward the north and west, where they'd have to skirt the chasm and then approach again from the city's western side, entering the deserted section through the abandoned western gate. Ty arranged an escort of enforcers to show them the way.

Kara leaned in toward Marcus. "You should go with them. Find Dylan. See if you two can tap into the ley lines and get some heating stones and ley globes working over there and get his report at the same time."

"Good idea. I'll send back for some of the other Wielders to come help."

"They look miserable," Hernande said as word spread—followed by groans—that they wouldn't be entering the city through this gate, that they'd have to travel west. Wagons began to turn, one getting caught in the runnel of mud alongside the stone road. But Hernande wasn't watching the Temerites. His eyes were locked on Allan. "You should send some healers as well. Some of them sound sick. We don't need influenza spreading through the Needle."

"I'll inform Freesia. She can rally the healers."

"Not all of them," Hernande said.

But before Kara could ask him what he meant, he stepped forward and snagged Allan's sleeve when it appeared Allan was going to follow Lienta, Boskell, Bryce, Ty, and the Matriarch toward their new enclave.

"What is it?" Allan asked, motioning the others to continue without him.

"It's Morrell." Allan stilled, body going rigid with tension, but Hernande continued, "She's fine—or at least she will be. She's resting in the hospital. I assumed you'd want to see her immediately. Drayden's watching over her."

Exhaustion and the chill from trudging through the rain over the last dozen miles to the Needle had seeped into Allan's bones, but as soon as he saw Morrell lying on the cot in the hospital, all his aches and pains doubled. He drew in a shuddering breath, staggering slightly, as if from a physical blow—

And then he was falling to his knees at his daughter's side, catching himself on the cot. The motion jolted Morrell awake; she drew back from his reaching hand in fear, startled, until recognition struck.

She lurched up from the bed and embraced him and he clung to her, even though the position was awkward and the muscles in his lower back protested. He breathed in the scent of her hair—tangy with salt from sand, with an underlying must from old stone—as he cradled her head and stroked her back. She half babbled, half sobbed, her voice rumbling in her chest as she tried to talk, her heart racing with excitement, but for a long moment Allan didn't hear a word she said. He merely held her, the world fading away—the long trek from Erenthrall with the Matriarch and Lienta and all of their people, the horror over what had happened in the city while they were there and as they left— all of it simply sluiced off him, released in a sigh of contentment.

But then he realized Morrell was trying to tell him something, something important, at least to her, and he forced himself back into the moment.

He opened his eyes, sought out Drayden, the mostly human man with a few remaining traces of Wolf in him crouched down against one wall of the hospital to one side. Morrell's self-proclaimed guardian nodded, his nostrils flaring as if he were scenting the air. One ear twitched. He didn't appear tense or worried.

Allan suddenly felt the eyes of those around them—Kara, Hernande, the healers, and the patients resting on cots—all focused on their reunion. He pulled back, hands shifting to Morrell's shoulders, but paused in shock when he saw her face, really saw it, without the overlay of expectation. Her hair was the same soft dirty blonde, although it was longer than before, fuller somehow, but her cheeks, her jawline, the tension in the skin around her eyes . . .

Morrell was growing up. She wasn't the waiflike child she'd been when he'd first taken her to Erenthrall, nor even the spindly adolescent transitioning toward adult. Somehow, in the last few months, the fullness of youth in her face had bled away, leaving behind the sharper angles of adulthood. He knew it couldn't have happened that fast, that it must have been happening there in the Hollow and he'd simply been ignoring it, but now it slammed into his gut with full force. He couldn't deny it any longer. His Morrell was an adult. A teenager, still young, but yet also an adult.

"—and that's when I healed her hand," Morrell gushed. "I just snipped the spindle off near her palm, and as soon as it fell out, I began sealing up the wound. But that isn't even the most astounding thing! With Hernande's help I've been practicing with the others from the University. He's been training me. At first, I didn't think it was helping—I couldn't seem to do anything more than usual—but then he took me to the outer wall, and—"

"Morrell," Allan said, trying to interrupt, but she continued, barely pausing to catch breath.

"—and I reached into the stone, I could feel it! I could sense the cracks in it, the hollows and imperfections! Then I did what all the other students have been telling me all along. I just released it all into—"

Allan shook her by the shoulders and shouted, "Morrell!" then chuckled at her shocked expression to take the sting out of it and hugged her close again. "You're talking too fast. I haven't followed a word you've said since I laid eyes on you."

When he pulled back again, she was smiling. "I'm just so happy to see you."

"And I'm happy to see you, poppet. Now, look at me." He squeezed her shoulders and looked her directly in the eyes, dark, like her mother's. "Are you all right?"

"I'm fine, Da." She sighed heavily, body slumping, as if the energy had suddenly drained out of her, but her smile didn't fade. "Hernande had me heal the wall, and it took more out of me than I expected, that's all. I'll be fine by morning." Her mouth twisted as her gaze flicked toward Hernande. "Maybe the afternoon."

"Good. Is there anything else that I need to know right now? That can't wait until tomorrow? I need to speak to Kara and Commander Ty about the people we brought from Erenthrall and what happened while we were there."

Morrell let herself fall back onto the cot. He expected a mild tirade, at least some huffiness and protest that he was abandoning her again so quickly, but she merely yawned, covering her mouth with one hand while pulling the disturbed blankets up around her again.

"Nothing that can't wait until tomorrow," she mumbled, already sounding half asleep. "Although I think Cerrin likes me. I'm not sure. He's acting weird."

Allan sat back, astounded, then turned toward Kara and Hernande. "What did you do to her? And who's Cerrin?"

"Cerrin is one of the other healers," Hernande said. "He's harmless. They'll work it out."

Allan wasn't certain he trusted Hernande's judgment, but he could find out more about Cerrin later. "And Morrell?"

Kara shrugged. "I haven't spent much time with her since you left," she admitted. "Just . . . too busy with the Nexus. And Tumbor. And Father Dalton." She grimaced and helped Allan up from the floor. "It's a long story."

"I'm afraid it's all my fault," Hernande said as they shifted away from Morrell toward the hospital's entrance. Allan noticed there were only two healers present; the others must have already left for the new Temerite camp across the chasm. He signaled to Drayden to keep watch over Morrell as they left, the answer coming as an acknowledging huff. "As she said, Cory and I took her under our wing after you left. She'd started healing people in the hospital on a regular basis and needed to talk. Some of the patients weren't treating her all that well, although most of them were grateful and pleasant."

"It only takes one or two bad individuals to discourage someone when they're that age," Kara said, without looking at either of them.

Hernande continued as if she hadn't spoken. "After working with her a little while, I decided it would be best if we began training her as a student of the University, such as it is. She began coming to some of our lessons with the remaining students who survived the Shattering, and a few others we've picked up along the way. My fellow mentors didn't know if we could help her or not, since we know nothing about her talents, but we thought we could offer her some guidance at least. School is more than simply learning rote lessons about the Tapestry or the ley or whatever talent you may have. It teaches you confidence and courage and other life lessons as well."

"Dylan and I have been talking about that very idea since we helped the Temerites escape Erenthrall."

"You mentioned that at the gates. What do you mean 'escaped'? They didn't come here willingly?"

They'd reached the temple, the streets of the outer city busier than usual this late at night, especially with the rain that had slowed to a drizzle now, the lightning having moved off to the east. Most of those out and about were enforcers and runners racing from the barracks and the temple on errands Allan assumed were related to the arrival of the Temerites.

They ducked into the shelter of the temple door, allowed through by a guard of six enforcers. More than had been on duty when Allan left.

"They came here willingly," Allan said, "but only after it became clear that there would be no refuge in Erenthrall for them." He paused, conscious of how his voice echoed in the strange corridors of the temple. "Devin has taken over what remained of Aurek's men in Haven. He's somehow managed to align the worst of the elements left in Erenthrall—the Rats, the Butcher to the east, a slew of other groups. They attacked the Temerite enclave while we were there, managed to take down the walls."

"How did they do that?" Hernande asked.

Allan shook his head. "Not here. And not in the orrery. You know how I affect the globes."

Kara had clearly forgotten how he disrupted the ley, for at the next intersection she turned right, away from the orrery, toward the kitchens. As soon as Allan smelled baking bread, his stomach growled.

"I'm starving for something other than dry journey bread and roasted prairie dog," he said.

"I figured we'd meet in one of the rooms off the kitchen," Kara said. "That way we can get you whatever you want that's available."

As soon as they reached the room—one wide and deep, with a long table down its center, benches on either side—Kara muttered directions to a few of the kitchen staff she caught in the hallway; one was sent running back toward the main kitchen, the other trotting off toward the outer city, her face scrunched up with whatever message she carried. All three of them settled onto the benches, the room obviously used to feed the staff and perhaps the enforcers who lived here in the temple. Within a few moments, the boy returned with a tray laden with a variety of meats, roasted vegetables, cheese, and bread. Allan grabbed a loaf of still warm rye, tore off a steaming piece, and loaded it with slices of ham. The ham was cold, fat congealed on its edges, but he didn't care. Salty juice dribbled down his chin as he bit into it.

The boy returned with a pitcher of water and another of ale.

"Do we have any kaffe?" Allan asked.

Hernande's eyes widened. "I didn't realize you drank kaffe. It's a Temerite drink."

"I didn't," Allan said through another mouthful. "Not until the trek back from Erenthrall with the Matriarch and Lienta. We had much to discuss, and the Matriarch drinks nothing but kaffe. She claims it keeps her energized."

"It contains some of the same compounds as tea leaves," Hernande agreed, "but in a much stronger and more bitter concentration."

Kara waved a hand in dismissal and said to the server, "See if we have some kaffe." When the boy left, she turned to Allan again, arms crossed over her chest. "Now, what happened in Erenthrall? How did Devin manage to defeat the Temerites?"

Allan took another bite of food, but suddenly he wasn't as hungry as before. He swallowed, the bread like a stone going down. The servant returned with his kaffe and he cupped the warm mug close and sipped with a sigh, his throat already tingling with the warmth. "They have Hounds."

"Who has Hounds?" Ty asked as he entered. His gaze shot immediately toward Allan. Cory entered behind him.

"I met him in the hallway on my way here," he said to Kara. "He was headed toward the orrery. I told him the meeting room had changed."

"I'm surprised you're back from getting the Temerites settled in," Hernande said.

Ty took a seat and stole some of Allan's food. "Marcus has everything in hand. And the Temerites and the others are more interested in sleeping than anything else. We can finish whatever needs to be finished tomorrow. Now, explain about the Hounds. I thought they'd all died in the Shattering."

"Obviously not," Allan said.

"It makes sense," Hernande said. "Their den was beneath the Dogs' in the Amber Tower, correct?" At Allan's brusque nod, he continued: "You, Kara, Morrell, and the others survived the blast because you were in the cells beneath the tower, protected by the stone. The Hounds would have been protected as well."

"Then why didn't we see them in Erenthrall before this? Where have they been?"

"We never saw them after the Shattering either. I'd surmise they never left the tower, or at least didn't stray that far from their den. They weren't trained to be independent, from what Allan has told us."

"And then they were caught in the distortion when it quickened," Kara said, sitting back in realization. "I released them when I healed it."

"Don't berate yourself. You released everyone and everything in the distortion. Don't forget the people trapped in the shard where we found the apothecary, the ones who gave up on being released and killed themselves. The distortion needed to be healed as soon as possible."

Kara's troubled expression smoothed as she let the momentary guilt go. She scrubbed at her face with her hands. "So Devin has control of the Hounds?"

"It would seem so. Which makes him infinitely more dangerous than Baron Aurek, if he uses them effectively. And from what I saw in Erenthrall, he's doing just that."

"He must have used the Hounds to coerce the other groups into following him," Hernande mused, "either as a threat, or he simply used them to eliminate any dissenting leaders."

"Like Baron Arent did during his rise to power," Ty said. "I suppose Devin's declared himself Baron of Erenthrall now?"

"We didn't stick around to find out. The Temerites used some of the old ley tunnels to escape their enclave as it was being attacked. Even then, we only survived because Dylan redirected the ley into the tunnels after we left, killing hundreds of Devin's men. He's been sickened over it ever since, which is why we were discussing how to handle those that can wield the ley or the Tapestry. There's too much raw power lying about in the cities that contained nodes now that the Baronial structure has collapsed. Anyone with the ability can use it however they wish. We've been lucky that no one has seized that raw power yet."

"Except for ourselves," Hernande interrupted.

Everyone looked at him, but Allan continued. "Except for ourselves. I see now why the Wielders set up their college, why they gathered up from the schools those that could manipulate the ley as soon as they reached young adulthood. They couldn't have random Wielders disturbing what they'd built. It's too powerful. It threatens everyone. We need to create our own college, for both Wielders and mages, so that we can protect ourselves from anyone who might attempt to use the ley or Tapestry against us."

"All of the Wielders we know of are already here, at the Needle," Kara said, "or at the node we established in the Hollow. They're already being trained."

"But not in a formal college setting," Hernande countered, "like what the other mentors and I have begun to do with the old University students." He stared at Allan as he considered what the ex-Dog had said, mouth pursed. "I agree with you in practical terms—we need to be able to defend ourselves if someone attempts to attack us with the ley or the Tapestry, especially since we now know that the two are inextricably connected. But in moral terms, what gives us the right to control the ley or the Tapestry? Look at what happened in Erenthrall when it was controlled by the Baron and the Primes."

Ty rapped the knuckles of one hand on the table forcefully, interrupting before Allan or anyone else could respond. "You're getting sidetracked. We can discuss the issues of politics and the ley later. We need to focus on more immediate concerns. What happened after you escaped the enclave?"

"We fled the city as fast as we could. A major auroral storm was descending on the central part of the city, near the University. The Gorrani were directly in its path. As we left, they were hit by the storm, which kept them from attacking Devin and his men as they secured the Temerite enclave. But it . . . changed them." He drew in a ragged breath, suddenly feeling the exhaustion he'd shrugged off upon seeing his daughter again. Not even the kaffe appeared to help. He met the eyes of everyone in the room. "The auroral lights twisted them, as it did with the Wolves. Only the Gorrani didn't shift into a wolf form. They changed into some type of hooded snakes. Those that survived the auroral storm anyway."

A heavy silence settled, Ty, Kara, Hernande, and Cory sharing startled glances.

"Don't tell me the bastard's vision is true," Kara said into the subdued quiet.

"It all fits," Hernande said. "We always thought the Gorrani were the snakes. And now we have Devin with Hounds. They could be the dogs he spoke of."

"Who are you talking about?" Allan said, the words sharper than he'd intended. The weariness had worn him thin. "What vision? What snakes? What dogs?"

"A lot has happened here at the Needle while you were gone."

"Enlighten me."

They explained it to him in pieces, Cory, Ty, Kara, and Hernande handing the story off one to the other with only a few occasions where someone broke in on someone else. Father Dalton breaking his pledge to keep his sermons to the preaching of Korma and a return to the natural order, his incendiary vision, his imprisonment in his rooms since then, and the subsequent discontent throughout the city that led to the riot. The continued unrest had only grown since then, with the emergence of the snake-dog symbol chalked onto every flat surface throughout the Needle. Hernande related Morrell's own experiences, from serving in the hospital, to joining the University students, to repairing part of the breach that the mentors had caused in the wall. Kara told of her attempts to increase the power of the Nexus and Iscivius' creation of another crystal, along with their thoughts on how to work with the mentors to heal the distortion over Tumbor.

"Iscivius?" Allan asked skeptically.

"Yes, Iscivius. Both he and Irmona began helping with the node after you left, on a daily basis."

Allan glanced around at the others. "No one found that . . . odd?"

"Of course, we did," Cory said. "Everyone was suspicious at first. But neither one of them did anything out of the ordinary. Although Irmona remained bitter and acerbic the entire time."

"In fact," Kara added, "Iscivius is still in a comatose state. We've tried everything. Even Morrell checked in on him. She found nothing wrong, nothing to repair. She said his body is fine, simply exhausted, almost completely drained. He's returning, but slowly, and she can't speed up the process."

"Or, at least, she doesn't know how yet," Hernande interposed.

"Regardless, it feels heartless to question his motives when it drove him into this state. Irmona has watched over him since the incident, refuses to help us any further with the Nexus. If anything, she's become more bitter toward us. I can't say I blame her."

"And what about the Nexus?" Allan asked. "Is it powerful enough now for you to heal the distortion?"

Kara pressed her lips into a thin line, staring off into space for a long moment. The others waited, no one daring to move. Finally, she turned to face Cory, watched him as she spoke. "I think so. It's difficult to tell. I . . ." She halted. Cory gave her a slight nod of encouragement, and she exhaled sharply. "I'm afraid to try. I've been putting off the attempt because I wanted to be certain it would succeed. I'm not a Prime, no matter what everyone thinks. I don't have the training or the experience. I don't want to fail."

Her voice had grown more and more ragged as she spoke, the effort to admit what she feared obvious. Cory shifted and wrapped his hand in hers, their fingers intertwined.

"It doesn't matter," Ty said, breaking the fragile silence. "You're the closest thing to a Prime we've got. Can you make another crystal? Can you increase the power of the Nexus any further?"

"Marcus and I have been practicing what we saw Iscivius doing, but we aren't even close to being able to replicate it. We don't have the speed and finesse required. And even if we could do it half as well, look at what happened to him. If we tried, I think it might kill us."

"Then you have to make the attempt with what you've got." Ty's tone left no room for argument.

"There's no rush," Cory said. "There hasn't been a significant surge of instability since the distortion over Erenthrall was healed."

"There's no reason to wait either," Ty countered.

Kara tightened with resolve. "No, Ty's right. Waiting won't give us a better chance. I'll start preparing the Wielders tomorrow. We need to start coordinating with the mentors and the University students. We'll make the attempt as soon as everyone is ready."

"How long will that take?" Ty asked.

"A few days. No more than a week."

Ty turned to Allan. "Dalton predicted that the Gorrani and this Devin would converge on the Needle. Did you see any signs that Devin and his forces were following you and the Temerites? What about the transformed Gorrani?"

"We kept scouts trailing a good distance behind us as we moved. They saw nothing. The last we knew, Devin was consolidating his forces in the Temerite stronghold, bringing in most of the more violent groups that had claimed territory in Erenthrall. The Gorrani who survived the auroral storm had retreated into the fissures and cracks in the southern cliffs."

"I don't think the snakes of Dalton's vision represent the transformed Gorrani in Erenthrall," Hernande interjected.

"The Haessan," Allan said. Then added in answer to the questioning looks: "That's what the Temerites are calling the transformed Gorrani. In the Temer language, it means snake."

"The Haessan, then." Hernande shifted forward and leaned both elbows on the table. "I know it makes sense that the Haessan would be the snakes in Dalton's vision, but his visions have never been that literal before. It makes more sense that the snakes represent the Gorrani to the south. Not only do the snakes in his vision come from the south, but we already have strong evidence that the Gorrani there are working their way northward."

"We're receiving more and more accounts of Gorrani attacks on settlements from my scouts daily. They're getting closer. And growing bolder." Ty turned to Allan. "We'll need to send out heavier patrols to the north, to keep an eye out for Devin and his forces. He may be settling into Erenthrall, but we know he has reason to hate you and the others here at the Needle. You killed Aurek. He's bound to come here eventually."

"We should warn those at the Hollow as well," Hernande said. "He may attack them, out of spite, if not revenge."

Allan attempted to stifle a yawn, but failed. He swallowed another gulp of kaffe, but it was cold and he could tell it was doing him little good. The weariness from days of walking and little sleep had accumulated too heavily. He heaved himself up from the bench, his body like a dead weight. "I need to rest. I can barely think, and I'm about ready to collapse."

Everyone else rose as well.

"We can speak more about Devin and what happened in Erenthrall tomorrow," Ty said. "I'll want to know details from both you and Bryce so that I can prepare the Needle if they do come."

Allan pushed back from the table. "You'll want Grant there as well. He and his Wolves explored more of the city than we did."

"How many Wolves did he find while he was there?" Hernande asked. "I saw two with him when you arrived, and one of them was new."

"Ten. He was going to give them the option of returning to human form again, but I suppose that will have to wait until my daughter recovers. There were a few others, but some had gone feral and refused to come with him."

He headed toward the door, but a wave of weakness washed through him and he was forced to lean against the table. Both Hernande and Cory reached forward to support him, but he waved them away. "I'm fine, just tired." Straightening, he gathered what remained of his strength and strode from the room.

He made it to his rooms, although he didn't recall anything about the corridors in between, and collapsed into bed without removing his clothes.

He was asleep before even the thought of removing his boots could register.

"He looked like death warmed up at the hearthside," Kara said as Allan left.

"I'm surprised he lasted as long as he did."

"It sounds like escaping Erenthrall was hell."

"I'm sure it was," Ty said, turning to face the rest of them, his expression grim. "And he didn't bring us good news. I was a Dog before the Shattering. I've dealt with the Hounds before. If Devin has Hounds, I'm not certain there's anything we can do to keep him from seizing the Needle and destroying everyone and everything here."

Marc hesitated at the door, uncertain, Armone already moving inside the smoke-hazed room and greeting those within. The nape of Marc's neck prickled with unease as he noted his fellow enforcers—the elderly Trenton, puffing on his pipe, and red-haired Cerena—sitting with Darius, Dierdre, and one other enforcer he didn't know, although he knew he was one of the twins. The lone twin looked enraged.

"They took Jonnas!" he spat. "Right off the street! Along with three others who have been helping us."

"Who took them?" Dierdre asked.

"Ty and his gods-damned enforcers!"

Cerena shot everyone around the room a startled look, then returned her gaze to the twin—Javers, Marc remembered, now that he'd heard the other twin's name. "Did you see them? Are you certain it was Ty and those loyal to him?"

"I didn't see the commander himself. And the men who grabbed them weren't dressed as enforcers. They were waiting for them, though. They leaped out of an alley as Jonnas and the others passed by, threw sacks over their heads, and then dragged them into the alley. It took less than thirty seconds. But you know Ty was behind it. Too many of our own people have disappeared over the last few weeks. He's hunting us down."

Trenton, who hadn't glanced away from Marc since he'd appeared, blew smoke into the air and asked, "Can we trust Jonnas not to talk? The others taken don't know any of us, not directly. But Jonnas could expose us all."

"He won't talk. You know him as well as I do. But what are we going to do to get him back?"

"Nothing." It was the first time Darius had spoken. Javers looked shocked, as if he'd been gut-punched. Before he could begin to protest, Darius added, "We don't know where Ty and his enforcers are keeping them, and asking questions will only draw attention to our own people. Jonnas won't talk, as you say. So we leave him. For now."

"Jonnas and these other three haven't been the only ones to disappear," Trenton said, still watching Marc. "Two others who aided us at the riot in the square vanished a few days ago."

"They're likely the ones who fingered Jonnas and the others." Darius raised a hand to forestall any more commentary, nodding toward Marc. "Who have you brought with you today, Armone?"

"Marc, the one I told you about earlier."

Darius' eyes narrowed. "I recognize you. You were sent out with Cutter's group to scout the area east of Tumbor."

Marc stepped into the room and everyone tensed. He halted and held up both hands, palms facing outward until everyone relaxed, then continued. "It should have been my group."

"And why is that?" Trenton asked.

"Cutter is one of those bastards from the Hollow. He hasn't been trained to be a Dog. He shouldn't be out there, leading scouting parties. He should be here, getting the shit beat out of him on our training grounds. Let him fight his way up the ranks like the rest of us."

Everyone nodded, even though Marc knew that not everyone here had been a Dog before the Shattering; at least a few of them had been enforcers in Tumbor under Baron Leethe.

Armone grinned, snatching up the dice and a cup. "That's why I brought him in," he said as he rattled the dice and then rolled, the bone cubes skittering across the table. They came up double snakes and Armone crowed. "Please tell me someone had already bet on that roll?"

Cerena snorted. "You aren't that lucky, Armone."

"Can we trust him?" Darius asked, and both Cerena and Armone fell abruptly silent, everyone now looking at Marc, hands on swords or fiddling with knives. All except Darius and Dierdre.

The silence stretched. Sweat broke out in Marc's armpits, made the back of his neck itch. He knew how to play Armone, had even had run-ins with Trenton and Cerena, but he didn't know how to handle them all as a group. He didn't know what the group wanted, which left him at a disadvantage. So he kept silent, let the awkwardness stretch, and kept his eyes on Darius.

Trenton suddenly leaned forward, his chair creaking. "We've been moving forward with your plans, Darius, but the loss of Jonnas and the others puts us in a bind. We won't be able to distribute the packages as quickly, which means there's a greater chance of discovery by Ty and the other enforcers, especially now that the Temerites have taken over the abandoned part of the city. If they find even one of the packages—"

"You're saying we're going to need more people," Darius cut in.

"Especially within the enforcers. Many of them will follow us as soon as we show we have a stronger hand, but there are few of them we can trust to carry out what needs to be done."

Darius' frown darkened.

"We can't leave Father up in that prison any longer, brother," Dierdre said. "He's been kept from his followers too long. Who knows what they've done to him?"

"I notice that your own attempts to sway your precious Marcus into freeing him haven't borne any fruit."

"I've managed to draw him away from that harlot Kara!"

"But have you done enough?" Darius faced Dierdre, Marc exhaling in relief as the second's gaze shifted away. "Will Marcus side with us when the time comes? We will need Wielders, Dierdre, to control the Nexus. We need him more than ever now that Iscivius is effectively useless."

Dierdre glared at her brother. "He will side with us," she said forcefully.

Yet Marc heard doubt in her voice, saw it flicker in her eyes as Darius turned back to him. The second enforcer drummed his fingers on the table while considering Marc. "Armone's instincts are usually dead on. We'll take you on his word. But we'll be keeping a careful eye on you."

"I understand. What is it you need me to do? What are you planning?"

Darius' suspicions rose again—Marc could see it in the twitch near the second's eyelid—but he leaned forward onto the table. "We intend to free Father and retake the Needle from Ty and this upstart Wielder, Kara."

Marc didn't try to hide his surprise. "And how are you going to do that?"

"Just as we did in Erenthrall—" Dierdre began.

But Darius cut her off. "You've already heard too much. No need for you to hear more until we're ready to begin . . . or until I'm convinced I can trust you."

Marc didn't respond. But Trenton stepped into what could have been another awkward silence.

"There is still the issue of when we should plan the attack. If we try to gather everyone together, it will be too obvious that we are about to act, and Ty and the others are already searching for us. They won't let a gathering like that first riot happen again. We need some other reason for everyone to converge on the square before the temple, something that won't arouse suspicions."

Marc suddenly smiled, the coiled tension in his chest releasing. He leaned forward onto the table from where he stood to catch both Trenton and Darius' attention.

"I know the perfect situation," he said, his voice a soft, confident rumble, "something you've obviously not heard about yet."

"And what is that?" Darius asked.

"In three days, the Wielders are going to attempt to heal the distortion over Tumbor."

Dierdre gasped, her surprise quickly turning to anger. "You lie! Marcus would have said something to me!"

Marc pushed back from the table. "Why would I lie about something so easily verified? The Wielders want the attempt to be kept secret, in case it fails. No spectacle, no forewarning."

"Then how did you find out about it?" Trenton demanded.

"I overheard some of them discussing it in the temple halls. In certain places, conversations carry far."

"If he's right, we can use this to bring everyone to the square, both civilian supporters and our own enforcers," Trenton said. "Everyone will want to be there to witness the healing. We can conceal our movements in the crowds. It's the perfect distraction."

"Unless Kara is successful," Dierdre said. "If she heals the distortion, it will counter everything Father has said about the Wielders since they seized the Needle."

"We've already taken care of that," Darius said. Marc wondered what he meant, but he didn't elaborate. Instead, he stared down at the table, thinking, one hand spinning an old erren coin distractedly.

"They obviously want their attempt to be kept secret," he muttered. "Otherwise, Marcus would have said something to Dierdre. But if no one knows about it, no one will gather . . ."

He halted the spinning coin with two fingers, snatching it up into his palm.

"I think it's time the Wielders' secret plans come out."

⌐

"The Gorrani are wiping out everyone left south of Grass," the Butcher rumbled. He was a hulking man, broad-shouldered and thick, but not with fat, merely dense muscle. He chewed on a piece of meat that the alpha Hound could smell had not come from any animal. "They'll come for us eventually. They've grown vicious since the aurora changed them."

Devin stood beside the fireplace in a ransacked room in what had once been the Temerite embassy. The scent of the Matriarch permeated every corner, laced with a medicinal unguent containing aloe and lavender. Even days after the Temerites had fled, he could smell her confidence, her power, in sharp contrast to Devin's musk.

Devin rapped his knuckles on the mantel, but didn't answer.

The Butcher gnawed on a piece of gristle, then spat it to one side as he rose from the battered settee he'd been resting on. His gaze flicked toward the alpha, then away. "We should send the Hounds after them, before they get here."

"Not even the Hounds could kill them all," Devin said, glancing up. "All it would take was one bite with whatever that venom is they have and the Hounds would be dead."

"It would give them pause."

"No. I won't risk the Hounds. I have something else I need them for."

"Then what?" the Butcher asked, voice twisted with derision. The alpha noted the lack of respect. Even Devin's own men were beginning to question him, after he'd lost hundreds in the ley tunnels and only managed to escape the Gorrani attack because the auroral storm had intervened. "Are we simply going to wait for them to attack us here? I didn't agree to be a part of your little army so that I could cower behind the Temerite walls. You promised us blood. You promised us flesh."

The alpha's nostrils flared at the implied threat, but Devin pushed away from the wall and faced the Butcher square on, even though the man towered nearly a foot over him. "Did you not get flesh? We took out the Temerites who'd been harassing you since the Shattering, didn't we?"

The Butcher's lip curled. "We took their enclave. They escaped."

"They're still gone. Besides, I didn't take their enclave so that we could settle in here." He stepped away from the Butcher, picked up a delicate statue from a nearby table that had somehow survived the seizure of the embassy, then tossed it to the floor where it shattered. "This was only one step on a long journey. We needed the supplies they had stored here."

"For what?"

"For the real goal. You want flesh? I know a place where there's plenty, and the Hounds are our ticket in."

"Where?" he asked suspiciously. The Butcher was ponderous, but he wasn't stupid.

"The Needle. Erenthrall has become too dangerous. We need someplace safer, a place easier to defend. The Needle has it all."

The alpha's ears twitched as the Butcher considered. He could hear the manipulation beneath the façade of truth. Devin didn't care about taking the Needle; he only wanted to see it—and those inside—destroyed.

He huffed in contempt. He could no longer think of Devin as a Baron, as his master, but there was no one else here who he could respect, who he could follow. What could he do? His two betas were on the verge of disobeying their commands, but who would they follow? There was no handler anymore.

The Butcher stirred. "I've heard snake meat is tough and stringy. Let the Gorrani have Erenthrall."

Devin grinned and the alpha's hackles rose as the so-called Baron turned to face his Hound. "Call your betas," he commanded. "I have a job for them."

The alpha's body trembled with the struggle between training and disobedience. In the end, training won.

He bowed his head to hide his snarl and asked, "What are our orders?"

Eleven

"HOW DID THEY FIND OUT?" Kara demanded, her voice echoing in the high ceiling of the Needle's node. Out of the corner of her eye, she caught some of the other Wielders turning in her direction—Okata, Carter, and Jenner. She was certain the others situated behind her were looking as well. She'd spoken louder than she'd intended, but Ty's news had startled her.

She lowered her voice. "How in hells did the people find out, Ty? We haven't told anyone except those within the council."

Ty grimaced, but waved a hand around the node. "And the Wielders. And the University students. Don't forget them."

Kara swore, glaring around at the others. All of them studiously returned to their manipulations of the ley and the crystals, practicing for their attempt at healing Tumbor, now only two days away. Except for Okata. The Gorrani Wielder met her gaze and asked a question with his eyes. She pressed her lips into a thin line but shook her head, and he returned to work.

"I can't believe one of them—" she began, but broke off and spun toward Ty. "Irmona."

"Did you tell her?"

"No. I left her out of the loop on purpose. I don't trust her not to sabotage our attempt in some way. But one of the other Wielders probably told her after our initial planning session." She bit her lower lip, a sudden wave of dread sweeping through her. She swore. "I wanted to do this without any fanfare, in case something went wrong and we're forced to halt the attempt. Maybe we should postpone it."

"You could, but I don't think that's wise."

"Why not?"

"Because for the past few weeks the mood of those outside the temple has been dark. It's not only about the fact that we haven't let Dalton speak, although his followers are the ones stoking the embers. They're able to rile everyone up because there's already a general sense of discontent."

"If there's one thing I've learned since ostensibly taking over the rule of this city," Kara said cynically, "it's that there's always a low level of discontent, no matter how bad or good the situation is."

"True, but this discontent has been growing, with Father Dalton and his vision as the focus. It's risen mostly unchecked. Until now. Once I heard that the Wielders' plans were being mentioned on the street, I went into the city to investigate. The news is everywhere, on almost every street corner, spoken of in every tent I passed. Everyone—from gossipmonger to enforcer—is excited about it. They want to see the distortion over Tumbor fall. Right now, it's a constant reminder that the world is broken. They may be able to forget about it briefly by hiding behind the Needle's walls, but it's still there the moment they leave and look up, a bright shiny blemish on the horizon."

"Healing the distortion over Tumbor won't return us to life as it was before the Shattering."

"But it will get rid of a constant and blatant reminder that the world is still messed up. Don't forget that is one of Dalton's central attacks on you and the Wielders: that you haven't managed to repair the ley system yet."

"Neglecting to point out that we haven't had a significant quake since we took over." She sighed in resignation. "So what are you suggesting, then?"

"Now that they know you're going to make an attempt, they're going to converge on the temple or the outer walls in an uncontrolled mob, all trying to score the best seats in the city facing Tumbor."

"You're afraid there will be another riot, like before."

"It didn't take much to ignite the last group, and it's only grown more volatile since then. I'm certain Dalton's followers will be in the crowds, trying to incite another angry mob. They'll be able to do it easily if the enforcers aren't there to regulate matters."

"Regulate them how?"

"We'll set up specific areas for viewing—sections of the steps on the temple, along some of the plazas on each tier, open up part of the wall's parapet so that people can stand and watch the distortion from there. We'll keep everyone in line by having enforcers everywhere."

Kara couldn't help flashing back to memories of the launch of the Baron's flyers in Seeley Park and the sowing of the central flyers' tower in Grass—the frenetic excitement of the crowds, its infectious thrill in her younger self's blood, the accelerated rush of her heart in her ears. Now that she thought about it, there hadn't been a moment like that since before the Shattering. It had all been pain and terror and uncertainty as the world fluctuated around them.

Perhaps it was time for something like this: a spectacle to draw all of those who had survived together.

Ty remained silent while she mulled it over.

"Go ahead with it," she said. "But I don't have time to help out. Talk to Hernande and Allan about it. I'm certain they'll have suggestions."

Ty moved toward the stairs leading up out of the pit. Kara watched him for a moment, worry niggling at her. She didn't relish having an audience for their attempt, but at this point it couldn't be helped.

She turned and stalked toward Okata, calling out, "Word about what we're doing has leaked out into the city. Everyone gather around. We can no longer afford any mistakes, since everyone in the Needle is going to be watching." She ushered the Wielders into a small group. As she looked into each of their faces, she couldn't help feeling a small surge of excitement, almost like what she'd felt when her father had taken her to see the sowing when she was twelve. "Everyone's going to have to have someone in support, someone to leap in if something goes wrong, either to take over your position, or to lend you strength if you begin to flag. I don't know how long it will take to heal the distortion. Marcus will be backing me up. Okata, you and Artras will be anchoring the flow from Erenthrall. We'll be drawing on the reservoir of ley beneath the city there, shunting it to the reservoirs that Jerrain, Hernande, and the other University students will be holding for us here. The rest of you need to keep the crystals locked in position and keep the flows from the other ley lines stable and shunt the ley in the reservoirs to wherever it's needed in Tumbor. Jenner, I'll pair you with Carter. You'll handle the line from the Hollow . . ."

"This is Hernande, one of the surviving mentors from the University, along with Cory, one of his students," Allan said. "You know Marcus, of course. And this is my daughter Morrell and her guardian Drayden, who used to be one of the Wolves."

The Matriarch of the Temerite enclave, now ensconced in the abandoned section of the Needle on the far side of the chasm, tilted her head slightly in acknowledgment of the introductions, her gaze fixed on Morrell and Drayden. "Please have a seat. It is a pleasure to meet you all."

The Temerites had taken control of ten square blocks of what remained of the outer circle of buildings within the broken walls of the Needle. When Allan and his group had arrived, they'd been met by Captain Lienta and Lieutenant Boskell at what had obviously become the outer defense of the Temerites. Rather than using the cracked and crumbling remains of the city wall, they'd secured a section in the city and were using the profusion of stone to wall up the streets and buildings around the enclave, much like what they'd done in Erenthrall, using the chasm as a natural barrier on one side. Lienta had led Allan's group through the streets, the surrounding buildings already being repaired, the windows lit with light from ley globes and lanterns, the mixture of white and flickering yellow strangely soothing. A few of the ley globes near the street flickered or dimmed when Allan came too close. Those Temerites on the streets nodded to Allan respectfully, staring at those with him they didn't recognize. Allan could tell from their expressions that they had not settled in completely, distrustful of those from the Needle. Their postures were guarded, movements tentative, even here within the rooms the Matriarch had claimed.

The building had once been a large mercantile house, the outer chamber's floor cracked white-gray marble flecked with green, the room open to two stories with columns up to the ceiling on both sides of the hall. Not as grand as the larger houses in Erenthrall before the Shattering, but still impressive. The Temerite guards had set up their operations on tables scavenged from the surrounding buildings, between the columns. The Matriarch had taken over the back rooms.

Allan settled into a chair that creaked with age, a pillow on top serving as a cushion. All except Drayden settled in around him in similar seats, the Matriarch situated behind her own table draped with cloth, its top littered with papers, an inkpot, quill, and a small stone serving as a paperweight. She was dressed as Allan had first seen her—the blocked tans and whites of Temer nobility, a few rings, a gold necklace— although during the journey from Erenthrall he had seen her in less formal clothing with vivid blues and greens that spoke of the livelier spirit he now knew lay beneath. Her aide, Janote, stood behind her, Lienta and Boskell taking up positions there as well, while servants appeared carrying trays of small sweet breads or pitchers of water or kaffe with a set of cups. Allan took a kaffe, surprised that the delicate cup had survived the trek from Erenthrall.

The Matriarch waited until they were seated and served, taking a cup of kaffe for herself, before leaning forward onto her desk and meeting Allan's gaze with a penetrating look. "To what do we owe this visit?"

"The formal reason for the visit," Marcus said, taking the lead, "is to see how well you are settling in and whether there is anything more that the Needle can provide."

The Matriarch held Allan's gaze a moment, as if searching for a hidden agenda, but then turned to Marcus, bowing her head slightly. She'd had weeks to get to know Allan, Bryce, and the others, and after the exhausting walk from Erenthrall, she and her people had initially been elated to reach the Needle, but now that they were here and had had a moment to rest, their natural wariness had returned.

"We are settling in nicely, as you no doubt saw while passing through the streets we've claimed as our own here. And the provisions you provided on our arrival have served us well. For the moment, there is nothing more that we require."

"Have you experienced any problems with the ley? The connection with this part of the city is tenuous, due to the shift in the relays caused by the quake and the chasm."

"No, we haven't. We are grateful for what access we do have to the ley, although many are still leery of it. We haven't had reliable use of it since the Shattering. In Erenthrall, we learned . . . not to trust it."

"Understandable. It couldn't be trusted even here until recently."

"Until the distortion over Erenthrall was healed, you mean."

"Yes. The distortion disrupted numerous ley lines integral to the system. It created a blockage that, if left alone, would have caused serious damage to the city and beyond."

"And did you think at all about what the destruction of the distortion in Erenthrall would do to those living there? Did you consider the consequences of your action? It left our enclave vulnerable, gave this Devin and his band of thieves and murderers and cannibals the opening they needed to attack us."

"At the time, the quakes brought on by the ley and the reverberations they caused in the Tapestry were destroying the entirety of the plains. We didn't consider anything except halting it before it destroyed us all."

The two glared at each other for a long, awkward moment, and then the Matriarch snorted and waved a hand. "I suppose we shouldn't argue over your intervention. The distortion had begun to collapse. Although there are some amongst my councillors who believe it was your interference here at the Needle that caused that collapse, that it was not natural."

Behind her, Captain Lienta stirred, gaze cast down to the floor. Lienta had said nothing to Allan on their way here. It must have been kept between himself, the Matriarch, and her closest advisers. The fact that they'd discussed what had happened in Erenthrall and the actions of those at the Needle without him present shouldn't have surprised him, but it did. He thought of all the long conversations he'd had with Lienta and the Matriarch over the course of the march, both together and separately, the pleasant memories now somewhat tainted.

Hernande suddenly leaned forward. "There is some argument about that here as well. It's possible that the collapse was initiated by Lecrucius' use of the Nexus here in defense of the Needle. Or it may have been natural, but untimely. I doubt we will ever know. Yet Kara Tremain did seize control and heal the distortion before it could destroy us. No one doubts that here."

The Matriarch raised her head. "So I hear. I've also heard that she is going to attempt to heal the distortion over Tumbor."

"That is true. We plan on bringing down the distortion in two days. We've already begun preparations in the node. Commander Ty is making a formal announcement about it today to the people of the Needle, along with information about where those who wish to see it can go for a viewing. You and the rest of the Temerites are invited to join Commander Ty and the others on the tiers of the temple beneath the Needle."

"Where will you be?"

"With Kara and the other Wielders in the node. We can't control the

Nexus from afar. We need to be there, in the pit, working the ley and the crystals that control it."

The Matriarch's lips pursed, her attention sliding to Allan. "And you?"

"I can accompany you, if you wish. Along with my daughter."

"Before you make a decision, though, you should be aware that there is some . . . unrest in the Needle," Hernande said.

Marcus frowned in disapproval, but said nothing.

"What kind of unrest?" Lienta asked, stepping forward protectively.

"Allan has already told you that we gained control of the Needle from Father Dalton and his Kormanley—"

"His White Cloaks," Boskell interrupted. "We know of them. They used and abused many of the survivors of the Shattering in Erenthrall, turned us against each other."

"So Allan said. When we took over here, most of those who already lived here didn't care. Kara had saved the Needle from destruction after all. The quakes had quieted, then stopped. Most of the people were content to leave it at that, but not all. There's a group loyal to Dalton that remains. They've been growing in strength and support since Dalton revealed a vision in which the Needle is attacked by two forces— dogs and snakes, one attacking from the north and the other from the south."

The Matriarch shot a glance at Lienta. "We've heard of this prophecy. We've found symbols chalked onto the stone here across the chasm. One of the rooms here in this building had it scrawled across the entirety of the floor, as if it had been used as a meeting place."

"It may have been," Marcus said. "We've had little luck finding out who's behind the group. They've been careful."

"What about Dalton himself?" Lienta asked.

Hernande shook his head. "He has nothing to do with the group, aside from being the focus of their fervor. Since he revealed his prophecy, he's been kept locked inside his rooms in the temple."

"Are you certain? If you don't know his accomplices . . ."

"No, we can't be certain. But Dalton has caused us no problems since being locked away, and Commander Ty has kept a guard on the door at all times. As far as we can tell, no one has visited him or spoken to him since he was secluded there."

"So what have his followers done, then?" the Matriarch asked.

"They've been protesting mostly, demanding that we release him and let him speak. They started a riot in the square before the temple a short time ago, halted by Ty and the enforcers. Since then, support for their group has grown. We're afraid that they'll attempt something similar when we heal Tumbor. It's the perfect opportunity to make themselves heard."

"Like the Kormanley before the Shattering," the Matriarch said.

"Yes. We've noticed the correlation."

The Matriarch said nothing, thinking.

Behind her, Lieutenant Boskell cleared his throat. "We should stay here. Wait. We've only just arrived. We don't know who to trust."

The Matriarch's lips twitched. She looked at Allan, even as she spoke to Marcus. "You said this was the formal part of your visit. Was there something else?"

"I've introduced you to my daughter, Morrell." At her name, Morrell shifted forward in her chair and Drayden stirred in his position near the door. She'd been quiet the entire conversation, but her eyes had never left the Matriarch. "What I didn't mention was that she is a Healer."

The Matriarch's brow creased in confusion, until the slight emphasis he'd put on the last word registered. Then her eyes snapped to Morrell. According to Freesia, Morrell hadn't fully recovered from her experiment repairing the outer wall, but she was strong enough that she couldn't be forced to remain at rest. Allan had been hesitant to bring her, but her obvious restrained enthusiasm now made him regret the protective thought.

"Captain Lienta," the Matriarch said, "I think it's time for us to go for that walk we spoke of before they arrived."

Even though the words were prosaic, Allan had spent enough time with the Matriarch to know that she was rattled. Without waiting for a response, she turned away, pushing back from the table in her wheeled chair, Janote coming forward to help her. Lienta gestured at Boskell, who nodded and departed, headed toward the outer room. Lienta then stepped forward, Allan and Marcus rising.

"Where are we going?" Marcus asked.

"To a balcony overlooking the chasm and the rest of the Needle."

Lienta offered nothing more.

They followed the Matriarch and her assistant out through a side door, passing through a corridor with rooms off to either side before emerging out into late afternoon sunlight in the lee of the old mercantile. Allan shaded his eyes as he glanced toward where the black spire of the Needle glinted, the top of the temple visible above the surrounding buildings. They crossed a street thronged with Temerites, most at work repairing the mercantile or digging out stone from collapsed walls farther down the street, then entered another building, this one an old manse with a small outer courtyard containing unkempt trees and some small brush. Allan wondered why the Matriarch hadn't used this as her residence, until they entered the lower floor and passed into the back rooms, where the entire northern corner of the building had crumbled into a pile of rubble. The southern corner remained intact, a staircase with deep steps leading up to the second floor. They ascended—Janote taking the Matriarch up in the wheeled chair, backward, step by step, Cory and Hernande helping—then headed down a small hall that ended in two double doors opening onto what had once been a grand sitting room with a bedroom off to the right. At the far end of the sitting room, an empty arched opening that had once held glass windows looked out onto a stone balcony. Allan could see the Needle and temple through the window as they approached, but when they stepped out onto the balcony, he realized the building stood near the edge of the chasm. It yawned beneath them, only a street and the stunted walls of half of another building between them and the drop-off.

On the far side of the chasm, the buildings of the outer city before the temple blocked out its base, those on the edge worse off than the manse they were in. Allan could pick out areas where the engineers of the Needle had demolished some walls and fortified others. The ragged edge of the chasm jutted out in one section, close to another section on the Temerite side, the gap narrow in comparison to the rest of the chasm. The sun glared down on the eastern edge, casting the buildings into stark gray angles and shadows, the whiter stone of the temple beyond and the Needle a sharp contrast against the blue sky scudded with clouds. People could be seen in the streets farther from the chasm's edge, and a few were visible on the tiers of the temple— enforcers, Allan presumed, already preparing for the healing of the distortion.

"As you probably guessed by the lieutenant's reaction, not all of my people are as willing to embrace the Needle as their new home as others. The White Cloaks were not welcome in Erenthrall after the Shattering. Their work there was destructive. Without them, we might have been able to rebuild Erenthrall as it was before. Instead, they drove wedges between the people who had survived. And all their actions were associated with the Needle. It's difficult to let those connotations go." She spun her wheeled chair around to face them. "Especially now that you tell me the Kormanley are still active here. Why did you not kill this Dalton as soon as you'd seized control?"

"The people here would have revolted," Marcus said. "He'd saved most of those staying here, offered them refuge, fed them. We needed him alive, to keep control, at least until we'd proven that we could offer the same stability."

"Which we have," Cory said.

"But it hasn't been enough," Marcus added. "That's why the healing of Tumbor's distortion is so important. It will prove that we don't need Dalton or his White Cloaks once and for all."

"And can you do it? Can you repair the distortion around Tumbor?"

"Yes," Cory said. "Kara says she can do it."

Marcus hesitated, but said, "We've made improvements to the Nexus here, made it stronger."

The Matriarch glanced from Marcus to Cory and back again, but turned to Morrell next. "So you're a Healer?"

Morrell stepped forward, confident, one hand reaching out toward the Matriarch. Lienta tensed. But she caught herself and bowed her head, although Allan wasn't convinced she was even aware Lienta was there. "Yes."

"And what exactly does that mean, child?"

"I can heal people. By touching them."

Cory shifted to her side. "It's true. She healed my foot after it was crushed beneath a boulder during one of the quakes. I should have lost my leg, if not my life."

"And she's healed many others besides," Hernande added. "She's even changed some of the Wolves back into their human forms—those that wished it. Drayden here is one of those." The Matriarch considered Drayden, standing back from the others, as Hernande continued. "A few had sunk too deeply into their animal forms, their humanity lost. Those she could not help."

Morrell raised her head again, chin lifted. "I might be able to heal your legs," she said boldly. "If you'll let me touch you, I'll be able to tell."

The Matriarch drew in a shuddering breath, one somehow filled with dread and hope and a deep-seated longing. She exhaled slowly. "Do you know how long I've been in this chair, child? Most of my life. I was twenty when the carriage I was riding in was attacked, the driver killed immediately. The horses panicked and bolted, while the guards held off the attackers. My retainer and I were thrown about the carriage, out of control, until it hit something in the road. We were flung off a ridge, tossed down a steep slope into a ravine. My retainer was killed. I barely survived. When my escort of guards finally found me and pulled me from the wreckage, I discovered I could no longer move my legs." She dropped her gaze to her lap. "They never did find out if it was bandits or an orchestrated attempt on my life by another holding. There was no one left to question."

She looked back up, her hands smoothing out the cloth of her dress. "The point being, child, that I've lived thirty-three years without the use of my legs. I've grown used to living without them. I'm not certain I'd remember how to use them even if you could heal them."

"So you don't even want me to check?" Disappointment tinged Morrell's voice, along with confusion.

"Not right now. I'll need time to think about it. It's . . . it's a big decision."

Morrell nodded as if she understood, although it was clear she didn't. She turned stunned, hurt eyes on Allan. He reached out and drew her close, kissed her forehead. "Don't fret," he said quietly. "You rattled her. She needs time to adjust."

The Matriarch had turned back to Marcus and Hernande. "As for the ceremony you have planned, I believe that the Temerites need to show our thanks for the help in escaping Erenthrall and the refuge you've provided here at the Needle. I will attend." When Lienta began to protest, she raised her hand to forestall him. "Along with a contingent of my guards, including Lienta and Boskell. And Janote, of course. We would appreciate your company, mentor, and your student, as well as you and your daughter, Allan."

Hernande bowed respectfully. "Cory and I would be delighted. Unfortunately, we'll be needed in the node with the Wielders, to help with the ley."

"Morrell and I would enjoy the company, as long as you bring along some of your kaffe."

The Matriarch laughed. "When you first drank of it on our journey here, you despised it."

"As you said then, it is an acquired taste. I appear to have acquired it."

"I see. Janote, make note of it."

Marcus and the rest turned to leave, ushered out by Lienta's guards.

Lienta stood next to the Matriarch on the balcony as they watched Allan, Marcus, and the others go. When they were safely out of hearing, he murmured, "I'm surprised, Matriarch."

"That I would attend the ceremony? Why would I not? I thought you agreed with me that an alliance with Commander Ty and Kara Tremain would be beneficial. Although I admit I hesitated upon hearing that the Kormanley were still active."

"I meant I was surprised you declined the girl's offer."

"Ah." The Matriarch remained silent a long moment, her hands fidgeting with her dress, but finally she sighed. "I gave up on ever having the use of legs again more than thirty years ago. The claim that she could heal me—" Her voice cracked and she raised a trembling hand to her face, shielding herself from them before forcing herself to continue. "It came as a shock."

Janote stirred. "As you said, you haven't had use of your legs for decades. I doubt you'd be dancing a sailor's jig any time soon."

The Matriarch barked an unsteady laugh. "Like in my wild younger days, before my marriage and slow submersion into politics? No, I'm certain it would be a struggle. Everything in life is."

"So you'll consider it, then?"

The Matriarch sobered. "I'll consider it. But it's not a decision to be made lightly. There's too much hope and fear involved."

"Have you found someplace to hide the package yet?"

Marc's cheek twitched, the only outward sign that Armone had startled him. "Not yet."

He turned from his perusal of the activities surrounding the large square beneath and on the first tier of the temple. Servants were scrubbing the stone, the mosaic with the central sun coming to startling life with vivid blues and greens that had been dulled by a coat of dirt and grit since their arrival. Others were hanging banners and folds of cloth from the tier's edge, while yet others brought out tables that would eventually hold food and drink. A few chairs had been arranged in strategic locations, but the majority of the people allowed onto this tier would have to stand.

The snap of cloth drew his attention upward, where the second tier—never before used—was getting similar treatment. He scanned all the enforcers and guardsmen he could see, hoping to spot Cutter or someone else he knew and trusted, but saw no one. He bit back a curse.

He was running out of time.

At his side, Armone scanned as well, but for a wholly different purpose. "Darius says the package will be small, no larger than a standard satchel, but it's more effective in a confined space. You'll need to hide it behind or beneath something, preferably something solid that will crack or shatter or burn and cause more confusion and damage."

"I don't see many options here on the tier. It's flat and open."

"I agree. Are you certain you'll be posted here during the Wielders' attempt?"

"That's what I've been told."

"Then it will have to be placed here somewhere."

"Why?" At Armone's look, he shrugged. "Anyone of consequence, such as Ty or the Temerites, will be up on the second tier, where the view of the distortion is better. The only people down here will be citizens. Why place anything here at all?"

"Because it will cause more panic, more chaos." Armone's gaze hardened. "You aren't wavering, are you? I gave Darius my word about you."

"I'm not wavering."

"Good." Armone turned back to the tier. They'd wandered from one edge of the mosaic to the other and now walked back, as if on patrol. The servants paid them no attention. "Remember that it will be packed with people during the attempt, so it won't be this open. You could simply drop the satchel in the center of the crowd and walk away. That worked well in Erenthrall."

Marc's stomach turned, an image of the butchered stockade village near Tumbor flashing across his mind.

He needed to warn Cutter or Ty. But Armone or one of the other

Kormanley enforcers had been in constant contact with him, if not actively working with him like Armone now, always within sight in the barracks or on the wall. The twin Javers had even followed him to the taverns the night before, although Marc didn't think Javers knew he'd been noticed. And he couldn't trust any of his fellow enforcers. He didn't know who else besides those he'd seen at the last meeting were with the Kormanley, but he knew there were others.

He hadn't been worried until today.

"I'll do that if necessary," he said, "but hopefully another opportunity will present itself."

Armone considered him a moment, then slapped him on the back and grinned—the easy, carefree grin he usually wore that set people at ease and hid the danger beneath. "Trust me, it always does."

"How many packages are there anyway?"

"Enough to take back the Needle and free Father."

They'd reached the stairs leading down from the tier and began to descend. Marc flung a last look back and cursed beneath his breath.

Where in hells was Cutter?

⌐⌐⌐

"Now, Cory, hold the reservoir." Hernande turned to Kara without waiting for a response. "Start siphoning ley from the node into the reservoir."

"Are you certain this is going to work?"

"Of course not, but I don't see any reason it won't work."

"It's just . . . the reservoir is here, inside the node. If it doesn't hold the ley, or if Cory loses control, it could drop the ley onto all of us."

Behind Kara, Hernande noticed Okata, Jenner, and the rest of the Wielders glancing toward the ceiling, where the reservoir Cory had created hovered, although they couldn't see anything there. The folds of Tapestry were only visible when they were filled with ley.

A few of the Wielders backed off a step or two.

"It won't drop onto us. I'm here as a failsafe, ready to intervene if it appears Cory can't handle it. But our theory is that the ley will cause little to no strain on us, unlike holding up, say, a person or something else more physically solid."

"But that's only a theory. We haven't tested it yet."

"We're testing it now."

Kara mumbled something under her breath that Hernande couldn't quite catch, but she turned to her Wielders. "Okata, you can sense the reservoir?"

"And the channel leading to it."

"Then I'll let you control the flow. Start off slow, see how the reservoir reacts. Everyone else, keep your eye on the crystal panes. We don't expect them to react, but I'm not certain of any of this. Be prepared for anything."

The Wielders shifted into position around the pit of the node, most of them focusing on the panes and the ley that fountained up from below. Okata drifted closer to Cory, his Gorrani visage concentrating on the air overhead, where Hernande could see the folds Cory had used to create a narrow conduit from the ley pit to a much larger circular construct that resembled the basin of a fountain. He raised his arms and closed his eyes and a moment later a plume of ley arched up from the pit and spilled down onto the conduit. Some of it splashed over the sides, the plume too large for the conduit to hold, but most of it began coursing down the conduit toward the basin. Within moments, the bottom of the reservoir had been filled, its contours now clearly visible.

Kara took a step forward. "Can you hold it, Cory?"

"I'm fine. As we suspected, the ley feels almost weightless. It's nothing like when we were holding up sand during our practice sessions."

"Then increase the flow, Okata. Let's see how much we can hold in this reservoir, and see how easy it is to siphon off again, before we get too excited. Let Okata know the moment you think there's too much ley, Cory."

Cory waved a hand in irritation. A moment later, the plume of ley increased in strength under Okata's administrations, although it narrowed so that there was no spillage as it hit the conduit. Looking at the configuration now, Hernande thought they could dispense with the conduit completely and simply pour the ley directly into the reservoir, but at the time they hadn't known how this would work. Or even if.

He found himself stroking his beard, but halted when Kara turned to him.

"You have that look, Hernande."

His eyebrows rose. "What look?"

"That smug look, as if you've just discovered fire."

"Ah, I see. Well, there's been a small bone of contention between myself, Jerrain, and Sovaan about the relationship between the ley and the Tapestry. What Cory experienced here today confirms that the theory proposed by Jerrain and myself is valid, while Sovaan's is not."

"And what theory is that?"

Around them, the node had grown appreciably brighter as more and more ley filled the reservoir. It was now a rather large pool of white light floating in midair, perhaps ten feet deep with a radius of twenty feet. Cory had expanded the basin's size to accommodate more of the ley.

"Jerrain and I have proposed that the ley and the Tapestry are linked, that in fact the Tapestry relies on the ley for its existence. We believe that the natural ley lines that thread their way around and through the land are in fact the foundations of reality, a skeletal structure upon which the Tapestry—reality—has been hung. When the nodes in Erenthrall were captured within the distortion, it severed many of the supports of this foundation, which sent shudders through reality. These manifested as quakes. Enough ley lines remained that the Tapestry could still sustain itself, but it had been strained by the lack of support. When the distortion quickened over Tumbor, cutting off even more supports, a ripple emanated through reality. All of us mentors and some of our students felt it in the Hollow. Unlike the quakes, which were localized along the ley lines, this ripple coursed through the entire system—both the ley lines and the Tapestry. It was as if someone had grabbed reality and given it a good shake, like snapping a rug to rid it of dust and dirt."

"And how does what Cory's doing here prove your theory?"

"Oh, it doesn't prove anything. But it does support it. In order for our theory to be correct, a necessary condition is that the Tapestry and the ley be . . . compatible. The ley being nearly weightless when supported by the Tapestry, and vice versa, indicates they are compatible at some fundamental level. Of course, this was suggested by how the mentors used the Tapestry to channel the ley for the Wielders in Erenthrall."

"It would be helpful if you knew how to fix these reservoirs into position without having a mentor holding it up."

"Yes, well, we haven't quite worked that out yet."

Kara was silent for a moment. Then: "If what you're saying is true, then when Prime Wielder Augustus created the Nexus in Erenthrall and shifted the nearest ley lines to that central location—"

"He was manipulating the foundations of reality. I doubt he realized it at the time, perhaps not even at the end. I'd guess that nothing came of his manipulations because he merely shifted existing ley lines slightly off course, from natural nodes in Erenthrall to his Nexus."

"Except something did come of it." Kara's voice had hardened. "His actions caused the blackouts and distortions in Erenthrall, if not the Shattering itself."

"Yes. The strain on the Tapestry for such minor shifts would have been subtle and obviously didn't start becoming apparent until the blackouts and distortions began. Augustus most likely never realized there was a connection between the ley and the Tapestry, which is why he could never determine what was causing the blackouts or distortions. The damage was being done to the Tapestry, even if the root cause was the shifts in the ley. Only the mentors from the University would have been able to identify the problem, and the rivalry between the Wielders and the University would have kept Augustus from seeking our help."

"His own need for complete control of the ley would have done that, even without the rivalry."

"I suppose. He was an arrogant bastard."

Before them, Cory suddenly waved a hand toward Okata. "That's enough. I can't expand the reservoir any further in here."

The plume of ley suddenly halted, dropping back down into the pit. Kara broke away, calling out to the other Wielders, confirming that the crystal panes hadn't shifted at all during the transference. Hernande stepped up to Cory's side, eyes raised to the white light hovering overhead. He inspected the folds of Tapestry holding it aloft unobtrusively, noting that if he stretched, he might be able to touch the bottom of the reservoir. Cory and Okata had nearly filled the entire pit with it.

"How much strain are you under?" he asked as he walked in a wide circle around the reservoir's edge.

"It's negligible, although I think the longer it needs to be held, the harder holding the reservoir will become, sort of like holding a weight with an outstretched arm at shoulder height. At first, it's easy, but the longer you hold it, the weaker your arm muscles become. They burn out."

He locked eyes with Cory, noted a small bead of sweat near Cory's temple. "How long do you think you can hold something like this?"

"Hours, perhaps even a day if necessary."

"Don't forget, this reservoir is small, merely a test run. For our attempt at healing the distortion, we'll need multiple reservoirs at least three times this size."

"We're ready to attempt siphoning the ley from the reservoir."

Both Cory and Hernande turned toward Kara. "Then go ahead and start," Cory said.

Kara glanced upward, Okata doing the same on the far side of the reservoir and conduit. Ley began streaming back toward the ley pit, much faster than it had left, and much more tightly controlled with Kara's help. Instead of a plume, it shot outward and down, straight and true, like the ley lines in Erenthrall. In less than half the time it had taken to fill, the reservoir lay empty.

"Congratulations," Kara said as the Wielders behind her relaxed into grins, a few patting each other on the back. "We may be able to heal Tumbor tomorrow after all."

Twelve

MARC STOOD TO ONE SIDE of the main door leading into the temple on the first tier. It was midmorning, clouds scudding across the sky overhead providing some scattered partial shade, but otherwise already hot. He wiped sweat from his forehead, thankful for the breeze that snapped in the banners strewn in intervals around the temple's edge. The tier was already crowded, people from the city below milling about, jostling for the best view of the distortion over Tumbor in the distance, conversations and laughter roiling all around. Marc could see the distortion's apex over the people's heads, hazy with distance, although its orange-pink-purple colors were still vibrant. He was certain, with the heat, that its base would be a shimmer of heat waves.

But his attention was focused on the stairs, where people were still ascending, even though there couldn't possibly be much room left on this tier. He searched for Cutter or Ty, knowing at least Ty would be up on the second tier, but he still hadn't seen either of them. This would be his last chance to warn them of the Kormanley's intent, perhaps his only chance, since he was supposed to plant the package himself and then leave discreetly before it exploded. He didn't know how Armone and the others planned on timing the explosions so they occurred at the same time, and he didn't care. All he wanted to do was warn everyone before it happened, and today would be the first day he'd be left alone.

On the stairs, a contingent of the new Temerites arrived, escorting their Matriarch up to the second tier. Her guards were vigilant, the captain leading the way, two others pulling the Matriarch's wheeled chair up one step at a time. Behind her, the ex-Dog Allan and his daughter were unobtrusively keeping her chair stable while conversing with her. Marc took an involuntary step toward Allan, thinking to warn him instead, but he was surrounded by the Temerite guard. They'd never let him in close enough to speak to him, not without drawing attention.

He stepped back beside the door and a hand clapped down onto his shoulder.

His blade was half drawn before Armone said, "Marc, where were you headed, my boy?"

The Kormanley guardsman slipped up to Marc's side, eyes on the Matriarch and her entourage as they continued their ascent to the second tier. He didn't drop his hand from Marc's shoulder, and he had a satchel slung across his chest.

"Nowhere," Marc said, surprised his voice held steady. The center of his back had prickled with nervous sweat. "For a moment, it looked like the old woman's chair was going to slip."

"Now that would be unfortunate, wouldn't it? Especially since we have something special planned for her and her Temerite guards."

Marc shrugged out from beneath Armone's arm. "Is that the package?"

Suspicion flickered across Armone's face, but he grinned and patted the satchel. "The very one."

"What do I have to do, besides place it?"

"Nothing. In fact, it turns out you don't even need to place it yourself. I managed to fit my package into a niche where no one will find it, which means I can stay here with you. Once we get the signal from the main gates, I'll pull the fuse and drop it. Then we'd better run like hell, because it's set to explode within ten breaths, maybe less. It's hard to be precise with these things."

For a moment, Marc couldn't breathe. He'd intended to hunt Cutter or Ty down the moment Armone left him alone with the package. Now . . .

"You're saying you don't need me?"

"Oh, we'll need you afterward, for when the real fighting begins. The packages are only to cause confusion. We'll have to take the enforcers still loyal to Ty and secure the temple after that."

"Then perhaps I should find a better location, to help with that. Maybe the commander's barracks in the temple or one of the temple doorways." Marc had half turned toward the entrance into the temple when Armone snagged his arm.

"I don't think so." The words were hard as crystal, even though Armone's grin hadn't faltered. "Darius has the barracks covered, as well as the main gates and entrances and Father's chambers. Everything's in place. You're needed here, in case something goes wrong on one of the tiers."

Marc considered breaking free and charging into the temple, but Armone's grip was tight, enough to cut off the circulation. His forearm was already tingling. He forced himself to relax and shrug. "All right, if you're certain I won't be needed elsewhere."

Armone hesitated a moment, then let him go. "Where were you planning on setting the package?"

"I thought I'd place it in the center of the sun emblem in the mosaic. I thought it somehow fitting. Plus, it should target the largest number of people."

"I don't see anything better. Let's head over there."

Armone gave him a nudge, indicating he should take the lead. With a last glance back toward the stairs on the outside of the temple, Marc began pushing through the throng toward the center of the mosaic, Armone on his heels. As he moved, he released the clasp on the small knife at his side.

"When does this attempt to heal the distortion start?" he asked.

"I heard around noon," Armone answered. "Our own little distraction should start soon after that."

Marc glanced toward the sun overhead. A little over an hour left. He swore silently to himself.

A sudden murmur ran through the crowd, someone shouting, "Look! Over the chasm!"

Everyone's attention shifted from the distortion to the southeast toward the west. Most of the chasm that had divided the city was obscured by the temple itself, but above what could be seen, a large pool of ley had begun to form. It appeared to be hovering in midair. Shifting to the right, Marc could see a large geyser of ley rising out of the chasm, splashing down into one edge of the growing pool. The excitement of those around them escalated, the level of conversation increasing. Someone at the far end of this side of the temple, near the corner, shouted, "There's another pool forming on the other side!"

"It's like Erenthrall all over again," Marc muttered.

"What's happening?" Armone demanded. He was too short to see over the rest of the people.

"The Wielders are using the ley, forming some kind of pool of it over the chasm."

For the first time in the past three days of dealing with Armone and the others, he saw a thread of uncertainty pass over the Kormanley's face. They hadn't known about the pools of ley, even with Dierdre's connection to Marcus. What else did they not know? What else had they not anticipated?

Armone's uncertainty didn't last. "It must be something they need for the healing," he said. "It doesn't affect our plans. Come on."

They headed back toward the center of the tier, fighting against the crowd now as everyone tried to push toward a better view of the chasm behind them. Mothers were hoisting their children up onto hips, fathers positioning them on shoulders so they could see. Everyone's eyes were wide with awe, all of them babbling about the Wielders, Erenthrall, and distortions. The air vibrated with hope.

Marc's gaze dropped from their faces toward the satchel Armone carried against his hip.

Reaching down, he drew his knife. He was out of time.

"How are the reservoirs holding?" Hernande shouted over the tumult in the pit. Wielders were scattered around the node, most of them channeling the ley out through the ley line that had been severed by the chasm and up into the reservoirs Jerrain and Sovaan were holding in place outside. Each mentor had one or two of the students with them for support. Marcus, Okata, Artras, Dylan, Jenner, and two others were holding the crystals in place. Kara paced back and forth between them all, listening to their comments as they manipulated the ley, pulling it from Erenthrall and storing it here at the Needle. Hernande watched her, noted the sweat that had plastered her hair to her forehead and the way her hands twitched.

When she passed by, he touched her arm to catch her attention. She flinched away from him. "What?"

"How are the reservoirs holding?" he repeated.

She closed her eyes and he could almost feel her reaching out toward the chasm through the ley. "They're fine," she said, opening her eyes again. "But we're going to need more power."

"Cory is ready. He can create a third reservoir if you think you'll need it."

"Do it."

He turned to pass the order on to one of their runners, but Kara halted him.

"Even with a third reservoir, I don't think we'll have enough power, Hernande."

"Then what do you suggest?"

Kara ground the heels of her hands into her eyes, then scrubbed at her face, glancing toward the crystals before she met his gaze. "We need to use a different configuration for the crystals."

"I assume it's one that's not naturally stable."

"No, it's not. We won't be able to hold it for as long as I'll need to heal Tumbor on our own."

"And we haven't figured out how to tie off our manipulations of the Tapestry to make them permanent, at least not for something of this magnitude." Hernande stared toward where the Wielders were keeping the crystals in position. He chewed on his lower lip before turning back to Kara. "I'd intended to help Cory and the others with the reservoirs, but I can stay here and hold the crystals in position with the Tapestry."

"Are you certain? What if you can't maintain their position for as long as I need it? I don't know how long this will take."

"I'll hold it as long as necessary."

"Then we'd better inform Marcus and the others. It will take a few moments to shift the crystals into their new position. But we'll wait until the reservoirs are full. I don't want to interrupt their preparations."

"I'll begin my own preparations. And send someone to warn the other mentors that I will not be joining them."

He turned to the runner, passing the messages along, then found a position near the edge of the ley pit, but far enough away that he'd be out of the Wielders' path. Sitting cross-legged, he began drawing in deep breaths, letting them out slow and steady, his eyes focused on the crystals where they hung suspended above the ley, refracting and refining its power, although with each breath he drew himself deeper inside himself, his body growing still. He hadn't performed the meditations of his training as an oransai since he'd fled Barakaldo and the Demesnes, at least not at such depths. But to control the crystals for such a length of time, he'd need to be completely centered, completely at peace. Nothing could disturb him.

The shouts and tension of the Wielders surrounding him faded and vanished, not even there as background noise. The sound of his heartbeat intervened and he consciously slowed it, synching it up with his breathing. Breathe in, breathe out, slow and steady, until even this faded, subsumed by silence. As his heart slowed, so did the world, the motions of Kara and the others becoming languid and fluid.

Without realizing it, he closed his eyes, although he could still sense the Wielders as they shifted position. Kara oversaw it all, her presence somehow more solid in this mental state, more vibrant. Through what the oransai called the Third Eye, he saw her approach, heard her say, "We're ready," even though the words were flattened and distant.

"Then begin."

She spun away. Through the Third Eye, he saw the ley surge upward as the crystals pivoted on multiple axes, settling into new positions. The tension between them vibrated through the foundations of Hernande's calmed state, but he reached out and plied the Tapestry, setting them against those tensions. Unlike the relatively simple folds used to obscure the cave entrances of the Hollower's retreat during the raid, however, when he attempted to tie the folds into place, that tension tugged at the knots, loosened, and undid them.

Resigned, he sank deeper into his meditation. "Do what you need to do now, Kara. I cannot hold the crystals indefinitely."

He didn't hear Kara's response—it was lost, like the noise of the Wielders and the thrum of his own heart—but he did sense the sudden release of the ley as she began to channel it toward Tumbor.

⁓

In a room that overlooked the Needle and the stellae that surrounded it, Irmona felt the surge in the ley as she knelt next to Iscivius' bed. She glanced out the opening that served as a window, to where the thin black spire of the Needle now pulsed with veins of blazing white ley light. It had never done that before, not on its exterior.

"They must be using one of their new configurations," she said to the empty air, before turning back to her brother's comatose body. "A configuration which wouldn't have been possible without your sacrifice."

She reached forward and laid her hand against her brother's cheek. Stubble pricked her skin—he hadn't been shaved in three days—but she gripped his chin, pinching tight.

"Are you in there, brother? Wake up, you bastard. Wake up!" She shook him, then released and struck his face, the sound of the slap sharp in the small space. Iscivius remained immobile, chest rising and falling with a slow, steady rhythm, as if he were in a trance.

Irmona jerked upright and swore. "You're going to leave this all up to me, aren't you?" Her hands closed into fists and she shot another glance toward the black tower. "Bastard."

Outside, someone cried out in surprise and a body thudded hard into the door. It rattled as something slid down it, a thread of blood snaking from beneath it and into the room. The lock clicked and it jerked open, the body of an enforcer with a slit throat tumbling to the floor.

Irmona glanced up at the black-haired woman who stood in the entrance with a small curved, bloodied blade. "Dierdre."

"Is he awake?" She flicked the blade toward Iscivius.

"Of course not."

"Then we'll have to do this on our own."

Irmona moved toward the door. "Is it just you?"

"Darius didn't have the men to spare."

Irmona stepped over the body into the hall, where another enforcer lay sprawled. "Only two guards?"

"They didn't consider you or Iscivius much of a threat. And the enforcers—those they can trust—are spread a little thin with practically the entire city on the walls or the sides of the temple."

"What about Father?"

"Darius is going to free Father himself, as soon as he takes care of Ty. But that won't start until Kara and the Wielders begin healing Tumbor."

They burst through a door onto the second tier of the temple, a roar from the hundreds of people gathered there and the tier below bringing them up short. Irmona shaded her eyes from the bright sunlight with one hand, her vision clearing to reveal the tier packed with enforcers, merchants, and citizens, all with their eyes locked on the distortion of Tumbor or the chasm behind. Huge vats of ley hovered over the chasm, three in all, the light pulsing so brightly it appeared to have a blue tinge to it. The fountains of ley that had filled the vats were beginning to fall away, the cheer from those gathered dying down, turning into a cacophony of babble.

Dierdre snagged Irmona's forearm and hauled her to the stairs, weaving through the crowd with slightly hunched shoulders, keeping them clear of any of the enforcers. Irmona spotted Ty, standing near the ex-Dog Allan and a small entourage of Temerites. She halted, had taken a step toward the betrayer, but Dierdre jerked her off balance and down another few steps, until the commander slipped from view.

"We don't have time!" Dierdre shouted.

"But—"

"Darius will deal with him."

Everyone's attention was shifting exclusively toward Tumbor now, or the pulsing of the Needle above them. They stumbled past two enforcers, necks craned back to see where the tip of the spire glowed a feral pinpoint white, like a second sun. As they reached the first tier, an altercation broke out near the center of those gathered, an enforcer roaring in pain and grappling with another, both snatching at a satchel, but Dierdre didn't pay any attention to them, dragging Irmona down the second set of steps, where the number of people thinned, the vantage not as good as up above. They flew down the last few steps and dodged into a set of doors at ground level.

"Hey! You can't be in here!" one of the guards inside the entrance yelled, stepping forward, his sword already drawn and streaked with blood. Four others rose from where they were shifting a body to one side.

Dierdre flashed a hand signal. "Like hells we can't. We've got our own business in the temple." She waved toward the stack of dead enforcers against one wall. "Is this entrance secure?"

The guard stood up straighter, dropping the tip of his blade to the floor. "Ty's men here have been taken care of. I've sent a few of our own men to check on the other entrances."

"Good. Make certain no one gets past you at this level."

The men pressed their backs to the corridor wall as Dierdre and Irmona passed them, then continued moving the bodies. There were two others farther down the hall, cut down from behind. Then they were jogging through mostly deserted hallways, all the enforcers and servants who lived in this section up on the walls or at the temple. Even those in the kitchen were sparse, too busy preparing for the feast after the healing to notice the two as they ran by. Irmona's chest began to hurt as they broke through the door into the stellae garden.

As soon as her feet touched the sand outside, she gasped. "Kara's already started. The ley's flowing toward Tumbor."

"Then we'd better get down to the pit." Dierdre started forward, her blade hidden behind her back as she stepped toward the Needle's entrance across the sand. A figure shifted out of the shadow of the Needle's doorway, an enforcer, one of Ty's.

"What are you doing here?" the woman asked.

"Kara asked me to bring all of the Wielders to the Needle immediately," Dierdre said. "She's going to need all the help she can get. I went to fetch Irmona."

Irmona caught the smile plastered onto Dierdre's face and the uncertainty on the woman enforcer's a moment before Dierdre stabbed her blade into the enforcer's throat.

At the same time, something exploded, the sound muffled by the temple.

∼

Sweat slicked the handle of Marc's knife as he slid up behind Armone and pressed it into the Kormanley's side. Armone stiffened and halted. They were crammed in between a group of shepherds, a family of five, and a man that smelled like a butcher near the center of the tier's mosaic. No one noticed them, most stepping around them in annoyance, straining to see either the pools of ley over the chasm or the distortion over Tumbor.

"What are you doing?" Armone's tone was light and calm.

"I'm going to take the satchel now," Marc said.

"I told you, I can place it."

"Hand it over." Marc pressed the knife harder into Armone's side, felt it slit through cloth and nick flesh. Armone hissed and twisted to face him.

"You want the satchel? Then here, take it." He lifted the strap of the satchel over his head and thrust it toward Marc, shoving him back into the shepherds behind him.

"Watch it!" one of the shepherds snapped.

Marc ignored him and clutched the weight of the satchel—heavier than he'd expected—to his chest. He didn't see Armone draw his own knife, but he felt it as it sank into his side.

He roared at the pain, slashed toward Armone as the Kormanley follower snatched at the satchel. Marc yanked it back toward him, the two circling each other as those around them began shouting and backing off.

"So Darius was right about you," Armone said as he jerked at the satchel. "He sent me here to make certain you followed through. I guess his instincts were right."

Marc didn't respond, his eyes locked on Armone's as he edged them both away from the center of the tier. Armone lunged, but Marc twisted the satchel between them, blocking his blade. Both men had a firm grip. He heard shouts from the other enforcers, but none of them were close. Someone was fighting their way there, but the crowd had become a crush of bodies pressing away from them.

"Not going to talk?" Armone asked. "Then I guess we'll have to start this early."

Reaching forward with his knife hand, he grabbed a loose strap that threaded into the satchel and yanked it free. Then he thrust the entire package at Marc and ran.

Marc stumbled backward, falling to one knee, a chill washing down his body from head to toe, tingling in his hands and toes. He lurched back to his feet, noted Armone surging away through the throng, fellow enforcers still struggling toward him, all of them too far away. The satchel felt hot in his grip, but he pulled it in tight and spun, bellowing, "Out of my way!" as he charged toward the edge of the tier. People screamed or gasped, but most of them attempted to clear a path. At the last moment, he tripped over someone's foot and fell against the stone edge of the tier between two of the animal statues that lined the open space. Pain flared up from the stab wound, but he flung the satchel over the side of the tier and collapsed against the nearest statue, a fox. Sweat flushed his body and blood coated his side. He pressed his free hand against the wound and shoved himself away from the statue, headed back toward the stairs. He didn't see Armone anywhere, so he cut toward the enforcers.

Three of them broke through the crowd, the one in the lead halting Marc with a grip on his shoulder that sent a dagger of pain into his arm.

"What in hells is happening here?" the lieutenant asked.

"It's the Kormanley." He couldn't seem to catch his breath. "They're planning an attack on the temple. It's probably already started. They've got bombs planted everywhere."

"Kormanley? Bombs?"

An explosion rocked the temple, felt through the stone at Marc's feet, the sound deafening. Everyone on the tier staggered, a plume of stone dust and debris jetting out from the side of the temple into the square below. Screams erupted from the tier, with men, women, and families staring around in confusion and clutching each other or cowering low to the ground. Marc stumbled toward the side of the tier, ears ringing, side aching, the hand holding his wound now coated in blood. The enforcers joined him. Those who were situated on the outer walls for the healing were pointing toward the side of the temple.

Marc leaned over the side, between an urn and a statue, the lieutenant beside him. Halfway down the slope of the temple, a hole gaped in the stone wall, debris still rolling down its side, the cloud of dust drifting off in the breeze.

"Bombs," Marc said, his voice sounding hollow. "Like that one."

The lieutenant reared back from the wall. "How many—"

And then the point of a sword emerged from his chest. He arched back, mouth agape, as the enforcer behind him said, "Sorry, Karl. You should have sided with Darius."

He withdrew the blade, shoving the lieutenant's body aside, as the other enforcer stepped around toward Marc. Behind them, fresh screams broke out, and Marc swore.

Dodging the enforcer's thrust, not even attempting to strike back, Marc threw himself into the surrounding crowd, heading toward the doorway into the temple at first, until he saw movement inside. Without pause, he veered right, toward the stairs again, the enforcers behind shouting toward those that emerged from the doorway. Sounds were still muted, but his hearing was returning.

When he reached the stairs, the world swayed as a wave of lightheadedness washed through him. He glanced back to see the enforcers converging on his position, and far beyond them, across the plains, the distortion over Tumbor suddenly lit up in a brilliant coruscation of white ley light, like the burning sun. He tore his gaze away and scrambled up the steps toward the second tier, shoving people aside. Someone shouted farther below him—more enforcers—but he didn't pause. He could see others looking down from the second tier, picked out Ty and Allan Garrett. Ty pulled back, yelling orders Marc couldn't make out. Allan stared down at him a moment longer, then retreated.

Marc dragged himself up the last few steps to the second tier, his energy flagging. He didn't know if it was because of the steepness of the stairs or blood loss. A group of enforcers pulled him up onto the tier but didn't let go, their handholds tight. Marc sagged into the support. Ty approached with Allan at his back, the commander's face lined with anger.

But before they reached him, Cutter shoved his way through those that held him.

"Marc, you're bleeding. What's going on?"

Marc snatched at Cutter's shirt, drew him in closer, the enforcers protesting. "It's the Kormanley. They're going to try to take over the Needle today, while the Wielders heal the distortion. They've got bombs everywhere. You have to get everyone off the tiers!"

"Is what he's saying true?" Ty had arrived, with Allan. "Can we trust him?"

Cutter hesitated, but only for a breath. "He was part of my patrol near Tumbor. We can trust him."

Ty waved the enforcers holding Marc off and he sagged into Cutter, unable to suppress a moan. Ty noticed the blood. "You're wounded. Who did this? What was that explosion?"

"One of them stabbed me when I tried to take the bomb from him. He armed the bomb before he fled, so I threw it over the side of the temple. Otherwise it would have exploded in the middle of the first tier." Allan shouted something, gesturing for someone to come closer. "They've got more bombs spread out on the temple and the walls."

"They who?"

"The Kormanley."

"I need names."

"Darius is behind it all, with Dierdre. They have multiple people in the enforcers—Trenton, Cerena, Armone."

Ty cut him off. He glanced around at the enforcers closest to them. "We need to get the Matriarch off the tier. She'll be a target."

"So will Kara and the rest of the Wielders who weren't originally White Cloaks, and the mentors from the University," Allan said. His hands rested on his daughter's shoulders. The young girl—young woman—dropped to her knees at Marc's side the moment she saw the blood, one hand reaching to clasp his own, the one pressing hard onto his wound. Marc gasped, but she glanced up and met his gaze.

"Don't struggle. Everything will be fine."

And then his skin prickled and a strange, calming warmth flooded through his side and abdomen. Vibrant blue-gold-purple light shimmered around the girl's hands, fading a few heartbeats later. The warmth in his gut seeped away, taking with it most of the pain but leaving behind a heavy lethargy.

"You're . . . the Healer," he managed.

She stood. "The wound was deep, and you've lost a lot of blood. You should rest."

"I don't think that's an option right now."

"No, it's not." Marc glanced up at the newcomer, one of the Temerites, a captain, standing to one side of Ty, Allan on the other. "We need to remove the Matriarch from the tier."

"Who can we trust?" Allan asked.

"Most of the enforcers on the first tier were with Darius," Marc said. "They killed the few I saw loyal to Ty."

All three looked down toward the first tier. "They aren't charging up here yet."

"They're waiting for the signal."

"What signal?"

"The explosives."

All three shared a look. "We'll have to take the Matriarch through the temple," the Temerite captain said. "We can't navigate the stairs here with her chair easily."

"I'll assume Darius has already begun securing the temple itself," Ty said. "Which means we'll get no support from the few men I left inside. And I'll need all of my enforcers here on the second tier to guard your retreat." He turned to Allan. "Who else can we trust?"

"Grant and the Wolves. They're still inside the temple, in the section they chose as their den. None of them were interested in the healing, and they don't like crowds."

"Good. Take the Matriarch and the Temerites and find the Wolves. Then get the hells out of the temple before Darius secures it completely. See if you can get Kara, the Wielders, and the mentors out as well."

The Temerite captain was already moving, the entire second tier suddenly in turmoil. The Healer hauled Marc's bloody arm over her shoulder and with Cutter's help, dragged him toward the entrance to the temple, another man who'd obviously once been a Wolf leading the way. The enforcers there were herding the Temerite guards through, Allan in the lead. The Temerite captain and the Matriarch were next, followed by her aide and more Temerite guards.

Cutter stepped forward with Marc and the Healer, but Ty halted them, squeezing Marc's shoulder. "Thank you for the warning." Then he motioned them after the ex-Wolf.

As they entered the doorway, the atonal bell at the main gates began to clang, the sound echoing oddly in the corridor behind them. Cutter and the Healer paused, looking back.

"That must be the signal," Marc said.

A few seconds later, a series of explosions shook the entire temple.

Kara gathered all the flows of ley—from Erenthrall, Farrade, and the Northern Reaches—through the crystals in their new configuration, amplifying its power and then channeling it down the tunnel leading to Tumbor. She traveled with it, vaguely aware as she passed out through the pit that something had happened at the Needle. It had sounded like a muffled explosion. Marcus said something she didn't catch, but she shrugged it aside as she focused on the ley. Hernande had warned her there was limited time. She needed to be as efficient as possible, and with the added crystal and the new configuration, the ley surged on the edges of her control. One small slip and it would break free.

And she hadn't even tapped into the reservoirs held by the mentors yet.

She felt the distortion of Tumbor long before she reached it, its presence more of a gaping absence of ley, where she should be able to sense some. A wound on the world, on reality, it loomed before her as she rode toward it.

Then the ley hit it, its shards slicing down through the ley's tunnel like a blade, severing the link between the Needle and Tumbor's center. The entire structure vibrated and for a moment Kara thought it would collapse with that slight disturbance. But the distortion held, the ley splashing out around the resistance, most of it funneling down into earth, a spume of it flaring up the distortion's side in a fan of white light. If someone had been standing near the distortion where the underground ley tunnel intersected the distortion, they would have seen a sudden fountain of ley emerging from the ground, churning upward like white rapids against a rock.

Kara steadied herself with a few deep breaths, then reached out into the turmoil and began guiding the ley around the distortion. Her first instinct was to surround the sphere with the ley and begin healing it as the Wielders in Erenthrall had healed distortions before the Shattering. But her experience with the distortion over Erenthrall told her that the technique wouldn't work here. Tumbor was too large, and even the smaller distortion over Erenthrall had begun to destabilize before she'd finished. The cracks in reality were too intricate, too complex to be smoothed and repaired from the outside in. Like Erenthrall, she'd need to heal Tumbor from the inside out.

But first she'd need an entry point, somewhere to focus her attack. In Erenthrall, she'd used the pit at the Nexus, which had extended all the way to the lake reservoir and provided a path of least resistance. She needed something similar here. All she had to do was find it.

Scouring over the distortion's surface on a wave of ley, she tested the exposed facets of the shards, pried her fingers into the cracks between, felt along their razored edges. The larger arms that formed the base structure of the distortion were easier to follow, the intricate layers and finer cracks between more difficult.

She'd covered only a quarter of the distortion's surface when she said, "It's too large. I can't piece together its overall structure, not like I did in Erenthrall. I'm not finding any sections that are significantly weaker than any other."

Back at the Needle, standing a few feet from her body, yet hundreds of miles distant, Marcus answered, "If you don't find a weaker point for entrance, then you'll have to use the ley tunnel from the

Needle." His words sounded oddly dampened, as if muffled by layers of cloth.

"It doesn't lead to the distortion's heart," Kara protested. She'd hoped to find something like the pit in Erenthrall, but she'd already finished checking the section beneath the distortion in Tumbor. The node in Tumbor hadn't been fed by a hidden lake far beneath the surface of the earth; it had been fed by the Nexus in Erenthrall.

She shifted her attention toward the northeastern section of the distortion, searching for that ley line, knowing it would be dead.

Back at the Needle, Marcus said, "Try the ley line to Erenthrall."

"I'm already looking. But it will have the same problem as the one from the Needle. All the ley lines will. None of them will feed directly into the distortion's center."

"Then use the ley line from the Needle to reach the node in Tumbor and redirect the ley from there to the heart."

"You make it sound so simple." She pulled back to the ley line from the Needle, began retracing her route. Searching for a weaker entry point was a waste of time. "I'm going to need you to direct the ley from the reservoirs into the line. I'll reshape it as the surge travels to Tumbor. Hopefully, it will be strong enough to pierce all the way to Tumbor's node."

"I'll inform Okata, Artras, and Jenner—" Marcus cut off, then swore. A hand wrapped around her upper arm and squeezed, the pain a sharp ache.

"What is it?"

"It's Dierdre. And Irmona. They're here, in the pit."

"What are they doing here?" As her attention shifted from the ley line toward the Needle, the ache in her arm escalated. Marcus must be digging his fingers into the muscle. "Get rid of them!"

Marcus suddenly released her. "I'll deal with them. Stay focused on the distortion."

Then he was gone. He shouted something toward Okata and Artras and then he was too distant for her to hear. She hesitated, wavering in the ley line between the Needle and Tumbor; she almost returned to the pit to help him.

But then she felt the surge from the redirected reservoirs heading toward her, and there was no time. If she was going to heal the distortion over Tumbor, it would have to happen now.

Marcus was on his own.

"What are you doing here?" Marcus shouted, letting his anger seep into his voice as he moved toward the bottom of the steps that encircled the pit. Dierdre and Irmona were already descending, Irmona's gaze locked on Kara, the crystals, and the Wielders that surrounded them all. Her look was hungry. "How did you even get in here? There were guards—"

Then he noticed the curved knife in Dierdre's hand, already covered in blood.

He halted in shock, then leaped forward, up the steps, blocking their descent. "What have you done?"

"What we should have done over a month ago, when Kara and Ty locked Father away inside his rooms. We're taking back the Needle."

"You can't. Not now. If you disturb us now—"

Dierdre grabbed him by the throat and slammed his back against the stone side of the pit, pinning him against the wall with the weight of her body. "Irmona, go."

Irmona didn't respond, merely slid behind the two and continued down the steps at a trot.

In the pit, the ley surged suddenly brighter, Okata, Artras, Dylan, and Jenner now focused so intently on controlling the addition of the reservoirs that they didn't notice Irmona approaching. The rest of the Wielders were also distracted, guiding the ley from Erenthrall and the other ley lines toward Kara's position or poised to seize control of the crystals if Hernande's precarious hold should waver.

Marcus snatched at the arm that clutched his throat and began to struggle. Dierdre held him, but she hadn't cut off his breath yet. "Stop this, Dierdre. If Irmona interferes, Kara could lose control. You could destroy us all!"

Dierdre's hand squeezed and he began to choke. "Is that all you care about? Kara? What happened to your concern for the Kormanley? What happened to us, Marcus?"

"What do you mean?" The words were wheezed out, her hold so tight he could barely speak. "I've spent all of my free time with you."

"Ha! What free time? You've spent nearly every waking moment here at the node for the past few months, here with *her*. It's time you make a real choice, Marcus. Me or her, the Kormanley or this pathetic attempt to recreate Erenthrall here at the Needle. Do you even see what's happening out in the city? She's letting everyone inside the gates! The city beyond the temple is overcrowded, the tent city even worse. People are living with the swine and the sheep in nothing but hovels. And now she's let in the Temerites! Who's next? The Gorrani?" Dierdre spat to one side. "She's going to destroy what Father built here. She's already halfway finished."

Irmona had reached the pit's floor, halted at the base of the stairs. She glared up at the crystals, at their new configuration, then toward Okata, Artras, Jenner, and the others. Marcus watched over Dierdre's shoulder as she considered each one, what they were doing, her attention falling finally on Kara.

Her look of naked hatred sent a shock through Marcus' entire body.

She drew a thin knife from the depths of one sleeve, stepped forward. But then she noticed Hernande, the mentor sitting off to one side, body perfectly still, eyes closed, expression serene except for a slight pinch of concentration between his eyes.

Irmona's arm twitched. Then she headed toward the mentor.

Marcus began to struggle harder, but Dierdre leaned her weight into his chest.

"Look at me!" she shouted into his face, and he stopped struggling, stared hard into her eyes. His nostrils flared and he drew in her scent, so familiar, so close. It reminded him of Erenthrall, before the Shattering, of the rooms that they'd claimed as their own here at the Needle. Through the anger, he could see how badly Dierdre hurt—damage caused by him, by his reaction when he'd found Kara, by his betrayal of Dalton and the Kormanley when he'd killed Lecrucius and helped Kara claim the Nexus here and, with Ty, the Needle. He could redeem himself in Dierdre's eyes, right here, right now. All he'd have to do was let Irmona and the Kormanley retake the node. "Choose, Marcus. Her or me?"

"Oh, Dierdre."

Her grip on his throat relaxed. The hard edges in her face softened and her shoulders sagged. A smile touched the corners of her mouth. In that moment, she was beautiful.

With a strangled grunt, Marcus shoved her hard, using the stone at his back as support. She tried to tighten her hand on his throat, but only managed to scratch him with her fingernails as she stumbled at the edge of the stair and then fell without a sound.

Irmona had reached Hernande. She raised her blade, the mentor completely unaware of her, lost in his trance.

Marcus reached for the ley in the Nexus, seized a small portion of the massive energy surging through the crystals from the ley lines and the reservoirs, and sent it arching toward Irmona. It hit her dead center, knocked her back from Hernande. She screamed as it engulfed her, in pain and rage and frustration, and then the metal blade of her knife clattered to the floor and there were only echoes.

Marcus sagged against the stone wall of the pit at his back, trembling, a belated flush of sweat breaking out over his entire body. He shoved forward again, halted at the edge of the steps, and stared down toward Dierdre's body.

The fall had been less than twenty feet, but she lay sprawled, arms and legs akimbo, neck at an unnatural angle. Her black hair fanned about her.

Marcus exhaled harshly, a wave of remorse forcing him to his knees. His gaze wandered over the pit, toward Hernande, still deep in trance, Okata, Artras, the others—all of them focused on the energy coursing through the Nexus. A raw energy. A wild energy, barely bridled. Not as intense as what Marcus had dealt with while altering the crystals of the original Nexus in Erenthrall, but it was somehow fiercer, more elemental.

And at its heart stood Kara.

Marcus stared at her, illuminated by the white force of the ley, then back down toward Dierdre. He pulled back from the ledge with a shudder and looked upward, toward the black base of the Needle streaked with pulsing light. His eyes were glazed with tears.

But then something struck him. "How did you get down here, Dierdre?"

Rising, he ascended the stairs, picking up momentum with each step. The first body was sprawling across the floor of the corridor outside, two more beyond that. The lieutenant who'd been set to guard them lay half in sunlight at the Needle's main entrance, the sand of the outer stellae garden soaking up her blood.

He gripped the slick obsidian of the Needle's doorway and stared up at the temple, the hollow sounds of the bell at the main gate muted here. "What are you up to, Darius?"

Except he already knew: it had to be about Father.

A sudden series of explosions rocked the temple, their concussions echoing down into the garden, the stone beneath Marcus' feet shuddering. Nothing like the quakes they'd experienced when the ley lines were unstable, but somehow more ominous.

High overhead, columns of black smoke and dust appeared over the top of the temple, followed by muted screams and the clash of weapons, all of it dampened and distant.

Marcus listened intently, then swore and ducked back into the Needle.

Kara shaped the surge of ley from the reservoirs into a sharp point as she rode it toward Tumbor, refining it into a thin spire, like the Needle itself. She let the momentum of the ley drive the spike through the ley line, so that when it struck the distortion, it carried behind it the force of the entire network, magnified by the crystal configuration at the Needle, augmented by the ley captured in the reservoirs.

It pierced all the way to the center of Tumbor, shards of reality shattering as it passed. A pang twisted in Kara's gut—how many people were still alive in those shards, how many trapped and now dead?—but she held the spike of ley until it reached the node in Tumbor. It collapsed instantly, ley filling the chamber, Kara already beginning to reshape it into another needle, this one aimed straight up from the pit toward the center of the distortion high above. The distortion itself shuddered around her, a reaction to the disturbance caused by what she'd done so far. It would collapse within moments, but she didn't spend a single heartbeat worrying about the collapse. She'd done this too many times to allow herself the luxury of fear.

But as she prepared to send the new spike on toward the heart of the distortion, she did take note of the pit here in Tumbor itself. Because it wasn't a pit, not like it should have been. It was much larger. As the ley branched out, seeking to fill the available space in the shard not still locked away inside the distortion, the magnitude of what she'd found hit her.

This was a Nexus, far surpassing the one built at the Needle. This one rivaled the original in Erenthrall in scope and capacity. Or it would have, if the crystals hadn't been shattered and the surrounding landscape destroyed. The destruction here was far worse than what she'd seen in Grass. The chamber she stood in was exposed to the distortion overhead, at the bottom of a crater obviously caused by an explosion. The towers had been sheared off much closer to the ground, the stone debris thrown much farther. Here, the devastation was nearly absolute. At least, what she could see of it in the freed shards.

She thought again about what Marcus had claimed upon her capture—that the Shattering hadn't been caused by the Kormanley, that it had been Baron Leethe. She hadn't believed him, had thought he was simply rationalizing his own culpability in what had happened.

But now . . .

Was it possible that all the cities had had their own Nexus? She hadn't been a Prime. She'd only known the nodes in a few districts in Erenthrall. Perhaps every city that had been connected to Erenthrall had a node such as this.

But no, that couldn't be true. She could sense through the ley a pit like the one she'd expected not that far away, built like the nodes she'd worked before the Shattering, except on a larger scale. The layout of that node and this one didn't make sense, unless one of them had been built in secret, had been used as an attempt to subvert or break free from the Nexus controlled by Prime Wielder Augustus and Baron Arent. Except something had gone wrong.

Marcus had said the pulse that caused the Shattering had come from Tumbor.

The distortion shuddered, a reverberation she felt in her teeth, even though her body stood hundreds of miles distant. She focused again on the second spike she'd created, gathered the strength of the ley now filling the dead husk of this new Nexus, and shot it upward, to where she could sense the heart of the distortion vibrating. It lacked the power of the spike she'd used to reach this node, but it still hit its target.

The entire distortion lit up with a fiery white light, blinding in its intensity. Kara screamed, her metaphysical form in Tumbor turning away, cowering down, even as her voice echoed in the chamber at the Needle. She lost her hold on the ley, let the raw power funnel unfettered through the crystals at the Needle toward her position, then channel upward through the distortion. In Erenthrall, that raw power had healed the shards from the inside out, branching along the distortion's main arms, then out through the secondary and tertiary filaments, down to the tiniest cracks and most minuscule shards. That feral energy had fused the fractured realities back together, even as the distortion over Erenthrall continued to collapse.

But that didn't happen here in Tumbor.

The distortion was too large. The energy spread to all the shards, through the arms, skating along the fractures, but by the time it reached the entire breadth of the shreds of reality, it had grown too dissipated. Kara choked on her own scream and lurched up in horror, reached out with one arm, fingers extended, as if trying to grasp tendrils of light from the air.

"No," she whispered.

The distortion began to collapse.

She should have fled back to the Needle. Instead, she solidified her connection to her own body through the ley and stayed. There was nothing she could do. All the power they had been able to produce at the Needle had already been brought to bear. There was nothing more to reach for, nothing left to grasp. And it hadn't been enough.

The ground began to rumble, like distant thunder, but it grew swiftly, became a growl, a howl of grinding stone, punctuated by a hissing slicing sound that shuddered in Kara's bones. A sound she remembered from the distortion that had maimed the seamstress' hand and killed her dog Max's original owner back in Erenthrall, as if the air were being shredded.

She flinched when the collapsing distortion reached her, the churning wall of destruction blasting past her with a concussive wave that wrenched at her spiritual body before abandoning her to an utter calm that felt surreal after the chaos. She hovered resolutely, staring after the wall of the distortion as it imploded, a sphere shrinking in size, whirling in upon itself, until it was nothing but a blazing, multicolored ball the size of her hand that flared once and winked out.

Her connection to herself at the Needle wavered, the ley lines between Tumbor and their Nexus destroyed. But still she didn't flee. She turned in a full circle, witnessed the destruction she had caused. The land around Tumbor had shattered, splinters of rock and dirt and debris jutting up at odd angles in all directions, nothing of Tumbor left. Nothing recognizable. The air felt edged, as if slivers of the fractured reality remained, the act of breathing enough to kill.

A wind tugged at her arm.

"It's gone," she said, her voice cracking. Her chest ached. Her cheeks were wet with tears. "It's all gone."

The wind again, at her arm, except this time it registered that there was no wind. Someone pulled at her arm. Someone was bellowing in her face.

Her metaphysical form faced the Needle. She considered staying, letting the thin tendril that connected her to her body snap. She'd failed. And now Tumbor and everyone and everything trapped within it was gone.

But the moment was fleeting.

She dragged herself back to the Needle, slamming into her body with a jerk.

"It's gone!" she shouted, before she realized Marcus was clutching at her arm, that he was holding her upright as the entire pit lurched around them. A quake. Because the ley lines had been stressed. Because the firmaments of reality had taken a significant hit.

"We have to get out of here," Marcus yelled over the roar of the quake.

"It's because the distortion in Tumbor collapsed! It's gone, all of it—Tumbor and everything trapped inside. This is the aftershock."

Marcus drew close, so he could shout in her ear. "That's not why we need to leave. The Kormanley are attacking the temple."

He dragged her toward Hernande, Okata and Artras hauling the mentor to his feet. He hung limp.

"He's still in the trance, holding the crystals," Artras said.

"We have to wake him."

"It will release the crystals!"

"Someone will have to stay and stabilize them."

"I'll stay," Kara said.

"Hells you will," Okata snapped. "The Kormanley want you more than anyone else here."

"Jenner and I will stay, with the other Wielders," Dylan said. "We'll hold the crystals. And someone has to stay to control the Nexus after this quake ends anyway. We can't all leave."

"Dylan—"

"Don't argue! Go!"

Marcus pulled Kara toward the stairs, stone and debris falling from overhead. Dylan said something to Artras, the elderly Wielder nodding once as he and Jenner ran toward the edge of the pit. The crystals were locked in place, strangely stable compared to the lurching stone around them. The other Wielders in the room had been thrown to the floor or were scrambling to escape, only a few attempting to hold the churning ley under control. Artras slapped Hernande hard, the mentor's head snapping back as his arms jerked upward. In the pit, the crystals began to tilt and twist, Dylan and Jenner shouting orders, dragging in a few others as they seized control.

Then Marcus was shoving Kara up the stairs, on her heels, Okata, Artras, and Hernande stumbling behind. She caught sight of Dierdre's body below, noticed a few others knocked unconscious or killed by debris, and then she passed up through the opening into the black corridors of the Needle, streaked with veins of ley, and the Nexus fell behind.

Thirteen

CORY HEARD THE FIRST EXPLOSION and saw the smoke out of the corner of his eye, but he couldn't afford to glance in that direction. He needed to concentrate on holding the reservoir. Sweat already beaded his forehead, and it didn't come from the heat of the sun. This field was ten times as large as the one he'd held inside the pit during their test run, and the Wielders hadn't yet begun siphoning off the ley energy.

"What in hells was that?" Sovaan asked from his position ten steps to Cory's right. Jerrain stood to his left.

"Does it look like I'm omniscient?" Jerrain answered. "Jasom, go see if you can figure out what's going on. Mirra and Keller, stay here in case we need the support. The rest of you stay put! I don't know what the Wielders are doing, but if they don't start using this ley, they're going to lose it."

Jasom trotted down the length of the temple. They were positioned on the second tier, but on the edge facing away from Tumbor, so they had it mostly to themselves. A few guardsmen were stationed at the edges, where those who'd arrived late were crowding to see around the two sides. There'd been a brief surge of people on their tier when they'd started filling the reservoirs, but that had already passed.

Jasom returned. "There's some sort of commotion with the enforcers on the first tier. Allan, Ty, and the Matriarch are retreating into the temple. I'm not certain what caused the explosion."

"What about—" Jerrain began, but he cut off as Cory felt the Wielders inside the temple begin to access the ley.

"What about what?" Jasom asked.

No one answered. Cory couldn't, too focused on keeping the reservoir stable; he assumed Sovaan and Jerrain were similarly occupied. The ley drained far faster than he expected, surging out of the containment and flowing down into the chasm toward what he assumed was a ley line. As it drained, the pressure on the folded Tapestry he held lessened.

Then light flashed overhead. Jasom, Mirra, Keller, and the other three students scrambled to the side of the tier, Keller crying out, "It's the distortion! It's completely white, blazing like the sun!"

Whatever was happening around the corner escalated. Cory could hear oaths, people yelping, a woman's curt scream, and swords clashing.

Then the bell over the main gates began to clang, a startling sound, reminding Cory viscerally of the bell they'd used in the Hollow as a warning.

A heartbeat later, explosions rocked the temple. Jerrain cursed as all of them staggered. Sovaan fell to one knee, his hold on the Tapestry slipping, what was left of his reservoir of ley dropping down into the chasm. Before Jerrain could berate him, choking black smoke billowed over them all. "Jasom and the rest of you, get back here!" Cory shouted, struggling to hold onto his portion of the Tapestry.

"No!" Keller yelled, his voice threaded with dismay. Cory couldn't see him through the smoke—couldn't see any of them, could only hear Jerrain gasping—but he knew he hadn't returned. He was still at the corner of the tier. "No, no, no!"

"Keller!" Three shapes emerged from the smoke, blurred by the tears in Cory's eyes—Mirra, Tara, and another student. Cory snatched Mirra's arm and dragged the other two closer. "Where are the others?"

"They're helping Sovaan and Jerrain. Something went wrong, Cory. The distortion—it . . . it collapsed! And the enforcers! They're fighting on the temple stairs. Commander Ty is holding them off right now, but he's outnumbered." Tears were beginning to form in Mirra's eyes. She wiped at her own face in disgust, her skin already blotchy, her breath beginning to hitch.

Cory fell to one knee, his attention half on the Tapestry, half on her. He grabbed both of her shoulders. "Mirra, listen to me. Are you certain the distortion collapsed? It didn't heal?"

"I'm certain. It wasn't . . . wasn't like Erenthrall. I saw it folding in upon itself."

Cory squeezed her arms in comfort, but stood. He tested the Tapestry near the reservoirs, but no one was drawing on the ley anymore. He didn't think the Wielders needed it any longer, now that the distortion had collapsed.

He sucked in a sudden breath, coughed, and shouted, "Jerrain, let the reservoir go! The distortion's collapsed! We need to get away from the temple as soon as possible, before the quake hits! Head for the northeastern corner of the tier now!"

He pulled Mirra and the other students after him, trying to keep low, beneath the smoke, but it cleared within a few paces, the bulk of the temple blocking it. Standing straight, he herded Mirra and the others toward Sovaan, the administrator staring back toward the smoke with a shocked look.

"This can't be happening again," he said as Cory approached. "The Needle was supposed to be safe."

"Nothing in the new world is safe! Now take the students and head toward the door near the corner. We need to get inside before—"

They heard it before it hit, a low, rumbling, grinding sound.

"Get down flat!" Cory shoved Sovaan to the stone tier, reached for Mirra, but then the temple lurched beneath them. He slammed into the stone chest-first, breath bursting from his lungs, but began crawling toward Jerrain's position without thought. They'd experienced too many quakes for him to be shaken by this one. He pushed a sobbing Mirra toward the temple entrance and kept going, not looking back to see if Sovaan or any of the others were trying to reach it. Beneath the smoke, he found Jasom protecting Jerrain and two other students, all of them flattened to the stone. He gestured toward the doorway, Jasom nodding in response, then pushed on. Stones rattled down onto the tier, dislodged from above, but he merely winced as some of them struck his shoulders, back, and legs.

Ten feet farther on, he ran across Keller. The brown-haired student lay crumpled on the stone, surrounded by three others—a woman and two men. Cory rushed forward on hands and knees, grabbed Keller's shoulder, then lurched back, his hands bloody.

Keller hadn't been killed by the quake. His entire side was soaked in blood from a sword wound in his chest.

Cory fought back the urge to vomit, checked the other bodies, and found similar wounds—one man with a vicious cut to the neck—then backed off. He scanned what he could see of the second side of the temple around the corner. Smoke still billowed up from multiple areas, the worst in the streets below and the square. It looked like the barracks was on fire. He spotted three craters on the second tier, bodies strewn on all sides, some burned and maimed by the blasts, others like those he'd found with Keller. Most of the dead were clustered near the main door. There were still pockets of fighting, mostly on the first tier, where a wave of stragglers was trying to reach the doubtful safety of the ground. He caught snatches of fighting on the outer walls, a few sections where explosions had torn at the parapet.

The ground lurched again, and he scrambled back toward the others.

"Where's Keller?" Jasom asked as he approached. He and Mirra were waiting at the door, the others already inside.

"Dead." Cory motioned them into the corridor. The hallway beyond was choked with dust and he covered his mouth with one arm as he followed the other mentors and students deeper inside the temple. One or two of them were sobbing.

When they reached a cross-corridor, Jerrain halted and snapped, "Quiet!"

Cory worked his way up through the six remaining students to Jerrain's side and listened. "They're fighting in the main corridor."

"Who's fighting?"

"I don't know." He glanced back at Sovaan and the rest. "We need to get out of the temple, without running into anyone."

"I only know the main corridors."

Someone screamed, high-pitched and gurgling.

Mirra tugged on Cory's shirt. "I know all the back halls. I've been exploring."

"Then you lead the way." Cory motioned her into the intersection of the halls. "Take us down and out as fast as you can."

Mirra nodded, then headed right, away from the sounds of fighting.

They wound through corridors, past doorways open and closed, pausing at every crossing to listen. The rest of the students had figured out something worse than the quake had happened, now that the ground had settled for the moment, and were trying to stifle their sobs. Mirra led them without hesitation, cutting left, then right again. An aftershock rattled the temple when they found a narrow set of servants' stairs down to the second level, but no one paused. They didn't see any enforcers or anyone else.

The second level was more difficult. At every intersection, there were one or two corridors with the sounds of conflict—fighting or screams. Twice they had to wait while guards ran across a corridor farther along. Bodies appeared, mostly enforcers, but a few servants slumped along with the rest.

Then they reached an intersection with activity in all directions, close, although they couldn't see anyone.

"Is there another way out or around?" Cory asked.

"Not that I know of. The first and second floors of the temple are more heavily used."

"We've already backtracked twice," Jerrain said. The others were crowding up close. "It was stupid to think we'd get out of the temple without running into someone. Not in a situation like this."

"Then we'd better hope we run into the right people." Cory concentrated, then motioned to the left. "We'll head for the orrery, try to slip past everyone there."

The group remained close as they picked their way down the corridor straight ahead, skirting the bodies, one or two moaning as they passed. They rushed past a cross-corridor, fighting going on to either side, then sidled up to another, Cory peeking around the corner. At least twenty enforcers were brawling ten paces away. He couldn't tell the two sides apart, not with such a quick glance. He motioned the others by, the main door to the orrery twenty paces beyond, then followed. Jerrain had cracked the massive double doors to look inside, had already shoved Mirra and Jasom through. Sovaan went next, Jerrain waiting until the other four students were through before pulling Cory in behind him and shutting the door.

The orrery was empty, the orbs representing the planets pulsing overhead, the bright white of a comet and its glittering tail somehow sharper than the others. With the door closed, and the quake quieted, it was eerily silent in the room.

"Where to next?" Jerrain asked.

"There's only one option," Sovaan declared in contempt. "Students, follow me."

He headed toward the far door. Jasom and the others hesitated, looking toward Jerrain and Cory.

"They're right behind us," Cory said. "Follow Sovaan."

The small group crossed the room in a huddle, Sovaan at least five paces out in front, but they hadn't made it halfway across when the far doors slammed open and enforcers spilled into the room. The mentors and students halted as the enforcers blocked their path, Cory only relaxing when Ty appeared.

"Commander Ty," he said, stepping past Sovaan toward the enforcer.

"What are you doing here?" Ty demanded as his enforcers shut the doors behind him, pressing their backs up against them. The rest spread out, searching for things to barricade them with. Ty was covered in sweat and blood, not all of it his own. A gash on his forehead dripped steadily, and he'd taken nicks and cuts to his arms and legs.

"We were on the third tier when the bombs went off, followed by the quake. We've been trying to escape the temple."

Ty scanned Cory and the others, then flicked a finger toward the door they'd come from. "Are they behind you?"

"Yes. Close."

Something crunched into the doorway Ty had just come from, the men there crying out as they were jolted inward. A roar of triumph came from the outer hall, muffled by the doors, along with shouted orders Cory couldn't make out.

Ty stalked to the side of the chamber, where the open windows looked out on the Needle and the stellae garden below. But Cory already knew the drop was too high, not without some kind of rope to climb down at least partway.

The door Cory and the others had used rattled, and Ty's men scrambled to hold it. But Ty halted them with a gesture. "Don't bother. There's nowhere to retreat. Let them in."

The men—no more than twenty, Cory realized, although it had seemed there were more—pulled back from both sets of doors, reforming around Cory and the others at Ty's command. They herded the mentors and students to one side, near the windows, Ty taking up a position before them all.

Moments later, something crashed into the doors to their right— once, twice—and then something splintered and enforcers charged into the room, each of them wearing a white linen tied to their upper arm stained with the black symbol of convergence adopted by the Kormanley. Cory hadn't noticed it on any of the men in the hallways, but he hadn't paid much attention then. As they filled the room, Darius stepping out into the forefront, Mirra twined her fingers into Cory's. He glanced down at her and squeezed.

"Halt!" Ty bellowed, his voice ringing through the chamber, startling Cory and the others. His men braced themselves, swords ready, stances wide. Darius' men continued to surge into the room, emerging from the other set of doors now, although they stayed behind Darius, who held up one hand, palm flat.

"Run out of places to hide?" Darius asked.

"There's no need to run anymore," Ty said. "By this time, Allan will have gotten the Matriarch and the Temerites out of the temple and to safety."

"I doubt he's even managed to get them to the first level. He had few enforcers with him."

"You forgot about the Wolves."

Darius twitched, a few of his own men sharing glances behind him. He dropped his hand and stepped forward. "It doesn't matter. The Temerites were never a significant problem. We have you, and my men are freeing Dalton from his prison as we speak. I'm certain Dierdre and Irmona are securing the Nexus and the Wielders." His gaze shifted toward Cory, who tried not to react to the sudden gut-wrenching worry about Kara. "And it appears we have the mages as well."

Jerrain stepped forward, hand outstretched, fingers curled. "We could kill you where you stand." Cory felt the Tapestry twist near Darius' heart. The students around him tensed.

"But you won't. I've been paying attention to your little school. You've been teaching the ethical use of the Tapestry, even have a code of conduct for your students, all because of what happened in your Hollow with the raiders. You've sworn to uphold that code. Killing me now would violate that."

"Oh, I don't know," Jerrain said. "Killing you would give me a certain satisfaction at the moment."

Jasom and Tara stepped forward next to Jerrain, hands poised as claws.

Darius stared at them a long moment, then shifted his attention to Ty. "Take them." When his men hesitated, he said, "Take them! The mages are bluffing."

They surged forward, Jerrain dropping his arm in disgust. Darius' men seized Ty first, forcing him to his knees before clouting him across the back of his head with the pommel of a sword. He collapsed, the rest of his men receiving the same treatment.

They approached Cory, Jerrain, and the rest of the mages more carefully. When one reached out to grab him, Jerrain said, "Unless you want to see exactly what I'm willing to do with the Tapestry, I'd suggest you simply lead us to whatever prison you have waiting."

The men shared a look, then stepped back, one of them saying, "This way."

As they were escorted out of the orrery, Cory glanced back at the black tower of the Needle through the windows and wondered silently what had become of Kara.

Allan flew down the stairs inside the temple, Lienta on his heels, both with swords drawn, but the corridor at the bottom was empty. They could hear fighting in the distance, but who knew exactly where. The corridors distorted sounds too much.

Behind them, an escort of Temerite watchmen kept track of Morrell, Drayden, Cutter, and Marc, Janote carrying the Matriarch in his arms, with one of the guards behind with her wheeled chair. As soon as they reached the first level, Janote settled the Matriarch back in her chair and took hold of the handles, the rest of the watchmen falling in behind.

"Ready," Janote said.

"Good," Allan said. "We'll leave the temple by the servants' entrance on the western side."

"What is happening?"

The entire Temerite guard snapped to attention, but Allan recognized the growling voice and turned to find Grant standing in the middle of the corridor. Three Wolves paced behind him, teeth bared and hackles raised. Allan wondered where the rest of the pack was.

"Darius has attacked the temple. We need to get the Matriarch out before he traps us here, but first we need to find Kara and the other Wielders."

Grant scanned the Matriarch and the Temerites, then returned to Allan. "What happened to the distortion?"

"We don't know," Lienta replied. "We never got a chance to see."

Grant suddenly looked up.

At the same moment, the Wolves behind him broke into ear-splintering howls. Everyone except Grant and Drayden clapped their hands to their ears.

"Why are they doing that?" Lienta shouted.

"Can't you feel it?" Grant answered, the fur on his face bristling.

The earth leaped upward, tossing Allan into the wall to one side. Pain shot through his shoulder, but he staggered toward Grant. "Take us to the Needle," he yelled. "We have to find Kara!"

Grant barked something at his Wolves, the three on four legs cutting their howls off and darting down the corridor behind them. More joined them from side halls before branching out in all directions. Lienta was already motioning everyone forward.

They scrambled after Grant and the Wolves, the temple shuddering around them, dust shaking down from overhead, accompanied by the occasional chunk of stone. Within two turns, they ran into enforcers, the Wolves ripping into them without pause, Allan and the others maneuvering around the mauled bodies. Servants screamed and ducked out of their way or suffered the same fate as the enforcers as they moved deeper into the temple.

They burst out into the stellae garden and the brilliant sunlight at the same moment Marcus, Kara, Artras, Okata, and Hernande emerged from the Needle. Kara stood stunned, as if unable to fathom what was happening, but Marcus stepped forward and yelled, "The distortion collapsed, and Irmona and Dierdre tried to kill Hernande! They're trying to take the temple!"

"They're succeeding," Allan answered. "Ty's holding them off on the second tier. We need to get whoever we can out of the temple now!" He turned to Grant. "The western servants' entrance. Go!"

Grant whistled; his Wolves dodged through the stones of the stellae garden, around the black spire of the Needle, and toward the entrance to the west. Lienta and the others followed, Janote once again carrying the Matriarch, another guard bringing her chair. It wouldn't navigate well through the sand.

"Where are the other Wielders?" Allan asked as Kara's group joined them, the rest of the Temerite watchmen bringing up the rear. He made certain Drayden stayed near Morrell, but still kept his daughter close.

"They remained behind. Dylan and Jenner and the rest need to be here to hold the ley lines, now that Tumbor is lost completely. And the others aren't of any interest to Darius and the Kormanley."

Allan hoped Marcus was right because they didn't have time to go grab them. As they rounded the side of the Needle, enforcers emerged from the entrance they'd come from. He noted white armbands on their upper arms as he and the rest of the Temerites ducked into the shadows of the western doors and slammed them shut behind them.

They met resistance on their path to the outside servants' entrance. Darius had made certain all entryways were covered by guards loyal to the Kormanley, but he hadn't counted on the Wolves. They left mangled bodies behind them in the corridors, Allan hearing only shrieks before coming up on the remains seconds later. They made short work of the five guards at the servants' entrance, and then the group spilled back into the sunlight, now on the streets of the outside city. Black smoke billowed up from what Allan guessed was the barracks off the main square. Craters stood out on the tiers of the temple. He couldn't see the walls, but knew there had been explosions from there as well. He could hear some fighting in the streets, but the sounds were distant. Windows and doors in the buildings within sight were closed and shuttered, although on closer scrutiny he found groups of people huddled in alcoves and corners, some racing away from the Wolves down the side streets.

"We're out," Grant said. "Now what?"

"Get us back to our enclave beyond the chasm to the southwest," the Matriarch said, surprisingly calm and composed. "You offered us shelter, and helped us escape Erenthrall. We'll return the favor and protect you now."

Lienta didn't appear happy. "How will we get there?"

Allan steadied himself as the quake quieted, wiped his face free of sweat and tension with one hand. "We can't use the main gates, they'll be too heavily guarded, even taking into account the Wolves. So it will have to be the southeastern gates. It's the only way out of the city."

"How will we get them open?" Lienta asked. "I doubt Darius has left them open for us."

"I'll take care of that," Marcus said, stepping forward.

"Marcus." Allan was glad to hear the edge of warning in Kara's voice.

He'd begun to wonder whether something more serious had happened to Kara back in the pit, but she appeared to be snapping out of it.

"We have to get out of here," Marcus said. "Darius will have no compunction killing you or the others, not after what you did to Dalton. And he'll flay me once he finds Dierdre's body."

"We don't have time to argue," Marc said. The enforcer guard still clutched his side, panting, even though Morrell had healed him on the tier.

"Agreed," Lienta said, motioning toward Grant with his sword. "The southeastern gates?"

Grant huffed, then flicked his hands, the Wolves taking off again. Now that they were in the open, Allan counted eleven of them, plus Drayden.

They edged through the streets, slowed by caution and their unfamiliarity with this area of the Needle. Aftershocks rattled through the ground beneath their feet, none as powerful as that first lurch, although Allan knew that meant nothing. The Icy system was adjusting to the loss of Tumbor. If Hernande's and Kara's theories were correct, the results could be more catastrophic than when they'd lost Erenthrall.

They'd nearly reached the edge of the outer ring of buildings, where the tent city began, when Kara suddenly gasped and jerked to a halt. She searched the group frantically, as if finally becoming aware of where they were and who was with them. Allan shifted toward her, Hernande coming in from the other side, before she spun and said, "Where's Cory?"

The others were moving past them, Marcus with a passing shrug, Artras pausing.

"We don't know, Kara," Allan said. "There wasn't time to find him."

Kara pulled away from Hernande's soothing reach. "We have to go back for him."

"We can't."

"We have to go back!"

"We can't! They were on the third tier, overseeing the reservoirs. We don't know where they went from there." When Kara began to turn away in defiance, he grabbed her shoulder and spun her toward him. "Kara, all I know is that Darius and his men were more interested in Ty and securing the temple than they were in Cory and the other mages.

Cory could have escaped the temple on his own. Charging back into the temple now would only give Darius and Dalton more prisoners."

"More *important* prisoners," Artras added. She touched Kara's back. "We'll find him and the others. *After* we've gotten everyone else to safety."

Lienta whistled, the noise piercing and urgent. Allan held Kara's gaze, her despair etched in the exhausted lines around her eyes and mouth, but he saw acceptance as well.

"Let's move."

He stayed by Kara's side, Hernande and Artras supporting her on the other, everyone else ranging out ahead of them except for a few of Lienta's watchmen as guards. They'd already begun pushing through the tents, the group scattering slightly as the pathways became narrower than the streets, littered with the detritus of those who were living there. Most of the occupants were huddled in their tents, mothers and fathers staring out in fear as they passed, children pulled in close. A few were guarded by men or women with makeshift weapons, threatening from behind half-pulled tent flaps. None of them attacked, especially after spying Grant and his Wolves, and they saw none of the enforcers. All the fighting appeared to be centered on the temple and the walls, but even that was dying down. Darius had planned well, the resistance from Ty's supporters minimal. The people of the Needle didn't care who was in charge as long as they were fed and could trade and live within the security of the walls. Allan saw the scrawled dog-snake symbol on at least twenty tents and chalked onto the flagstones near the rounded basin of a fountain.

The walls reared up before them and they slowed, gathering together into a tighter group once again. Allan worked his way back to the front, where Lienta, Grant, and Marcus were scanning the wooden gates from cover deep inside the tents.

"Only twenty feet of free space from the gate to where the tents begin," Lienta was saying. "Not much room."

"We aren't going to be fighting," Marcus countered. "We're going to be running."

"How are you going to get the gates open?" Grant rumbled.

"Hernande can blast them open," Allan said, "using the Tapestry."

"You're assuming he has the strength after holding the crystals in the Nexus stable for us."

"Then what else?" Lienta waved toward the gates. "There are at least thirty guards on the ground, probably another twenty up above, possibly with arrows."

"There won't be any guards when I'm done." Marcus stepped forward, through the tents, visible from the wall now. "Get the others and get ready to run."

Lienta shook his head. "What's he doing?"

"He's going to use the ley."

As he spoke, Marcus raised his hands. Allan motioned Janote and the Matriarch forward with their covey of watchmen, Hernande, Kara, Morrell, Drayden, and the others coming up behind. Grant whistled for his Wolves. "Get ready to charge straight for the gates!"

Ley erupted from the ground in front of Marcus, surging forward from his position straight toward the gates. The men in front cried out in alarm, began to fling themselves out of the way, but the ley widened as it shot forward, growing taller, until it reached higher than the wall itself. It struck without a sound, engulfing the entire tower, the guards in front, and those above.

"Marcus!" Kara gasped in horror.

"Run!" he bellowed.

Allan caught hold of Morrell and the nearest watchman's arm and dragged them forward, the others jerking into motion, Janote rushing past, pushing the Matriarch in her wheeled chair. The Wolves streaked out ahead. They shied away from Marcus to either side, chasing after the billowing flames of ley, which receded before them. Allan and Lienta made certain everyone had sped past him, then came up behind, Allan tapping Marcus on the shoulder. The Wielder let his arms fall, the ley dying down. The ground before the gaping hole where the gate had stood was littered with swords and buckles, rings and pins. The wooden gates had been annihilated; only the metal braces and hinges remained, jutting out from the walls as if they still supported massive doors. No one fired at them from above as they funneled through the short stone archway and onto the arid plains beyond. No one dropped oil down through the murder holes or lowered the portcullis. There was no one left alive in the tower above.

Shouts rose from the walls farther down, Allan glancing back to see men waving and pointing in their direction. "Head straight out onto the plains. Get over the ridge before they organize a group to follow us. We'll circle back to the Temerite enclave on the other side of the chasm overnight."

Lienta seconded the orders, then fell back to trot alongside Allan. "My men will have taken full control of the entire section on the far side of the chasm, including the outer wall and gates before nightfall. We'd already secured most of that area as a precaution."

Before them, Hernande appeared on the verge of collapse, Kara not much better. Morrell and Cutter helped Marc trudge forward up the strange circular ridge that surrounded the Needle, Drayden close by Morrell's side. Grant's Wolves had ranged out farther ahead, already beyond the ridge, while Lienta's watchmen had formed up around the group in a loose protective circle. The other Wielders—Artras, Okata, and Marcus—had clumped together near the Matriarch and Janote.

When he reached the ridge, Allan stared off into the east, his shadow stretching out before him. The sky on the horizon seemed empty, as if there were a hole where the distortion over Tumbor had been. It pulled at him, as if it had its own gravity. He knew what the land where Tumbor had stood would look like; he'd seen it in the ring of devastation surrounding Erenthrall, where the distortion there had begun to collapse before Kara had healed it.

Shouts echoed up from behind him, and Lienta, who'd halted with him, clapped a hand on his shoulder.

"Time to disappear," the Temerite said.

"For now."

They slipped down off the ridge and rejoined the others as the sun began to sink into the western horizon.

"What have you done?"

Darius turned from the window in the orrery at the question as his enforcers led Father Dalton into the room. The man's milky eyes bored into him and he lowered his head, gesturing toward the window. "I've secured the temple and the Needle for you, Father. My men have captured the Wielders that remained at the Nexus, as well as the mages and the traitor Commander Ty, along with some of the Hollowers that supported him. Kara Tremain eluded us, with Marcus' help, along with the mentor Hernande, Allan Garrett, and a few others, including the Matriarch and the Wolves."

"The Matriarch? She's here?"

He'd forgotten that Dalton had been isolated during recent events. "Yes, Allan Garrett brought her back from Erenthrall. Devin and those from Haven have taken over the ruined city, or so they claim."

Dalton shifted forward, heading unerringly to Darius' side. "And what of the Gorrani?"

"We haven't heard or seen the Gorrani for weeks now."

Dalton glared down at the stellae garden and the Needle. "They're coming. We'll have to deal with them ourselves now. Where are Iscivius and Irmona?"

Darius sucked in a bitter breath. "Iscivius is in his rooms, unconscious. Irmona and Dierdre"—his breath caught in his throat, but he forced the words out—"they were both killed by Marcus."

Dalton faced him. "We'll deal with Marcus, in time. We'll need someone to control the Nexus, someone we trust."

"None of the Wielders we captured can be trusted completely. They're either loyal to Kara, or aren't powerful enough to manipulate the Nexus beyond mere stabilization."

"You said Iscivius is unconscious?"

"He's been in a coma for weeks now."

"Take me to him."

They made their way to Iscivius' room, through halls littered with bodies, most of them servants or enforcers loyal to Ty. Father Dalton stepped over them all, as if his eyes weren't occluded. The bodies of the guards Ty had set on Iscivius' door still lay in their own pools of blood, but Dalton's attention fixed on Iscivius immediately.

Darius stood aside as Father walked to Iscivius' bed. He stared down at Iscivius' prone form, then reached down and touched Iscivius' forehead.

Iscivius gasped, back arched, and then collapsed back onto the bed. His eyes fluttered open, then focused on Dalton. "Father?"

Dalton held out his hand, Iscivius reaching up to grasp it, as if it were a lifeline. "Get up. We have work to do."

PART II:

Erenthrall

Fourteen

BRYCE'S LEG THROBBED like an unholy forge being beaten by the hammer of a god.

He'd been in the barracks when the Kormanley attacked. At least a third of the men there "resting up" with him for the next watch on the wall had turned on the rest. The fight had been short but fierce, Bryce taking out at least twenty men and women, three of them bare-handed before he'd managed to snag a sword. He'd have gotten at least a few more if an explosion hadn't ripped through the barracks wall and thrown him across the room. When his vision had stopped blurring, he'd found himself choking on smoke, with a foot-long wooden shard jutting out of his thigh. Before he could recover, Trenton had emerged from the black smoke and the Kormanley had surrounded him.

"You should have stayed in the Hollow," the erstwhile enforcer said.

"You should have stayed in hiding."

"Take him with the others to the temple."

Bryce had reached for the nearest Kormanley, intending to snap his neck, but one of the others jerked the wooden shard out of his leg and he'd screamed and passed out.

They'd done a piss-poor job in patching it up, nothing but an old shirt wrapped around it and tied tight. Blood had already seeped through and trailed down one side, and it had begun to itch. Swollen and hot, he couldn't stand, could barely move without his sight going blurry. He massaged the muscles above the wound and wondered where everyone else was. Captured? Dead? There were twelve others in the makeshift cell with him, sitting against the walls or lying flat on the bare stone, but he barely knew them.

The door to the room groaned open and enforcers entered, swords drawn, but no one stood to oppose them. Most were wounded, although none as badly as Bryce, but he still suppressed a surge of contempt.

When the guards lowered their swords and stepped to either side of the door, more prisoners were shoved inside. Enforcers at first, but then Cory, Jerrain, Sovaan, the mage students, and finally—

"Ty!"

Bryce attempted to stand as the commander stepped inside—rigid with contemptuous dignity, even though he'd obviously been beaten— but the agony was too intense. He collapsed back against the stone wall with gritted teeth and a fresh sheen of rank sweat.

"Bryce." Cory knelt beside him, Jerrain and a few of the students joining them. Cory began inspecting his leg. "What happened?"

"The damn Kormanley attacked the barracks. I got caught in one of the explosions."

At the doorway, Sovaan had halted a few steps behind Ty. "I demand to speak to whoever's in charge!"

Trenton stepped into the room. "Darius and Father are a little busy right now, calming the fearful citizens and subduing the rest." His attention shifted to Ty. "I'm certain one of them will deal with you shortly. I wouldn't get too comfortable."

Ty didn't respond, and Trenton and the enforcers filed out, drawing the door closed behind them. It shut with a clang.

Cory prodded Bryce's leg, and he yelped, slapping the mage's hand away. "What in hells do you think you're doing?"

Cory sat back. "It doesn't look good. You need to have a healer look at it, or Morrell."

"I don't see any healers here, and I suspect Darius isn't all that inclined to provide one. There'd be no point."

"What do you mean?" Jerrain asked.

"He means," Ty said, coming closer, "that it's unlikely we'll survive the next few days."

The mages all shared a look, while the rest of the enforcers around the room drew closer, pulled by Ty's presence.

"You mean they'll kill us?" Sovaan asked. "But why?"

"Because as long as we're alive, we're a threat." Ty scanned everyone. "At least some of us. I'm not certain about all of you."

"Why haven't they slaughtered us already?" Jerrain asked. "Why keep us prisoner? They could have cut us down in the orrery, or even here."

Bryce shifted his weight, regretting the movement of his leg almost immediately. "Because they want witnesses. They want an execution. They'll kill those of us recognizable—Ty, myself, perhaps some of you mages—publicly, to make certain the citizens know who's in power. It's what Baron Arent would have done."

"Yes, but it may be more than that."

"Why?"

Ty waved a hand around the room. "Look who's here . . . and who's not."

Everyone glanced around. "The Wielders," Jerrain said. "Kara, Artras, Okata. They're missing."

"Allan and Morrell, Hernande and Cutter as well," Bryce added.

"Which means that either they're being kept in a separate room, or they somehow managed to escape. I don't think Darius could have prepared many rooms like this one, not without someone noticing. If they don't have the Wielders or the others, then they'll want to know where they went. They're going to want information, especially from me."

"Why you?"

"Because when the Kormanley first started showing themselves—with their staged riots and that snake-dog symbol—I started kidnapping some of their members. We still have them, unless they've managed to find the location where we've been interrogating them."

"Kara would never have condoned kidnapping," Cory said.

"No, she wouldn't have."

"She didn't know about it?"

"Marcus didn't think—"

"Marcus! He doesn't think, that's the problem! He—"

"This isn't getting us anywhere," Bryce interjected. "If they've been captured and are simply being held somewhere else, then we're on our own. If they're free, then they'll likely try to free us if they can. In either case, I don't feel like waiting here for Darius to decide to kill us. We need to find a way out of this room, and then the temple."

"We don't have any weapons," one of the enforcers said.

Bryce pointed to the mages. "We have them."

"Lieutenant Boskell, close the gates and seal the enclave. We're taking over this section of the Needle."

"Yes, Captain Lienta." Boskell began shouting orders, watchmen already racing away toward the gate tower and deeper into the sector the Temerites had taken over as their own upon their arrival. As soon as he was satisfied his men were following orders, the lieutenant faced Lienta again. "What shall we do with them?"

He jutted his chin out toward Kara, Marcus, Allan, and the others behind Lienta, all of them hanging back beneath the cracked arch of the gateway, Lienta's men circling them, although they kept their distance from Grant and the Wolves.

The Matriarch wheeled her way forward with Janote. "There's been a coup at the Needle. We will hide them here for now. Pretend you never saw them."

Boskell bowed stiffly, a flash of relief crossing his face as the Matriarch motioned Lienta forward. Two months ago, he would have scowled. Allan and the others had grown on him.

"Take them to the embassy. Make certain they're seen to."

Allan stepped up. "We'll need to speak about what's happened. Soon."

"I know. But first we need to rest, and Lienta's watchmen need to find out what's happened at the Needle. We can't make plans until we have information. Now go, follow Captain Lienta. We'll talk in the morning."

Kara drew breath as if to protest, but Marcus caught her arm and whispered something in her ear. She subsided.

"This way," Lienta said, and the entire group passed through the gates into the section of the Needle that had been cut off by the chasm. Behind them, the portcullis lowered with a screech, its metal bent by the quakes months before and repaired by the Temerites. The gates groaned closed and metal braces were set across them.

At intervals, through the darkness and the shadows cast by the buildings, snatches of fighting could still be heard from the main part of the Needle. Ley globes still lined the walls and temple, the buildings outside mostly lit with candlelight, but the white light that had veined the black spire of the Needle itself had died down. The ground shook and trembled at odd moments, unsteady, but overhead the hard glitter of the stars remained constant. The moon hung heavy and half-full on the horizon, for once not shadowed by the glow of a distortion.

When they reached the mercantile that the Matriarch had transformed into their embassy, Lienta ushered Kara, Allan, and the rest into the inner rooms, Janote taking the Matriarch herself aside with an escort.

"Will she be all right?" Kara asked. Lienta hadn't heard her approach.

"She'll be fine. Janote will take care of her."

"If there's anything we can do—"

"I'll let her know." He halted at the end of the hallway, where it branched left and right, doorways opening off on either side. "Use these rooms for now. They're secluded from the rest of the embassy. Stay here. The Matriarch doesn't want the general populace to know you're here, at least not for now."

"What does she intend to do about Father Dalton and Darius?"

"I don't know, but as she said at the temple, we'll shelter you here until we figure out what to do. The Kormanley won't get in. We've made certain we can hold this sector if necessary."

Marcus laid a hand on Kara's shoulder. "There's nothing we can do right now anyway."

"We could check on the stability of the Nexus and the ley—"

"Kara! Let's get some sleep first. We're all exhausted."

They were, Lienta realized. Hernande looked ready to collapse at any moment, supported by Cutter and Morrell. Marcus' eyes were hollows, and the enforcer Marc—someone Lienta barely knew—looked drained. Only Allan appeared ready and willing to face the Kormanley, but like Lienta and the rest of the guards, he'd done almost nothing in their escape.

Marcus guided Kara to one of the rooms with Artras, the rest dividing up into pairs, Allan and Morrell together, Cutter taking Hernande's weight. Drayden crouched down outside Morrell's door. Marc joined the Wielders.

Lienta turned to find Grant standing immediately behind him.

"We'll need . . . other accommodations." Behind him, one of the Wolves growled, a low ominous sound.

"Right."

Darius found Father on the second tier, staring northward with his clouded eyes. The moonlight made the stone of the temple glow a lambent white, the Needle above nearly invisible except where it occluded the stars. A breeze cooled the sweat on Darius' neck, making him feel the grit that had caught between his skin and armor. He strode directly to Father's side.

"We've secured the city."

"And the walls? They weren't too severely damaged by the explosives?"

"Nothing we can't repair easily. However, the southeastern gates are completely destroyed."

Father's lips pursed. "That presents a problem."

"Do we have time to repair it?"

"I don't think so." Father's gaze—which Darius realized had been fixated on the Three Sisters glittering far to the north—shifted toward the east. "Look at Erenthrall."

Darius stepped forward and squinted, but he didn't need to search long. The horizon in the direction of their old home glowed a fervent piercing white. "What is it?"

"It's the Nexus." The ground trembled beneath them, a low rumble. Father didn't even pause. "It's cracked. What you see is the ambient light of the ley being vomited up out of the earth. Or perhaps hemorrhaging is a better term. The destruction of Tumbor has finally violently wounded the ley, perhaps beyond repair. The signs of its collapse have already begun. Look to the north. The Sisters have been destabilized. They've begun to quicken. If you watch carefully, you can see them pulse. And there will be more signs in the coming days."

Darius stared at the Sisters, caught the faintest pulse of light, like a heartbeat, from all three, all at different intervals. He swallowed back bitter fear. "What does that mean for us?"

Father faced him. "It means that the dogs of Erenthrall, this Devin and his men, are already on their way to the Needle because they believe we are a safe haven now that Erenthrall has cracked. The Gorrani, the serpents, are headed here as well. They simply want revenge."

"Your vision. It's coming true."

"Did you doubt, Darius?"

"Never!"

Father's mouth twitched. "It does not matter. We must prepare for the arrival of the dogs and snakes. Don't bother repairing the south-eastern gates. Simply close them off with stone, as quickly as the masons can manage. Seal it off."

"That will leave us with only one gate."

"One entrance to guard, rather than two."

"Only one exit as well."

"We will either stand here, or fall. And if we fall, then there will be no chance to stop the destruction of everything that we hold sacred. The ley will destroy us all."

Father began walking toward the temple entrance, his pace sedate. Darius glanced back toward the flickering lights over Erenthrall and the pulsing distortions to the north. "What will we do about Erenthrall and the Sisters?"

"Nothing. It is in Iscivius' and the Wielders' hands now. All we can do is pray. Korma will either see fit to aid Iscivius in saving us all or, in His wisdom, He will destroy the world and create it anew. That is up to His judgment."

Darius began to trail after him. "Then where are you going?"

Father paused, half turned back. "You captured mages when you took over the temple. Have you forgotten how they entered the Needle the first time? They must be dealt with immediately."

"That's already been taken care of. They won't be blasting their way out of the temple. They won't be doing much of anything until we're ready."

"—so as soon as the debris settles from the back wall, we'll push through into the corridor beyond—"

"You're certain there's a corridor there?" Sovaan asked.

"—and clear it if necessary. We'll keep the mages in the middle of the group." Ty looked up at Cory. "If we're trapped at any point, don't hesitate to blast through a wall on either side."

"What will we do with the wounded?" Cory asked.

"Nothing." Bryce motioned down at his leg. If possible, it looked worse than when Cory had first inspected it upon arriving, the blood leaking out of the wound now darker, thicker. "There's no way you can carry me with you and still make it out alive. Anyone who can't walk will have to stay behind."

"But—"

"No," Ty interrupted. "Bryce is correct. We can't afford to be slowed down, by anyone or anything. Got it?"

Cory clenched his teeth. The other mages stirred.

Then the door to the room groaned open. Half of those gathered around stood abruptly; no one had heard anyone approaching from outside. Most reached for nonexistent swords.

From outside, someone shoved a half-barrel into the room, what looked like water sloshing over the side.

"Don't touch it!" Ty shouted.

Someone tossed something else through the door, a sachet of some kind. It hit the water and sank.

The door pulled closed. No one moved, looking at each other in confusion.

Seconds later, those closest to the barrel gagged and began coughing. Hands raised to their mouths, they lurched away, but stumbled and within three steps had fallen to their knees and slumped to one side.

"What in hells?" someone mumbled in stark terror.

"It's a gas." Ty pointed at Cory. "We have to go now!"

Cory twisted toward the wall they'd chosen as their exit, reached for the Tapestry, but then the gas slammed into his senses. With a single indrawn breath, it burned from mouth to sinuses to throat and down into his chest. He tried to exhale, but his lungs wouldn't work. His eyes teared as he grasped at his shirt, the stone wall before him wavering. Men were collapsing on all sides, eyes red, tongues distended. He fell forward onto hands and knees, Jerrain hitting the floor on his left, Ty on the right. Bryce clutched at his throat. Cory reached for the Tapestry again, felt its folds as he tried to knot it within the nearest wall, but it slipped from his fingers as he fell onto his side.

Stone pressing into his cheek, he watched as Bryce's head finally slumped to the side and rocked forward. His last thought was that it was strange that the Dog was still breathing.

Fifteen

"NONE OF YOU look like you slept at all," Allan said from his seat as Kara entered the Temerite main chamber, followed by Artras and Marcus.

Kara barked laughter. "I destroyed Tumbor yesterday and you thought I'd sleep?" She crossed the room and leaned on the table, more to hide the trembling of her hands than for any other reason. Her skin felt drawn, her eyes bruised, her entire body somehow both light and heavy at the same time.

She glanced around the table. The Matriarch was there with Janote, of course, and Lienta and Boskell. The others in their group from the temple were present as well—Allan, Cutter, Marc; Grant and Hernande; Morrell and Drayden; Okata. Only the Wolves were absent.

The Matriarch pushed a cup across the table. "Have some kaffe. It will renew your energy for a while."

Kara picked it up and smelled the steaming liquid, tart and pungent, like ground-up earth. She took a sip and almost spit it back out. "Bitter," she managed after a swallow.

"Some people add milk or sugar, although we consider those who do so heathens."

Cups were poured for Artras and Marcus as the Matriarch gestured toward three free chairs. "Sit. We have much to discuss."

"So do we." At Allan's raised eyebrow, she added, "Did you think I simply sat around and wallowed in anguish all night?"

"It crossed my mind."

"She worked both of us to an extreme," Marcus said, grabbing his cup and gulping it without thought. He immediately began coughing. "Gods, what is this!"

"Steeped ground roasted cacao beans."

Marcus continued gagging, while Kara took another sip. "It does seem to work. My arms are tingling. And it's spreading."

"The body's reaction is blunted after multiple uses, but the first time can be rather pleasant," the Matriarch said.

Kara set her cup down. "What's the report on the Needle?"

Lienta leaned forward. "The Kormanley have taken over the city east of the chasm. The populace doesn't seem inclined to rebel against them, at least not yet. Most appear ecstatic that their Father has been released. He spoke to them this morning at dawn from the temple's tier. We couldn't hear all that he said, but it sounded as if he reassured them but was also riling them up. He mentioned snakes and dogs repeatedly, and he pointed toward the north and toward Erenthrall."

At mention of the city, he deferred to Allan, but before the ex-Dog could speak, Kara said, "We already know about Erenthrall."

"What do you know?" the Matriarch asked.

"The ley system there has ruptured. It's spewing out of the ground, like a volcano, ley flowing through the streets like lava. Whatever support it had, even with the distortion over Tumbor, has collapsed now that the nodes within Tumbor have been completely destroyed. If Hernande's theory that the ley lines form the underlying structure of reality and the Tapestry is draped over it is correct, then—in essence—a cornerstone of the foundation has been knocked away. The entire system is fluctuating, and something within Erenthrall gave way."

"The repercussions are worse than that," Boskell broke in. "The watchmen have reported a change in the Three Sisters to the north. They've begun to pulse. Also, they swear that they've seen the land to the west and south . . . rippling."

"Rippling? Like when the auroral lights pass over something?"

"No. As if the earth itself were rising and falling, like a wave on water."

"Quakes," Hernande said.

"Worse than anything we've experienced so far. The men also report more sightings of auroral storms. Nothing close to us yet, but they're fearful."

"It would appear that the Kormanley seizing the Needle is the least of our problems," Marc said.

"No, it's a significant problem," Kara said instantly. "The pulsing of the Three Sisters and the quakes are simply effects. The root of the problem is the ley. And in order to solve the problems with the ley, we're going to need access to the Nexus at the Needle."

Hernande raised a hand to stop her. "We've already tried that. It didn't work."

Kara winced as if physically struck and bowed her head. Then she gathered herself and pushed herself away from the support of the table. "You're right. We tried that. It failed. I failed. But we're still going to need the power of the Nexus if we're going to heal anything and stop whatever's happening to the land. It's gone too far to be halted by an individual."

As if in answer, another quake struck. Not as strong as the ones immediately after Tumbor's distortion collapsed, but it lasted for at least five minutes, everyone glancing upward at first, then hunkering down and holding onto the table and chairs, cups and saucers. Janote grabbed the porcelain kettle holding the kaffe. Dust sifted down from the ceiling, everyone covering their drinks.

When it finally faded away, watchmen raced into the room. "Matriarch!"

"I'm fine." She waved them away, though they were reluctant to leave. "Boskell, deal with them. Have the servants bring us something more substantial than kaffe, please."

The lieutenant stood and joined the watchmen at the door, escorting them outside. He returned a moment later, servants trailing behind him with trays of fruit and bread. As they set the food around the table, the Matriarch again motioned to the three empty chairs. "I assume you've come up with some type of plan."

Artras sat without preamble, drawing her own cup of kaffe toward her and snatching up a few grapes. Marcus followed suit, cutting a slice of bread, but Kara remained standing, crossing her arms over her chest. "We need access to the Nexus," she said.

"That's only one of our problems," Hernande countered. "Can you repair the rupture in Erenthrall from the Nexus?"

Kara began pacing back and forth, everyone remaining silent. "I don't know," she finally said. "Probably not. The ley is wild in Erenthrall, and because of the lake beneath the ground, it's strong. In order to repair it, I'll have to be in Erenthrall. But I'll need the power of the

Nexus to do it. Someone will have to funnel the ley from the Nexus here toward Erenthrall so that I can use it."

"Which means we'll have to retake the Nexus, if not the entire Needle," Marcus said. "But there's more."

Artras spit the seeds from her grapes into the palm of her hand. "Based on our observations of the ley last night—as Marcus said earlier, extensive observations—it would seem that even if we can get control of the Nexus here and Kara can repair the rupture in Erenthrall, that won't be enough to keep the ley from ripping reality apart."

"Why not?"

Artras faced Okata. "Because there's a gap in the foundation of the Tapestry. It will continue to ripple, as Boskell described it. Think of a flag flapping in the wind. Eventually, unless the flag is tied down, it will tatter and fray. The Tapestry will do the same thing."

"Unless we tie it down," Hernande said. He'd begun to stroke his beard. His eyes were squinted in thought, focused on Kara. "The issue is the lost nodes that were inside the distortion over Tumbor, isn't it? They were destroyed. They were anchors for the ley, and thus for the Tapestry."

"Yes."

Boskell threw his hands up in disgust. "Then we're lost. There's no way to tie them down again. All of this discussion is useless."

Hernande made a noise of disagreement. He'd progressed to chewing on his beard, and his gaze had shifted to Morrell. "In essence," he said, musing to himself, "we need a node in Tumbor, something for the ley to connect to, to use as an anchor."

"But there's nothing left," Kara said, sinking down into her chair and resting her head in her hands, despair welling up from her chest. When she spoke, her voice was ragged. "I was there during the collapse. I saw it. The distortion shattered everything, broke the ground into splinters, reduced the buildings to rubble. *There is nothing left.* Nothing." She suppressed a shudder.

"But the earth remembers," Hernande said.

Kara raised her head. "What does that mean?"

The others looked as confused as she felt.

Hernande spat out his beard and leaned toward her, one finger poking the wooden table for emphasis. "The earth remembers. The stone. It remembers what it once was. Tumbor must have been built over a natural node, one that Prime Wielder Augustus used as a focal point to shape his network. The earth will remember that node, its shape, its structure. For the stone, it will feel natural."

"I don't see how that helps us," Marcus said. "None of us know how to construct a node. Based on the pits and the Nexi here and in Erenthrall, it's not something easily done. The placement of the stones, the order." He shook his head. "Constructing a new node without any foreknowledge of how to do it could take months, if not years. I doubt we have that much time."

Kara drew breath to agree, but Morrell spoke first.

"He means me."

Her voice was soft, so it took a moment for most of those at the table to realize it was Morrell who'd spoken. But eventually everyone focused on her small-framed body, her soft blonde hair. Drayden sat beside her, nostrils flaring as he returned everyone's stare. He growled, but Morrell placed a hand on his arm and he quieted.

"Hernande means me," she said again, her tone stronger. She straightened in her seat, glanced apologetically to her father. "I can build a new node. If he's right and the earth remembers, I can heal it, return it back to what it once was. I did it with the stone of the walls here at the Needle. I'd need to go there, to Tumbor, or where Tumbor used to be. I'd need to touch the earth there, but I could do it."

"No," Allan said instantly.

Morrell smiled. "You can go with me, Dad."

"No!" Allan shoved back from the table, his chair clattering to the floor. "I can't let you—I can't—" He balled his hands up into fists and nearly beat them against the table, catching himself at the last minute and placing them down gently, even though he gave an inarticulate cry of frustration.

"What he's trying to say," Lienta said into the startled quiet, "is that he can't go with you."

Morrell looked stricken. "Why not?"

"Because I have to go with Kara," Allan answered. He faced Kara. "Isn't that right? I have to go with you, because you'll need to get to the Nexus in the center of Erenthrall and right now it's in the middle of a geyser of ley. The only way to get through that is if I'm there, to suppress the ley."

Kara opened her mouth to answer, but the words halted in her throat. Allan so obviously wanted her to deny it, so that he could accompany his daughter to Tumbor, to protect her, but she couldn't. She did need Allan and whatever talent he had that canceled out the effects of the ley.

Allan cried out and stalked away from the table, away from them all, halting a short distance off. Morrell leaped up and joined him. Kara couldn't hear what she said, but Allan hugged her tight and rested his chin on top of her head.

"Every time I think we can finally stay together," he said, his voice barely audible, "something sends us apart again."

Morrell answered, but her words were muffled by her father's chest. He chuckled and stepped back to look down at her. "One day, yes. Both of us together."

"I will protect her," Drayden said, his rumbling, animalistic voice loud. He startled as it echoed in the room, but glared around at everyone defiantly. "I will go with her and keep her safe."

"She'll need more protection than a single half-Wolf," Lienta said.

Drayden bared his teeth, but Lienta halted him with a raised palm.

"I simply meant that you'll be traveling through Gorrani territory and they will show you no mercy."

Okata stirred. "Perhaps if they have a Gorrani in their party, they will have a better chance." He faced Kara. "If she is creating a node, a Wielder should be with her. I may be needed to help connect the ley lines to the new node when it is finished."

"That makes sense."

"Who else?" Allan asked, stepping away from Morrell.

Lienta and Boskell looked at the Matriarch. She bowed her head. "Send as many of our watchmen as needed. If she fails to create the new node, everyone is lost."

"I'll go," Boskell said immediately, "with a few watchmen as a guard. I owe Allan my life, after all."

"Not many," Okata warned. "It will be easier to evade the Gorrani if there are fewer of us to notice."

Allan didn't appear satisfied, but he said nothing.

"Who will go with Allan and myself, then?" Kara asked.

"I will go with you to Erenthrall." Everyone turned to face Grant, the pack leader lounging back in his chair, arms over his chest. "I am still searching for my wife, even if it is unlikely I will find her now. My Wolves will protect us all."

After seeing how they'd handled the Kormanley guards in their escape, Kara didn't question him, turning to the Matriarch instead. "That only leaves the problem of seizing the Nexus."

"Leave that to us," the Matriarch said. "The Temerites will make certain that Marcus—"

"And me," Artras interrupted.

"—that all of the Wielders needed are at the Nexus when necessary." She tapped the table with her knuckles in contemplation. "Which brings up an interesting issue. The Wielders here will need to know when to send the ley to Erenthrall for your use, Kara. Yet we may not be able to seize control of the Needle completely. Our hold may only be temporary. We should time this so that you are already in Erenthrall when we attack. How can we do this?"

No one spoke until Hernande said, "You will all have to be in place and ready on an agreed upon day, at the same time. Morrell, you must have constructed the node before then. Marcus, Lienta, you must seize control of the Nexus here and hold it for as long as Kara needs. And Kara, you'll have to be ready and prepared in Erenthrall."

"How long will it take Kara to travel to Erenthrall, and Morrell to Tumbor?"

"The parties will be small," Allan said, "and I assume they'll have horses?"

The Matriarch nodded. "Whatever we have is yours."

"Then two weeks."

Boskell snorted. "You'd better factor in some time for delays."

"And I don't know how long it will take me to create the node in Tumbor." Morrell had drifted back to the table. Her father enfolded her in one arm. "It may require more than one attempt."

"Let's say three weeks," the Matriarch said, with the tone of finality. She pointed to Kara, Artras, and Marcus. "You three need to get some rest. Actual sleep this time. Leave the preparations to Lienta. Now go."

Kara rose, but staggered. Now that decisions had been made, her exhaustion settled into her muscles like stone. Marcus caught her arm, but he was as weary as she was. Allan came forward and led her back toward their room deeper inside the embassy. She couldn't even dredge up the words to thank him. Artras and Marcus trailed behind them.

The ex-Dog left them in their rooms, each crawling into separate beds. Kara pulled the thin blanket up over her legs, then let it drop. She stared up at the stone overhead, heard Marcus shifting into a new position, knew that Artras had already fallen asleep by her snores. Concern over Cory caught at her attention, brought her back from the brink of unconsciousness for an anguished moment, but even that wasn't enough to keep her eyes open.

As she fell into darkness, she muttered to herself, "Three weeks."

The darkness surrounding Cory appeared complete, until he heard a murmur of sound. It was muddy, softened and distorted, but it was a voice. He concentrated, the ethereal feel of being submerged in water receding, but not far. A dim light appeared, blurred and muddied like the sound, as if it were above the surface of the water.

He pushed toward it, and the closer he came, the more sensation coursed through him. The darkness resolved into the shape of his body—arms, legs, torso—but it remained disconnected from him, distant. His mouth, sinuses, and throat burned. His lungs were hollows of liquid fire. A roaring sound pulsed in the background and it took him a long moment to realize it was his heartbeat, slowed down tenfold, barely sustaining his life.

Movement above the water reclaimed his attention and he pushed closer, running up against a wall, a slick surface, like glass. But he was close enough now that he could discern figures beyond the glass, could hear words and phrases. And the longer he listened, the clearer it became.

"... take his ... get arms. Drag him ..."

Two men, close to him. One leaned down and hoisted up his legs, close enough Cory could see his face, but he didn't recognize him. An enforcer, though. Someone else leaned down and pulled up Cory's arms. Or at least, he assumed they were his arms and legs, since when the two enforcers began to drag the body, his perspective shifted. He felt nothing, no tingling in his extremities at all.

They dropped him near the wall and his head rolled to one side. Jerrain and Sovaan were stacked next to him, some of the other students beyond. Bryce sat upright against the wall, head forward, Ty beside him. They were still in their prison cell beneath the temple then.

". . . others with them . . ."

". . . freaky that their eyes are still open."

"Get over it. Let's move the . . . Darius wants at least five for . . ."

"What about . . . damned mages?"

Cory beat against the glass wall, screamed Bryce's name, bellowed at Ty, but his body didn't even twitch.

The guards dropped another body near Cory, one of Ty's supporters.

"Dalton wants them for something . . ."

"I don't see why we just don't kill them all. They've been nothing but . . ."

Another body, then two more, mostly out of Cory's sight, although he could see at least one of the guards most of the time.

"There. That's all of them."

"Except these seven."

The two guards shifted back into Cory's view, both standing over Bryce and Ty. Except Cory noticed they were blurrier than before, mere black smears against the torchlight. He couldn't pick out Ty's features anymore either. Bryce had faded into the background of stone.

One of the guards kicked Bryce's wounded thigh, then laughed. "Whatever that gas was, it knocked them out good. He didn't even flinch."

Cory slammed against the glass again, strained against it, but his vision kept fading, as if he were sinking. Yet his hearing continued to improve.

"Are you ready?" a new voice asked.

The two bleary guards shifted. "We've got Ty, Bryce, and five others picked out, as Darius ordered. What do we do with them?"

"Find some others to help you haul them up to the first tier. Commander Darius and Father have plans for them, some kind of sermon."

"What about the rest?"

"As soon as you've removed these seven, give them another dose of that gas. Darius doesn't want the mages to awaken until Father's ready for them. They can do too much damage on their own."

The dark swatches moved, the light almost gone. Belatedly, Cory reached out for the Tapestry, cursed when he easily passed beyond the glass wall. He focused on the guards, but his grip on the Tapestry was tenuous. Like silk, it slid from his mental fingers and with a final outraged cry, complete darkness enveloped him again.

Ty woke when someone slapped him hard across the face. He sucked in a breath, then immediately leaned over and vomited, his throat, lungs, and mouth burning as if coated with oil and lit on fire. The bile made it worse. He heaved a second time, then spat, not surprised to see blood in the vomit. His hands were tied behind his back, his legs bound at the ankles and knees, straight out in front of him. His body leaned back against a wall, one of the temple corridors, since it tilted forward.

Drawing in shallow breaths, he looked around without raising his head. Five—no, six—others were bound and seated like himself down the corridor, Bryce to his left. No one sat to his right, where he'd puked. But Darius squatted before him, a slew of enforcers behind him.

"How do you feel?" Darius asked.

Ty swirled the bitter taste around in his mouth and spat again before raising his head. "Like shit." It hurt to talk, his voice a croaking growl, nearly unrecognizable. Something leaked from his nose. Blood.

Darius chuckled. "Glad to hear it."

From the far end of the corridor, where the sun blazed in the ruddy colors of dusk, the roar of a thousand voices rose in a shout. From the other direction, someone moaned as they began to come around.

Darius gestured toward the enforcers behind him and they shifted farther down the corridor, standing over the rest of those tied up with Ty.

"What's going on?" Ty asked. "Father giving one of his sermons? Trying to appease the people?"

"Not appease. Trying to allay their fears."

"They should be afraid, with you in power."

Darius reached out and grabbed hold of Ty's chin with one hand, pinching his cheeks tight as he searched Ty's eyes. Ty struggled, but his entire body ached, his muscles weak. He couldn't break Darius' grip, defiantly refused to look away.

Next to him, Bryce moaned.

Teeth grinding together, he funneled all his hatred for Darius and

Father Dalton and the Kormanley into his gaze, breath heaving out through his nostrils.

Darius finally grunted and thrust Ty's head back as he stood. "Father was right. You'll never tell us where your men are keeping Jonnas and the others you captured. We'll have to find them ourselves." He stalked away, toward the sunlight and the tier.

"They haven't found them yet?" Bryce asked, keeping his voice low.

"You sound like hell."

"I feel like it."

"At least you didn't puke." Farther down the hall, the other guards with them were waking up. "How's your leg?"

"Is it still there? I can't tell."

Ty grunted at the gallows humor. If it *was* gallows humor. "I don't see any of the mages."

"Maybe they escaped."

"Somehow I doubt it. My last memory before waking here was Cory on his hands and knees, reaching for something."

"Shut it!" one of the enforcers ordered, stepping in front of both Ty and Bryce. Both guardsmen looked up at him as another roar reverberated down the corridor.

"I don't see the point in listening to you," Bryce said. "I'm already three-quarters dead as it is, and it sounds like your cursed Father Dalton is getting ready to hand me the other quarter."

The guard didn't answer, merely stalked off toward the sunlight, vanishing in the glare.

"He didn't take that well," Bryce said.

"He never took well to honesty."

Someone emerged from the light, resolving into Darius. "Get them all up and out onto the tier. Father's ready."

The men moved forward, Darius coming for Ty himself. Ty's erstwhile second jerked him up by the arm, slashing the ties at his knees and ankles so he could walk, even though Ty's legs gave out almost instantly, numbed from the gas and immobility.

"Time to face Korma for your betrayals," Darius said as he hauled Ty forward.

They emerged onto the first tier, passing through ranks of enforcers, headed toward the stone platform that jutted out over the massive square below. Kormanley banners flapped in the brisk breeze on all sides, ley globes blazing on the edge of the tier and along the length of the walls. Ty's eyes teared up at the brilliant sunset, the orange-red-gold of the light on the horizon and burning in the clouds intense. He blinked as Darius dragged him to a halt at the start of the platform, Father twenty strides ahead in a blazing white robe, hands raised to the sky.

Below, what appeared to be every soul who resided in the Needle stood in the square, most with hands raised toward Dalton.

"These are the men who led you astray!" Dalton bellowed, his voice somehow echoing through the surrounding buildings to those below. "These are those who would control the ley, instead of letting it return to its natural order! You've witnessed how destructive they can be. Tumbor has been destroyed! Erenthrall is consumed by white fire!" Ty shot a glance toward the northeast, where the white glow above Erenthrall was clearly visible. "And far to the north, the Three Sisters tremble, on the verge of quickening, as I foresaw in my vision! All that I have said will come true, unless we seize control and stop it ourselves! And the first step in our quest of purification, of renewal, of a return to the natural order as Korma demands, is the judgment of those who sought to destroy us."

Dalton turned to face Ty with his clouded eyes, his arms dropping. In a much softer voice, he said, "Welcome, Commander. I'm glad you could join us."

The door to Kara's room slammed open, startling all of them, and Lieutenant Boskell stepped in, surveying everyone present with one swift glance.

"Kara, Allan, Marcus," he said, "you need to follow me now."

Allan stood. "Why? What's happening?"

"Father Dalton is in the middle of a sermon and he's brought prisoners forth as part of the show."

Kara immediately thought of Cory and the other mages. "Who?"

"I didn't stay to find out. The Matriarch ordered me to find you and bring you to the embassy roof."

"Then let's go."

Boskell led all three of them out the door, cutting left and taking them into corridors and stairs they hadn't been privy to yet. They ascended swiftly, emerging on the roof in a matter of minutes. Kara's hands were clenched into fists as she looked toward the temple, but it was too distant and the light too odd to make out faces. She could see a figure she assumed to be Dalton in a white robe at the end of the stone walk jutting from the first tier, assorted figures arrayed around him. A smaller group stood out up front, near Father.

Kara twisted and found the Matriarch, Janote, and Lienta at one edge of the roof, the captain with a spyglass raised to his eye.

"Who's being held prisoner?" Kara demanded as she moved toward them. "Is it Cory?"

"No," Lienta answered, lowering the glass and handing it over before Kara could ask for it. "It appears to be Commander Ty, Bryce, and a few other enforcers."

"They only just emerged," the Matriarch said. "Our men have only caught snatches of Dalton's sermon, but it appears to be a trial."

"Not a trial," Allan said at Kara's side. "An execution."

But Kara wasn't listening. As soon as Lienta gave her the glass, she raised it to her eye. She searched wildly for a breath, then forced herself to calm down, focus. Even though Lienta had said Cory wasn't present, her heartblood still roared in her ears. She found the temple, centered herself on the first tier, the ledge, the front ranks.

Dalton blazed in his robes, lit by the ley and the lurid colors of the sunset. Ty stood with Darius at the edge of the jutting stone walk, but as she watched, the two traded places with Dalton. The others were each led up to the edge of the tier on either side, Bryce practically carried by two guardsmen because one of his legs was a bloody mess. She didn't recognize any of the other men, except as a vague recollection of seeing them around the temple.

No Cory. None of the University mentors or their students.

A surge of relief shuddered through her, followed by shame.

"What's happening?" Allan asked.

Kara started, her attention returning to the temple. "Darius has taken Ty out onto the end of the jut over the square. He's got a wicked dagger with him. Bryce and the others have been positioned at the edge of the tier."

"Where's Dalton?"

"He's still near the front, but not out over the crowd." She drew in a ragged breath. "We have to do something."

"What?" Marcus asked, his frustration clear. "What can we do?"

The Matriarch placed a hand on Kara's arm. "There's nothing that can be done. There's no need for you to watch."

Kara shrugged her off, suddenly angry. "I have to watch. I owe Bryce and Ty and all of them that." Her voice had become choked. "He stayed behind so that you could reach me, so that you could escape and save the Wielders."

"That does not mean you are required to watch. Only that you grieve."

"I'll watch."

The Matriarch's soothing grip dropped away.

Through the glass, Kara shifted between Ty's stoic face, Dalton's exultant one, and Bryce's, more a rictus of pain.

As Dalton raised his arms once again, head lifted, words Kara could not hear spilling from his mouth, she trembled with energy she couldn't expend to save them and tears burned her eyes.

Ty stood at the end of the jut, a sea of people beneath him, Darius at his side, holding him in check. Wind gusted into his face, but he held himself stiff, back rigid, formal. Behind, Dalton spouted words about justice, about faith, about a coming battle to be fought here at the Needle, to be fought by all of them, but the words were meaningless. Ty stared out at the horizon, sunset to the west, out of sight, but its colors caught in the clouds above and highlighting the mountains to the northwest. Those colors faded into dusk in the east, pinpricks of stars barely visible, Erenthrall burning off to the side, the Three Sisters pulsing straight ahead. The pulses were clear; a flash of brighter light from each one, all three at different intervals, but all still spaced far apart. They'd been unbalanced, had begun to quicken. That, at least, of what Dalton had said, was true.

Dalton's voice rose to a crescendo and Darius shifted beside him, his eagerness radiating off his skin like heat. He spun Ty toward him, dagger ready. To one side, he could see Bryce and a few of the other guards lined up on the side of the tier, an enforcer with a dagger standing behind each one.

"You realize that the god Korma doesn't preach about returning everything to its natural order." Ty was surprised at how calm his voice sounded, how serene.

Darius hesitated. "What do you mean?"

"Korma is all about balance."

Ty threw himself backward off the stone jut, Darius realizing his intent a few seconds too late. The Kormanley usurper swung his dagger at Ty's gut, the blade scoring a thin line across Ty's stomach, but not cutting deep enough to disembowel him. Darius' hand tightened on Ty's arm, but then released. Still, it was enough to make Darius stumble to his knees at the edge of the jut to keep himself from following Ty, his face a rigid mask of hatred. He screamed something Ty couldn't hear past the rush of air in his ears.

On the edges of the tier, the enforcers slit the throats of their prisoners and shoved them down onto the steps of the temple. Bryce's body struck the stairs and crumpled, rolling and twisting like a rag doll before coming to a sprawled halt.

Then Ty hit the flagstones of the square.

⌔

On the roof of the Temerite embassy, Kara choked on a gasp and staggered, someone catching the spyglass as she crumpled forward, leaning on the lip of the roof for support.

"They slit their throats," she gulped, "and threw them . . . from the tier . . . onto the steps."

Hands were supporting her—Allan's, Marcus', Lienta's—she didn't know. She couldn't seem to catch her breath. The world had gone dark; or perhaps it was simply that the sun had set.

"Breathe, Kara," Allan said into her ear. Someone pounded her on the back. "Breathe."

She sucked in a breath, coughed it back out, then tried again. After a painful hitch in her lungs, she began to breathe normally again. She straightened slightly, then suddenly stiffened. With a lurch, she batted away the concern and grabbed Marcus by the shirt, dragging him close.

"I know you and Cory don't get along, but you'd better do everything in your power to save him while I'm gone, to save *all* of the mentors and their students. Do you hear me?"

"Of course—"

Kara shook him. "Don't give me the age-old platitudes, Marcus. I know you too well. Swear it. Swear on Korma or Bastion or even the gods-damned Kormanley if that's what you care about, but swear you'll get Cory and the others out of there alive."

Marcus met her gaze, held it. "I'll get as many of them out alive as I can. I swear it."

Kara held him, her arms trembling, then thrust him aside. She stalked back to the stairs, her sight blurring. She moved without thought, without emotion, until someone caught her shoulders in the middle of the corridor where the Temerites had given them rooms. Hernande had halted her, Artras and some of the others behind him.

"What is it?" Hernande asked, stark fear in his eyes. "What's happened?"

"Ty and Bryce are dead. Dalton had them killed on the tier and threw their bodies onto the steps of the temple."

Then she broke Hernande's grip, stepped into her room, and closed the door behind her.

Sixteen

"YOU'LL HAVE TO LEAVE at night. All of you." Lienta spoke in general, but he looked toward Allan. "We've been watching Darius' patrols since they seized control last evening. He has men on the walls, but not that many patrolling outside the Needle."

"Why is that?" Allan asked.

Boskell answered. "Our best guess is that there's too much going on inside the city. He doesn't have the men. At least half of his enforcers are on the wall or overseeing the reconstruction of it. They've elected to seal up the southeastern gates, with masons working since last night's execution. All of their efforts appear to be in preparation for a fight."

"Dalton believes in his visions," Marcus said. "He'll take them as fact. To him, the dogs and snakes are coming. He's getting ready for them."

"As long as it benefits us." Allan turned back to Lienta. "So how do you propose we slip past the patrols and those who are standing watch on the walls? The Needle is dead center in the middle of this crater, with no appreciable cover between the walls and the outer ridge."

"The patrols will be easy. There's a pattern, with enough space between groups that they won't be able to see you in the dark. Evading those on the walls is a little trickier, but if you leave through the gates and follow our own walls toward a specific location near the second tower on the left, then the temple and Needle itself will block your path from nearly everyone on Darius' walls. We're also planning on a diversion at my signal."

"What kind of diversion?"

"It doesn't matter," Boskell said. "As soon as it starts, we'll head straight out from the wall as fast as we can without calling attention to ourselves. We should be over the ridge in fifteen minutes, maybe twenty."

"And then we travel."

Allan, Lienta, Boskell, and the Matriarch faced Kara, who straightened in her seat. None of the others present—Morrell, Grant, Drayden, and Okata—had said anything during the short planning session.

"Then you travel," the Matriarch agreed, "as swiftly as you can, because three weeks does not give you much leeway if something goes wrong. And experience shows that something will always go wrong."

Everyone around the table stirred. No one had touched the food or drink the Temerite servants had put out. Kara looked resolved, although still haunted by the collapse of Tumbor and the deaths of Ty and Bryce. Morrell was moody and introspective, her eyes downcast.

"How long do we have?" Allan asked, searching his daughter's face.

"Three hours. That's when the moon will be lowest and the darkness most complete."

Allan stood. "All right. Three hours, then. Everyone pack whatever you plan on taking with you, if you haven't already, and meet at the Temerite gates."

The group disbanded, all but Morrell and Drayden drifting away, Lienta and Boskell in discussion over final details, Grant with a word saying he'd ready the Wolves. Kara hesitated the longest, before noticing that Morrell hadn't moved. She left with a quick backward glance of understanding.

Allan moved down the table, closer to Morrell's seat. "Are you ready?"

"Yes. No. It's hard to tell." She looked up finally, the fear evident in the lines of her face. "I don't know if I can do it."

Allan sat on the edge of the table. "Yesterday, you were confident you could."

"Yesterday. Now I've had a night to think about it. Everything relies on me succeeding."

Allan took her hand, busy shredding a slice of bread into tiny pieces. "I know you can do it. You've always done what's necessary before."

"Like what?"

"Healed Cory and the others, repaired the wall for Hernande. Reverted Drayden from Wolf back to man." Drayden huffed at his name. "Mostly." Drayden growled, and Morrell's mouth twitched into a smile. "The point is, you do what's necessary. You'll be fine. Think of it as healing the land."

"Do you ever doubt yourself?"

"All the time. I'm better at hiding it than you, though." He squeezed her hand and let it go. "Go collect your things. At least some food, if nothing else. I need to do the same."

Morrell pushed her chair back and stood, heading toward the door to their rooms at the far end of the embassy. Drayden lingered long enough to murmur in his rough, wolfish voice, "I will take care of her," before following her.

Allan watched them both, until Morrell paused and turned back.

"I miss Janis and the Hollow. Maybe, when this is over, we could go back there again?"

He didn't think she meant simply to visit. "Of course, poppet."

She made a face at the nickname, but said nothing.

When they were gone, Allan stared around at the empty room, then rapped his knuckles on the wooden table before rising to collect his own things.

***

Lienta was waiting with Boskell, Okata, Grant and his Wolves, and two other watchmen when Allan, Morrell, and the rest arrived at the gates, escorted by the Matriarch, Janote, and her own guardsmen. Hernande, Artras, and Marcus stood beside her as the rest of them each claimed one of the horses off to one side. The small group was sparsely lit by torches. Night had fallen two hours before, so the light kept most of them in flickering shadows as they moved about. Allan's horse snorted as he approached, then snuffled his hair and ear as he snagged the reins and brought it forward. Kara said something to Marcus, but all three of them responded, Hernande and Artras giving the Wielder a hug. Then Boskell called them all to the gates and within moments they were passing beneath the stone wall and outside into the night.

Grant's Wolves slipped out into the darkness, merging with the shadows within the blink of an eye. Grant and Drayden kept back from the main group, so as not to spook their mounts. Boskell cut immediately right, taking them along the wall, its immense height looming at Allan's shoulder, close enough he could touch it with an outstretched hand. They passed the first tower, but drew up short of the second.

Then they waited.

The animals shifted restlessly, leather saddles and straps creaking, even though no one had mounted up yet. Their scent was strong. Allan stroked his own horse's neck as he stared out at the plains. Clouds obscured most of the sky, leaving the stone and grass beneath heavily shadowed, but the moon broke through in patches and stars were occasionally visible. He thought he caught sight of one of the Wolves once, but couldn't be certain.

"Mount up."

Boskell's voice from the shadows gave Allan a start, but he pulled himself up into the saddle without a word, the others doing the same around him.

"How will we know—" Kara began, but then three distinct cracks sounded from the far side of the wall, muted by its bulk. Silence followed, but Boskell said, "Go, go now! Straight onto the plains!" and they were moving.

Within thirty feet of the wall, something in the city behind them exploded, followed an instant later by two more explosions. Shouts began to fill the night, strangely distant. Halfway to the ridgeline ahead, the atonal bell at the Needle's gates began to clang, the shouts growing louder, even over the thud of the horses' hooves surrounding Allan and the wind in his ears. He didn't dare look back to see what was happening, not without risking losing control of his horse's pace, but as they reached the ridge—the lead riders climbing up and over, then out of sight—he heard another few cracks and two more explosions.

Boskell didn't pause on the far side. He rode them hard deeper onto the plains, the Needle and the activity there falling behind and out of sight. At one point, Allan realized they were being paced by the Wolves, Grant, and Drayden on either side, they and the rest of his group only distinguishable when they passed through a patch of moonlight.

Half an hour later, Boskell slowed. They hadn't been racing, but the horses were lathered with sweat and needed the break. Allan immediately slipped from his saddle and found the Temerite lieutenant.

"Were we followed? Did they see us leave?"

"We weren't followed," Grant said, emerging from the night with one of his Wolves. "My Wolves made certain of that."

"But were we seen?"

Grant shrugged.

"They should have been distracted by our attack," Boskell said.

Allan turned back to him. "You attacked? With what?"

"Catapults. Nothing more." Boskell began checking his horse for injury. "We built them for the outer wall, but moved them to the lip of the chasm last night. That should have kept the Kormanley's attention on their own buildings, not the plains."

"You had catapults?" Kara asked. Allan hadn't heard her approach. He glanced back, but the rest of their group were keeping their distance, checking their own harness and saddles, Boskell's few watchmen eyeing the open plains.

"We're more prepared for an attack than you might think. Initially, it was for our own protection and for the Gorrani threat you warned us of to the south." He picked a stone out of his horse's hoof and tossed it aside, letting the animal's leg go. "But if we need to use it against the Kormanley, all the better."

"You've given up a distinct advantage," Grant muttered, "revealing you have catapults."

"Lienta and the Matriarch felt it necessary. They both believe that you, Kara, and Morrell represent our only chance at repairing the ley. You had to escape the Needle. There was no other option." He raised his voice, so that everyone could hear, although not so loud that it would easily carry across the grassland. "We'll walk the horses to a creek to our west, give them a rest and feed and water them. Then we'll split up, my group heading south, Allan's group north."

The night felt suddenly still and cold. Allan moved to his horse and patted it down, the animal musky with sweat, his motions mechanical. They shifted to the stream to let them drink, and he dipped his hands into the chill water until they were numb.

Then Boskell called an end to the break.

Morrell came to hug him, and he pulled her in tight, drawing in the scent of her hair in a deep breath. She broke away first.

"I'll be fine," she said, her voice only quavering a little.

Then she turned and mounted up, hesitating before Boskell kicked his horse into motion and he, Morrell, Drayden, Okata, and the two watchmen with them faded into the dark.

"She'll be fine, you know. She's stronger than she looks." Kara stood at his side, but he didn't dare turn, could barely bring himself to speak.

"She reminds me of her mother."

Kara said nothing, but Grant cleared his throat. "We should leave. Three weeks is not long, and we have far to go."

Allan forced himself to look away from where Morrell had vanished. He knelt and tossed some of the frigid water onto his face to shock himself into focus.

Then he stood. "Let's move."

"The Wolves will scout ahead for signs of Devin's forces," Grant said as Allan and Kara mounted up.

"Let's hope Boskell and his watchmen can keep Morrell safe from the Gorrani," Allan added.

They kicked their horses into motion, headed to the north, with Grant falling into a loping gait behind them.

⟜

Hernande stood in awkward silence with Marcus, Artras, the Matriarch, Lienta, and Janote at the gate to the Temerite section of the Needle after it closed. He chewed on the end of his beard as men raced back and forth on the walls above, eyes narrowed. He caught the signal as it passed from the wall to the inner buildings along the chasm that split the city, but even so, he jolted when the first three catapults launched.

"What was that?" Artras asked, shaken.

"Catapults," Hernande answered, before either Lienta or the Matriarch had a chance.

The three volleys exploded in the city, immediately followed by shouting, the panic escalating, until the clang of the main city's gates filled the night.

"How did you know—"

"I didn't know you had them. But I recognize the sound of their launch from my days in the Demesnes before I fled to Erenthrall." He listened as the second volley launched. From their vantage beneath the gates, he could only see a brightening of the darkness as the fiery projectiles reached the peak of their arcs before falling back into the city, brighter flares following when they struck. "Light catapults by the sound of the release. Pitch-filled shells?"

"Designed to explode on impact and spread the fire over as wide an area as possible." Lienta contemplated the flicker of orange light from the attack on the bottom of the clouds as three more volleys were launched. "They'll continue this for the next half hour, as a diversion and as a warning, if Dalton was considering an attack on our enclave."

Hernande turned back to the gates, once again chewing on his beard in apprehension. "Did they make it out unnoticed?"

"I have men watching them and how Dalton reacts. We should know something shortly."

Marcus hadn't turned away from the continued catapult attack. "How many catapults do you have?"

"Five light catapults, with three more under construction."

"What other long-range weapons do you have?"

Lienta eyed Marcus, then glanced at the Matriarch.

She waved a hand. "We have three weeks to plan an attack on the Needle that will get these three into the Nexus. They're going to find out what our assets are at some point."

Lienta's shoulders tensed, but he said, "We have ten ballistae as well. We are somewhat limited on spears for their use, but we have plenty of pitch-pots for the catapults."

"And how were you expecting to get us inside?" Artras asked.

"We've done little planning so far, but the general idea was to attack their weakest point, the secondary gate that you used to escape."

"They will have sealed it or rebuilt it by then," Hernande pointed out.

"But we have you and Artras and Marcus. If you can't burn it out with the ley as you did when you escaped, then Hernande can use the Tapestry to blast it open again or blast our way through another section of the wall."

Hernande tugged on his beard in annoyance. "Someone told you about how we got in the first time, I see."

"Secrets such as that are hard to keep," the Matriarch said.

"I suppose. But don't you think Dalton will have anticipated an attack on the secondary gates? Even the main gates? And you forget that there are two other armies out there, converging on the Needle as we speak. In three weeks, we may not have access to those gates, or even the outer walls. We may be surrounded by the Gorrani, or Devin's men, or both."

"What do we do then?" Artras asked.

The Matriarch motioned to Lienta. "Have our scouts returned from the north and south yet? Do we know how close the Gorrani or Devin's men are?"

"No. According to Allan, the Gorrani were within two weeks' march of the Needle. That report was a few days old."

"And Devin?"

He shrugged. "We have no word on his men at all. He may not have even left Erenthrall. We saw him last fighting the Gorrani outside our old enclave in the city. But if he left now and pushed hard, he could make it here with an army within three weeks."

"It's unlikely that he's waited until now to follow us. We killed a significant number of his men during our escape. He would have left as soon as he felt his hold on Erenthrall secure."

"Then we can expect him to arrive before we can act to take the Nexus."

"That could be useful," Marcus interrupted. Both Lienta and the Matriarch faced him as he continued. "Devin or the Gorrani could be the diversion we need to get into the temple. If Dalton and Darius are occupied on the walls, defending the Needle, we can slip in during the chaos."

"How?" Artras demanded.

"I may have an idea," Hernande said carefully. "It will put your own watchmen under minimal risk, Matriarch, but will keep Dalton and Darius occupied and our infiltration will come from a direction they won't suspect. However, it does carry an extremely significant risk."

Lienta straightened. "What is it?"

Before Hernande could answer, a runner arrived and gave a whispered report to Lienta, then departed.

"The two groups made it outside of Dalton's patrols without being seen. That's all we know for now."

A tension that had crept into Hernande's shoulders eased. Both Marcus' and Artras' shoulders slumped, Artras bowing her head as if in prayer.

The Matriarch touched Janote's hand. "Then we should return to the embassy. We can continue planning our insurgency tomorrow. We have three weeks to discuss every possibility, after all."

Beneath their feet, the ground shuddered with a light tremor. They all shared a look, but no one said out loud what everyone was thinking:

The Tapestry could give way before Kara and the others were able to repair it.

～

Dalton stood over the massive table to one side of the orrery and stared down at its surface. He could see it clearly through the cataracts that hazed his eyes, but not as he'd been able to see it before the Shattering. Now, it was riddled with shifting colors, and occasionally he'd receive flashes of insight or visions. These flashes were extremely short and difficult to follow while he was awake, but when he slept, they played out in his mind like dreams, longer if not always as clear.

The map had been left untouched by Darius and the rest of the enforcers, the markers depicting the last known placements of the Gorrani and any other faction of note within range. But Dalton knew that some of the information was old. As he watched, a large black stone blurred and shifted closer to the Needle's spire, smaller stones around it also edging closer. The convergence was clear, even though the pieces returned to their original positions when Dalton blinked. The entire table rippled with movement, blocks of wood and stone sliding left or right, up or down, some vanishing while others appeared out of nothing. The colors and movements were fluid and mesmerizing.

And revealed to Dalton so much of what was to come.

The doors to the orrery opened and Darius entered, his steps hard and angry as he headed toward Dalton and the table.

"What in hells are they doing?"

"They, who?" Dalton didn't turn, didn't even look up.

"The Temerites! They're bombarding the western edge of the city near the chasm with catapult fire."

Dalton squinted and leaned forward. At the edge of the Needle, two pebbles had appeared. Through his cataracts, the pebbles split, one heading northward, the other southeast, moving fast, but his vision faded before he could determine where they were going.

"I suspect it has something to do with the two groups that have left the Needle."

"What two groups?" Darius halted next to the table. "We've closed the gates, and those on the walls and on patrol have reported nothing."

Dalton straightened. "The bombardment is a distraction. The groups have already slipped out beyond your patrols."

Darius swore and leaned onto the table, even though there was nothing there to see. "I need more men. Men I can trust. Should I send someone to intercept and stop them?"

Dalton considered, but his insights from the table were incomplete. Perhaps he'd learn more tonight while he slept. "No, not now. Perhaps later. The two groups are small, no more than ten in each. As you say, we have minimal enforcers we can trust. We need them here, preparing for the Gorrani and the dogs."

"Devin's army." He motioned to the map. "These placements are old. Where are the Gorrani now?"

Dalton shifted the large black stone and some of the smaller ones near it. He reached for a small block of polished wood set off to one side and placed it on the map northeast of Erenthrall. "Devin left Erenthrall with his men four days ago."

"How long until he arrives?"

"Difficult to say. At minimum, ten days, more likely longer."

"The Gorrani are closer than that."

"But they are moving slowly, cautiously. I'd say we have ten days before they appear on our horizon as well."

Darius scanned the new placements on the map, then shoved back from the table. "We'll be ready for them."

The door to the orrery opened again as Dalton said, "Yes, we will."

Iscivius entered, followed by a contingent of enforcers with the Wielders Dylan and Jenner in tow. Both were restrained, hands cinched behind their backs, but neither one of them struggled. They stepped forward reluctantly. Oddly, Dylan appeared more vibrant than Jenner, his body brighter and more blurred with potential. When he'd been brought before Dalton that first time, after being captured in Erenthrall, he'd carried fewer possibilities around him. But perhaps that was because Kara had outshone him.

"I brought the two Wielders as you requested." Iscivius' tone was curt and distracted. He hadn't believed Dalton or the other Wielders that Marcus had killed his sister Irmona; refused to accept it, even though it had been verified by multiple observers within the pit. His obstinance irritated Dalton, but he could understand why Irmona's death was hard to accept. There was no body, unlike Dierdre. "I fail to see why you need them. They've refused to help with the Nexus, and we cannot trust them."

"We do need them," Dalton answered, "more than you know."

He drifted across the room, eyes locked on Dylan. The Wielder fidgeted, but held his gaze far longer than Dalton expected. But eventually he dropped it, as nearly everyone did, the cataracts and the intensity of Dalton's look too difficult to withstand. Dalton halted before him, not even glancing toward Jenner. The potentials of the two told him that Dylan was the key. Jenner would follow Dylan's lead.

"You aren't cooperating with Iscivius."

Dylan raised his head. "Why should we? He's with the Kormanley."

"Because all of our lives depend on it." Dalton spun back toward the table, motioned the guards to bring Dylan and Jenner forward. Iscivius and Darius trailed behind.

Dalton pointed to the map and the icons that dotted it. "See those black stones? Those represent the Gorrani forces headed in our direction right now. They're upset because we destroyed nearly all their forces the last time they attacked the Needle. They won't care who's in control here at the Needle. They'll slaughter every last non-Gorrani inside these walls, whether you're Kormanley or not.

"And this lacquered block represents Baron Devin's forces, coming from Erenthrall, which is currently spewing ley hundreds of feet into the air, thanks to Kara Tremain's failed attempt to heal the distortion over Tumbor. Even without the ley making Erenthrall unlivable, Devin has no love for you Hollowers. You killed Aurek and a significant portion of his men. Some might say you lured Aurek and his followers to their deaths here. I'm certain Devin believes that.

"Both these forces are coming here, to the Needle, as I foresaw. The serpents and the dogs. They will clash here, and unless we can protect ourselves—protect the Needle—they will destroy us all."

"You have your Kormanley enforcers to protect you," Dylan said.

"According to Darius, Allan Garrett claimed Devin had Hounds with him. Our enforcers would be no match against Hounds. They will find a way inside and open the gates, as they did with the Temerites in Erenthrall. We need something that the Hounds can't circumvent."

"And what would that be?" Jenner asked.

Iscivius answered. "The ley."

Jenner still appeared confused, but Dylan understood. "He wants us to create another wall of ley, like Lecrucius did to stop the Gorrani. The Hounds won't be able to penetrate it. But Lecrucius was a Prime."

Dalton faced Iscivius. "Can you recreate Lecrucius' wall?"

Iscivius drew himself up. "I can." Then he glanced toward Dylan and Jenner and added grudgingly, "But not without support."

"Which is why we need you," Dalton said, stepping closer to Dylan, close enough they were nearly face-to-face. Dylan attempted to step back, but the enforcers halted him. "If you do not help, the Hounds will slip behind our walls within hours after Devin's forces arrive. They will slaughter the guards on the gate and open it. Devin's men will pour into the city. They will kill everyone they encounter, indiscriminately. The Needle will fall within a day. I have foreseen it."

Dylan shot a look at Jenner, but the former White Cloak merely shrugged.

Clearly unnerved by Dalton's nearness, Dylan exhaled harshly and said, "We'll help, but only to protect the Needle. We won't use the ley to kill the Hounds or Devin's forces."

Dalton backed off. "We won't have the chance. The ley wall will have to be in place before Devin arrives, or we risk giving the Hounds the opportunity to slip inside ahead of time." He shifted his attention to the enforcers. "Return them to their rooms. Release them, but place guards on their doors. They are not permitted to leave their chambers until we have need of them."

Dalton, Darius, and Iscivius watched the two Wielders being escorted from the room in silence. As soon as the doors to the orrery closed, Iscivius said, "We still cannot trust them."

"We must. It is the only way to stop the Hounds."

A tremor shook the temple, the strongest one since the day before. Dalton steadied himself using the table, the pieces on its surface juddering in place. A few near the edges toppled to the floor.

After a few minutes, the shuddering ended.

"It will still require all of the Wielders here at the temple," Iscivius said, as if nothing had happened.

"They will follow Dylan and Jenner."

Iscivius appeared doubtful. "There's another problem. The structure Lecrucius created for the wall was complex. I don't understand all its intricacies. I won't be able to modify it without being uncertain of the results."

Dalton reached for the fallen pieces. "What is the issue?"

"The wall will encircle the entire Needle, including the section where the Temerites have seized control. They'll be inside it, with us."

Setting the pieces back on the table, Dalton turned to Darius. "Then we will have to be ready for an attack from the Temerites."

Seventeen

"I THOUGHT YOU SAID we wouldn't run into the Gorrani this close to the Needle," Boskell said under his breath.

Hidden in a dry culvert behind Boskell and Okata, Morrell soothed the horses, which were picking up on the tension between Boskell, the two watchmen, and Okata. Drayden's close presence wasn't helping. Their nostrils flared as he paced back and forth between the narrow edges of the dry streambed, the nearest shying away from him and stamping its feet. Morrell moved among the animals carefully, muttering nonsense phrases beneath her breath as she strained to hear Boskell and Okata.

"There shouldn't be," Okata answered. Morrell glanced to where the two were lying on the ground at the edge of the culvert. The two other watchmen were stationed on the other side, watching for others approaching from their flanks. Okata held a small spyglass, peering through the screen of grass into the distance. "According to our last reports, the Gorrani were amassing south of here, still days distant from the Needle. The area between should have been empty. The Gorrani have been approaching with stealth. They would not want those at the Needle to be aware of their true location."

"Then I'd say we're unaware. How many of them are there?"

"A thousand, more or less. I see the markings of at least ten sects."

Boskell swore, looked down at Morrell, then back into the distance. Morrell silently wished she could see what they were seeing, even though her heart was already beating faster than normal. They'd been riding hard for the past seven days, almost directly east. The initial excitement over leaving the Needle, of heading off into territory she'd

Reaping the Aurora   301

never seen, of being part of a group with a mission like her father, had worn off within the first few days as the reality of what they were attempting sank in. Everyone was depending on her. What if she couldn't rebuild the node? What if it was too much for her to handle?

She'd spent the last three days wallowing in self-doubt. Now she wondered if they'd even reach Tumbor.

"Where are they headed?" Boskell finally asked.

"West. They're going to pass south of us. The closest they'll be is perhaps a mile. We should be outside of their patrols."

"Should? I don't like the sound of that. I'd be more comfortable if we were farther away."

"They'll spot us as soon as we move. The plains are relatively flat here."

A horse snorted, and Morrell shushed it before saying, "Can we follow the culvert?"

Both Okata and Boskell stared down at her, then each other, before Boskell motioned toward one of the watchmen. "Sesali, follow it. Find out where it leads and if it will continue to provide enough cover for us and the horses."

The woman trotted down the dry streambed heading away from the Gorrani, careful of the sandy bottom, short bow at the ready. Boskell and Okata returned to watching the Gorrani's movements, the other watchman—Hanter—shifting position to cover both his own and Sesali's watch.

Morrell drifted away from the horses toward Drayden, who still paced back and forth. Every few minutes, he lifted his nose into the air and sniffed.

"What do you smell?" Morrell asked.

He eyed her, then flicked a hand behind her. "Mostly horses." He hesitated, then added, "We are safe here for now. No one has been near here today."

"Unless the Gorrani have sent out scouts."

"You are nervous. I can smell it."

"You aren't?" she asked, incredulous.

He huffed a chuckle. "We are downwind of the Gorrani. I would smell their scouts before they arrived."

Morrell rolled her eyes, kicked at the sandy bottom of the culvert. It didn't appear to have had water recently. Now that she thought about it, all of the streambeds they'd passed since leaving the Needle had been dry. She recalled Hernande—or perhaps it was Cory—talking about how the quakes and distortions over Erenthrall and Tumbor had altered the shape of the land, diverting rivers into new paths. The entire region had gone dry, even the air tasting of dirt. The only relief had come from the rainstorms.

If it continued, this region would be a desert before long.

"If the Gorrani are here, where we weren't expecting them, doesn't that mean that the Needle is in trouble?"

"We cannot warn them. We have no one to send back."

Morrell didn't like it. Lienta and the Matriarch should know about the Gorrani. Hernande as well. But Drayden was right—they had no one to spare.

Sesali returned, short of breath and flushed. "The culvert runs mostly northeast. There are a few sections where we'd be partially visible, but it should suffice."

"I'll take it," Boskell said, climbing down from his position with Okata, dislodging a shower of dirt and stone. "Lead the way. We'll walk our mounts."

Taking hold of their mounts' reins, the group followed Sesali down the winding streambed. Okata and Hanter took up the rearguard, Okata halting every so often to check on the Gorrani. Over the course of the next half day, they were forced to run across areas where the banks of the stream were shorter, the bed wider, their heads and torsos visible above the surrounding dried grass. Okata watched for signs the Gorrani had seen them, but there was no reaction. Twice, the earth shook with quakes, the sand-and-stone bed strangely fluid during the rumbling, Morrell's feet half buried by the time the tremors ended. No one said anything. They simply pulled themselves from the sand and continued moving.

Only toward sunset did Okata and Boskell begin to relax, the Gorrani force now southwest of their position. As the sky began to darken to the east, Boskell ordered a halt and began to make camp for the night in the middle of the culvert.

"We'll scan for the Gorrani in the morning," he said. "If we can no longer see them through the spyglass, we'll leave the protection of the culvert. It's taken us off course, so we'll have to make up some time, but I'd rather we go unnoticed."

Everyone settled onto separate patches of the rocky bottom, Boskell setting up watches. As night fell, Drayden slipped out into the darkness to prowl around. Morrell suspected he was searching for something bloodier and rawer than the dried biscuits and salted jerky they'd had earlier, since they didn't dare risk a fire.

She lay down on her pallet, squirmed around until the rocks had shifted to either side, then curled up, staring out at the shadowed forms of the others. But she couldn't sleep, her thoughts churning around the Gorrani, worry over what had happened to Cory and the other mentors and students at the Needle, and where Kara and her father were and what they might encounter in Erenthrall.

After rolling over for the fifth time, she heard someone hissing. She shifted and found Okata motioning her up to the edge of the culvert where he stood watch. She glanced around to make certain he wasn't looking for someone else, then abandoned her pallet and crawled up to Okata's side. The earth felt cool beneath her, the night air smelling of chaff and dust.

"Couldn't sleep?" Okata asked.

"I'm worried about Cory and Hernande and Kara. My father. Everyone."

"Understandable." He motioned out beyond the culvert, to the southeast. "Look."

Morrell parted the stalks of grass before her, then inhaled sharply.

The plains were silvered by the moon, stretching into the distance, but far distant auroral storms played across the land. She counted at least four distinct areas, the ripples of light dancing, as if caught in invisible winds. They were all moving in the same general direction, changing colors as they went. Vibrant blues, incandescent greens, breathtaking reds and purples and yellows. One of the storms began to rise toward the heavens, fading into wisps before it vanished. Farther east, two more storms blossomed into existence, expanding with startling swiftness.

"They're beautiful."

Okata shifted uneasily beside her. "They're dangerous. And they're drifting through what used to be Tumbor."

⟶

Light bloomed and Cory struggled toward it, recognizing it as the fading effects of the drug they were using. Like the last twenty times, he struck the glass wall between lucidity and true consciousness, but he immediately looked beyond.

The room was full of enforcers and servants, all of them smears of color and light that slowly solidified and cleared. Most were kneeling next to the cots of the other mentors and students, either washing them or feeding them. Two servants sat next to Cory, one holding him up-right, the other with a bowl of soup and a spoon.

Since they'd taken Bryce, Ty, and the others, the Kormanley had come on a regular basis to feed them and take care of them. Cory still couldn't feel his arms or legs, but they'd lessened the dosage enough that during these times he could swallow, even though his throat and lungs were raw. Each time, he forced himself to eat to keep his strength up. So when the servants began spooning the soup into his mouth, he swallowed it all.

Today was vegetable stew, mostly broth.

He scanned the room, counting the enforcers and servants, and swore. Over thirty in all. Too many for him to handle alone. He sought out Jerrain and Sovaan, but both of them looked worse off than he felt. The servants had to force Jerrain to swallow reflexively. Most of his broth ended up dribbling out of the corners of his mouth. Sovaan ac-tively fought his handlers. He had enough mobility that he could clamp his mouth shut and jerk his head to one side. The rest of the students were in similar situations.

He focused on the guards. All enforcers, all looking slightly bored, a few uneasy. Cory didn't know how long they'd been held here, but it must have been days. Long enough for the guards to relax. They weren't afraid that the mages would waken fully and attempt something anymore.

Cory reached beyond the wall and snagged a piece of the Tapestry near a small stool one of the servants had brought to use as a table when feeding Jerrain. The Tapestry felt oddly loose in his mental grip, as if it had once been pulled taut, but now some of those ties had given way. He tried to ignore the implications of that as he tweaked it into a small fold, then released it.

The stool jounced and scraped across the floor an inch.

One of the servants feeding Jerrain screamed and leaped to her feet. "It did it again! Did you see?"

"See what?" an enforcer asked, shifting away from the wall toward the two women.

"That stool," the first woman said, pointing to where the stool now sat, bowl still on it, but now with stew sloshed over the side and dripping off one edge. "The last three times we've been here, it's suddenly moved on its own at some point during feeding. I swear it's these damned mages!"

The guard laughed. "The mages?" He leaned down and gripped Jerrain's chin, staring hard into his eyes, then released him. "There's nothing they can do. They're too drugged up. See?" He slapped Jerrain with the palm of his hand. "They're paralyzed, barely conscious, only brought out of it enough you can feed them. If we woke them up any more, they'd be blowing holes in the walls. Now finish up with this one. Darius and Father want him."

He stalked off, as Cory's heart stuttered. What could Darius and Dalton want with Jerrain?

The spooked servant slapped her helper. "Was it you? Have you been kicking it?"

The second woman fended her off with one hand. "It wasn't me, I swear!"

Cory ignored the two, focused on Jerrain's face, on his eyes. Mostly paralyzed, it was difficult to read anyone's expression, but he thought Jerrain's gaze fixed on the stool then shifted toward Cory. He couldn't tell for certain. The startled woman knelt again and jerked the stool closer, spilling more stew. She tilted Jerrain's head back and shoved in a spoonful, the other woman massaging his throat to make him swallow. Cory couldn't see his eyes.

But a moment later he felt a flick against his chest. It couldn't have come from the two feeding him; it must have come from Jerrain or Sovaan. They were the only two with enough skill to risk something that precise near someone's body. Even Cory didn't trust himself to do that. If he used too much force, it could have bruised Jerrain, or worse.

Before he could decide what to do next, the servant who'd been startled stood and grabbed her stool. "We're finished here. You can have him."

She stalked out of the room, her helper trailing behind. The enforcer stepped forward.

"That's enough for today. All of you, get out. You two, grab the mage and bring him with us."

Two enforcers trotted forward, sheathing their swords, then hauled Jerrain up, throwing an arm over a shoulder. They dragged him from the room, his feet scraping on the floor behind them. Two others brought in another one of the damned buckets of water as the rest in the room filed out, the servants hurrying to get out of the way. The gas was already filling the room, burning into Cory's lungs, by the time they closed the door. The bloom of light and the glass wall fell away.

When consciousness returned, he searched immediately for Jerrain.

His cot was empty.

The servants filed in again, began bathing everyone using sponges and towels. They'd brought some kind of oatmeal or gruel that slid down Cory's throat like thick paste. He barely noticed, consumed by worry over Jerrain. He tried to use the Tapestry to catch Sovaan's attention, even considered flicking Sovaan's chest like Jerrain had flicked his own—the bastard deserved a few bruises—but didn't get up enough nerve. Instead, he tried to tug on Sovaan's loose shirt. Sovaan didn't appear to notice, and at the end of the visit the enforcer had Sovaan taken from the room.

Cory flailed against the glass wall, frantically searching the room for some option that didn't involve killing everyone present except the mages, but the gas was already starting to spread as the last enforcer slipped out of the room.

As it began to burn down his throat, his gaze met Mirra's on a cot across the room. Even with a mostly paralyzed face, the undergraduate looked terrified.

They took Cory next. Neither Sovaan nor Jerrain had been returned, their cots empty, the blankets still rumpled. Cory reached out for the enforcers' hearts as he was pulled upright and manhandled through the door. They nearly dropped him into the bucket of water, the two hauling it cursing. The corridor outside was filled with enforcers. Even if he dropped the two carrying him in their tracks, he'd never have enough time to take care of the rest before one of them bludgeoned him unconscious.

He voiced an inarticulate cry of frustration from behind his glass wall and let the men's hearts go.

They dragged him through corridors Cory didn't recognize, his head hanging forward. His view consisted of the familiar rough stone floor of the temple, the occasional niche for a doorway or cross-corridor, and the enforcers' feet. He heard the lead enforcer ahead of them, calling out orders, and the tread of others both in front and behind. The scent of spice and charred meat hit him, his stomach cramping with hunger, but then they turned another corridor and it faded. The smell told him they'd been near the kitchens, on the first level of the temple, and were now in the rooms and halls to the north, a section he'd always assumed was servants' quarters.

The enforcers paused and a door opened. They entered and tossed Cory onto another cot. The glimpse of the corridor outside while they shifted his body gave him no new information about his location, but he did catch sight of Darius speaking to the lead enforcer.

Then his head rolled, and he was left staring up at the ceiling overhead. The door closed, the sounds of conversation and footfalls outside fading. He unconsciously tried to hold his breath, so he wouldn't breathe in the burning gas, but it never came.

He didn't know how long he lay there, mind drifting, before he realized that the skin of his face prickled, as if being stabbed with thousands of tiny needles. It started beneath his eyes and spread across his cheeks to his ears and down toward his neck. His lips burned, the sensation twice as intense there, and he moaned, shocked when he actually heard a sound. He tried to say his name with nothing more than a forceful exhale, but his mouth twitched.

With agonizing slowness, the paralysis around his face and down into his chest released. He laughed when he first managed to mutter, "Cor," then, an eternity later, "Cory."

His shoulders had begun to tingle when the door opened. Without thought, he twisted his head, the muscles stiff and protesting, as Darius and Dalton stepped through with two enforcers, at least four others visible outside. The two enforcers set chairs in front of Cory's cot, then stood back as Darius and Dalton seated themselves.

"I see you've regained some mobility," Dalton said. "Can you speak yet?"

"Where Jerrain Sovaan?" It came out as an angry choked croak.

"I see you can. Good. It will get easier as the gas wears off." Dalton leaned forward, searching him with his pale, milky eyes before sitting back again. "We have a proposal for you. Darius?"

"The Gorrani and Baron Devin are coming—the serpents and the dogs—just as Father predicted. We're going to have to defend the Needle once they get here. You and the other mages could help us with that. We've seen what you can do, what damage you can inflict. You infiltrated our walls in a matter of minutes, blasting your way in through solid stone. We want you to turn that power against the Gorrani and Baron Devin's forces when they arrive."

"You can hurt them significantly from the walls," Dalton said. "We can place you on one of the towers of the main gate and you can do whatever it is that you do with the Tapestry and destroy them before they come within a hundred yards of the Needle."

"And if you agree, the others will follow," Darius added. "They are only students."

The two fell silent. They stared at Cory, waiting.

He coughed, then said brokenly, "Where are Jerrain and Sovaan?"

"Dead," Darius said.

"They both proved to be uncooperative," Dalton added.

Cory strained to leap from the cot for Dalton's throat, his entire chest constricting with the effort, but he only managed to lift his head. The cords on his neck stretched and stood out, but he finally collapsed back to the cot with a strangled cry. His breath came in gasping pants. Tears burned at the corners of his eyes, but he fought them back. He fought all of it back—the rage, the grief—his breath leveling out.

He stared at the ceiling until he was composed, then rolled his head to one side. The fingers of his right hand twitched. He didn't think that was supposed to happen so early based on what Dalton had said about the gas, so he clamped his teeth together and glared at the two Kormanley, hoping they wouldn't notice.

"Jerrain didn't deserve that," he finally said, voice low but still cracking, still rough. He didn't think it would ever return to normal; his throat felt too raw for that. "Neither did Sovaan."

"They chose not to help us." Dalton lifted his chin. "What do you choose?"

Cory laughed, a dark sound. "And if I say no, you'll kill me, too, then move on to Mirra or one of the others?"

"If necessary."

"That's not much of a choice."

Darius stood, loomed over him, one hand resting on the hilt of his sword. "It's what you've been given."

Cory stared up at him, then down at Dalton, who remained seated. "They're only students."

"Students who hold the power to destroy stone and earth, flesh and blood. To kill with a thought."

Cory wanted to spit in their faces, but he drew in a breath through his nose and said, "I'll help you." As soon as he was free from the damned paralysis, he'd find a way to get the rest of the students out of Dalton's hands and away from the temple. Let Dalton think he would help until then.

Darius immediately moved to open the door, gesturing toward the guards outside. Dalton stood, blocking Cory's view.

"You made a wise decision, Cory. If we can't hold the Needle, none of us will survive. Neither Devin nor the Gorrani will use it as is needed."

He shifted away, revealing a small table with a bowl sitting on top, brought in by the enforcers. Darius and the other guards had already exited. Dalton halted at the door.

"We'll wake you fully once the Gorrani have arrived. Until then . . ."

He pulled a small packet from his pocket and dropped it in the bowl, then stepped outside, the door closing softly behind him.

Seconds later, the stench of the gas hit him and Cory cursed as it dragged him back down behind the glass wall and into the dark.

⌖

Morrell spluttered as the wind tore the edge of the oiled leather coverlet from her hand and lashed the heavy rain into her face. She snatched at the flailing coverlet and dragged it back into place, hunkering down lower in the shallow depression where she and the rest of her group cowered as the storm raged above. Lightning flared, followed almost instantly by thunder, and the wind once again tried to tear her minimal protection from the sting of the rain away. She gripped it tighter and cursed, her teeth chattering. The rain was cold and had already soaked her through to the skin. It came in sheets and vicious gusts.

She glanced around at the others, the watchmen with their heads bowed down to shield them, Okata looking up toward the sky, his beard glistening as more lightning danced across the plains all around them. Boskell looked miserable, while Drayden hadn't even bothered with a coverlet, merely sat and let the rain wash off him. They'd searched for some kind of shelter before the clouds from the northwest overtook them, but they'd found nothing. The horses were standing a short distance away, rumps to the fiercest wind, heads lowered, black shapes in the frigid gray. One occasionally shook its head.

"How much longer will it last?" Boskell shouted.

Okata lowered his head, rain streaming from his face. He didn't seem to mind it at all. "Do I look like a weather-witch?"

And suddenly three figures emerged from the grayness behind them. In a flare of light, Morrell caught the Gorrani's startled faces.

She screamed and pointed, Okata and Hanter reacting the swiftest, rising, blades already being drawn. But the Gorrani were quicker and Hanter the closest. A curved Gorrani sword cut across his chest and he fell without a sound, Sesali and Boskell surging upright and forward, out of their reach, toward Morrell. Okata took their place, his own sword clashing with the other two, fending both of them off as the man who'd hit Hanter stepped toward Boskell and Sesali. Drayden shoved Morrell back toward the horses, her coverlet snapped away by the wind in the process, then turned to join the others. She caught the fight in flashes as she tried to circle around toward Hanter. Her fingers scrabbled for the knife at her belt, mostly used for eating, then pulled it free.

Behind, one of the horses screamed, and she spun as arms closed around her and dragged her tight against someone's chest.

"Drayden!" She squirmed in the man's grip, feet kicking as they hauled her up and back, the arm holding her knife trapped. Her free hand clamped down on the man's upper arm, her fingers digging into the muscle. He wrenched back with a curse in the Gorrani language, his shirt ripping. Morrell grabbed at him again, her fingers slipping through the tear, touching flesh. She dove through the contact into the man's body, merged with him in the space of a breath, and then tweaked a few muscles in his shoulders and sent a bolt of pain into his stomach.

His arms went lax, numbed, and she wrenched herself from his grasp a moment before he folded over his gut and vomited into the trampled grass. She kicked him in the head, hard, then thought better of it as he moaned and rolled onto his side. Reaching down, she touched his forehead and said, "Sleep."

He slumped into unconsciousness.

A hand clamped down onto her shoulder and she spun, knife reaching, but another hand grabbed her wrist. "It's me, Morrell."

She recognized Boskell's voice before lightning revealed his face. Blood snaked down from a cut on his forehead, black against his pale skin. Okata finished off the last Gorrani, Drayden standing over three others Morrell hadn't seen arrive, his eyes feral. Sesali stood off to one side, her face a portrait of grim pain as she held her arm to her side. Morrell counted seven Gorrani. She guessed all of them were dead except for the one who'd grabbed her.

Her gaze fell on Hanter.

She ran to his side, pulled him over onto his back, and grabbed the sides of his head with both hands. The aurora came easily, flickering into existence practically before she'd called it, far stronger than anything she'd felt while practicing at the Needle. She rode it into Hanter's body.

"He's still alive."

The others gathered around. "Can you—"

"Quiet."

Morrell raised her face to the rain. It pelted her skin, stinging as if it were hail, but she hardly felt it. Hanter consumed her, the wound across his chest raw and open and horrendous. The sword had sliced through cloth and skin and muscle, had slipped between two ribs and caught the lungs, nicked the heart. The blood loss was monumental. Hanter's consciousness had dwindled down to a faint light, like a firefly, sputtering to life, then dying, each resurgence fainter than the last.

When it surged to life again, Morrell snagged it and held on tight, allowing herself to merge completely with Hanter's body. She gasped at the agony, but flooded the wound with the aurora, let it suffuse her skin, sink deeper into the tissue, into muscle, into bone. The firefly in her grasp flickered and she grappled with it, drew it closer, stared into its yellow-green vibrancy.

Emotions and images washed through her, a scattering of disjointed,

intense memories: profound grief as she gathered her eight-year-old
son's pale body up into her arms and clutched him to her chest, her
wife's hands resting lightly on her hunched shoulders, the healer standing awkwardly to one side; a wild burst of laughter exploding from her
gut as she danced madly with a beautiful young girl with flaxen hair, the
world beyond a blur of music and a smear of color; her heart thundering through her entire body with raw panic as she raced through the
streets of Erenthrall, her wife's hand clenched tight in her own, the
distortion an ear-piercing shriek overhead, threatening to quicken, men
and women screaming to either side as the entire world shuddered
around them.

The memories began to die, fading in clarity, in focus. The firefly
began to die. Morrell reached for it, even as she began healing Hanter's
wounds, starting with the heart. But as soon as she drew on the essence
of the aurora, as soon as the heart began to knit back together, the firefly
began fading even faster. She could no longer hold it close. The memories leached from her, stretching and pulling free with painful snaps.

Before she'd even begun, the firefly sputtered out.

A darkness began to close in, smothering, implacable, a darkness she
remembered from healing Cory when his leg was trapped beneath the
boulder in the caves at the Hollow. His foot had begun to die, the blood
flow cut off.

That darkness began to suffuse Hanter's body—*her* body. She was
still entangled in it, down to her core.

She lurched away, the darkness dragging at her, pulling her down,
sinking into her own flesh. Someone was bellowing at the top of their
lungs, but she could barely hear them. With the darkness came ice, a
frisson of cold that lacerated her muscles with a delectable, shivering
pain before all sensation ended. Part of her leaned into that pain, even
as she struggled to free herself.

Then hands gripped her shoulders and yanked her backward, her
fingers ripping away from Hanter's face, her essence sucked up and out
of Hanter's body like boots from thick mud. Boskell threw her onto her
back, straddled her. Lightning flared and thunder growled, rain lashing
down from the sky. Boskell slapped her. But she couldn't feel it. Couldn't
feel anything. All sensation—dead. She'd brought death with her. Its ice
bit into her, seeped deeper as Boskell hit her again.

She could let it claim her. Its touch wasn't unpleasant. An aching pain, followed by exquisite numbness.

But then it touched her lungs and her breathing hitched. With effort, she reached for the aurora. It answered as swiftly as it had for Hanter, slammed into her with a heated fire to counter the ice. Boskell barked a curse and leaped off her as it enfolded her in shimmering light. Morrell arched her back as the fire seared the ice from her, then collapsed back to the soaked grass. The auroral lights faded.

She reached up to touch her face. "I can feel the rain again."

Drayden appeared. "Are you all right?" he growled. He searched her from head to foot, nostrils flared as if he could scent death, grunting with each exhale.

Morrell sat up. "I couldn't save him." She sucked in a steadying breath, recalled what Freesia had said about how healing drained the healer and the victim alike. "I think . . . I think my attempt to heal him actually killed him."

"He would never have survived the wound," Boskell said.

From the shadows of the storm, Okata arrived with the horses and Sesali, her arm cradled at her side. "We must leave. Now. This was not a scouting party, it was a patrol. There's a Gorrani encampment close by. The patrol will be missed."

Drayden's hand clenched protectively on Morrell's arm. "She's not recovered yet."

"Can you ride?" Boskell asked.

"I can."

"Then let's ride."

Drayden snorted in disapproval, but Morrell ignored him. "What about Hanter? We can't just leave him here, out in the open!"

"We don't have a choice. The Gorrani are too close."

"At least let me try to heal Sesali's arm first."

Boskell hesitated, then nodded.

Sesali hissed as Morrell gripped her arm, the guardsman's blood slick beneath Morrell's fingers, but when she tried to call forth the aurora it merely spluttered. A wave of dizziness enfolded Morrell, and Drayden barked once as she began to fall, then caught her.

"I'm sorry," Morrell murmured, the words slurred.

Sesali looked disappointed, but ripped her sleeve off and wound it tight around the wound. "It's not that deep," she said, then motioned to Boskell.

But Morrell had connected with her enough to know she lied. She'd have to try to heal it as soon as she could.

She tried to tell Sesali, but Drayden had already handed her off to Okata, who seated her before him in the saddle and took the reins of both his own horse and hers. Then Boskell and Sesali mounted, Sesali taking control of Hanter's horse, and they took off into the storm.

Morrell clung to the pommel, the world a tattered cloth of biting wind, chill rain, lightning and thunder. She couldn't shake the sensation of ice—it clung to her skin like a shroud—nor Hanter, who she'd hardly known. She clutched the memories she'd lived to her, afraid they would slip away as the firefly had. She forced herself to experience them again and again as they rode, so she would never forget. The tears she shed were lost to the rain, but she knew she cried. Her entire body ached with the grief.

An hour later—maybe more, time had ceased to exist for Morrell—the intensity of the storm faded and Okata slowed. The rain slackened and the winds died. The clouds tore and sunlight lanced down onto the plains.

"What's that?" Sesali asked, pointing.

A short distance away, the grassland ended and shattered earth began, shards of rock jutting up into the air in all directions, some with edges as sharp as a blade, others towering overhead. It looked like a field of broken glass, except it was stone. At various places, auroral storms danced and flickered, encompassing acres of land.

"That's what's left of Tumbor," Okata said. "We're at the outer edge of where the distortion sat."

Morrell stared in mute horror. There was nothing recognizable left, the landscape completely altered, unfamiliar, and utterly foreign.

Okata didn't slow.

An hour later, they entered the shattered land. They had ten days left to reach the heart of Tumbor.

Eighteen

KARA SAT ON A BOULDER at the top of a small rise beneath the brittle stars and stared at the far northern skyline. The stars there were swallowed by a churning mass of clouds lit almost constantly by internal lightning and ethereal flares of purple-and-blue light. They made the horizon appear bruised. But brighter than even that were the Three Sisters, the three distortions over Ikanth, Severen, and Dunmara. Severen's pulsed the brightest, the other two mere echoes. But it wasn't its brightness that troubled Kara, it was its heartbeat.

She chewed on her lower lip, contemplating the distortions, the maelstrom that surrounded them, and the shudders of the earth that had continued as they traveled northeast in an arc toward Erenthrall. Her palms ground into the rough stone beneath her, grit gouging into her skin. The pain was remote, her attention fixated on the Three Sisters, on the steady flash of their lights, on counting the interval between each one.

She didn't hear Allan's approach until he was at the rock. She spun with a curse, lurching away before she recognized him.

"Allan!" She pressed a hand to her chest, the scrapes from the stone finally registering as her hands began to burn. "You startled me."

"Obviously." He waved a hand at the stone for her to sit back down, Allan settling in beside her.

She brushed her hands together, picked a fleck of lichen from one palm with a grimace. "What are you doing up? Your watch ended hours ago."

"I woke during that last quake, couldn't fall back to sleep." He lifted his chin toward the north. "What are you watching?"

"The Three Sisters. Their heartbeats. They're speeding up. The one over Severen is the fastest. It's doubled since we left the Needle. It will be the first to quicken, but it will likely trigger the others when it goes."

"Will it quicken before we reach Erenthrall?"

"How much longer do we have?"

"Eight days. We'll reach the city tomorrow, perhaps the day after."

"So I could start work early."

"I didn't say we'd reach the Nexus tomorrow. Once we hit the city, we'll have to find a way to the Nexus. That won't be easy."

Kara considered that in silence, then said, "I can't tell when it will quicken. The pulse is accelerating. It might even be exponential. But it doesn't matter whether it quickens or not before we reach the Nexus. This isn't about one distortion, or three. This is about the entire world. We broke the world, Allan. We've damaged reality itself." Tears burned her eyes, and she rubbed them with her fingers.

Allan grabbed her hands, holding them tightly before he caught her wince. He turned them over, so he could see where she'd scraped them raw. He looked up into her eyes. "You didn't break the world," he said, his voice angry. "You healed the distortion over Erenthrall."

"Yes, I healed Erenthrall, and because of that I thought I could heal Tumbor. I risked everyone's lives because I was too arrogant to back off when Dalton pressed me, when the Kormanley pressed me. I knew the Nexus at the Needle wasn't strong enough! I knew the distortion over Tumbor was too large! Yet I tried to heal it anyway. And look!" She stood, pulling free of Allan's loose grasp so she could wave to the north, to the east, to the southeast. "The Three Sisters are on the verge of quickening, the Reaches and the Steppe are covered with unnatural storms! Erenthrall has erupted into a geyser of ley! And where Tumbor used to stand, there's nothing but auroral lights! It all started when the distortion over Tumbor collapsed. I caused it all!"

"The Kormanley—"

"Stop it! Just stop it! It wasn't the Kormanley. It never was. *We* caused this all, Allan. *Us*. The Wielders, the Barons, the people in Erenthrall, everyone who demanded access to the ley lines. We all want to blame the Kormanley for the Shattering because it's convenient, but the truth is that we all brought it upon ourselves. Prime Wielder Augustus created the Nexus and subverted the ley, all at Baron Arent's command. But Baron Arent wouldn't have risen to power, wouldn't have controlled all the Baronies and beyond, without us. We gave him power, because we wanted the ley. We wanted heat and light, all of which we had before, but using the ley made it easier. *We* created this problem. Everyone who used the ley in their everyday lives."

"But Marcus—"

Kara cut him off with a slice of her hand. "He had nothing to do with the Shattering. Neither did the Kormanley nor Baron Leethe. The blackouts and distortions were already appearing in Erenthrall, were already escalating in strength. I think even without the Kormanley's interference—or Baron Leethe—the Nexus would have Shattered eventually. Reality was already being torn, even before they began to meddle with it. If anything, they brought the Shattering on earlier, perhaps made it worse."

"Or perhaps they lessened it, made it more manageable, gave us a chance to fix it. Left on its own, maybe the Nexus would have collapsed all of the ley lines simultaneously and ended everything all at once."

Kara simply stared at him from a few paces away, her wild anger cut short. "I suppose we'll never know."

A Wolf padded up to the stone, snout lifted to scent the air. It ignored them both. Grant came up behind it.

"Are Devin's men close?" Allan asked, rising.

"If they were, they'd have heard you and attacked by now." The Wolf at his feet swung its head toward him, ears back at the reprimand. It whined, but Grant reached down to ruffle the fur on its head in reassurance. "They're where they've been for the last five days—marching toward the Needle. After today, we won't be able to track them. They'll be too far away."

"So we managed to evade them," Kara said.

Grant's glare shifted to her. "They're too intent on the Needle. They didn't even send out scouts to watch their flank."

"How long until they reach the Needle?"

"Five days."

Allan shot a glance at Kara. "Let's hope Dalton and the others can hold it for at least five days after that, otherwise Marcus won't have a chance to seize the Nexus there."

"You worry about too many things," Grant growled. "It is out of your control. Worry about Erenthrall and what we will find there. Everything else is meaningless."

He'd addressed the comment to Kara. She stiffened in response.

But then a low rumble came out of the west. Kara braced for a quake, the others doing the same, but the earth remained stationary. Yet the rumble grew louder, the sound like stone grinding against stone. The Wolf at Grant's feet sank to its haunches, lifted its head, and howled into the night sky, the two others in their group doing the same from different points on the plains around them, joined by other animals—their own horses hobbled a short distance away, coyotes, the screech of hunting night birds, the baying of bison. And still the noise escalated, until it drowned out the Wolves, until Kara was forced to clap her hands to her ears, the grinding now like mountains colliding and crumbling into dust. A pressure built, deep inside her head, and she screamed, but she couldn't even hear herself. She squeezed her eyes tight against the pain—

Then the wall of sound surged past them. The pressure dropped off sharply, Kara's ears popping. She opened her eyes in time to catch the grass flattening to the ground in a ripple that sped away from them into the distance. The grinding sound faded as swiftly as the pressure.

Kara tentatively pulled her hands away from her ears and worked her jaw until her hearing returned to normal, a faint ringing in the background. She was surprised there was no blood.

She stood, uncertain when she'd fallen to her knees. "What in hells was that?" Her own words sounded flat and dull to her, but the ringing had begun to fade.

The Wolf lay on the ground, whimpering, Grant stroking its side in comfort. "Something has happened to the west," he said. "Something . . . terrible."

Allan stood slowly, shaking his head as he stuck a finger in his own ears as if to dislodge something. In a voice that was too loud for general conversation, he said, "It sounded as if the earth itself cracked."

As if Kara needed any further incentive.

"We need to get to Erenthrall," she said. "We need to get to the Nexus."

The grinding sound of stone jerked Dalton from ragged dreams of the white fire of the ley and the howl of dogs. He sat up abruptly, then clapped his hands to his ears, momentarily disoriented as the baying of dogs continued. He'd already stumbled from his bed when guards slammed through his door.

"Father!"

"Find Darius!" Dalton shouted, not certain he'd been heard. But the captain of his guard snapped his fingers at those behind and two guards ran off. Dalton dragged on a robe over his sleeping clothes.

The captain ripped his helm off and covered his own ears with his hands. "What is it?"

"Take me to the orrery!"

The captain led him from the room, through corridors mostly empty. Everyone they ran into had their ears covered, leaning against the wall or crouched down, cowering against its base. One or two were bleeding from the ears or nose as the noise escalated.

They were outside the orrery doors when it suddenly ended. Dalton staggered against the nearest wall and leaned against it for support before tentatively uncovering his ears. His head throbbed, and a wave of nausea swept through him. He choked it back, but one of the guards succumbed and vomited in a corner. In irritation, Dalton motioned to the captain to open the door as the stench of bile filled the corridor.

Dalton moved immediately to the table, the captain closing the door behind himself and two other guards, who took up their position on either side of the door. The captain joined him.

"That wasn't a quake," the man said.

"No." Dalton glanced up, noticed a bead of dark blood beneath the captain's nostril. "You're bleeding."

The captain touched the blood with a finger, then wiped at it with the back of his hand, leaving a smear across his upper lip. "It's nothing."

The far door to the chamber opened and Darius stepped inside. "What was that?" he asked as he crossed the room to Dalton's side. "The Needle is in chaos. The animals went berserk, and half of the people I ran into on the way here are bleeding from the nose or ears. A few passed out."

"I haven't had a chance to look," Dalton said. "Give me a moment."

He stepped up to the map, as the captain said, "I think it came from the west."

Focusing his attention toward the Demesnes, Dalton let his strange vision play across the landscape. The few pieces placed on the map shifted and danced, but he ignored them. This hadn't come from a person. This had been more fundamental.

Then he caught sight of a fracture in the map. He leaned forward, part of the map risen out of the surface of the table in his vision. He traced the crack, unease growing in the pit of his stomach as he edged around the table to see it all. Then he remembered the scale of the map and he stood up straight, staring at nothing.

"What did you see?" Darius asked.

Dalton shifted his gaze toward him. For a moment, a dagger jutted from Darius' chest, blood coating the front of his armor, but then the dagger blurred and vanished.

"The land has broken to the west. The center of the Demesnes has . . . has risen. It's created an escarpment a few thousand feet high."

"So it was a quake," the captain said.

"No. This is more significant. The land has begun tearing itself apart."

The look of horror on the captain's face was almost comical. "What . . . what can we do about it?"

Dalton forced his features into a calm expression. "Nothing. We must wait and see what Korma intends."

The captain glanced toward Darius for reassurance, but Darius merely bowed his head and stared at the floor. The captain turned and walked stiffly toward the door to stand with his guards.

"Is there truly nothing that can be done?" Darius asked. "Iscivius—"

"You would have the Wielders attempt to repair the damage with the ley? That is what Kara preached, and look where it has driven us. No, we can do nothing about the ley except pray that it repairs itself before destroying us all. We have a more pressing issue." He tapped the table near their representation of the Gorrani. Nearly all of the markers for the Gorrani had gathered in one spot, a day's march from the Needle. "They've gathered. They will arrive tomorrow. Go to the Wielder's pit, find Iscivius, and tell him it is time."

Darius hesitated, jaw clenched, then bowed his head and departed, moving swiftly.

Dalton returned to the map, leaning forward as he scanned the escarpment that the others could not see. "May Korma protect us."

Hernande dabbed at the blood that had seeped from one ear with a wet cloth as he, Marcus, and Lienta emerged onto the roof of the embassy in the Temerite quarter of the Needle. They were escorted by three watchmen.

All three of them immediately scanned the rest of the Needle across the chasm. Fire lit the base of a column of smoke in one area and there were occasional screams and the panicked braying of animals—all muffled and softened by the damage to Hernande's ear—but the ley globes on the outer walls were still lit and the Needle itself appeared untouched. Figures moved in the streets, but it was difficult to tell whether they were citizens or enforcers or both.

"It doesn't appear that the noise was caused by Dalton," Marcus said. The Wielder tilted his head and shook it, as if trying to rattle something loose. "Not that we thought so to begin with."

"Those on the wall report it came from the west," Lienta said.

They all turned in that direction, but the night cloaked everything beyond the wall. Only the stars could be seen overhead. Even those would be obscured soon if the storm raging to the east came in their direction.

Hernande looked up, resisting the urge to massage his left ear. "Look at that."

Both Marcus and Lienta followed his line of sight, gazing up into the night sky. A single point of light blazed brighter than the rest, trailing a faint tail behind it.

"That can't be a distortion, can it?" Lienta asked sharply.

"I don't think anything can be ruled out now," Hernande said, "but it's not a distortion. It's a comet. The one depicted in the orrery at the temple. It's close enough to be visible now."

Both Marcus' and Lienta's shoulders relaxed.

"Then it's nothing we need to worry about." Lienta leaned forward onto the edge of the wall. "We'll send some scouts out to the west to see if we can determine what caused that grating noise."

"Do we have the men to spare?" Marcus asked.

"We have enough to hold the wall and the chasm if necessary."

"And are we ready for our attack?" Marcus turned to Hernande. "Are *you* ready?"

Hernande didn't drop his gaze from the comet. He realized he was chewing on the end of his beard and forced himself to stop, began pulling on it instead. In a distracted voice, he answered, "I'll be ready."

Marcus hesitated, then faced Lienta. They began discussing the preparations for the excursion into the Needle and how they intended to get into the pit. Hernande lowered his gaze and stared at the stone roof, calculations racing through his head.

After a moment, he grunted and shot another glance toward the comet. "It's going to be on its closest approach the day of the attack. But is it significant or just coincidence?"

"What was that, Hernande?" Lienta asked.

Hernande waved a hand in dismissal. "It is nothing. Merely that the gods meddle in mysterious ways."

Both Marcus and Lienta looked confused.

Then the watchmen in their escort began to shout, drawing their attention toward the east again. White ley fountained up beyond the Needle's far wall, a plume at first, but then it began to spread, reaching out to either side. It rose to a height half again as tall as the wall itself and it continued to encircle the Needle.

"What in hells is it?" Lienta asked.

Hernande suddenly realized Lienta had been in Erenthrall during the last attack on the Needle. "It's a wall of ley."

"Prime Lecrucius used it to halt the Gorrani attack, at Dalton's order," Marcus added. "It killed thousands of them."

"This could change everything," Hernande said, stepping forward sharply. "If they use it to seal off their section of the Needle—"

But even as he spoke, the spreading ley reached the chasm. Instead of following the chasm, separating Dalton's section from that taken over by the Temerites, as Hernande had feared, it continued on across, joining up with the wall on the far side.

Hernande sighed in relief.

Lienta spun and shouted, "Get everyone off the walls! Now!"

Half of their escort charged to the stairs, already shouting orders ahead of them. Hernande didn't think they'd reach the walls before the ley finished forming, but he merely said, "I don't think those on the walls are at risk. It appears that Dalton is repeating what he did before. The ley is merely encircling the Needle."

"I don't trust Dalton or his Wielders," Lienta said. "We'll retreat from the walls for now. Wait and see."

Marcus had edged up to Hernande's side. "It does beg the question, though: who's creating the wall of ley? None of the Wielders we left behind were strong enough, even if they had seen Lecrucius' construction."

Hernande grabbed his upper arm. They both said at the same time, "Iscivius."

"He must have woken up from his coma," Marcus said, then swore. "That means I'll have to deal with him when I reach the pit. Damn, damn, damn."

"Will it be a problem?" Lienta asked.

Marcus considered, then drew in a deep breath and exhaled slowly. "No. No, I can deal with Iscivius. It simply means I'll have to be more on guard."

Behind them, the two edges of the wall of ley connected, sealing them in.

***

Kara, Allan, and Grant reached the edges of the cliffs overlooking Erenthrall midmorning two days later. Grant had sent the Wolves into the cracked lands that surrounded the city to find a path down to where Erenthrall had sunk, but the others had decided to dismount and scout from the heights while they waited.

"Oh, gods," Kara said. She shaded her eyes against the glare of the sun overhead and the harsh white light of the ley shooting up from the center of what used to be Grass in huge spumes. In a weak, sickened voice, she added, "It's changed so much since we were captured by the White Cloaks."

Allan removed a spyglass from his pack and focused it on the center of Erenthrall. "It looks like it's spewing directly out of the old Nexus. I can see the edges of the old crystal dome through the sheared towers." He shifted the glass around. "The nearest streets are flooded with ley. It's running off on all sides. The surrounding land doesn't reabsorb it for at least ten blocks."

"That means that the ley is concentrated and the land in that area is already saturated with it. It shouldn't change our approach, though."

"This might. It looks like the Gorrani—no, not the Gorrani, the Haessan, the Gorrani that have been altered by the aurora into serpent creatures—have moved to the center of the city. I can see them in the streets." He paused, then pulled the spyglass away from his eye. "It looks like they've surrounded the geyser. And there's a heavier concentration of them around the University walls. I'd say they're laying siege to it."

Kara held out her hand and Allan gave her the glass. She brought it up to her right eye, began fiddling with it. She wasn't as skilled with its use as Allan, but she managed to find the center of Grass and the University. They were too distant for her to get a good look at the Haessan; they were merely blurred figures shifting through the streets.

"Why would they do that?" Grant rumbled.

"Last I knew, the Tunnelers had taken control of the University," Allan answered.

"They're still there. I can see some of them on the walls." Kara began lowering the spyglass, but movement caught her eye. She refocused, farther away from the confluence of the two rivers, where the University had been built. "The Haessan aren't just near the center of the city. They're farther out as well. I see a group of them in what used to be Tallow."

"Let me look again."

Kara handed the glass to Allan and stepped back to where Grant stood with arms crossed over his chest, the horses a few paces beyond.

"I do not like this," Grant said. "How will we get past these Haessan?" His lip curled in disdain at the name.

Allan rejoined them. "That group you saw was a patrol. They have them scattered throughout the city. We'll have to evade them as we approach."

"And what about those surrounding Grass? How are we going to sneak by them? They're everywhere."

"We'll find a way."

One of the Wolves trotted up to Grant and whined.

"They've found a path down to the city," he said. "Come."

The Wolf loped off ahead of them, Grant following immediately.

Kara and Allan shared a look. "We only have six days to get to the Nexus," she said.

"I know."

They caught up to Grant and led their horses after the Wolf, following the edge of shattered roadway with the scattered remains of buildings on either side. This section of the old Erenthrall hadn't been built up as much as the rest, so only a few walls remained standing, the rest merely piles of rubble. Already, the debris had begun to lose its shape, the edges worn off, the lines of walls and doorways merging with the surrounding land. In another ten years, it wouldn't even be recognizable as a street or as buildings. It would simply be landscape.

They bypassed numerous fissures, then followed a wide crevice until it began to narrow and eventually ended in a steep slope of rocky debris. One of the other Wolves waited for them there. Both led them down into the depths of the cracked land, over heaps of fallen sandstone and collapsed walls. The earth shook at one point, dirt and stone raining down from overhead, where the sky was a thin, jagged blade of blue. Kara cringed, an arm raised over her head protectively, reins held tight in her other hand, and alternately cursed and prayed until the quake stopped. Her limbs shook long after they'd continued moving on, the fear of being buried in a slide in one of the crevices too powerful to shrug off.

After backtracking twice and taking too many turns and switchbacks for Kara to keep herself oriented, they emerged from the side of the thousand-foot cliff onto the edges of the sunken Erenthrall. It felt strange to step from rock-strewn sand and dirt onto a cobbled street with the walls of storefronts and houses on either side. Most had been damaged severely by the Shattering and the subsequent sinking of the city, but enough remained here to make the transition surreal. The third Wolf waited for them here, all three of them glancing back toward the three humans and their horses before jogging out onto the street ahead, heading straight toward Grass.

Kara's foot nudged something in the dust and she reached down and pulled a toy cart with a wooden horse attached from the dirt. A smudge of what looked like blood stained one broken wheel.

She stood staring at the handcrafted cart until Allan touched her hand.

"We need to move. Only six days, remember?"

She glanced at the sky, surprised it was midafternoon. It had taken them half the day to get down to the city.

She dropped the horse and cart. "Let's go."

They mounted and headed down the street with Grant in the front, the Wolves breaking apart, one taking point, the other two vanishing to either side. They moved swiftly, pausing only to drink and eat and wipe the sweat from their foreheads. The only sounds were the clop of their horses' shod feet or their own footfalls, the barking of wild dogs in the distance, and a low rumble that throbbed in Kara's teeth. The presence of the ley prickled her skin, so powerful she could taste it, like metal against her tongue. At one point, one of the Wolves reappeared and warned them of people ahead—not the Haessan, but someone else—and Grant took them seven blocks north before turning back toward Grass. The buildings changed, from the rough storefronts and houses in that outer district to more solid brick-and-stone apartments. An entire block had been burned to the ground, reminding Kara of West Forks after the Shattering. Then they shifted again, to ware-houses whose roofs had mostly collapsed, empty windows looking up onto blue sky.

They dodged two more groups of scattered people and then slowed, keeping close to the buildings now, everyone on foot, leading their horses. The low rumble had increased in volume, and Kara realized with a shock it was the sound of the geyser, heard even from this dis-tance. The sun had shifted, resting on top of the cliffs to the west, the area they'd traversed now steeped in black shadow, with only a few sections lit by torchlight where some straggling survivors lived. There was no sign of the ley globes Allan had reported being in use when he'd been here months earlier, but that made sense considering the state of the ley.

Grant halted them in what had once been the Candle District, blocks from the Tiana riverbed. He drew them into an abandoned shop, the counters bare, only a few signs that it had once sold leather shoes scat-tered on the dust-covered floor.

"The Haessan are close," Grant said. He kept his voice low, but it was hard to soften the growl. He motioned toward the counters. "We should hide here, wait for the Wolves to return. Put the horses in the back room."

Allan led the horses through the inner door, returning a moment later. They settled in, Kara clearing a space to sit, tossing a few leather soles to one side, along with a shoe form. She tried to disturb the dust as little as possible. Across from her, Allan did the same, while Grant remained at the counter's edge to keep watch outside.

A short time later, the sunlight faded, the shop falling into a strange gray dusk. White light from the ley lit the street beyond the shop, brightening as the geyser fountained higher for a moment, then died down. Aside from the rumble of the geyser, the street had gone eerily silent.

Kara shifted forward to say something to Allan, feet scraping across the floor, but Grant reached back and snapped his fingers in warning, his entire body bristling. One of the horses snorted, the sound muffled, then settled again.

A breath later she heard the clink of metal against metal from out in the street beyond. She pressed her back against the counter, then leaned forward far enough she could peer around its other edge.

A strong animal scent hit her first, a heavy musk, dry and spicy, almost like cinnamon. The Haessan moved into sight and she stifled a gasp. Like the Wolves, they retained some of their human form, standing upright, with arms that ended in five-fingered talons, some of them gripping the hilts of curved Gorrani swords. But the humanity ended there. Their skin was scaled and patterned, like a snake, their necks protruding from their armor, rounding out into snouts, their eyes circular black pits. Forked tongues tasted the air as they passed, five in all.

Then they were gone.

Kara slumped back against the counter, exhaled slowly, but said nothing until Grant shifted toward them and said, "They're gone."

"They're . . . unspeakable." She shuddered. "Why didn't they scent us? Or the horses?"

Grant shrugged. "The scent of leather in here is strong; it may have hidden us. And there are others living close by. Perhaps they thought we were part of that group."

Kara choked back a scream as a Wolf rounded the side of the counter. It eyed her with a cold inhuman stare, then huffed and focused on Grant. With a low growl and a few yips and whines, it reported in, then lowered itself onto its stomach, laying its head on its front paws.

"She says the Haessan are everywhere. They control all the bridges leading across the rivers. There's no way to cross without them seeing us."

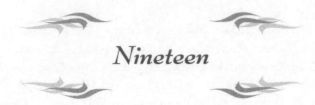

Nineteen

"WE HAVE TO GET ACROSS!" Kara said, half rising. "Morrell and Marcus expect us to be there!"

"Hush," Allan said, holding up a hand to halt her. "We've got five days to figure it out."

"No, we don't. We've got four days. I need to be in the Nexus on the fifth day, because who knows when Marcus will manage to get into the Nexus at the Needle, or how long he can hold it."

"Agreed, but charging out into the middle of the Haessan and getting killed or captured isn't a good option either. We need to rest and think."

"While you rest, my Wolves will keep an eye on the Haessan," Grant said. "They can keep track of their patrols, get close enough, unseen, that perhaps they can find a way past them all."

Kara glanced between the two, then settled back down. She couldn't deny her exhaustion. "We'll rest for tonight. But tomorrow we need to find a way past the Haessan. Don't forget that we still have to make it through the ley as well."

Allan's gaze dropped to his hands, palms up in his lap. "I haven't forgotten."

Grant grumbled something, and the Wolf jumped to its feet and padded out into the deepening night without a sound. "We should stay here," Grant said after she left, "in case the leather is hiding our scent. Perhaps there are rooms upstairs."

The second floor had obviously been the cobbler's home, divided up into a kitchen area, a workroom, and two bedrooms. Shoe forms filled the workroom, but someone had stripped it of all leather but some scraps. The kitchen was bare, some plates and cups still in the cupboards, a few broken on the floor. But there were still beds in both bedrooms, one large one in the first, two smaller ones for children in the second. It reminded Kara forcibly of the apartment she and her parents had had before the Kormanley bombing in Seeley Park had taken their lives and Ischua had taken her to the Wielder's college, except their apartment had been filled with clocks.

Grant and Allan traded looks, then took over the children's room, leaving Kara the large bed. She tossed her pack to the floor and crawled onto the bed, the straw-stuffed mattress having long dried out completely. It reeked of dust and hay and had settled into a hard, flat surface, but she didn't care. She sneezed as she set her head on her hands as a pillow and closed her eyes.

But her heart still thrummed from the horror of seeing the twisted Haessan. She couldn't sleep. She rolled onto her back, the mattress crackling as she did so, and stared up into the darkness at the ceiling. Thoughts of Cory flashed through her head, her hands clenching into fists, but she forced herself to set that worry aside. Instead, she cycled through their plans to heal the ley network: Morrell in Tumbor, Marcus at the Needle, and her here. If any one of them failed . . .

The terrifying grinding sound that had roared over them a few days before echoed in her mind. She knew in her gut that it was a consequence of the destroyed nodes and the loosening of reality. Whatever had caused that noise would continue, would likely grow worse.

Which meant they had to get to the Nexus. But how could they get past the Haessan? They held the bridges over the river, at least those closest. Maybe they could travel farther upriver, cross there, then return. But did they have time?

She tossed onto her side. There had to be another way.

At some point she fell asleep, deep enough that when she woke again she couldn't remember dreaming. But she bolted upright and then sprang for the door, where she found Grant and Allan already awake, seated at the table in the kitchen, one of the Wolves at their feet. Both of them looked up from their conversation.

"I know how we can get past the Haessan."

Allan sat back. "We were just discussing that. The Haessan have surrounded the geyser on all sides. They appear to be worshipping it. Grant doesn't see how we'll be able to get past them."

Kara stepped forward and tapped the table with one finger. "We go beneath them. We use the ley tunnels, like the Tunnelers did."

Dead silence.

Then Allan leaned forward. "What about the ley?"

"Not all of the lines will be flooded. Remember, some of them had been blocked—by us, by the White Cloaks before us. Besides, if we run into a line that is flooded, we can still pass through it. We have you. It's how we planned on getting to the Nexus to begin with."

Allan scrubbed at his face with both hands. "We'd have to leave the horses behind."

"But it would get us across the river," Grant rumbled. "The tunnels run beneath it."

Allan tilted his chair onto its two back legs, balancing as he thought.

Kara leaned onto the table, both palms flat. "The tunnels might even take us all the way to the Nexus itself."

Allan stared at her, then swore. He let the chair fall back onto four legs. "Where's the nearest node?"

Two hours later, they were descending the spiral stairs of the pit in Candle, the horses let loose near the leather shop, the Wolves scouting out the pit and tunnels below, noses in the air. There were three tunnels, all of them free of ley, like the pit itself. Kara reached out on all three, then selected the one heading north. "This one goes beneath the river."

Allan stepped forward, torch held high, one of the Wolves slipping out ahead of him. The ex-Dog scanned the tunnel ahead, then turned to her. "I vowed not to come down here ever again, after the last time."

"Do you have a better option?"

Behind them, Grant chuckled, a deeply disturbing sound as it echoed in the pit.

Allan motioned with the torch. "After you."

⟳

"Father! Commander! The Gorrani are arriving."

Dalton glanced back from his inspection of the secondary gate that had been destroyed by ley as Marcus and the others escaped. The gaping hole where the gate had been was now a wall of solid rock, albeit hastily patched and mortared. He couldn't help but compare it to the wall that had been breached by the Hollowers when they came to rescue their Wielder, Kara. That wall now looked more solid than those around it, as if the granite used to repair it had somehow been fused together. He'd been told it was the work of Allan Garrett's daughter, a report substantiated by the rumors floating around the city.

This wall looked as if it would collapse if someone simply came and knocked on it.

As if sensing his assessment, Darius said, "At least it's been sealed."

"This is the best the masons could do?"

"So they say, given the time constraint and what they had to work with."

Through his vision, Dalton received an image of the wall crumbled, shattered stone littering the ground beneath it. "It will not hold long. It will be one of the first breaches in our defenses as soon as the ley wall collapses."

Both looked up at the white flames of ley towering above them. The men manning the gate towers kept well back from the edges, most of them pacing nervously or trying to ignore the danger that burned a few feet from their position. Dalton would have ordered them off the wall if Iscivius could have convinced him the ley would hold, but he couldn't risk it.

He turned his back on the old gates and headed toward the temple. "To the Needle." It was the only place within the city where they could see beyond the ley wall.

Darius and the lieutenant who'd delivered the news fell in behind him.

They reached the temple and its inner stellae garden in short order. Dalton paused within the entrance to the Needle itself, the smooth pitch-black walls veined with pulsing ley. He wanted to go down to check in on Iscivius, but he'd already pestered the Wielder repeatedly since the ley wall went up. The last time, Iscivius had snapped at him. The toll of keeping the wall in place had begun to show through, Iscivius' face lined with tension, his eyes somehow hollow. He didn't need to disturb him, especially now.

Instead, he ascended the stairs to the right, his escort trailing behind him. They spiraled up around the center of the tower, windows occasionally looking out upon the temple and the city beyond.

When they'd climbed high enough to see beyond the ley wall and found a window facing the south, he halted. Darius joined him, motioning the others back.

"They've halted at the rim of the crater," Darius said, stepping closer to the window and removing a spyglass from a pocket. "Perhaps the ley will convince them to turn back."

"No. Their scouts would have told them of it long before this." Dalton shifted forward. A warm wind gusted into his face, sending the sleeves of his robes fluttering, but he merely squinted into the distance. "What do you see?"

"A grouping of ten Gorrani warriors at the lip of the crater. They appear to be discussing something. I can see their banners behind them, but not their men. It looks like all of the sects are represented. Now they're arguing. Their leader has just cut them all off. He's motioning to both sides with his arms. Half of the group has disappeared over the rim." Darius paused, then added, "The banners have moved beyond sight."

Dalton lowered his head and closed his eyes, tried to pull at the fabric of his sight, to suss out what the Gorrani would do. Would they attack, regardless of the ley wall? Would they retreat, as Darius suggested? He didn't believe that. He couldn't see how an attack would represent any threat to the temple or the city, as long as the ley wall remained standing.

His sight remained unchanged. Not even a flash of insight as he'd seen at the gates.

"Something's happening." Darius tensed, straining forward with the spyglass. "Gods, there are so many of them."

Dalton's eyes snapped open. In the distance, spread out in a long line, the Gorrani suddenly emerged from behind the crater's rim. They stretched to either side, far enough that Dalton was forced to lean out of the window to see either edge. Multicolored banners snapped in the gusts, the warriors themselves dressed in armor that matched their sect's colors. Sunlight glinted on hilts and bracers, although most of the Gorrani armor was hardened leather, leaving their arms and legs exposed. The men at the center were mounted, seated higher than the rest.

Drums suddenly echoed across the dry plains. Within moments, a contingent of a hundred men appeared from behind the line along the crater and charged on horseback down toward the Needle and its walls, the men screaming an incoherent battle cry. A chant began, the warriors along the crater suddenly drawing their swords and pointing them toward the heavens. Those on horseback continued straight toward the ley wall, a plume of dust rising behind them. Apprehension seized Dalton's chest, but he remained where he stood, his grip tightening on the edges of the window.

"What do they intend to do?" Darius asked. "Charge straight into the ley? They must know what happened last time."

The charge didn't falter. The group fell from sight, hidden by the ley wall.

Darius lowered the spyglass and spun toward the lieutenant who'd brought them here. "Go to the walls. Tell the lieutenant commanders to ready—"

"Wait." Dalton touched Darius' arm. "Look."

Below, the plume of dust had shifted direction, cutting left along the edge of the wall. As soon as it did, the sound of the drums changed and all of the Gorrani along the lip of the crater stepped forward, marching toward the Needle. Their ranks were five deep, but behind them came camels and horse-driven carts and more Gorrani, although these were not dressed in armor. The group of one hundred hidden by the ley wall changed direction again, angling back out toward their own ranks. They reappeared, their muted battle cries echoing up from the plains, mingling oddly with the chant. Beneath the drums, the tread of thousands of feet marching in rhythm provided a counterbeat.

Then the chanting and the drums halted, as if cut short by a knife. The warriors on foot stopped where they stood, holding position, along with the support forces behind them. Only the hundred on horseback still moved, although their battle cry had ended.

Once the hundred rejoined their forces, the Gorrani shouted a single word in their own language at the Needle, punctuated by a sword thrust into the air. They did this three times, the same word, and then suddenly their carefully arranged ranks broke. Those behind began unloading their carts and erecting tents. The warriors split into groups by sect, the leaders who'd remained at the front rejoining their men.

"They're making camp," Darius said with a hint of derision. "Settling in. It was all for show."

"How many men do they have?"

Darius brought the spyglass back up, scanned the forces, his lips moving without sound as he counted. "I'd say three thousand warriors, with maybe twice that many in their supply train."

"Nearly twice what they brought before."

"I see women and children in the supply train, helping out." Darius lowered the spyglass. "This may be all the Gorrani that remain."

Dalton stared out at the warriors and their support, smaller tents already erected, larger ones going up behind them. Could this be all the Gorrani left in the Flats? He'd heard there were hundreds of tribes, but he knew that the Gorrani were not numerous, even before the Shattering. They kept to themselves, did not build cities, living in groupings of rock that jutted up from the Flats called cenotan, where water collected in pools. Trade was done at specific locations on the edges of the Flats. Few non-Gorrani were allowed into the Flats to see the cenotans.

So it was possible these were the last of the Gorrani. It would explain why they'd become so vicious. They were desperate.

"They're obviously not going to attack with the ley wall in place," he said. "Keep the men on the walls ready, just in case."

He turned from the window and headed for the stairs again.

"Should we wake the mages?"

He paused, considering, then shook his head. "Leave them. Unless the ley wall falls."

Darius began issuing orders behind him as they descended. They were halfway down the tower when Dalton glanced out the window to one side and caught movement in the Temerite section. He stopped dead in his tracks.

"Darius! The Temerites—they're doing something on the edge of the chasm!"

His commander came up behind him to see, leaning out of the window, but then the tension in his shoulders relaxed and he drew back inside.

"They're fortifying their edge of the chasm wall, that's all. They've been working on it for the past few weeks. We've been keeping a careful eye on them, but they haven't done anything more than reinforce walls, build up a few barricades, and shift the few ballistae and catapults they have. It's nothing."

As Darius motioned to his men to continue down the stairs, Dalton squinted at the Temerite watchmen on the roofs of the buildings below. For a moment, his odd vision flickered and he thought he saw watchmen racing across the depths of the chasm, but there was no bridge.

He closed his eyes and rubbed at his temples, a minor headache forming, then looked again, but there was nothing except watchmen repositioning a ballista while others hauled stone to the roof to build up its edge for protection. Nothing he saw hinted at an attempt to build a bridge, and the chasm was too wide to simply throw down any kind of wooden construct. It would never have the proper support and would snap in the middle.

Yet he couldn't shake the feeling they were up to something.

After watching for another five minutes, he finally stepped away, making a note to have a watch set on them in the future. For now, the Gorrani arrival was more worrisome.

❧

"It's no use," Allan said, stumbling back from the ley line that blocked their path. "The ley current here is too strong. If I try to step farther out into the tunnel, it's going to knock me off balance, just like a strong current in a river. I'd be washed away."

Kara swore, viciously, Grant raising an eyebrow in surprise from where he stood with the three Wolves behind them.

They'd traveled the ley tunnels for what Kara felt was at least a day already, although it was hard to tell since they'd remained under ground. During that time, they'd encountered tunnels filled with the ley, but they'd been able to pass through them, Kara, Grant, and the Wolves huddling close to Allan, everyone moving mostly in sync, slowly and carefully, making certain they remained in the bubble of protection that surrounded the ex-Dog. They'd discovered that the bubble changed size depending on the strength of the ley—the stronger the ley, the smaller the radius of protection. The tunnels were a maze of twists and turns, but they'd passed from junction to node to barge station, crossing beneath the river and into the section near Grass on the far side.

But now they'd run into a junction completely filled with the ley where the current was too strong. If Allan were shoved off balance and swept away, he'd take his protection with him, leaving Kara, Grant, and the Wolves to burn in the ley itself.

Kara turned away from them both and leaned forward into her hands in frustration, pressing them into the smoothed surface of the river stones that had been used to construct this part of the ley network. The fact that they were river stones told her they were in one of the oldest parts of the system. They had to be close to Grass.

She shoved back from the wall. "Then we'll have to find another tunnel, one where the ley isn't flowing at all, or at a lower strength."

Allan and Grant shared a look.

"The strength of the ley lines has been increasing the closer we get to the old Nexus, where the geyser is," Grant said. "What if there isn't another approach underground?"

"There has to be," Kara snapped and stalked away from both of them, down the tunnel they'd traversed to get there. The last junction wasn't that far back, and there'd been other tunnel options. They'd only chosen this one because it angled toward Grass.

At the junction, she chose another tunnel, two levels down. They descended the side of the pit, from ledge to ledge, using insets that had obviously been constructed as a ladder. But the new tunnel ended at another junction with only tunnels leading away from where Kara could feel the geyser, so they returned and chose another. It ended in a wall of ley like the first, the current even faster here than before.

"The tunnel's narrower," Allan said. "The force has to be stronger to push the ley through."

Kara didn't care. They needed to get to the Nexus. She'd thought the ley tunnels were the perfect solution.

"Now what?" Grant growled. His ear twitched with his own frustration.

"We go back to the junction. There was one more tunnel. It doesn't head straight toward Grass, but maybe it will take us somewhere with more options."

Both men nodded, and the Wolves led them back the way they'd come, tongues lolling out of their mouths. They'd been traipsing through tunnels for hours.

The new tunnel ran parallel to the geyser, neither heading toward it, nor farther away. As soon as they stepped into it, Kara noticed ley coursed through it, but it was weak enough that it couldn't be seen. It merely prickled her skin, the fine hairs on her arms stirring. The Wolves protested slightly, until Grant uttered an impatient bark.

Twenty minutes later, Allan held his torch higher and said, "There's something ahead."

They slowed, the object emerging from the darkness as Allan pressed forward. It hung from a wide crack in the ceiling, stone and a heap of sand littering the floor of the tunnel, obviously a cave-in from the many quakes that had shaken Erenthrall both before and after the Shattering. Allan stepped toward it, then reached out and touched it, setting it swinging slightly.

"It's a ladder."

Kara joined Allan, the rope ladder clearer once she stepped to one side. The wooden rungs looked well used. She stared up into the shadows of the fissure above. It reminded her of the short time she'd spent with the Tunnelers, who'd used ladders such as this throughout their warren. "I wonder where it leads?"

"Should we find out?"

"No. We don't want to go up, we want to get to the Nexus."

Neither Grant nor Allan disagreed with her, but when they continued, Grant ordered one of the Wolves to watch their backs.

The tunnel continued for another few thousand feet, then ended in a much more significant cave-in. Stone and dirt filled its entire width. Allan climbed the debris, scanning the top with his torch.

"It's completely blocked." He faced them both, the flames of the torch casting his features in feral yellow light. "Either we check out that ladder, or we backtrack further and try to find another junction leading toward Grass."

"I think you'll do neither."

The new voice echoed down the tunnel from behind them. Kara and Grant spun, the two Wolves leaping to join the third, all of them breaking into low, menacing growls. Allan hopped down from the debris, coming to Kara's side. Kara couldn't see anything, even when Allan shifted forward, bringing the light with him, but Grant lifted his head and sniffed the air, nose wrinkling in distaste.

"Rabbits," he huffed.

Footsteps approached, causing the fur on the three Wolves to bristle. They didn't charge, though, Grant keeping them in check.

Four figures appeared, swords drawn and leveled. They halted just within the reach of the torch, the leader dressed in scratched armor with a dented helm, the others in tattered clothes.

"I think," the leader said, "you'll be coming with us."

Kara tensed, and then Allan said incredulously, "Cason?"

The leader hesitated, eyes squinting. "Allan?" She swore and reached to pull the helm from her head, tucking it under her arm. She didn't lower her sword, and her expression wasn't welcoming. "And Kara. What in hells are you doing here? And why do you have Wolves? Have you finally come to kill us for trading you to the White Cloaks?"

One of the Wolves lunged forward with a snarl, the three younger men with Cason scrambling backward. Cason didn't move, and a sharp word from Grant brought the Wolf up short, just out of Cason's reach. The Wolf continued to growl, saliva dripping from its jaws, then began to pace back and forth across the width of the tunnel.

Cason kept her eyes on it. "I see you've got them trained now."

"Not trained," Kara said. "They're allies."

Cason glanced toward her. "So I've heard. I thought it merely rumor. I've heard many things about you and the White Cloaks and what you've done at the Needle. I've heard that you purposely destroyed Tumbor by collapsing the distortion, that you've set the ley here in Erenthrall out of control in order to destroy us all so you can take the city. Or what's left of it."

"That isn't true! Tumbor was an accident. The ley geyser here was a direct result of that. I'm here to fix it."

Cason's eyes narrowed. "Why should I believe you?"

"You don't need to believe us," Allan answered. His hand rested on the hilt of his own sword. "Just stay out of our way."

"And let you cause another 'accident'? I don't think so."

Behind her, one of the others whispered something, but Cason held up a hand to silence him.

"How did you get here?" she asked.

Even Kara heard the desperation beneath the too casual tone of the question. "Why do you want to know?"

Cason shifted her gaze from Allan to Kara. Another of her followers hissed a warning. "Never mind. It doesn't matter. You'll have to come with us. Your Wolves will stay here."

She turned her back on the still growling Wolf a few paces in front of her and headed back toward the ladder. The three with her retreated as well with a sharp word of command. Two of them kept Allan, Grant,

Kara, and the Wolves in sight, weapons still drawn, faces twisted with suspicion.

Kara stepped up to Allan's side. "Should we go with them? We could simply backtrack. She doesn't seem intent on capturing us."

"Not right now, but that's because we have the Wolves. They'd never be able to take us. She's probably headed back to the ladder to get reinforcements."

"Then we'd better decide fast," Grant rumbled, his voice deeper than normal. "My Wolves can take them before they reach the ladder."

Kara hesitated.

"Remember," Allan said, "they traded us away last time for food and supplies."

"But they may know of a way to get into Grass."

Kara started forward, bypassing the Wolves. Allan and Grant conversed briefly, then Grant growled low in his throat. One of the Wolves whined in protest, but they all quieted.

Allan and Grant caught up to her before she reached the ladder, where Cason and her escort of three had been joined by seven others. Kara recognized Sorelle and Jaimes, the two of them looking more strained and haggard than before. Sorelle glared at the three of them, but Jaimes actually smiled. Kara remembered the young man trying to warn her as they were being led to the meeting with the White Cloaks, heard again his mouthed "Run!" moments before the White Cloaks first appeared.

"Up," Cason commanded, one hand holding the side of the makeshift ladder. Those around her bristled.

Kara went first, then Allan and Grant. Cason came up behind them. The ladder was difficult to climb, since it wasn't anchored at its base, but Kara managed. She passed into the crevice in the tunnel's roof, its sides scraping her shoulders and back, a jagged rift lit above by torchlight. Dirt and stones dislodged by her movement rained down on those below. When she reached the top, hands grabbed her by the shirt and underneath the shoulders and hauled her up into a shallow room with an arched ceiling, all built with river stone. It smelled of dry earth with a faint hint of ancient spices. Ten more of Cason's Tunnelers watched her warily. Kara dusted herself off as Allan and Grant emerged from the rift, the ladder tied off to one side of the room to metal rings that studded one wall.

Cason followed Grant, then the ten Tunnelers below scrambled up after her. Without a word, Cason led them all out of the low-ceilinged room into a corridor, similar rooms opening off to either side, all of them empty. Sounds echoed strangely in the hollow spaces, the scrapes and clanks of their feet and clothing and armor amplified until they hit a steep stairwell that spiraled up to a heavy wooden door with a massive iron lock that looked like it hadn't been used in decades. The door's hinges squealed as Cason pulled it open and passed through.

Kara gasped as she emerged into a familiar hallway with a series of doors on either side. "This is the University! We're in the corridor of practice rooms!"

Cason halted ahead of her and turned. "Welcome to our new home. Or should I say prison."

"What do you mean?" Allan asked.

Cason considered him for a moment, then spun and continued moving forward as she spoke.

"After we traded you to the White Cloaks—or attempted to trade you to the White Cloaks—we had a few weeks of peace before the Rats decided they'd had enough. They invaded the tunnels from every direction, intent on finding our base camp. We were fighting them on all fronts, collapsing tunnels to cut them off, slaughtering them in junctions, doing everything we could to keep them at bay. They were losing three people for every one of us, but we were still in retreat. They'd nearly made it to our main camp when the earthquakes began."

She'd reached the end of the corridor of practice rooms and ascended another set of stairs to a set of double doors that opened onto one of the University's main halls. The entire room had been converted into living quarters. Pallets covered the floor, most of them occupied by men and women and children either sleeping or sitting, working on mending clothing, repairing weapons, cutting up carrots, or peeling potatoes. It reminded Kara of the tent city outside the ring of buildings surrounding the temple at the Needle, except here there were no tents, no privacy at all. The Tunnelers were tattered and worn, their clothes in worse shape than when Kara had seen them before, their faces more gaunt and creased, hollowed and dulled somehow. A fire roared in the massive hearth on the far side of the room and a cluster of men and women worked around it, mostly dealing with the pots that hung on hooks over the flames. Kara scanned the people and estimated there were only a third of those she'd seen at their previous base camp.

"Except for those keeping guard on the walls and at the gates of the University, these are the only ones of my group left," Cason said, her tone harsh and bitter. "The quakes killed many of them, the tunnels collapsing as the shaking escalated and we attempted to flee to the surface. Many more were lost as we ran, carrying whatever we could with us. Not because of the Rats—they were scrambling to save themselves—but because of the ley. Tunnels that had always been safe were suddenly flooded with it, cutting off our routes. A few flooded even as we were using them. A little less than half of us made it out of the tunnels alive.

"Once we were free, we discovered the entire city of Erenthrall was coming apart, and we could see why. The distortion was collapsing. The sound of the earth grinding together, of the distortion chewing it up as it imploded, was deafening. Most of us cowered on the flagstones of the ley barge station where we'd emerged, or simply stood and waited for it to end us. But then a spear of light shot up through the core of the distortion from the earth and struck its center. It flared so bright that those who didn't turn away were blinded, some of them permanently. When it ended, when my vision returned, the distortion had vanished, and the first thing I saw were the walls of the University. We needed a place of refuge. We needed a place we could defend. Without giving anyone a chance to recover, I got my people onto their feet and moving. The city was shockingly quiet after the quakes. No one on the streets. No one moving except us. We managed to seize control of the University before anyone could react.

"Then, of course, the city sank into the plains." She motioned toward one of the narrow windows, the glass long shattered. As they approached, a throbbing background noise that Kara couldn't place grew in intensity, but she couldn't see what caused it. Beyond the window, the University commons was filled with rubble. "I lost more of my people when some of the University buildings we were living in collapsed. I thought we'd seen the worst of it after that. For months, we held the walls and slipped out into the city to scavenge through the tunnels beneath us, accessed through that crack in the cellar's floor. We watched as that damn Baron convinced the Rats and the Butcher and all of the others to join him. We watched as the Gorrani became more violent, killing everyone who wasn't Gorrani that they encountered. We watched as the Baron attacked the Temerite enclave, and then watched as the Gorrani attacked them. It would have been a bloodbath if the auroral storm hadn't come. That storm allowed the Temerites to escape, cut the fight between the Baron and the Gorrani short. And even then, the Gorrani didn't escape. They were caught in the middle of the storm as they fled and it changed them."

"We saw," Kara said. "We ran into some of them on our way here."

Cason stared at her, then continued without responding, heading toward another doorway, to stairs leading upward through one of the mansion's small towers. Sorelle, Jaimes, and some of the others trailed behind them. "The Gorrani have surrounded our walls ever since. They've kept us caged in here, or so they thought. We could get out through the tunnels. As long as they couldn't breach our walls, we were safe, and we always had a way out if they did.

"Until Tumbor collapsed. Until the geyser of ley erupted from the center of Grass and the tunnels beneath us—tunnels that had once been free—were flooded with ley again."

She thrust through another door onto the roof of the mansion, the dull roar that Kara had heard since they'd entered the mansion now a throb of thunder, like a thousand waterfalls all cascading down a thousand-foot fall into a pool of water. Except as the group spread out on the roof, their gazes moving inexorably toward the north, toward Grass, Kara realized it wasn't water. It was the ley of the geyser, shooting far above their heads in the near distance, where the shorn-off towers of Grass ringed the building that had once been the Nexus. Kara drifted toward the edge of the roof, eyes locked on the geyser, her skin prickling with the intensity of the ley now that they were this close. She wanted to reach out and join with it, knew that she could, but that it would sweep her away.

"I need to get there. I need to reach the Nexus." Her gaze dropped from the tower of ley, to the streets outside the University lined with the Gorrani. "I need to get past the Gorrani."

"And I and my people need to get out from behind these walls," Cason said from behind her. "You got through the tunnels somehow. You managed to reach us. How?"

Kara turned her back on the Gorrani, on the geyser that was so close, yet still so distant. She caught Allan's attention. He gave a subtle nod and she faced Cason, voice hardening.

"You like to trade, right? Use your fighters to get us through the Gorrani to the Nexus, and I'll get you and your people out of the University."

Behind her, Sorelle, Jaimes, and the others began to protest. Sorelle straightened and began, "Cason, you can't—"

"Quiet," the Tunneler leader said.

Sorelle clamped her mouth shut and crossed her arms over her chest.

Silence held on the roof, interrupted only by the thunderous roar of the geyser. The tension between the Tunnelers and Kara's group was palpable.

Then Cason stirred. "No." Those of her group on the roof relaxed as she continued. "No, I won't risk what few people I have left. Not against the Gorrani. But I can get you to the Nexus, if you're willing."

Kara didn't even hesitate. "How?"

Twenty

DRAYDEN LIFTED HIS HEAD to a sky covered with black storm clouds and flared his nostrils. "They're still behind us. Closer now."

Boskell swore. "How many? Can you tell?"

Drayden scented the air again, turning his head in different directions. Morrell watched intently, aware of the roiling clouds overhead, the prickling of the air against her skin, of the vibrant aurora that washed across the lands in nearly every direction here on what had once been the streets of Tumbor. The landscape was nightmarish, the earth splintered into mostly unrecognizable shards that jutted up from the ground at odd angles, some as large as the buildings she remembered in Erenthrall, others as tall as the trees in the Hollow. The ground beneath their feet crackled with every step, even the flat surfaces shattering like glass, the stone brittle. Scattered among the otherworldly shards of stone and earth were shockingly recognizable glimpses of the old Tumbor—an arched stone doorway opening onto nothing; the head of a solemn-faced, bearded man from a statue; a rounded balcony half buried in the debris. All of it was lit by the coruscating auroral lights and erratic flashes of lightning from the storms. Sporadic gusts of wind picked up sand and grit and brought with it odd scents, fresh rain one moment, the sulfur smell of a spoiled egg the next. The horror of it all—the randomness, the strangeness—lay against Morrell's skin like a cold, wet blanket, even days after entering the region.

Days in which they'd been dodging the auroral storms and the Gorrani who'd followed them into the wasteland.

Drayden huffed, blowing air out through his nose, then shook his head. "Hard to say. At least a dozen, maybe more."

"It's not a scouting party, then," Okata said. "They've sent a yavun."

"What's a yavun?" Morrell asked. Lightning flared, not far distant, and a blast of wind sent her hair streaming out to one side. It smelled like dew on a spring morning.

"An elite warrior unit. It usually contains fifteen men, composed of our best fighters."

Boskell stared off into the distance, as if he could see the men. "You said they were closer now. How close?"

"No more than a day." Drayden faced Morrell. For a moment, his eyes glowed a feral yellow. "Let me hunt them as they approach. I will take care of them."

Morrell shuddered at the intensity of his voice, the raw power rumbling beneath it, like the thunder rolling through the air.

"No," Boskell said. "I want you to stay with Morrell." Drayden's lips parted in a silent snarl, his teeth gleaming white. Boskell didn't see, his focus now on Morrell. "How close are we to Tumbor's center? Can you tell?"

"We're close. I think we'll reach it today, maybe tomorrow."

Boskell looked to the sky, then swore again. They hadn't been able to see the sky for days. "Anyone know how much longer we have to get ready?"

Sesali spoke up for the first time. "Three days."

"You're certain?"

"Yes. Three days."

"Is that enough time, Morrell?"

She straightened. "It has to be."

Boskell eyed her solemnly, then glanced at both Okata and Sesali. Both of them nodded in agreement, and with that Boskell began to move. "Then we're going to send you and Drayden on ahead. No arguments!" He shot that toward Drayden. "You keep her alive, Wolf, you hear me? The three of us will take care of this yavun. If we can't kill them all, we'll slow them down. We'll try to catch up to you if we can."

Okata and Sesali were also moving, both checking weapons, rooting through their knapsacks, handing off supplies to Boskell. Drayden hopped down from the stone he'd been standing on to scent the air, heading toward Morrell. Boskell was stuffing whatever Okata and Sesali gave him into his own satchel. All of a sudden, events were beginning to move too fast, and Morrell realized that Boskell and the others had already discussed what they were going to do, without her or Drayden's knowledge.

"Wait—"

Boskell thrust his satchel into Morrell's hands, then grabbed her shoulders and looked her square in the eyes. "You have to get to the center of Tumbor and do whatever it is you need to do as fast as you can. We'll hold them off, hopefully kill them, but you have to get that node built within three days. Don't wait for us. Don't even think about us. Get that node built, understand?"

Morrell drew in a breath, her chest hot and achy. "I understand."

Boskell looked over her shoulder at Drayden. "Get her out of here."

Drayden gave a short growl, then caught Morrell's arm and tugged her toward the east. Morrell resisted, watching as Boskell conversed briefly with Okata and Sesali, motioning to the north and south, the three of them breaking apart, Boskell heading west. They clambered over the shattered remains of Tumbor and vanished in the shadows and crevices within moments.

Morrell's throat closed up and for a few moments she couldn't breathe. She turned and stared off into the distance, toward the center of Tumbor, auroral storms surging across the broken landscape, lightning walking jaggedly across the horizon. She was suddenly glad she'd been able to heal Sesali's arm a few days before.

"We must go," Drayden said in his guttural voice, not without a thread of sympathy.

"Yes." Morrell coughed, the word coming out as a dry, weak croak. She steeled herself. "Yes, let's go."

Hernande startled awake to the strident sounds of horns. He sat bolt upright in his bed, blankets tangled in his legs, and stared bleary-eyed at the wall as he tried to sort out the sounds.

"Two different calls. The Kormanley . . . and the Gorrani."

He lurched out of bed and snatched at clean clothes. What sounded like the footsteps of a hundred men pounded past his closed door, shouts muffled by the wood. He dragged a shirt over his head and stuffed its tail into his breeches as he flung the door open and stalked down the hall, heading toward the main hall. Three doors down from his own, Marcus' door flew open, the Wielder stepping out in front of him.

"What's happening?" he demanded.

"I don't know. The horns woke me."

Marcus had already turned away, jogging toward the main hall. Hernande followed.

The Matriarch's embassy was abuzz with activity, most of the Temerite watchmen sprinting toward the doors. Lienta stood in the center of the hall, issuing orders, the only center of calm in the area. Hernande didn't see the Matriarch anywhere.

Marcus bulled his way through to Lienta.

"What's happening?" he demanded again.

Lienta spared him an irritated glance, then finished his orders and held up a hand for the rest as he turned to Marcus. "Baron Devin and his army have arrived. Father's forces are scrambling for the walls, even though Devin's men have only been sighted on the horizon. The Gorrani are reacting as well."

"Are the Gorrani readying to attack?" Hernande asked.

"It's hard to tell. I've ordered my own forces to the walls, although the ley barrier is still in place. If the Kormanley drop it, we may have to defend ourselves." More watchmen had arrived, were demanding Lienta's attention. "You two should get our teams together and prepare for an attack on the temple."

"It's not time yet," Marcus said instantly. "It's too early. The comet isn't overhead."

"We may not have a choice," Lienta snapped. "If the Baron and Gorrani attack the Needle, it presents our best chance of taking the Nexus and holding it, while the Kormanley are focused on the others. Get your teams ready. Right now."

He turned back to his men, pointing to one of the lieutenants, who began a report on the walls.

Marcus spun on Hernande. "It's too early!" He began pushing back out through the watchmen.

"But Lienta is right. If the Kormanley are distracted by the Baron and the Gorrani, we'll have a better chance of taking control of the Nexus."

"We'll never be able to hold it long enough to use it, though!"

"Do you have a better idea?" Marcus didn't answer, continuing toward the corridor that contained their bedrooms. Hernande snagged his arm to halt him. "Go find Cutter, Marc, and the rest of our own men. I'll get Artras and everything else we'll need. Meet at the edge of the chasm."

Marcus tensed in indecision, then muttered, "We'll never hold it for three days," before sprinting away toward where the others were housed.

Hernande turned to find Artras standing behind him. She held up a couple of satchels.

"I heard the horns and grabbed what we'd need, just in case."

Hernande pulled two of the satchels over his head, adjusting them on his shoulders.

"Marcus is right, you know. If we're forced to take the Nexus—"

"I learned in my youth that sometimes the gods and the universe are playing with a different set of rules than you are. That sometimes you must simply let the game play you."

Artras snorted. "And sometimes you need to break the rules."

Hernande stared at her a moment, then smiled. "Perhaps."

They made their way through the mostly empty outer hall—Lienta presumably having moved to the walls—and out a side door into the reclaimed streets of the Temerite section. Hernande was surprised to find it still night, at least a few hours left until dawn. But the buildings were lit by the towering white wall of ley that still encircled the Needle, its ambient light obscuring nearly all the stars overhead. Only the moon, the brightest stars, and the smudge of the comet could be seen from the streets. Those outside were either headed toward the outer walls or scrambling to their assigned stations inside the city. Hernande and Artras ran in the opposite direction, toward one of the half-ruined buildings overlooking the chasm.

When they arrived, they found it empty except for the weapons cached here earlier. Hernande motioned to the stairs leading to the roof.

They ascended, coming back out into the night air with a vantage on the depths of the chasm and the Kormanley controlled Needle on the far side. The light from the ley was lessened here, but they shifted into a patch of shadow nonetheless, hoping that none of the Kormanley enforcers stationed on the far side of the chasm would notice them.

They needn't have bothered. All of those they saw on the short walls overlooking the chasm were focused on what was happening closer to the temple.

"Like Lienta, Darius isn't taking any chances," Hernande said. "He's sending everyone to the walls."

"How long do you think Iscivius can keep the wall of ley going?" Artras asked.

"You could answer that better than I."

Artras considered for a long moment, both of them watching the activity at the temple and in the streets below, then said, "He's been holding it up for days now, probably with the support of the Wielders that stayed behind. But he can't keep it up indefinitely. And I don't think any of the others are strong enough to hold it for him. It's going to fall. It's only a matter of time."

"And then the Gorrani and Devin's men will attack. The serpents and the dogs, just as Dalton predicted."

Both of them looked to the north, although they couldn't see the piercing white lights of the Three Sisters on the horizon because of the wall of ley. Neither of them said anything about the rest of Dalton's prophecy.

Marcus and Cutter emerged from the rooftop door and spotted them.

"Have you heard anything?" Artras asked as they joined them. "We can't see beyond the ley wall."

"Lienta says the Gorrani are shifting their men to face northward. He thinks they intend to attack. We'll know for certain when their drums start up." He scanned the temple and the Kormanley's men. "Right now, he's waiting to see what happens."

"Neither Devin nor the Gorrani can do anything to us or the Kormanley until the ley wall comes down," Cutter said.

"Lienta's thinking that perhaps we should force the ley wall to come down."

Hernande's eyebrows rose. "He wants us to go across now and take out Iscivius?"

"It's a possibility. But, for now, we wait." Marcus shifted restlessly before settling down near Hernande. "How long will it take you to get ready once we know we're going?"

Hernande shrugged. "I've been practicing entering the meditative state since we devised the plan. I can be ready within minutes. Someone will have to carry me across, though. I won't be able to walk and remain focused at the same time. If my concentration is interrupted—"

"It would be disastrous." Marcus stared down into the chasm, then sighed and stood. "Unless Lienta orders otherwise, we'll go as soon as the ley wall falls. Be ready."

He and Cutter returned below.

Artras watched their retreat, then said, "That could be minutes, or hours, or days from now."

"Somehow, I don't think it's the latter."

"The Gorrani are already here," the Butcher complained. "And the Needle looks like it's already been consumed by ley."

Devin trudged up the last of the slope of the crater surrounding the Needle, coming to a halt opposite the Butcher's giant ax. It hung listlessly from his hand. The alpha Hound watched them both from six paces back. He already knew the situation at the Needle. His beta had reported in nearly a day ago, but he'd decided that the "Baron" didn't need to be informed.

What the alpha really wanted to know was what Devin would do now.

"The Needle hasn't been consumed by ley," Devin said with a hint of derision. "It's a wall. They used it the last time the Gorrani attacked."

"So what do we do?"

Devin considered in silence, the Butcher's shoulders twitching with impatience. The alpha could smell the bulkier man's frustration. He'd come here to fight, to butcher, to feed.

Behind them, the combined forces from Erenthrall—the Rats, the Butcher's men, and those from Haven—approached, the noise of their march growing.

"We won't be able to attack the Needle, not with the ley wall in place," Devin finally said.

"What about the Gorrani? We can attack them."

"They're already encamped. They'll be rested, ready for us."

The Butcher reached out and casually grabbed Devin by the throat with his free hand. The alpha tensed, nearly rushed forward to protect his master, the instincts drilled into him in the den at the Amber Tower, but he fought them back, nearly choking with the effort.

"You promised us blood," the Butcher said. His grip tightened and Devin's hands shot up and snatched ineffectively at the larger man's wrist.

"We'll attack . . . at dawn," Devin choked out. "Our men . . . need to rest . . . at least a few hours."

The Butcher's eyes narrowed and then he released him. "Dawn." He turned and loped down the slope toward the approaching army, casting the alpha a dismissive look.

The alpha bristled—he'd killed men for less—but Devin snapped, "Why didn't you do anything? He could have killed me!"

The alpha didn't answer. His fingers itched for the hilt of his dagger.

Massaging his throat, Devin bent over and coughed, then spat into the grass. When he recovered, he straightened and shot a glance toward the Gorrani. "We'll never be able to take the Gorrani, not exhausted from the march and without some preparation. Unless . . ." He turned back to the Hound, then grinned. "Unless they're distracted by something else."

Stepping down from the ridge, he halted directly before the Hound. "I order you to infiltrate the Gorrani camp and kill all of their sects' leaders. Then move on to their warriors. Kill as many of them as you can, quietly, before dawn."

The alpha stared into Devin's eyes, his hackles raised in hatred, but he didn't think Devin noticed. He was so weak, he couldn't even scent the enmity from his own Hounds.

Without a word, he stalked off into the night, heading toward the darkness where he knew his beta waited, leaving Devin behind. When his beta emerged from the night shadows, he asked, "You saw? You heard?"

His beta nodded. "Are we going to follow his orders?"

"No." The simple word sent a frisson of ingrained fear through the alpha's body and he flinched, but when the expected blow in reprimand did not come, he felt elated. Freed. As far as he knew, no Hound had ever refused an order. No Hound had ever defied his master and survived. But the world had changed, had been reshaped, and with it, the Hounds had been unleashed. "No," he said again, the word hard and harsh. "The Hounds will follow no master. We will follow no orders but our own. Let the Baron"—he twisted the title—"fight the Gorrani on his own."

He could smell his beta's pleasure as they angled away from the army, away from the crater and its Needle surrounded in harsh white ley light.

"What about our third?"

The alpha's steps faltered. He glanced back toward the Needle, even though they were below the ridge and could only see the glow of the ley wall over its edge. "We cannot reach him. Let him carry out his orders. We will find him after."

He turned back to the darkness. "And then we will find our own way in this new world."

A ragged, tortured scream cut through the crunch of Morrell's footsteps on the shale of Tumbor and she ground to a halt, head lifted. Behind her, Drayden mimicked her, one of his ears twitching. The scream trailed down into silence.

"It was a woman," he said. "Not Boskell or Okata."

"But it could have been Sesali."

"It could have been one of the Gorrani as well."

Heartsick, Morrell turned away and took up a careful trot. Moving too fast with the strange earth would cause her to trip—she had the sliced hands to prove it—but she didn't dare walk. She didn't know how long it would be before the Gorrani yavun caught up to her.

But the location of the old node was close. She could feel it.

They struggled onward through the broken shards of the city, climbing up splinters of stone, then down the far sides. Blade-sharp edges slit open clothes and skin at odd moments, to the point where Morrell no longer felt the individual cuts. She didn't dare heal herself or Drayden, because she didn't know how much strength she'd need to create the node. Lightning surrounded them, thunder rolling in from all directions. The wind picked up, whistling in the strange crevices created by the shards, until an auroral storm danced overhead like sheets of clouds, then died back down to gusts. At one point, they were forced to cower beneath an overhang as another auroral storm abruptly blossomed in front of them, going from nothing to flaring waves of blue and gold within a few heartbeats, completely blocking their path, all in an eerie silence. When it touched land, the earth seethed and shattered like glass.

Hours later, Morrell stumbled beneath an arch of shards onto the flat face of what appeared to be actual crystal. Details were etched into the face. Words. It had once been the wall of a building, the words some kind of quotation, outlined in scrollwork and pictures. She fell to her hands and knees, grit grinding into the cuts on her palms. Her mouth was dry—they'd drunk sparingly—and her stomach was a hollow pit. She hung her head down between her arms.

Drayden rushed forward and knelt beside her. "We can't stop. You need to keep moving. The Gorrani are close. I can smell them."

"We're here," Morrell said, raising her head. "The node used to be right here, beneath the earth."

Drayden glanced around at the heap of shards, no different than any of the landscape they'd already traversed, but he didn't question her. "Do what you need to do. I'll protect you."

He rose and moved away, his feet crunching in the earth as soon as he left the crystal's smoother, harder surface. But the sound faded as Morrell closed her eyes and reached down into the stone beneath her, as she'd reached into the wall surrounding the Needle to repair it.

She immediately recoiled, jerking her hands free of the crystal with an anguished cry.

"What is it?" Drayden called from the archway.

"The stone," she said. "It's screaming."

She dashed away the tears, then reached and placed her hands against the crystal again, ready for the earth's agony this time. It shuddered through her body as she joined with it, her instinct to reach out and heal it. But this damage was too extensive, too deep, and she didn't have the time or the strength to deal with it now. The Gorrani were too close, and Kara and Marcus and the others were counting on her. Boskell, Okata, and Sesali were counting on her.

She tilted her head back, her eyes closed, and let the pain slough off her, shunting it to one side as she dove deeper beneath the surface, down beneath where Tumbor had once thrived. The ancient node that had once been a part of the ley network before Prime Augustus had created the Nexus had been underground. Deep. Beneath even the barge system. Augustus had supplanted the original node with his own on the surface, had shifted the natural ley lines slightly to accommodate the Wielders. But even the original node had been caught in the distortion over Tumbor.

When she reached where it had originally rested, she discovered it had been sundered into a thousand pieces. But those pieces were easy to identify. They didn't match the density, texture, or color of the stone that surrounded them. As she allowed herself to meld with them, a sense of incredible age settled over her, along with a burning cold. Her skin pulsed with an innate magnetic force, one that pulled her in a thousand directions at once, toward all the other nodes throughout the plains and beyond. Each of them called to the others, each of them drawn to the others, like metal to a lodestone. And all of them were foreign.

As she merged deeper into the fragments, she realized the cold seeping into her bones came from outside the earth, from the heavens. Like the comet above, the node stones had once traveled the stars, and at some point in the far past had plummeted down to the earth. In her mind's eye, Morrell suddenly saw the Needle with its protective ridge of earth for what it was—an impact crater. Erenthrall and Tumbor—all the major cities with a node—must have all once been craters, all signs of the long-forgotten impacts lost as the cities grew, the contours of the land plowed under and reshaped.

But the force that connected Tumbor's node to the others had been weakened when it was first cut off by the distortion, then shattered. The individual shards weren't strong enough alone. And the ley traveled the invisible lines of force between the stones. That's what created the ley lines between the cities, lines that spanned the entire continent and beyond.

The node here in Tumbor had been one of the largest. Morrell could feel it in the shape of the rock. Its loss had disrupted the entire network. There were other, smaller nodes scattered throughout what remained of Tumbor—fragments that had broken off from this one as it crashed into the earth, or simply other stones that had fallen from the skies— but this one dwarfed them all. This one was what she needed to heal for Kara to restore the ley lines and stability to the ley. She could sense how all of the fragments would fuse together to make it whole again, just as she could sense how bones and tissue should be knit back together. It was all the same process.

The tingling sensation she associated with the auroral lights prickled her fingers and hands where they pressed hard into the surface of the crystal beneath her. The auroral storms surrounding them responded as well. Their energies shifted, drawn toward her. She gathered that power—power that had been set free and ran wild on all sides—to her, pulled it in tight. The prickling sensation traveled up her arms and into her shoulders, her hair beginning to stir with its energy, as if caught in a wind. It dove down into her chest, her breath catching, her heart speeding up, then down into her gut, through her legs, and into her feet. Her entire body vibrated with it, and still she drew in more. The node was huge, as large as one of the ley barge stations in Erenthrall. It would require all her strength to heal.

When she felt she had enough gathered, she focused on the node stone below and tensed.

Then a snarl ripped through her concentration and someone shouted, "Morrell!"

Her eyes flared open to find a Gorrani warrior charging straight toward her across the crystal wall, strangely curved blade drawn, an intense purpose blazing in the woman's eyes. Morrell screamed and scrambled back, her connection to the node below crumbling as the Gorrani warrior raised her sword to strike. Morrell brought her hands up to ward off the blow, noted the coruscating auroral lights that still surrounded her, then shoved that energy outward without thought.

The Gorrani woman shrieked as the threads of light enveloped her and flung her back. Bones cracked and flesh tore as the aurora transformed her, as it had transformed the Wolves in Erenthrall. But Morrell had released the aurora wildly. It had no shape, no direction, no purpose.

In the space of a breath, it stretched one of the woman's arms to twice its normal length, the skin rippling and smeared, while the other arm compacted down closer to the woman's body, melded with her torso. The skin on the right side of her head split open and fell away, revealing scales like that of a snake, the eye bulging and turning yellow, the iris a slit of black in the center. The scream stretched and broke into a serpentine hiss. Then the transformations became too intense and the woman's heart spasmed and stopped. Morrell felt it, still connected partially with the aurora, and felt the smothering black of death encroaching on her as it had with Hanter. She pulled herself free as the aurora dissipated and the woman's body fell onto the crystal shard, twitching once.

Morrell heaved in a lungful of air, choked on it, nearly gagged, but a vicious growl broke through her panic. Near the arched shards, Drayden leaped at another Gorrani warrior with wicked speed, batting away the man's sword arm with one hand while using the other to catch him behind the head. He yanked hard and Morrell heard the crack of the man's neck from a hundred feet away, the body crumpling. A second Gorrani appeared from the right, blade slicing down Drayden's back before he could turn. He howled and arched, blood already appearing through the cut on his shirt, but even as Morrell lurched forward, he twisted and lunged. The two fell to the ground, the second Gorrani screaming before his outcry was cut short with a ragged gurgle, Drayden stumbling back and away from the limp form. His hands and neck were sheathed in blood.

He caught sight of her, panting heavily, then stumbled toward her. He made it three steps before falling face-first to the ground. Even then, he lifted his head and one arm and growled, attempting to drag himself forward.

Morrell spun to find two more Gorrani approaching from behind her. Another emerged from the shards to her left, then two more back at the arch near Drayden. There were too many of them, coming from too many sides. Wind lashed her hair about her as one hand balled into a fist near her chest in indecision. The auroral storms that had been drawn to her use of her power were bearing down on them all, their pressure building. The air felt heavy and thick as she heaved in breath after breath.

Drayden dragged himself another body's length closer, then growled, "Run," before collapsing. He didn't move again.

Morrell sucked in a deep breath, but this time held it. Her hand dropped from her chest.

"No," she whispered to herself. "Not this time."

She reached for the storms, pulled the auroral energies toward her, gathering them as she had before. Sheets of auroral light sprang up around her, the wind picking up to a gale force. Dust and dirt exploded away from her, the lights expanding outward, twisting and weaving, as she drew more and more of their energy to her.

On all sides, the remaining Gorrani of the yavun hesitated. Those that didn't have their blades already drawn drew them now.

Morrell swallowed, her mouth dry. "Don't come any closer!"

The closest Gorrani grinned, his teeth shockingly white beneath the darkness of the storm overhead. "We are yavun and you are the target. You will have to kill us, as you did our sister."

Morrell's gaze dropped to the tortured body of the woman warrior and tasted bile at the back of her throat. She hadn't meant for the woman to die like that. She hadn't meant for the woman to die at all.

She lifted her head. "That was a mistake. I didn't intend to kill her. I'm a healer."

The Gorrani warrior chuckled and began to advance again, the others following suit. "Then you will die here, healer."

"I don't think so."

She reached down into the stone beneath her as the Gorrani broke into a run. Before they'd gone three steps, the earth heaved, a column rising out of the ground, shoving Morrell and Drayden up into the air, splinters of rock shattering outward. The Gorrani cried out, hands raised to protect their faces, a few of them knocked to the ground. When the column had risen thirty feet into the air, Morrell released the auroral energy with a gasp. She fell to one knee, holding herself steady with one hand, then scrambled toward Drayden. She rolled him onto his back, already reaching into his body to determine the damage. Auroral lights leaped from her hands, sheathing him in waves of color and she laughed out loud in relief when she realized he still lived. Without thought—the power coming swift and easy because of the storms—she healed the grievous wound across his back, his cuts and bruises. A ragged howl rose from his chest as he arched his back at the pain, but Morrell held him down.

"I'm sorry!" she shouted, the wind still surging around them. "There's too much energy here! I should have gone slower, but it's hard to control!"

Drayden fell back to the stone and lay there, his breath coming in harsh, short pants. "Where . . . are the . . . Gorrani?"

"I took care of them."

Drayden's breath caught. Then he tried to get up.

"Don't!" Morrell shoved him back down, but he snarled at her, snapping with his teeth. She leaned back and let him rise with a disgusted shake of her head. "I healed you too fast. You're still recovering."

He ignored her, although he hesitated as soon as he looked around. Auroral storms were still approaching, easier to see at the height of the column of stone, and lightning continued to fork in the distance all around them. He limped toward the edge of the column and stared down.

"They're trying to scale the rock," he said.

Morrell stood and ran to his side, grabbed his arm for support when the wind threatened to shove her over the side.

Below, the Gorrani had regrouped. There were seven of them now, four on the ground staring upward, three of them attempting to climb the column. One of them had already made it a third of the way up, the sides of the column ragged, with numerous places for a handhold or ledge for a foot.

Morrell stepped away from the edge. "I couldn't kill them. I couldn't! Not like the Gorrani woman. That was an accident. I didn't know the aurora would do that to her. I just threw it at her! She was going to kill me. I—I couldn't do that to them, too. I'm a healer! I'm supposed to heal people!"

Drayden caught her shoulder and the ragged flow of words cut off. He met her gaze. "Have you rebuilt the node?"

She opened her mouth to protest, then shook her head. "No. Not yet."

"Then do it. Now. I'll take care of the Gorrani."

"There are too many of them!"

Drayden grinned. "But they have to come at me from below."

A sudden shout echoed up toward them, followed by the clash of swords. Both of them stepped back to the edge to find the four Gorrani on the ground fighting a fifth, swords flaring in the darkness, the motions of all five of them a hypnotic dance from this height. The four men of the yavun spun around the fifth, none of them able to get in a significant blow. The three men scaling the wall had halted to watch the action below, but now they turned back and continued to climb.

"Who—?"

"Okata," Drayden answered, then gently pushed her back from the edge. "Go. Repair the node. Prepare it for Kara, no matter what happens to me or Okata."

Morrell backed away, toward the center of the column where the crystal wall lay, the Gorrani warrior's twisted body a black shadow to one side. She paused when she caught sight of it, but then shoved the gruesome death out of her mind and reached for the aurora.

The storms were close. Their energy leaped through her body, tingling through every pore, her hair writhing around her face. She pulled it in with ease, even more than she had gathered before, and the center of the column erupted in ethereal sheets of blue, gold, and green lights, with hints of purple threaded throughout. She closed her eyes and lifted her arms to the sky, diving deep into the earth again, toward the fractured stone. Drayden snarled and she flinched, but forced the sudden desperate sounds of fighting away, merged herself with the strange metallic nature of the shattered node below. It wanted to be whole. She could feel how its pieces fit together, could sense its oblong, rough, imperfect shape that had somehow, with the other nodes that had fallen from the sky, reacted with the ley and created a natural network across the plains. She drew on the energy of the wild aurora and began fusing the rock back together.

The first few pieces merged slowly, almost reluctantly, but the next few went faster, then faster still, until a cascade effect began, the thousands of shards suddenly pulling together as Morrell poured the changeling energy of the aurora down from the skies, through her body, and deep into the earth. It sizzled through her, every nerve on fire. Vaguely, she heard someone screaming, realized it was her own voice, but the raw power dampened her hearing.

Then it was over, the node whole again. She cut off the flow of the aurora, even as the invisible force that the node exuded reached out toward the other stones and reconnected. She opened her eyes, the auroral lights still swirling around her. Waves of weakness washed through her and she wavered where she stood, her arms dropping. A figure walked toward her, three bodies sprawled across the column's top behind him. But she wasn't finished. The large node below had been restored, but like Erenthrall, Tumbor had contained more than one. The others were smaller, but she had enough residual auroral energy captured within her she could heal the others as well.

Reaching out, she sought out the strange metals she'd tasted in the stone in the surrounding area, fusing the shards together as she found them. The figure continued to approach as the auroral lights that wove around her faded. She tensed as he drew closer, knowing that she wouldn't be able to defend herself once she finished with the smaller nodes. She could barely stand even now, her strength drained. And she couldn't use the aurora as she'd done before. Not on another human. The result was too horrifying.

So she used the last of the gathered aurora and her strength to piece together one more minor node at the edge of what had once been Tumbor and then faced the figure, now only a few paces away.

"It's done," she said, her voice cracked and gravelly. "The nodes have been repaired."

"Good."

She sobbed at hearing Drayden's voice, then fell forward. The Wolf caught her and held her, even though she could sense he had been wounded again. His blood saturated his shirt, rubbed against her face as he shifted her and laid her down on the etched crystal beneath them.

"I can't heal you," she said, tears mixing with his blood. "I'm too drained."

"It's all right. None of my wounds are mortal."

But she couldn't stop crying, or clutching at him with one hand. He hurt—the pain deep—but didn't protest.

"Where's Okata?" she asked between hitching breaths.

"Here."

Both of them turned to see Okata dragging himself up over the edge of the column. Drayden leaped to help him, supporting the Gorrani Wielder as they both returned to Morrell's side. Okata limped, his left leg almost useless. Morrell didn't understand how he'd made it up the face of the column.

Drayden set Okata down beside Morrell, who reached out to touch his blood-coated hand. She closed her eyes and surveyed his wounds as well, even though she could do nothing to help him right now. His left leg had been broken and she lost count of his cuts and bruises, but like Drayden, he'd survive until she'd recovered.

She let her hand drop from his. "Boskell? Sesali?"

Okata shrugged. "I do not know. I did not see them when I followed you here."

"I'll watch for them," Drayden said.

"There are still members of the yavun missing. I killed two before coming here, but there were likely fifteen, which means three are un-accounted for."

"Perhaps Boskell and Sesali took care of them."

"Or the Gorrani took care of *them*."

Morrell wanted to protest, but she knew it was likely. The tears that had begun to calm started up again. She couldn't stop them. Her chest ached and a tremendous lassitude began to settle over her body.

"Did she repair the nodes?" Okata asked. He sounded as if he sat a thousand feet away.

"Yes."

"Then why haven't the auroral storms abated?"

Morrell roused herself enough to answer. "Because Kara hasn't restored the ley lines yet. The nodes only created the channels."

"Then we should leave these shattered lands before the rest of the Gorrani's yavun find us. If they still live."

Morrell's eyes popped open and she managed to roll onto one side to face Okata and Drayden. "We can't leave. Not yet. There's something more I need to do here before we go, and I'll need the auroral storms to do it."

Twenty-One

THE DARKNESS BEGAN TO RECEDE, and Cory struggled up into the burning ache left behind by the gas being used to subdue him and the rest of the University students. He struck the glass wall and cursed, peering out from behind it at the blurry, distorted image beyond. He was still too deep. He could pick out a brighter patch of white, marked with a few smears of color and dabs of shadow, nothing more. Some of those shadows moved, so he knew there were people in the chamber with him and the others. Probably enforcers, maybe the servants that fed and bathed them. He didn't know how long he'd been under this time, but based on his protesting muscles, even without attempting to move, and the hollow pit of his stomach, he assumed it had been days.

The passage of time hadn't blunted his anger. It seethed with him behind the wall, hotter than the raw burn of the gas left in his lungs and throat.

He pushed at the glass wall briefly, testing it, then settled back down to wait and plan. Baron Devin and the Gorrani must have arrived, might be attacking the walls of the Needle even now, but he had no intention of helping Father Dalton or Darius fight them. He could care less about the Kormanley.

But the University students in the room—Mirra, Jasom, Tara, the three others—they were his responsibility now that Jerrain and Sovaan were both dead. He'd see them free of the Kormanley no matter what the cost.

As the first rays of dawn began to lighten the horizon, Hernande glanced up toward the thin streak of light from the comet, now only two days away from its closest approach if his calculations were correct, then tugged on Marcus' sleeve. "We should retreat inside before one of the Kormanley enforcers sees us."

Marcus shifted toward the roof door that led down into the half-crumbled building, sticking to the fading shadows. Hernande closed the door behind them.

They found Artras, Cutter, Marc, and twenty Temerite watchmen huddled in the rooms below, the lieutenant in charge of the watchmen pacing back and forth. By the track worn into the dust and dirt of the floor, he'd been doing so for a while.

"What's his problem?" Marcus asked as they joined Artras and the others.

"He feels he's being wasted here, that he should be on the walls." Artras shrugged. "Did you see anything from the roof?"

"Nothing. The Kormanley scrambled to man the walls at first, but they haven't done anything but wait for the last few hours, just like us."

"Lienta did say—"

A horn cry cut through their muffled voices and nearly everyone in the wide room looked up or stood, head cocked, listening. The lieutenant bolted for the doorway, halting just inside and glaring outward, his jaw muscles twitching.

"That's coming from the Kormanley," Marc said.

Before anyone else could respond, the thunder of drums rolled across them.

"The Gorrani."

The Kormanley horns fell silent. Hernande drifted toward the nearest windows facing away from the chasm and the Kormanley's section of the Needle, the others following.

"What are you looking at?" Cutter asked.

"The wall of ley. It's still up."

"Which means the Gorrani are getting ready to fight Baron Devin," Marc said in understanding. "Maybe they'll annihilate one another and leave the rest of us in peace."

Hernande faced them all. "You forget Father's prophecy. It won't matter if they kill each other, it's the Three Sisters' quickening that destroys us all."

A deafening roar—of a thousand voices—washed over them, muted by the walls of the building and distance, but recognized by everyone who'd witnessed the Gorrani attack on the Needle earlier. It faded, replaced by the rumble of thousands of feet as the Gorrani charged. There was too much stone between their location and the fight for Hernande to feel the earth trembling beneath, but they could hear the screams when the two forces finally met.

The faces of the watchmen around them turned grim; it was obvious they wanted to be near the battle. An itch began in Hernande's feet and across his shoulders. He shrugged, but fought the urge to move. Artras also appeared twitchy, her hands clenching and unclenching. At a questioning look from Cutter, she snapped, "I'd like to be able to at least *see* the battle, that's all."

Hernande faced the windows again, then suddenly stepped forward.

"What?" Marcus asked, joining him. Apparently, they were all anxious. "What is it?"

"Is it my imagination, or is the ley wall shorter than before?"

Everyone crowded closer, peering through the window. Then someone cursed.

"It is shorter," Marc said.

"By at least a few feet," Artras added. "It's hard to tell, since it flickers at the top, but it's definitely smaller. And I don't think it's burning as intensely as before."

"Iscivius and the other Wielders must be exhausted by now. They've held the wall for days."

"I'd say they're about ready to collapse."

The lieutenant abruptly stepped back from the door and called, "At attention!" The watchmen scrambled into a semblance of order a few seconds before Lienta strode into the room, followed by three high-ranking officers. An entire squad of watchmen could be seen outside, huddled close to the building.

"Report," Lienta said.

"We've been watching the Kormanley on the walls near the chasm," the lieutenant said. "They do not appear to have noticed our activities here. Their focus has been on their own walls, although they have kept a cursory watch on our ballistae."

"Good. The ballistae are going to provide a distraction, hopefully pull all of the Kormanley on the far side of the chasm away from this area. Our watchmen on the walls report that the ley has started to fall. Everyone here has exactly one hour to prepare for a crossing into the main part of the city and an attack on the temple." Lienta caught Hernande's attention. "You'll be ready? Everything depends on you."

"I'll be ready."

Lienta didn't respond, merely stepped outside to pass on orders to those waiting there. The lieutenant motioned the men inside toward the back rooms, everyone reaching to strap on weapons and anything else they'd set to one side while they waited.

Hernande stepped away from the window toward the back as well, Marcus and the others following. He'd already picked out a secure location on the edge of a collapsed wall, one that gave him a view on the chasm, but kept him out of sight of the enforcers there. He hesitated as he stepped into the sunlight pouring through the broken wall, revealing heaps of rubble, but only long enough to take a single, centering breath. Then he picked his way around the debris to a roughly circular space he'd cleared a few days after Kara and the others had left. He heard the others following him, but he'd already begun his focusing exercises. As he pulled a candle from its niche to one side, the noises from the fight between the Gorrani and Devin's men—along with the rattle and clank of Lienta's watchmen—faded away. He placed the candle at the edge of the circle, in the lee of the debris there, so its light would remain hidden. From the same niche, he pulled out a small rolled rug and snapped it open, setting it on the stone floor of what had once been a ballroom. He knelt on the rug, centered on the intricate design woven into it in shades of brown, tan, and burnt reds, weight resting back on his heels. Then he lit the candle, the scent of the match sharp, stinging his nostrils, its yellowed glow as brilliant as the sun, the guttering of its flame like gusts of wind. His awareness of his immediate surroundings had already heightened.

He eased back, hands clasped loosely in his lap, back straight. He could see the gaping rent of the chasm through the crumbled wall, the slight promontory that jutted out toward the buildings, city, and temple on the far side. This was the narrowest section of the chasm within the Needle, the most obvious section for a bridge. Except he wouldn't be building a bridge of stone or even wood.

He intended to build a bridge of air.

He filled his lungs, exhaled slowly, then did it again. He'd intended to use the flame of the candle as a focus, but he could already feel the meditative state rushing forward to engulf him. He'd been practicing for days now, so he wasn't surprised. He opened himself up, let the calmness flow into him, fill him, like water filling a pitcher. He blinked a few times, then his eyes closed, yet he could still see the chasm and promontory outside the shattered wall. The water continued to fill him, and he sank into its depths, releasing his ties to the physical world. The scent of the smoke from the candle died out. The delicate taste of ash and stone faded from his tongue. The anxious rustle of Marcus, Artras, Cutter, and Marc silenced, followed by that of Lienta's men. The weave of the rug biting into his knees and toes flattened out into nothing.

All that remained was his vision of the chasm, the jut of stone, and the buildings on the far side, the temple and the spire of the Needle piercing up into the sky beyond them.

From where he floated in the depths between consciousness and unconsciousness, he reached forward and began to fold the Tapestry into layer upon layer upon layer, each tighter than the last.

Marcus watched Hernande as he settled himself upon the small rectangular rug with what looked like a depiction of a sun at its center, surrounded by thousands of tiny symbols and pictograms. If it was a language, it was one that Marcus had never seen before. He wondered where Hernande had found it, although he supposed the mentor could have carried it all the way from Erenthrall after the Shattering. The University had been spared most of the initial damage because of its walls and the fact its buildings had been made of stone. Not many of those who'd fled Erenthrall had been able to take such personal possessions with them. Not many personal possessions had survived in the months since. He knew he'd kept hold of very little, although he had a few prized pieces in his room.

Hernande drew in several deep breaths, then stilled, his back rigid. His breathing slowed. His eyes fluttered, then closed. Slowly, his head sagged forward until his chin hit his chest.

Everyone around them quieted, even Lienta's watchmen. The Temerite captain had brought twenty armed with swords and ten archers. With the watchmen that had already been stationed in the building, that brought the Temerites up to fifty, plus Lienta, Marc, Cutter, Artras, and himself. Not that large a force.

But all they had to do was get to the Nexus and hold it until Kara could finish her work in Erenthrall. Assuming Morrell could repair the node in Tumbor.

For a moment, the impossibility of it all overwhelmed him.

Then Artras tugged on his arm. "Is he even breathing?"

He pulled himself back into the moment to focus on Hernande again. "I'll check."

He edged through the rubble to Hernande's position, careful to keep out of sight. He crouched down at Hernande's side, leaned in close.

The University mentor didn't move. Marcus shifted closer, so he could listen for Hernande's breath as he watched the man's chest.

Nothing happened for what felt like an eternity. Then Hernande's chest rose slowly. He exhaled even slower, the entire process taking at least ten of Marcus' own breaths. Then the mentor stilled again.

Marcus' skin prickled with unease, but he pulled back and made his way toward the others.

"He's breathing. Barely."

"He said he'd be so far under that we could move him," Artras said, "but he didn't warn us he'd basically be dead."

"He's not dead."

"Did you listen for a heartbeat?"

Marcus didn't answer.

"How will we know when we can move across?" Lienta asked. Marcus hadn't realized he'd shifted close enough to overhear them. "I'm not asking any of my watchmen to walk out into thin air to test it out."

The men close behind him pretending they weren't listening in began to fidget.

Marcus glanced around at the rest of them. Artras shrugged.

He contemplated Hernande for a long moment, then said, "Wait here."

Before anyone could protest, he climbed up the small pile of rubble and stepped out onto the jut of rock that protruded into the chasm. It had once been part of a decorative garden, with a flagstone walkway and patches of earth where grass and shrubs and flowers had grown. Now it was riddled with weeds, the flagstones canted or broken. As he walked up to the edge of the chasm, he reached down and scooped up a few chunks of stone.

He stared down into the rent in the earth stretching away to either side, slicing down through the city and its walls. Water cascaded down into the darkened depths in various places from underground streams. A few ley lines were visible as well, angled toward the Needle, throbbing with white light.

He gazed across toward the buildings on the far side, noticed a few Kormanley guards take notice of him. He waved, then hefted a stone in one hand and casually tossed it out into the chasm.

It struck something in midair and bounced off to one side.

Marcus choked on his next breath as something lodged in the back of his throat. He shot a look toward the Kormanley to see if they'd noticed, but they weren't watching him anymore. Still, sweat prickled his forehead as he bent down and tossed a handful of dirt and sand toward the edge of the chasm a few feet away.

Most of it hit something that wasn't there, remaining suspended in air, a few pebbles bouncing and rolling out another foot or two from the edge. To either side, the dirt fell into the chasm.

Marcus stood slowly, tossed a few more of his stones out toward the abyss as if bored, then forced himself to walk slowly back to the darkened ballroom.

As soon as he was out of sight of the Kormanley guards, he said, "The bridge is already there. It's about five feet across. We'll have to be careful, but we can cross now."

"What about the Kormanley?" Marc asked.

"There are four guards directly across from us, but they aren't particularly vigilant right now. There are more to the north and south."

"We should wait for the ballistae to begin their bombardment," one of Lienta's lieutenants said.

The Temerite captain considered. "We don't know how long Hernande can hold the bridge. Send one of the watchmen to the ballistae. Tell them to begin their assault now." The lieutenant immediately turned and selected someone, the man running back into the inner rooms. "We'll send the archers across first. They can take out the Kormanley as they go."

"They won't know where the bridge is," Artras said. "You'll lose half of them because they'll be trying to shoot and walk across nothing at the same time. It won't work."

"I'll go first," Marcus interrupted, already impatient. "I'll mark the bridge with dirt so that everyone can see it. Someone get me a pouch and fill it."

Lienta snapped his fingers and five men began scrambling to empty out a sack and fill it with whatever they could find inside the hall.

"I'll follow you," Cutter said. He rolled his wounded shoulder, stretching it out, then began to string his bow. "It's time I started putting all of my efforts to practical use."

No one questioned him.

One of the guards set to keep watch suddenly shouted. "Captain Lienta! The ley wall!"

Everyone headed toward the inner rooms and the windows that allowed them to see the ley wall, but Lienta ordered all but one of his lieutenants back. Marcus, Artras, and Cutter joined them.

All along the outer wall, the fiery ley wall was in flux, its flames shooting high, then collapsing again, rising and falling in waves around the perimeter.

"It's failing," Artras said curtly. "They're fighting to keep it up, but it's failing."

"We may not need the ballistae as a distraction after all."

Without a sound, the entire ley wall sank out of sight.

A hush fell, everyone in the room holding their breath. Lienta looked up.

Marcus started when the horn sounded, closer than he expected.

"The ley wall is down," Lienta said, stalking back toward the demolished ballroom. As soon as he entered, he asked the watchmen, "What are the Kormanley doing?"

"They're scrambling for the outer walls!"

"What about those at the chasm?"

"Those closest to the outer walls are leaving. Most of those stationed farther in as well. The four nearest our position are agitated, as if they don't know what they should do. It appears the one in control is ordering them to stay. They're arguing."

"We aren't waiting—for them or the ballistae. Marcus and Cutter, the bridge."

Marcus had already snagged the bag of dirt from the watchmen. He sprinted up the debris and out onto the promontory of rock, not even looking toward the far side, his eyes locked on the few specks of dirt and stone that appeared to be hanging in midair. Reaching into the bag as he ran, he grabbed a handful and threw it out ahead of him, slowing only as he neared the edge of solid stone. His heart faltered once, painfully, a rush of adrenaline shivering through his body, as he took the first step out into what appeared to be a vertical drop into nothing. But his foot landed on a solid surface, the dirt he'd already thrown grinding under his heel. Emboldened, he continued forward, tossing dirt and stone before him, making certain he spread it wide enough that the edges of the bridge could be easily seen. Shouts echoed across the chasm, but he didn't dare look up. Behind him, he heard Cutter swear, followed by the sound of feet crunching on gravel and the snap of an arrow being released. Two more shots and Marcus was standing over nothing, the gaping maw of the chasm below. His breath began to catch in his throat, drowning out the growing shouts from both ahead and behind. He began to shake, an involuntary reaction to the impossibility of what his eyes were convinced was a drop to his death. But he forged onward, throwing dirt haphazardly now, intent only on getting to the far side safely, before something happened to Hernande and the bridge vanished. An arrow skittered across the invisible surface at his feet and he nearly jerked to the side and over the edge. Another shattered as it struck, flecking him with slivers of wood. But then he could see the rugged chasm wall before him, its edge near. He glanced upward with an inarticulate cry of relief—

And saw one of the enforcers waiting for him at the makeshift wall they'd erected at the chasm's edge, sword at the ready. The man grinned in anticipation, stepping up onto the top of the wall and over. He'd already thrown gravel over the edge, outlining the bridge, his foot kicking a chunk to the side and over into the chasm. His eyes didn't waver.

Marcus halted, began to step back. But an arrow sprouted in the enforcer's throat. The man staggered against the chasm wall in surprise, then slumped to the side and fell off the bridge. His body struck the chasm wall and flailed as it faded into the darkness below.

Marcus almost followed when Cutter's hand shoved him forward from behind.

"Move! Lienta and the others are right behind us."

"The Kormanley—"

"We've taken care of everyone close."

Marcus didn't need any more prompting. He lurched to the wall and crawled over the top, allowing himself to succumb to tremors as his feet touched solid, visible stone again. He dropped the bag and clutched at the gritty reality of the building that paralleled the chasm at this point with one hand, steadying himself as he caught his breath. Cutter stalked along the wall to the north, bow ready, arrow trained forward.

"You don't even seem short of breath," Marcus said, wiping at his face with his other hand. He was still trembling.

"I didn't think about it," Cutter answered, without even glancing back.

Marcus barked a short laugh.

Lienta suddenly appeared, stepping down from the wall, as nonchalant as Cutter. His watchmen came after, spilling over the edge in various states of shock and agitation. Most were stoic, but a few were white-faced, with widened eyes. One dropped to his knees and vomited off to one side.

Artras and Marc came toward the end, Hernande thrown over Marc's shoulder, his body limp, two watchmen behind them.

"That's it," one of the lieutenants said. "That's the last of our group."

His words were punctuated by a sudden crack of wood, followed by two more. Everyone turned northward, where three boulders the size of Marcus' head arched out over the chasm and crashed into the Kormanley side of the Needle with shattering impacts. The catapults had begun their assault.

"What's next?" one of the watchmen asked.

Marc and Artras settled Hernande's body against the short wall, Marc still supporting him. The University mentor's head hung at an odd angle, his features locked in rigid contemplation, brow slightly creased.

"How do we wake him up?" Artras asked.

Marc slapped the mentor, hard, Hernande's head cracking into the stone wall behind him. Artras gasped, then hit Marc on the shoulder. "How dare you!"

Marc didn't seem affected at all. "I don't think he's going to wake up. Not for one of us anyway."

"He'll come out of it on his own," Marcus said.

"You'll have to carry him," Lienta said. "We aren't waiting here." He picked out five watchmen. "You're on point. Head for the temple. Avoid as many people as possible, especially enforcers. Go."

As soon as the five men left, he turned to Marcus. "We'll keep your group in the middle until we reach the temple. Once we've taken the Nexus, we'll hold the Needle while you do whatever needs to be done."

He motioned to the rest of his men. Marc hefted Hernande up onto his shoulder like a sack of grain. "Let's go."

From behind the glass wall, three enforcers stood guard over five servants as they fed the rest of the University students. They'd already fed Cory, one of the servants even using a damp cloth to wash his face. He still couldn't move, not even to swallow on his own, but his throat and lungs burned with the raw fire from the gas. He hadn't tried to speak yet; it was too early, and he didn't want to give the guards any reason to call for reinforcements. There'd been twice as many a short time ago, but something had happened and the other three had been pulled away.

Of the three that remained, two kept close to the door and glanced outward every few seconds, unable to keep still. The third glared at the University students as the women worked. He was older, grizzled, and kept playing with the handle of a pipe attached to his belt next to a small bag that Cory assumed contained leaf for smoking. One of the other guards had called him Trenton.

Surreptitiously, Cory attempted to move the fingers of his left hand, hidden from the others by his body. He was shocked when they twitched. He tested the glass wall again, pushed himself closer to consciousness. He tried swallowing, felt the muscles in his throat pulse.

He glanced to where three of the women were feeding Mirra, the two others finishing up with Jasom. He was running out of time.

From behind the glass wall, he reached forward on the Tapestry and encircled the hearts of all three of the enforcers. Then he squeezed.

All three dropped to the floor, dead before their bodies hit the ground.

The five servants jerked, one of them crying out, two of them standing, including the eldest, the one who'd washed them as they were fed.

"What happened?" one of them asked.

The matron shook her head. "Go find the other guards."

"Don't," Cory said. The word came out as a dry croak, barely audible, but it caught the matron's attention. She stepped toward him.

"Did you do this?"

"Yes. I can do the same . . . to all of you . . . if any of you . . . step out of this room."

For emphasis, he gave the matron's heart a tweak. She sucked in a sharp breath through her teeth, her hand rising to clutch at her chest. The women behind her cried out or shrank back.

"We've fed you, washed you, kept you alive!" the matron said in reproach.

"You've kept us sedated!" Cory croaked. He was regaining his voice, even though it hurt to speak. "Imprisoned!"

"Because Father demanded it. You're dangerous. As you've demonstrated."

"I won't hurt you unless you force me to." Cory tilted his chin toward the open door. "Close the door."

The matron glanced toward the opening, then back toward him, clearly considering escape. But she pointed to one of the others. "Close it. Don't do anything stupid."

The girl, no more than twelve, hesitantly approached the door, then closed it and ran back to the others.

The matron turned back to Cory. "Now what?"

"Now you help me get the others awake and mobile. I've had enough of your Father. We're leaving."

～

"Commander! The ley wall has collapsed!"

"I can see that," Darius snapped as he reached the top of the Needle's outer wall and strode to its edge. He placed his hands against the stone parapet and gazed out at the battlefield, where Baron Devin's men from Erenthrall and the Gorrani from the south were pummeling each other, the ground already littered with bodies and soaked with blood. Dust raised from the fighting obscured most of the details, but it was obvious that neither side had made a significant advance toward victory. They were evenly matched. But it was difficult to tell, regardless. There were no lines, no obvious strategies at play. The crater of the Needle had become a melee.

As yet, only a few of those outside the walls had noticed that the ley wall had fallen. That wouldn't last for long.

"We have to hold the gates," he said, turning to face the enforcers that lined the wall. "If either the Gorrani or Baron Devin breach the wall before Iscivius has a chance to rest—"

He choked on the words as a freshet of blood arched across his face. He tasted blood as the throat of the lieutenant to whom he'd been speaking gaped wide, slit from behind. The man's eyes were opened in shock. Darius' entire body went numb as the lieutenant toppled to the side, revealing another man, one Darius didn't recognize. He held a small dagger in one hand, tilted downward, blood dripping from its edge. There were streaks of blood across the man's clothing. Even so, he was hard to see. Darius' eyes kept sliding away from him, the man fading in and out of sight.

"What—?"

"I've been inside for days," the man said. He didn't move, kept his eyes locked on Darius. "I've been waiting for the ley wall to fall. It didn't make any sense to open the gate with the ley wall still up."

Darius stopped trying to discern the man's features—his face a blur of mouth, nose, dark hair like a mustache—and took in the rest of the near wall. All the men who'd been stationed there were dead, their bodies slumped where they'd fallen, crumpled to the stone floor or draped over the parapet. Close to twenty men, all taken out without a sound.

He faced the man in sudden horror, took a step back as he reached for his sword. His back came up against the edge of the parapet. "You're a Hound."

The man looked out at the battle below. "Where's Father?"

Darius drew his blade, the knot of terror in his gut twisting into anger. "You won't make it off this wall."

"You won't stop me."

"Why not?"

"Because you're already dead."

Darius started to draw a breath to laugh, to protest, perhaps both, but suddenly the Hound stood in front of him, the man's motion a mere blur. Something punched into his chest and shoved him back against the stone edge behind him. With a scrape of leather armor against stone, he tumbled through the crenellation and over the wall.

Wind and the flapping of his clothes muffled all other sounds as he fell. He had time to notice a knife had sprouted in the center of his chest, that it somehow constricted his breathing, that his chest felt tight.

The pain ripped through him a moment before he struck the ground. Bones in his body cracked. His sword clanged against stone and jolted from his grip. He bounced slightly, but settled, his body arched over a boulder to the left of the gates, arms and legs at odd angles, head tilted to one side. But he was still alive. He exhaled, the breath leaving him in a gurgling moan. Blood trailed from the corner of his mouth. He could taste it, thick and syrupy, draining from him in a thin stream. He thought some dripped from his nose, but he couldn't be certain. A dull throb had begun in the base of his skull, had begun to crescendo. Most of his body was numb, nothing but vague twinges of pain or phantom twitches, but he knew the building throb was pain. He braced himself for the agony.

But then a sound caught his attention: the clank of the gate mechanism, then the clangor of its chains as the massive doors began to open.

He tried to bellow in fury, but all that came out was a weak gargle and a bubble of blood from his nose. It burst, splattering him with a spray of droplets.

Then the Hound stepped out of the door and raised a horn to his lips.

The peal of the horn calling Baron Devin and his dogs to the Needle's doors was deep and hollow and beautiful.

It was the last thing Darius heard before choking to death on his own blood.

�

"Where is everyone?" Lienta asked as they ran through the mostly deserted streets toward the temple. The few people they saw moved quickly into doorways and niches, those in the buildings closing shutters and bolting doors. Many of them were elderly, or mothers or teenagers who were guarding children.

They passed a cross street and a sudden roar echoed down its length.

"There!" Artras shouted, pointing with one hand.

The group ground to a halt. At the far end of the cross street they could see a crowd of people gathered in an open plaza, hands raised to the heavens. Another wave of sound rolled toward them, what sounded like a chant.

Marcus swore. "It's Father. He's holding another one of his sermons, probably to keep the people of the Needle calm."

"Let him," Lienta said. "It will help us gain access to the temple."

He whistled and the group broke back into a trot, five men still out in front on point, Marcus and the rest in the middle. They cut toward the temple's side entrances, parallel to the plaza before the temple, slowing as they drew nearer. Marc was gasping under Hernande's weight by the time Lienta motioned them to a halt. They huddled up against one of the buildings. Artras helped Marc set Hernande's body on the ground, the bulky guardsman wiping sweat from his face.

"He's heavier than he looks."

Marcus edged forward with Cutter until they were at the edge of the building, and he could see why Lienta had called a halt. They were at the edge of the temple, the first tier rising above them, lit with mid-morning sunlight, its steps glowing. Some of the stone was marred with burn marks where the Kormanley bombs had gone off during the coup. Some stone debris still lay in the street, especially around the entrance. It was obvious a bomb had gone off here, probably to keep some of Kara's people from escaping.

A half dozen guards surrounded the damaged doorway, all of them casting occasional glances to the northeast, agitated.

"Something's changed," Lienta said when he noticed Marcus behind him.

"What do you mean?"

"Listen."

Marcus paused. He could still hear the chanting from the sermon, muffled by the buildings, and beyond that the fighting outside the walls. Nothing sounded different. "I don't—"

"The fighting," Cutter said, cutting him off. "It's closer."

"That's why the enforcers look so anxious," Lienta said. "They can see the ley wall is down and those outside have noticed."

Marcus strained his hearing, filtering out the chanting. "The fighting sounds closer than the outer walls, though."

At the same moment, a horn blared to the northwest, picked up by at least three other horns at various points around the wall on all sides, all Kormanley signals. Lienta perked up when a Temerite horn joined them, listening intently.

His expression turned grim. "The gates in the outer wall are already open. Baron Devin and his men have already secured them and are beginning to fight their way through the tent city toward the temple."

"What about the Gorrani?"

"No word. I assume they're attacking the Baron from outside. With Devin at the walls, we need to take the Nexus before he reaches the temple. No more time for subtlety." He gestured at the archers. "Take out the enforcers. Everyone else, get ready to run. Be ready for whatever we might encounter once we're inside the temple."

Marcus and Cutter headed back to Marc and Artras, passing on the orders. Cutter strung his bow and made certain his sword was ready to draw once they were inside. Marc did the same, although he wouldn't be able to fight while carrying Hernande.

"Why don't you just"—the enforcer waved with one hand—"with the ley?"

"Because it may draw attention," Artras said, her wicked dagger appearing in her hand. She tested the sharpness of its blade with her thumb.

Marc's eyes went wide.

"I'll save the ley for when we're inside," Marcus added. "If we need it at all. I don't want to exhaust myself getting to the Nexus and then not have enough strength to do whatever Kara needs me to do when she's ready."

"Lienta is ready," Cutter said.

"Right."

Marc hefted Hernande back onto his shoulder with a tight groan, and the small group joined the Temerites. At a signal, the archers stepped out from the behind the edge of the building and fired.

The rest ran. Four of the six guards fell in the first volley, one arrow missing its target entirely, the other embedding itself in the guard's arm. The man grunted and stared down at the shaft in surprise, then looked toward Lienta. He drew breath to shout, arm already reaching for his sword, but an arrow took him in the eye, his head snapping back. As he fell, two more arrows took out the last guard.

Then Lienta was at the entrance. Without a word, he jerked the door open and four Temerite watchmen ducked inside, a terse "Clear!" coming a breath later. Lienta began ushering the rest of them inside. "Move, move, move!"

Marcus dashed in behind the last of the Temerite front guard, the darkness within blinding him for a moment. He blinked rapidly, eyes adjusting to the ley- and torch-lit interior corridors with their oddly slanted walls. Shouts broke out ahead, punctuated by the clang of swords on metal and stone, but the Temerites didn't slow. Twenty paces farther on, he stumbled over a body, a servant, then an enforcer, blood still spurting from a neck wound.

They passed two corridors, turned right, past more shouts and fighting, then the Temerites ahead of Marcus suddenly halted. He could hear arguing, loud even though they were trying to be quiet. Blood pounded in Marcus' ears, and his breath came in tight gasps.

From behind, Lienta shouted, "What's the holdup?"

"We don't know the way to the Nexus!"

Marcus cursed and began shoving forward. "Let me through!" The Temerites backed into the sides of the corridor, opening a path. He came up on a cross-corridor, three dead enforcers at the intersection. After a quick look around, he said, "This way."

The lieutenant in charge nodded. "We'll lead, but stay close."

They began moving again and ran into four servants, the lieutenant pushing them into a room to one side and jamming a knife into the lock. Marcus called out directions as they moved deeper into the temple, toward its center, where the Needle rose into the sky. The corridors widened and narrowed until they spilled out into one of the main corridors that could hold four abreast.

"This way!" Marcus charged down the corridor toward the double doors at the end, which led to the stellae garden surrounding the Needle and the node beneath.

When they were twenty paces distant, a group of twenty enforcers emerged from a side corridor. Both groups halted abruptly, the enforcers obviously caught off guard.

Before either group could react, there was a muffled explosion from somewhere else in the temple.

"What in hells?" the enforcer's leader said, looking upward as if trying to pinpoint where the explosion had come from. Then his face hardened, and he pointed with his sword. "Kill them."

An arrow shot by Marcus' head close enough it tugged at his hair, and one of the enforcers went down. By then, the two groups had collided, Marcus dragged forward with the Temerites as they charged. A knot of grappling men formed in the corridor, Marcus shoving his way toward the doors. Another explosion echoed over the clamor of the fight, and then Marcus was able to stumble free from the main knot of guardsmen. He headed toward the node, but halted when he heard Artras call his name. She and Cutter were protecting Marc, fending off random attacks that slipped by the Temerites. Marc attempted to keep Hernande's body as far from the flailing blades as possible. They were all pressed up close to the corridor wall, but they'd made it most of the way through the fray.

Swallowing a curse, Marcus dodged back into the edge of the fighting, taking a hard elbow to the gut from one of the Temerites as he repositioned himself. Clutching his side, Marcus reached over another man and grabbed Marc's shirt near his shoulder, hauling him and Hernande into the clear. Artras and Cutter followed, blood staining both of their blades and their clothes. A cut slashed Artras' cheek, but she didn't appear to notice.

"The node," she said.

They ran the few feet to the doors and burst out into the bright sunlight of the stellae garden. But Marcus didn't stop, plowing forward even though he was half blinded until he reached the black side of the Needle and the door into its inner rooms. Before heading down the stairs, he glanced back to see Cutter jam a sword through the handles of the double doors, and then all four of them, Hernande still slung over Marc's shoulder, sprinted down the stairs.

They didn't slow until they neared the opening that led down into the main chamber, where the black walls pulsing with white ley light gave way to stone.

Motioning Artras, Marc, and Cutter to stay back, Marcus edged forward and peered down into the pit. White ley light fountained up in the middle of the well at its center, Wielders scattered all around it, manipulating the ley and the crystals that amplified it inside. The Nexus appeared stable, the ley energetic, but not chaotic. It didn't appear as robust as when Kara had attempted to heal the distortion over Tumbor, as if some of the ley lines that had fed it then had been diverted or had shifted elsewhere. Or perhaps it was simply a consequence of the eruption in Erenthrall, drawing energy away from this node. Shifting ley lines would have caused significant earthquakes, and they'd felt nothing since Tumbor fell.

Marcus' attention drifted from the ley to the Wielders. He recognized all of them, including the three who were standing over the collapsed body of Iscivius near the lip of the well. Carter and Jenner appeared to be arguing with Dylan, although Marcus couldn't pick out about what.

Carter's gaze flicked toward Marcus, and he pulled back.

"What's going on?" Artras whispered.

Marcus hushed her with a gesture.

They waited in silence, Marcus barely daring to breathe.

"Marcus, if that's you, you can come down into the pit. Iscivius is unconscious, and the rest of us are either exhausted or have no intention of harming you or whoever's with you."

Marcus hesitated, sharing a look with Artras, Cutter, and Marc. The large guardsman merely shrugged, leaving the decision up to him.

He turned and began descending into the pit. "That's a fairly broad statement, Jenner, especially when you have no idea why we're here."

"I'm hoping it's to take control, now that Iscivius is out of the picture."

Dylan stepped forward. "Is Kara with you?"

"No, she's in Erenthrall."

Marcus fought back the twinge of jealousy and hurt that twisted inside him at the raw disappointment in the Wielder's face.

"Erenthrall!" Jenner exclaimed. "What in hells is she doing there?"

"Trying to save us all."

The Wielders in the pit not actively controlling the Nexus looked confused. Dylan's gaze landed on Hernande. "What happened to him?"

Artras motioned Marc toward the side of the chamber, where he let Hernande slip to the floor and stretched his back. Artras began checking the University mentor over for wounds. "He's in some kind of self-induced trance or coma and hasn't snapped out of it yet."

"Self-induced? But why?"

"That's not important right now," Marcus cut in impatiently. "What is important is that we need to seize control of the Nexus and then hold it for at least two days—from Father Dalton, from Darius and the Kormanley, from everyone."

"And why is that?"

"Because within the next two days, Kara's going to need everything we've got if she's going to have any chance at all of healing the ley."

No one said anything, the Wielders in the pit all stunned. Marcus decided not to mention that it also relied on Morrell repairing the nodes destroyed in Tumbor in time and Kara actually making it to the original Nexus in Erenthrall. Or that there was no way of knowing whether either of them had succeeded.

Before anyone could ask any questions, there was a crack of splintering wood and Cutter leaped toward the stairs, followed by Marc. "They've broken through the doors," Cutter shouted as he ascended.

"Wait!" Cutter and Marc halted near the entrance to the pit in consternation as Marcus spun toward Dylan. "Can you control the ley enough to flood the lower floor with it? Or at least fill the doorway? We only need to keep them out."

"I think so."

Marcus waved Cutter and Marc down from the stairs. They descended reluctantly, Cutter craning his neck so he could see up into the upper floor. "I can hear them in the sand outside," he said. "They're being cautious." He listened, everyone in the room silent, breath held. Then he turned and trotted down the steps. "They're entering the Needle. Whatever you're going to do, you'd better do it now."

"Dylan?"

"I've got it."

Ley arced away from the well, a thin stream curling overhead toward the top of the stairs and out into the corridor beyond. Panicked shouts echoed down from the outer hallway, followed by the sound of a scrambled retreat.

"Without one of the mentors here to create a reservoir, the best I can do is keep up a steady flow through the corridor and out into the stellae garden," Dylan said. His voice already shook with strain. "I'm letting the ley drain into the sands there."

Marcus glanced toward Hernande, Artras crouched over his slumped body. She shook her head. "No signs he's coming out of it at all."

Marcus gripped Dylan's shoulder. "Do what you can."

"When he gets tired, one of the other Wielders can take over," Jenner said. "What do you need us to do to help Kara?"

"We need to prepare to send as much of the ley to Erenthrall as possible. Sometime between now and the end of the day tomorrow, Kara's going to need it. Now, let me see what Iscivius has done to the Nexus."

Marcus stepped up to the edge of the pit, Jenner on one side, Artras joining him on the other. He rucked up the sleeves of his shirt, ran his hands through his hair, then dove into the ley.

⟐

"How are you doing?" Cory asked.

Mirra swallowed down another sip of water from the cup the matron held out for her with a pained grimace, then coughed. "It hurts, but I can move." Her voice sounded like gravel being crushed underfoot.

"Good. We're leaving." He stood and glanced around at the rest of his five charges, all undergraduate students from the University. He briefly wondered where Hernande was, whether his own mentor was still alive, but he shoved that concern aside. "Can all of you move?" At their nods and cracked-voice responses, he continued. "I need you all to focus. We're going to get out of the temple—out of the Needle entirely if we can—and we're not going to be subtle. Jasom, Tara, and a few of you others were trained in using the Tapestry as a weapon in the Hollow: I know that some argued against it, Jerrain in particular, and some of us even vowed not to use it as a weapon ever again, myself included. But circumstances have changed." He motioned toward the bodies of the guards he'd killed, that had been dragged to one side. "On my authority, you all are granted the right to use the Tapestry to get us out of here, whatever it takes."

"Even killing someone?" Jasom asked.

"Even killing someone."

"But what about the oath Sovaan made us swear in order for us to continue training as students?" Tara asked. "We pledged to do no harm."

Cory closed his eyes and bowed his head, then opened them and caught Tara's gaze. "The oath is a good oath, one you should take seriously, one that you shouldn't throw away carelessly. But I doubt Sovaan, Jerrain, or even Hernande could predict the situation we're in right now. I believe that, if they were here with us, they'd condone using the Tapestry to do whatever is necessary to escape from the Kormanley."

Tara pressed her lips together, but gave a terse nod. She reached down to help one of the younger students up. Jasom did the same, Mirra handing the cup of water back to the matron with a hoarse thank you.

In the corridor outside, someone shouted. Footsteps charged toward the door, which Cory had barricaded with whatever stools and benches had been in the room. Someone hammered on it from the outside, the thuds sounding hollow. They tried the handle, but Cory had unleashed a tight knot inside the lock, destroying it. A curse, then more shouting and the sound of retreating feet.

"Looks like you've lost your opportunity," the matron said. She motioned the rest of her own charges to her, backing up against the wall to one side. Her tone was gloating, but it held a tremor of uncertainty.

Outside, what sounded like the tread of a dozen guardsmen ground to a halt in front of the cell. They began beating on the door again. Someone had brought an ax.

Cory shifted to the center of the room, gathering the rest of the undergraduates around him.

"What are you going to do?" the matron asked. "You can't escape now. They're waiting for you!"

"I never intended to leave through the door."

He held his hand out toward the wall opposite the door and released a knot in the rock itself.

The explosion sent shards of stone skittering through the room, the matron and her charges shrieking, some of the students yelping. But most of the debris was flung away into the room on the other side of the wall. Outside their door, the thudding of the ax paused, then resumed with greater vigor as part of the group broke away, their footfalls fading into the distance. Without waiting for the dust to settle, Cory stepped into the next room, glancing around briefly as the other students followed. Mirra stayed close to his side.

"I think they're circling around," she said.

"I know." He picked his way through the chunks of stone to the only door, ready to blow it off its frame, but it was unlocked. He flung it open and stepped into the corridor beyond, poised to wield the Tapestry if necessary, but the hall was empty.

He motioned everyone out of the room and pointed down the hall. "Head that way, turn right at the end of the corridor."

"What about you?" Mirra asked.

"I'll be right behind you."

She looked uncertain, but Tara grabbed her hand and they both trotted down the hall, the rest trailing behind. Cory urged them on, the sounds of the approaching guards already echoing down the hall. Tara and Mirra paused near the end of the corridor at a door and he swore under his breath, waving them onward, but Tara shook her head and pointed.

"What is it?" he asked when he reached them, but he could already hear someone pounding on the door.

"Cory, is that you?" a muffled voice asked. It was cracked and raw, but Cory instantly recognized Sovaan's grating tone. His heart leaped in his chest. "Let us out!"

"Us?" he shouted, pushing Tara and Mirra out of the way. With a gesture, he ordered them to continue down the hall. "Is Jerrain in there with you?"

"Yes, yes, he's here as well. Stop stalling."

Cory tried the door, but it was locked. He stepped back and released a small knot in the stone to one side. Stone cracked with a dull popping noise and the door swung open, revealing Sovaan, clutching his side.

"You could have warned me," the administrator snapped.

"I thought you were both dead. Where's Jerrain?"

"Here, here. He's not well."

Cory sucked in a shocked breath when he saw the elderly mentor. He'd been frail before, spindly, but now he appeared emaciated. He shot a glance toward Sovaan and noticed that the administrator looked gaunt as well. Sovaan was leaning heavily against the wall, using it for support as he shifted closer to Jerrain's cot.

"He didn't react well to the recent doses of the gas," Sovaan explained. "They've barely fed either of us. I'm not certain why they roused us completely out of our stupor now."

"I'd guess because the ley wall has fallen and the Gorrani or Devin and his men have arrived and are attacking the wall. That's the only reason they kept us alive to begin with."

Sovaan coughed, the sound ragged. "That makes sense." He motioned toward Jerrain. "I haven't been able to wake him since this morning."

Cory stood, Tara suddenly appearing in the door.

"They're coming!"

"Tara, help Sovaan." He reached out and picked Jerrain's body up carefully into his arms. He hefted him off the cot, shocked by how light he felt. He spun and found the room empty, Tara and Sovaan gone, then hustled to the door, Jerrain slack in his arms but still breathing.

As soon as he stepped out into the hallway, someone shouted, "There they are!"

Without thought, anger surging through his body, he released a large knot in the center of the floor halfway down the hall. The explosion shook the entire corridor, gouts of stone rocketing up from below, tearing into the ceiling. The side walls cracked and rock began to cascade down into the corridor. A slew of Kormanley guards—at least ten that Cory could see—shouted and cursed as they fell back. Those in the front screamed as they were caught in the rock fall.

Dust billowed toward them, and Cory turned away from it to find Tara staring at him from the corner, Sovaan beside her. The administrator's mouth was pressed into a thin line, but not in disapproval. His gaze was locked on the collapsing stone.

Then it shifted toward Cory. He gave a slight nod and asked, "Where should we go from here?"

It took a moment for Cory to realize Sovaan was ceding control to him, but then he shifted Jerrain into a slightly less awkward position and said, "To the outer walls."

Twenty-Two

"WHAT IS IT?" Grant asked.

Kara stepped forward into the storage room and ran her hands over the supple material. It had been discarded in a heap atop a crate with straw jutting out of the sides, what looked like spars thrown on top. As the material shifted beneath her hand, it shimmered.

"It's a sail," she said, her mind already racing.

"A sail for what?" Allan demanded from her right shoulder.

"One of the ley barges." Kara faced Cason, the Tunneler leader standing in the doorway to the room, arms crossed. "Where's the barge?"

"Outside. It's mostly intact."

"Mostly?"

"There's a hole in one side of the hull. My guess is that it crashed before the Shattering and the lord or lady who owned it didn't want it anymore. They wouldn't want to appear to have damaged goods. So they donated it to the University. But a hole shouldn't affect its flight."

Grant rumbled. "How will this help us?"

"If we can get it rigged up, if I can channel the ley appropriately"— Kara drew in a steadying breath—"then we can fly over the Gorrani outside, straight to the Nexus."

Both Grant and Allan shifted uncomfortably, sharing a look. Allan leaned in to whisper, "Don't forget how the ley reacts to my presence. I've been on a ley barge before. It nearly fell out of the sky because of me."

"We'll work something out."

Cason coughed to catch their attention. "Will this work? Will it get you to the Nexus?"

Kara hesitated. "Let me see the barge."

They followed Cason, Sorelle, and Jaimes out of the storage area through a slew of corridors and hallways, emerging into blinding sunlight punctuated by the fierce white geyser of ley to the east. Kara shaded her eyes and blinked as they rounded the University building and halted next to what had once been a training yard. Everything on the University grounds had changed so much since the Shattering that she barely recognized it from her time here working with Hernande and Cory with the sands.

The barge took up most of one side of the yard, the beams along one side stove in. There was little damage elsewhere. It appeared as if someone had simply run the barge into the corner of a building, like a water barge hitting a submerged rock. Splintered wood jutted both inside the hull and out, a few chunks dangling at odd angles.

"I don't remember this barge being here after the Shattering," Allan said as they approached.

"It couldn't have been. It would have been annihilated when the ley from the explosion passed over the University."

Sorelle answered, her voice tense and angry. "It wasn't in the yard. We found it inside one of the other storage rooms and moved it out here to make room for our wounded. It took nearly twenty of us to get it out."

Cason cut her off with a gesture. "Can you use it?" she repeated.

"If I can figure out how the sails were rigged to the hull."

"Sorelle and Jaimes will help you figure that out. She lived near the docks before the Shattering and knows a little about ships." Sorelle began to protest, but Cason overrode her, raising her voice as she continued. "Are you satisfied? Is this enough to seal the trade?"

Kara looked to Allan, who shrugged, and Grant, whose lips twitched into an anxious half snarl.

She scanned the barge once again. "It's enough."

Cason instantly motioned to some of her people watching from a cautious distance. "Get a crew together and bring all of the spars and sails out from the storage room." The group raced off, half of them splitting away toward the main hall, the others heading toward storage.

Cason faced Kara again. "Now, tell us how to get out of the University through the tunnels without running into the Gorrani."

"Allan will show you."

The ex-Dog stepped forward. "Not until you help us bring the Wolves up from below."

"Deal. Sorelle and Jaimes, stay here and help her set up the barge. As soon as you're done, find us in the tunnels down below. Allan, come with me."

Allan turned back to Kara, almost said something, then shifted toward Grant instead. "Don't let her leave without me."

"I can't," Kara said. "You're the only one who can get me close to the Nexus."

"I don't trust you not to try on your own."

He left before Kara could protest, trailing after Cason. A group carrying spars and rope appeared from the direction of the storage room. Three others held folds of the sail up overhead, grunting under its weight, their sinuous form like a snake. The ley fabric sparkled in the sunlight.

Sorelle planted herself in front of Kara, blocking her view; Grant emitted a low growl of warning. "You'd better have a way to get us out of here."

"I don't lie, and I don't trade in people's lives."

Sorelle flinched, her face going slack, revealing the scared young girl beneath the tough façade. Then the scowl returned. "I'll be watching. Don't try anything."

The first of the spars arrived and she, Sorelle, and Jaimes began attempting to sort them out, Jaimes climbing up on the deck of the barge to scout out the layout of the rigging there. One of the young boys hauling the sail had worked on a river ship and joined him. Between them and Sorelle, they managed to lay out the rigging on the ground, others spreading out the sail so they could align the grommets at the edge of the cloth with the attachments on the spars and the hull.

"That's it!" Jaimes shouted from up above, pointing with one hand as he spoke. "The rope must run from there, through those holes in the sail there, then back through these hooks on the spar, back and forth, until it reaches the end. This section here attaches to the short mast in the middle, and that larger spar works the same as the smaller one, but at the back end of the barge. The sail lays flat."

"But what about this piece?" someone yelled from the ground. "And what's this hook for?"

Jaimes looked toward his helper, who shrugged. "You've got me. I've only ever worked with vertical sails."

Sorelle snatched the piece from the boy on the ground and inspected it. "This is used to keep the ropes from tangling when you're up in the air. And that hook is to help guide the barge into its berth at one of the towers."

"I don't think we're going to need that," Kara said.

"Right." Sorelle turned away from her. "We need to start handing up the spars and sail. Are you ready?"

"Yes, Captain."

Jaimes grinned at Sorelle's "I'm not the captain!" reply, then vanished over the deck railing. A bunch of those on the ground began handing up the spars. The rope had already been taken up to the deck.

Someone ran up to Sorelle from the direction of the main hall. "Sorelle! They're starting to bring up the Wolves."

"Grant, you'd better go keep the Wolves under control." When he hesitated, Kara motioned him away with one hand. "I'll be fine. Now go, before someone gets eaten."

Grant gave a grin that was a little too full of teeth, then trotted away.

The next few hours were full of grunting, sweat, and curses as Sorelle, Jaimes, Kara, and the rest of Cason's crew hauled the spars and sails up onto the top of the barge and rigged them to the stump of the mast and the mechanisms at the prow and stern. The edges of the mainsail were tied to the sides of the craft as well. It was a smaller vessel than the ones Kara had witnessed for the first time rising above Seeley's Park, moments before the explosion that had killed her parents. Those ships had been built by the Baron for show, to stun the crowds gathered in the park. After that, the lords and ladies and merchants—anyone with enough influence and money—had built their own craft, with the permission of the Baron and the Primes. This craft could carry maybe twenty people. That, coupled with the fact that all the work had to be done beneath the smothering folds of the sail itself, caused more than a few short-tempered arguments and at least one brawl. Thankfully, these kinds of barges had flat bottoms, so the deck was level and not canted to one side.

It was dark before Jaimes and Sorelle agreed that the setup was as good as it was going to get. They stood next to Kara, staring up at the ship in the light thrown by the ley geyser, the folds of the sail draped over its sides, rope hanging down, slack. Grant stood behind them, a Wolf at his heel. The other two Wolves were roaming about the yard.

"Are you going to be able to make it fly?" Sorelle asked.

"What do you mean?" Jaimes asked, wide-eyed.

"Before the Shattering, there was a whole system of towers built to make these things fly," Sorelle explained. "All those towers are gone."

Jaimes shot a look at Kara. "Don't tell me we spent most of the day rigging this up when you can't make it fly."

"I can make it fly," Kara said, with more conviction than she felt. "The towers were built to create enough ley energy to keep the ships in the air without individual Wielders or Primes watching over them." She gestured toward the tower of ley light beyond the walls. "I'd say we have plenty of ley energy unleashed at the moment."

"Besides," someone said from behind them, "that's not our concern."

Kara faced Cason, approaching with a small escort of her own people. "Where's Allan?"

"Down below, in the tunnels. That's a neat trick of his, blocking the ley."

"What do you mean?" Sorelle asked suspiciously.

"You'll see soon enough. I have the rest of our group packing up as many of our supplies as we can manage to carry. I've already sent a scouting party into the tunnels beyond the nearest blockage, searching for the easiest way out that puts us well beyond the Gorrani's territory. Allan is keeping the way open as we shift supplies into a temporary staging area on the far side. If you two are done here, I need you to go help with that."

"I want to see if this will work," Jaimes said, crossing his arms and staring at Kara in expectation.

Both Cason and Sorelle shifted toward Kara as well. Even Grant moved forward.

Kara shook her head, then reached for the ley as she focused on the ship.

She'd done this once before, before the Shattering. During one of the blackouts, she'd used the sails of a crashed barge to lift the mast off a trapped man's leg, freeing him. This shouldn't be any different, even if the towers that had been built back then had been destroyed. In fact, this should be easier; she'd been working during a blackout back at that time, when the ley was at its weakest.

The moment she touched the ley, it surged through her, fierce, chaotic, and breathtakingly strong. She hissed as she caught it and reined it in.

"What's wrong?" Cason asked, tense.

"Nothing." Kara steadied herself. "Nothing. The ley is stronger than I expected here, that's all."

"It will be worse near the Nexus," Grant said.

Kara ignored him. Drawing the ley from beneath them, she sent it surging upward, through the barge and into the sail.

The cloth rippled down one edge, the shimmering that appeared embedded in the material intensifying, glinting like stars. All of those watching gasped. Kara let the flow of ley increase steadily, tight and controlled, and the sail belled out and lifted, the far end snapping once before the ropes pulled taut. Sorelle drifted forward in awe. The sail—attached at either end to the ship by long horizontal bars—looked exactly like a hammock, except upside down.

Kara edged the strength of the ley higher. With creaks and groans, the prow lifted from the ground, then the stern. Within moments, the entire ship was hovering ten feet off the ground. But it was pitched to one side, and the bow was lower than the stern. Kara adjusted the flow of the ley, increasing it in some areas, lessening it in others, the ship rocking this way and that before leveling out.

"There," Cason said, "you've seen it. Now go help with the supplies. I don't want to be inside these walls when dawn breaks." She turned to shout at the rest of the Tunnelers who'd gathered to watch, everyone scurrying back to the main hall. Kara let the ship settle back to the ground, the wood of the hull cracking and popping ominously. Sorelle and Jaimes watched with disappointment. Then Sorelle shook herself, resuming her usual scowl, before glaring at Kara and following the others. Jaimes departed reluctantly, casting a few last glances back as he crossed the yard.

Cason held Kara's gaze. "You're an extremely dangerous woman."

Kara didn't know how to respond, so she kept silent.

Cason finally looked away, toward the ship. "I'll send Allan up as soon as all of my people are on the far side of the ley tunnels. If you are here to fix the ley, I wish you luck."

Then she spun on her heel and didn't look back.

One of the Wolves brushed up against Kara's leg and sat down on its haunches. She ruffled the fur on its head between its ears without thinking.

"Let's load our own supplies onto the barge while we wait. As soon as Allan shows up, I want to lift off. We need to be at the Nexus tomorrow."

Grant tilted his head back to the stars, the streak of the comet blazing across the constellations. It had grown, its tail now twice as long as when they'd watched it from the plains.

"Are you concerned about Morrell and Marcus? Will they be ready?"

Kara headed toward the main hall, where they'd left their satchels. "It doesn't matter. I'll do whatever I can once we reach the Nexus, whether Morrell has managed to rebuild the node in Tumbor or Marcus has regained control of the Nexus at the Needle."

Grant huffed, then whistled, the Wolves loping toward them both.

The main hall was in uproar, Cason's Tunnelers racing in all directions, carrying bags and satchels and crates, or hastily packing whatever materials remained. But the frenetic activity had taken on a hopeful note, one far different from what they'd encountered when they'd first entered the hall the day before. The expressions on the Tunnelers' faces were excited, the noises of the hasty exodus punctuated by bursts of laughter and chatter. Everyone steered clear of Kara, Grant, and the Wolves. Cason watched over it all, hands on hips, occasionally issuing an order or helping heft a particularly heavy sack or basket.

Kara had slung her satchel over one shoulder, was reaching for Allan's, when a hollow thud echoed through the building.

Around the hall, everyone halted whatever they were doing. Someone asked, "What in hells was that?"

Cason started toward the door to the hall. She hadn't made it halfway there when it burst open and some of the Tunnelers dressed as guards stumbled into the room in a panic. "It's the Gorrani!" one of them shouted. "They're attacking the main gates with a battering ram!"

Cason swore. "Couldn't they have waited one more gods-damned night?" She didn't wait for an answer, another hollow boom echoing through the chamber. "Jaimes, get everyone down to the tunnels. Get them through. Leave the damned supplies! Everyone move, move, move! Sorelle, get as many competent men together as you can and head to the wall. Stall them. Keep them from breaking through for as long as you can. I'll join you in a moment."

The entire room exploded into action, Sorelle calling out names as she raced for the door, the rest of the people dropping the heaviest bags and crates and racing toward the doorway leading to the storage room and the crack that led to the tunnels below. Cason herded people out, forcing some to abandon their supplies. Kara flung Allan's satchel over her shoulder and thrust Grant's into his chest, catching his attention.

"Come on. We're leaving."

He gave a short, rumbling bark and the Wolves streaked out ahead of them, following in Sorelle's wake, but cutting right toward the barge. Grant and Kara raced behind, Kara reaching out to snatch up the sail that had settled back down over the deck with the ley. It billowed up fast enough to lift the front of the barge from the ground, her control of the ley less finessed than before. Restraining it, the barge settled again. The Wolves leaped through the shattered hole in the side of the hull. Kara climbed the ladder leaning against the barge's side, the booms from the battering ram louder outside than in. Grant guarded the base of the ladder until she'd reached the top, then climbed up beside her. They flung their satchels to the deck, Kara moving to the side railing to where she could see the main hall and could watch for Allan. She couldn't see the gates from this vantage.

"Should we lift off?" Grant asked.

"No. We have to wait for Allan. There's no way we'll make it to the Nexus without him."

Kara began drumming her fingers against the wood of the railing. The thuds from the gates continued, although now they were joined by shouts and screams from the wall. An occasional stray arrow shot up from over the roof of the building beside them, visible against the ambient light from the ley geyser. Moments later, something caught fire, the glow of the flames washing the buildings yellow-red. A column of black smoke appeared, rising from somewhere beyond the wall.

Cason emerged from the main hall, charging toward the gates with a small group of five at her heels. The sounds of the fighting escalated for a short time, and then suddenly a large group of Tunnelers raced toward the main hall, funneling inside.

"They've abandoned the front gates," Grant said.

The booming of the battering ram increased, coming in shorter intervals, as if the Gorrani had been energized by the Tunnelers' retreat. It was joined by the pounding of drums, a strange counterpoint that thrummed in Kara's skin.

She kept her eyes locked on the doors of the main hall. "Come on, Allan, where are you?"

She flinched when the next thud was accompanied by a crack and a roar of triumph rose from the Gorrani. The next was followed by a groan of wood and the third with the splintering of the gate's massive planks.

Kara reached for more of the ley as the Gorrani drums began beating out in frenzy and their roar of triumph broke into hissing chants. She could feel them pouring through the breach, invading the University grounds. The sound of their outcry changed, no longer muted by the wall itself.

The first of the changed Gorrani appeared on the open grounds before the main hall at the same time Kara increased the flow of ley to the sails. The barge lurched upward, one of the Wolves in the hull below howling in protest as Grant and Kara both snatched at the railing to steady themselves. Kara clenched her jaw as she concentrated, attempting to even out the flows and keep the barge level. She only partially succeeded, the vessel rising canted to the port side. The Gorrani hissed, a few of them flaring flaps of skin from the sides of their necks and head as they pointed toward the barge. Some of them appeared to spit venom.

The ladder clattered down the side of the barge as it rose, then dropped to the ground. More and more Gorrani appeared, spreading out, a large group gathering beneath the barge. Archers appeared and Kara felt small thuds through the railing she gripped with whitened knuckles as arrows punched into the flat bottom. A few shot up from the side, embedding in the ley-shimmered sail. Both she and Grant ducked, Grant grabbing her shoulder and shoving her toward the center of the craft, where the shortened mast stood.

As they moved, they rose above the roof of the storage building, the wall and gates coming into view. Gorrani leaped over the discarded battering ram, the gates stove in like the hole in the barge, one torn from its hinges and leaning against the other. The ley geyser appeared over the wall, then the harsher flames of the fire. One of the buildings across the street from the University's wall was ablaze.

As soon as they rose above the gates, the entire barge shuddered.

"What was that?" Grant asked.

"I'm getting interference from the ley geyser. There are eddies of ley here, like currents in a river. They're more intense above the buildings. I wasn't expecting it, but I think I can control it." The shuddering lessened, but didn't go away. "That's the best I can do."

Grant craned his neck. "We're drifting. We're now over the second storage building."

"I know. I'm trying to keep us inside the University grounds. It's harder than I anticipated."

"It will likely only get harder as we get closer to the geyser."

"I know."

Grant paused. "The Gorrani have stopped shooting arrows at us."

"Good. We need to keep an eye out for Allan."

Grant edged back toward the railing, growling once in warning when the barge lurched hard to starboard. The Wolves below howled.

"Sorry!" She muttered something else under her breath thinking that Grant wouldn't hear, but his ear twitched and he gave her a baleful look. She waved him toward the edge. "Watch for Allan!"

Grant cautiously peered over the side. "The Gorrani are attacking the main hall. Cason must have had her people blockade the doorway as they fled. The building is surrounded."

A small hollow of emptiness carved itself out of Kara's chest but she couldn't spare the attention to let it overwhelm her. Keeping the barge more-or-less stationary in the ever-shifting currents of ley didn't allow for any distraction. She couldn't think about what it would mean if Allan were trapped underground, if he couldn't reach them, or even if he'd been killed. She'd have to risk repairing the ley from a distance in that situation. It was the only option.

She twisted her neck so she could see the far northern skies. She'd taken the barge high enough—out of bowshot—that they could see over the edge of the surrounding cliffs toward the mountains of the Steppe. The light from the ley geyser washed out most of the stars, but it couldn't obliterate the harsh pinpricks of the Three Sisters, nor hide their steady pulse. The largest had accelerated since the last time they'd seen it, before descending into the sunken city. It beat faster than her own heart. The other two weren't far behind.

Below, the strange hissing chants of the Gorrani grew into a roar, mingled with the sound of shattering glass and splintered wood.

"They've broken through the doors," Grant said, pulling back from the railing slightly. He glanced toward Kara, his thoughts clear on his face. "They're storming the main hall."

"I won't leave him," Kara said.

Grant said nothing, stoic, implacable. One of the Wolves howled again, the sound forlorn.

"We can't reach the Nexus without him!" Kara shouted, ignoring the tears that pricked the corners of her eyes.

"If he isn't already dead, he's trapped—"

Grant's words cut off as something caught his attention below. He stepped to the railing, hands gripping onto the wood so tight his knuckles turned white.

"What is it?"

"It's Allan," Grant snapped. "Take us down! He's climbing out onto the roof of the main hall."

Kara let the strength of the ley lessen, causing the ship to descend, as Grant began frantically searching the deck. But she couldn't see where she needed to go, not standing at the mast.

Biting back a curse, she inched to the port side, what remained of the University coming into view. The barge shuddered as some of her control slipped, her concentration split between plying the ley and searching for Allan. She cried out when she found him, scrambling up the steep slope of the roof toward its peak. Leaning onto the rail, risking an arrow from the Gorrani who were swarming the hall below, she shouted, "Allan!"

The ex-Dog didn't respond, struggling up the last of the slate shingles onto the peak.

"Allan!"

"Descend faster," Grant growled, giving her a start as he appeared at her side, a rope in hand. He began tying it off on the railing.

Kara focused on the ley.

The ship dropped suddenly, her stomach rising into her throat as they dipped and dove toward the hall's roof. Allan looked up at them, crouched over the roofline. Then he glanced down.

Gorrani were beginning to climb out of the upper-story window, where Kara assumed Allan had emerged. One of them was already on the roof, but he slipped on the steep pitch and plummeted to the ground below with a hissed scream. The closer they came to the roof, the louder the enraged shouts of the Gorrani inside the building and the University grounds grew, a strange combination of battle cries, chanting, and destruction. It sounded like they were tearing the interior of the main hall apart.

A few arrows slammed into the side of the barge, one shattering on impact, but Kara merely ducked back slightly. She didn't let go of the railing. Wind whipped her hair behind her as they fell toward the roof, directly toward Allan.

Then Grant shouted, "Kara!" and she let the ley surge upward again, catching the sail and lifting the prow of the barge. Grant heaved the coils of rope over the side and Kara heard them slap onto the slate. The arrows halted as they passed over the building and she leaned forward again, caught sight of Allan snatching for the rope, three Gorrani already halfway to his position.

Allan snagged a coil, looped it around one arm once, twice, then grabbed on as the rope pulled taut.

The barge lurched as he lifted from the roof, swinging wildly. Kara seized the ley and held on tight, carrying them out over the building and up as fast as possible. Fresh arrows shot toward them, the deck and rail shuddering as Allan flailed around in the open below. Grant reached over the rail and began hauling him up, grunting with effort as the muscles in his arms and back bulged.

Moments later, Allan appeared, Grant grasping at his free arm and heaving him over the side. He sprawled on the deck, gasping and heaving, before rolling onto his back. He patted himself down, still breathing hard, then reached out a hand so Grant could help him up.

"Thanks."

"Not a problem."

The entire ship suddenly listed hard to starboard, everyone snatching at the railing for support.

Through gritted teeth, Kara said, "Allan, get as far away from the sail as possible. I'm barely holding the ship up."

Allan scrambled for the hatch leading down to the hold below, the ship continuing to list as he moved. Kara wrapped an arm around the railing as the deck canted down, Grant doing the same. Allan began to slide across the deck but grabbed onto the hatch's handle. Their satchels slid to the railing, catching on the edge. The wood of the ship groaned as Allan heaved the hatch open and dove headfirst inside. They heard him drop to the shallow hull beneath and roll, followed by the scratch of claws as the Wolves moved about.

As soon as he fell below the deck, the obstruction in the ley causing the list abated. She immediately began leveling the ship out, although it continued to shudder at odd moments.

When Kara felt stable enough to release her death grip on the railing, Grant grasped her shoulder. "Are you all right?"

"I'm fine." She wiped at her face—at the residue of tears and the tightness of the skin. "He's blocking the ley, like a stone in a river. On deck, he's too close to the sails for me to maneuver the ley around him. If he's near the hull, I have enough room."

"Good." He looked over the side, the University and the Gorrani snake people dropping away behind them. "Now what?"

Kara coughed and pulled a few strands of her hair away from her face, letting the wind take them. She faced forward, toward the prow, the shattered towers of Grass and the towering ley geyser rising before them. "Now we get as close to the Nexus as we can in this ship. After that, it's up to Allan."

". . . will protect you! Korma will guide us through these troubled times! Commander Darius is at the gates, the enforcers on the walls. Iscivius protected us with the ley for as long as he could, until he collapsed in exhaustion within the Nexus. But fear not! The walls will hold! Put your faith in Korma, cast out your doubts. Recall that it was the abuse of the ley by the Baron of Erenthrall and all the surrounding Baronies and nations that brought us to this place! It was their meddling with the natural order that caused the Shattering and brought this retaliation by nature upon us all! Did we not reclaim our control from the usurpers? Did we not seize control when yet another attempt to abuse the ley failed with catastrophic results, destroying Tumbor? We do not need the ley to protect us! We do not need to use natural powers that we do not understand! We have ourselves, our enforcers, and our faith in Korma and our belief in the natural order! Our walls will hold! Commander Darius and his men will—"

Father Dalton's words faltered when he saw the main gates of the outer wall swing open.

He'd come to the jut of stone overlooking the square where he'd given his sermons as soon as he realized Iscivius wouldn't be able to hold the ley wall any longer. He'd started preaching before it fell, first to only a smattering of people from the city, but word had spread. By the time the protection of the ley collapsed, the plaza below had been filled. He didn't know how much the citizens below could hear—not with the gusts of wind carrying his voice away—but it didn't seem to matter. The populace was terrified. He could feel it coming up from the square in almost physical waves. He'd scoffed at them, at their lack of faith.

Until the gates opened. Then, as his words broke and dragged down into silence, the first niggling worms of fear began to gnaw into his gut.

The specter of his own vision—of the serpents and the dogs, of the pulsing light of the Three Sisters exploding—suddenly crawled up onto his back and sank claws into his shoulders, its weight significant. He'd used the vision to unseat Kara Tremain and the Wielders from their grip on the Needle, but he hadn't seriously considered the ramifications of what it meant. He hadn't actually *believed* in it.

Until now.

He let his arms fall to his sides, the wind blasting his face, the banners of the Kormanley snapping fitfully on either side along the mostly empty tier behind him. Four enforcers had remained with him, at the insistence of Darius, but the rest had been sent to the walls.

They wouldn't be enough. Not against the dogs or the serpents. Most certainly useless against the annihilation promised by the Three Sisters, pulsing far to the north even now.

He dropped his gaze from the gates—still surprisingly empty—and stared down at the mass of people below, jammed in between the buildings on either side. Their hands were raised toward him, their cries of fear and adoration rising from below in counterpoint to the screams and beating drums and clash of the fighting outside the walls, muted by distance but still audible, carried by the wind.

His vision flickered, and he saw the entire plaza below littered with bodies. The building off to the right was burning. Gorrani were picking their way through the slaughter.

He choked and stepped back, shot a glance back toward the main gates. Men were pouring in through the opening now. It was too distant to be certain, but he thought they were Devin's men, not the Gorrani.

Footsteps behind him. Then one of the enforcers said, "Father? Is everything all right?"

He opened his mouth to respond, but only one word came out: "How?"

An uncertain shuffling of feet from behind. "I don't understand. How what?"

Dalton spun, anger spiking up through his fear. "How are the gates open? How could Darius have failed me so miserably? How could all of you have failed me?" He seized the man by the front of his armor and dragged him closer, began shaking him. The guard's eyes widened, but he didn't resist. "I did everything the visions that Korma sent told me to do! I did everything I could to warn everyone, to guide people, to keep everyone safe! And look what has happened! *Look what has happened!*"

"But . . . didn't you predict all of this?"

Dalton halted at the profound look of confusion on the man's face, then shoved him backward. His arms dropped. He turned and faced the auroral lights flickering far out over the plains in the direction of Tumbor, then shifted so he could see the Three Sisters. Shouts and the sounds of fighting began to rise through the gusts from the direction of the city below. The clamor of those in the plaza had risen, steeped now with uncertainty brought on by his sudden silence. And perhaps they could hear the fighting inside the city as well. Perhaps they could hear the cold serpents' hiss and feel the hot breath of the dogs on the backs of their necks, as he did.

"I survived the Shattering," he said to himself. "I will survive this as well."

Something wet splashed the back of his neck. He reached up in annoyance, his fingers returning with dabs of thick blood.

He spun in time to see a man tip the body of the enforcer he'd yelled at over the edge of the stone, the guard's throat slit. The other three guards lay dead on the tier behind them.

The man who'd killed them all said, "I don't think you will."

Dalton took a step back, but his heel found the edge of the jut of stone. He swallowed.

"Who are you?" He found it difficult to focus on the man, his gaze sliding off to one side. Even his special vision was unsettled, as if somehow the man wasn't really there.

The man stepped forward, the motion casual, as if he were unconcerned they were standing on a thin outcropping of rock with a deadly drop on either side. "I'm a Hound."

Dalton saw the knife flicker on his vision seconds before the Hound actually moved. He lurched back in response, foot stepping out into empty air, and the blade merely nicked his throat, the pain icy sharp and sweet.

The Hound reacted instantly, free hand snapping out and catching hold of Dalton's shirt front before he could plummet to the square below.

Irritation flashed across the Hound's face. "You can't escape that easily."

The Hound swung again and Dalton felt a tug beneath his jawbone from side to side. Blood spurted onto the Hound, who stepped back. Dalton's hands shot up to his throat, to the gash there that felt horrendously wide, his fingers coated instantly as he tried to stem the flow, his blood shockingly warm. He staggered forward, tried to speak, but fell to his knees instead, then forward onto the stone. His lower body had gone completely numb, his upper torso cold, his arms tingling, one hanging over the side of the jut. As blood pooled beneath him, began to drip over the edge of the stone, he heard the first screams of terror from his followers below.

Except they weren't screaming for him, he realized, as his vision began to fade.

Devin's men had reached the square.

❧

Cory stood as soon as the sounds of fighting in the corridor outside faded. The rest of the members of the University watched as he shifted toward the door—now concealed behind a fold of Tapestry that created the illusion that no door existed here at all—and listened.

Sovaan rose and joined him, still using the wall for support. "Should we leave?"

"Not yet. We need to wait to make certain the fighting has shifted to another part of the temple."

He glanced over the exhausted group. They'd hunkered down in this room as soon as Cory realized they wouldn't make it to the wall, not with Sovaan and Jerrain barely able to walk. When they'd run across this storage room containing food, and with no one currently trailing them, he'd forced them all inside to rest and created the illusion to hide the door. It wouldn't hold forever—someone was bound to come looking for the food in here eventually—but as far as he could tell, everyone was preoccupied with whatever was happening outside the temple. Everyone they'd run into had been scrambling toward the front of the temple, guards and servants alike, or barricading themselves behind their own doors.

Everyone had eaten, even Jerrain, who'd roused long enough to get food and drink before fading away again. Even that small period of consciousness had been encouraging.

While they'd remained hidden, the fighting had escalated and surrounded them, like a wave. At one point, the clash of swords and the screams of the dying had echoed through the hidden door in the hall just outside. It had lasted for an eternity, a pool of blood seeping beneath the door and into the room. Then the fighting shifted down the hall, farther away but still close. Someone had lain outside, moaning, until even that choked off into silence.

They'd huddled in the darkness without speaking, Tara with a hand clamped over Mirra's mouth to keep her quiet as she sobbed.

But now Cory couldn't hear anything, not even distant fighting.

They waited until Cory couldn't stand it anymore.

He tugged on Sovaan's sleeve to catch the administrator's attention. "I'm going outside to see if it's safe."

"I think I've regained enough strength I can conceal the door again after you've left. The others are looking better as well." He dropped his voice. "If you think we can reach the walls, I'd advise doing so now, while we still have a chance."

Cory dropped the illusion on the door and pulled it open. Torchlight spilled into the room, everyone blinking and holding up hands to block the sudden brightness. Bodies littered the floor outside, enforcers, servants, and others dressed in dirtier clothes with makeshift armor that reminded Cory forcibly of the bandits that had attacked the Hollow under Baron Aurek.

He pointed a few of them out to Sovaan. "I'd guess Devin has attacked the Needle with his men from Erenthrall. Somehow they breached the walls." He glanced back toward the others. "Scavenge whatever weapons you can from them, just in case."

He stepped through the bodies, finding it difficult to get decent footing. He pulled in breaths shallowly through his nose, the stench of blood and vomit and innards worse than a slaughterhouse. At the end of the hall, he turned back to see Sovaan and Tara pulling knives from those that still had them. Then he stepped around the corner.

The temple was quiet. Doors had been splintered open, the occupants killed inside or dragged out into the hall and slaughtered. Some of those hiding had fought back, one of Devin's men occasionally mixed in with the bodies, but most were servants from the temple and enforcers.

He found the kitchens, the fires in the ovens still roaring, although the cooks had either run or lay dead. Using a basket, he loaded up whatever he could find that didn't look ruined by the bloodshed, then stepped back into the hall.

Distantly, he could hear fighting again.

He stood rooted to the spot, his entire body vibrating as he listened. But the fighting didn't get closer.

Relaxing, he turned back in the direction of the hidden room just as two men rounded the corner at the far end of the corridor.

Everyone stilled. They had swords drawn, were streaked with blood. Four more guards dressed the same appeared behind them, and Cory could swear there were others out of sight.

He reached for the Tapestry.

"Cory?"

Hesitating, he squinted. "Lienta?"

The swords lowered, and the men began moving closer at a trot. As they drew near, Cory could see the Temerite uniforms through the blood. He shuddered in relief, nearly sagged against the wall.

"What are you doing here?" he asked.

"We came across the chasm with Marcus and some others so they could seize control of the Nexus here, but we got separated before the real fighting began. Since then, we've been combing the temple corridors trying to find a way out or find Marcus and the others."

"Why is he trying to get to the Nexus?"

"So he can help Kara repair the ley network."

"Kara's alive?" The words came out without any strength. He hadn't allowed himself to think about anyone else since they'd been captured. He hadn't had time, didn't need the emotional turmoil it would cause. Not that he'd been aware or lucid during most of his imprisonment.

"We assume," Lienta said. "She, Allan, Grant, and a few of the Wolves went to Erenthrall."

"Erenthrall!"

Lienta shot a glance down the hall, then grabbed Cory by the upper arm. "Quiet. It's a long story, one I can't relate right now. Are you alone?"

"No, the rest of those of us from the University they captured are hiding in a room not far away."

Lienta's eyebrows rose in surprise. "They didn't find you? Devin's men ransacked this section fairly well."

"We hid the doorway. They didn't know it was there."

Lienta looked as if he wanted to ask more questions, but he simply said, "Take us there."

Cory led Lienta and his men—twenty-three in all—back through the corridors until he reached the hall where they'd hidden. The illusion was back up, the wall where the doorway stood appearing to be solid stone. He recognized the bodies immediately in front of the door, then groped through the illusion until he'd found it and knocked lightly. "Sovaan, it's Cory."

The illusion wavered and dropped, some of Lienta's men shifting and mumbling behind him, then the door opened cautiously, Sovaan peering out.

As soon as he recognized Cory, then Lienta and the others, he ushered them inside. Cory reset the illusion outside. The room was crowded, but no one complained. One of the watchmen had brought in a torch. Cory handed out the food he'd found, then turned to Lienta.

"How did you plan to get out of here?" he asked.

"We were hoping to get back to the chasm. Hernande created a bridge, so we can cross, but I don't know if it's still there. We'd intended to stay with Marcus and the others, but he's sealed himself and the

Wielders inside the Nexus using the ley. He's completely flooded the lower levels of the Needle. No one can get through." He glanced over the University students and mentors. "How were you planning on getting out?"

"Through the outer wall."

Lienta stared at him mutely, then said, "Right. Outer wall, it is." He surveyed the students and mentors, their emaciated, bedraggled appearance. "We have enough watchmen to guard us until we reach the wall. Then it's up to you."

"I'll be ready."

Lienta issued orders, some of the watchmen supporting Sovaan and the others, a few simply lifting the weaker students up into their arms or carrying them over a shoulder. One of them cradled Jerrain in his arms. Only Jasom and Tara were strong enough to move without help.

They left the room, skulking through the empty halls of the temple toward the eastern entrance. Bodies continued to riddle the corridor, sometimes four or five fallen together in a group, other times a single body lying sprawled in an otherwise empty hallway. The sounds of the fighting escalated and receded, Lienta angling away whenever possible. Once, they hid in side rooms as a contingent of Kormanley enforcers raced past a cross-corridor.

They reached the eastern entrance, the door smashed in, bodies lying stacked on either side, the walls splashed with blood. The fighting here had been intense, but no one remained behind. As they picked their way down the last of the hall, the sounds of fighting grew louder in the outer city.

Crouching down in the doorway, Lienta and another watchman in front of him, Cory was shocked to discover it was nighttime. Parts of the city were ablaze, the red-orange glow of fires on all sides, outlining black columns of smoke. The stars overhead were completely blotted out, the air even within the entrance thick with flakes of ash. Cory coughed and pulled his shirt up to filter some of it out.

"The fighting appears to have shifted southward," Lienta said. "When we tried this entrance earlier, the Kormanley were still holding it against Devin's men. But I think we can make it to the nearest buildings without being seen."

He singled out five watchmen, who escorted Cory, Sovaan, and Mirra across the open area toward a darkened alley on the far side.

They ran hunched over, careful not to trip on the bodies on the ground. The shouts and screams from the surrounding city were louder outside, closer, and Mirra burrowed herself deeper against Cory's side as they ran. Cory's heart raced until they reached the protection of the walls, the open night sky overhead making him feel exposed and vulnerable.

Sovaan, Jasom, and two other students came next, with ten watchmen.

As soon as the remaining group headed across, Lienta and Tara in the lead, a mob of armored men appeared from around the southern corner of the temple. They immediately shouted, those at the front pointing toward Lienta and the rest with their swords, then charged as a group.

Lienta and the rest of the watchmen with him hesitated, as if considering making a stand, but Cory stepped out of the alley and yelled, "Run!" At the same time, he reached out on the Tapestry and released a barrage of knots beneath the paving stones between the mob and Lienta's group. Rock exploded upward, the echoes of the explosions rolling between the buildings on all sides. Those at the front of the mob faltered, then were overrun by those behind. Jasom stepped up to Cory's side and together they unleashed another string of explosions, the mob—some of Devin's group, Cory was certain—falling back.

Another large group appeared to the north. "Gorrani," Jasom muttered.

Lienta, Tara, and the rest reached the alley, Lienta motioning with one hand and shouting, "Go, go, go!"

They took off down the alley, heading deeper into the buildings. Cory turned halfway down and released two knots inside the buildings on either side, the walls exploding outward and down, choking the opening with stone debris. From the far side, he heard the two groups—Devin's men and the Gorrani; dogs and snakes—roar challenges at each other, followed by the clang of metal as swords met armor.

Then they ran, not stopping at corners or intersections, racing toward the outer wall. People retreated out of their way, slamming doors or cowering in corners, most clutching meager belongings or attempting to protect children or loved ones. A few carried weapons. No one group had more than ten people. Only once did Lienta backtrack, when the street was blocked by the collapse of a still-burning building.

They emerged from the outer city into the tent city before the southeastern gates. More people were huddled beneath the canvas here, entire families grasping hold of each other in fear, or frantically gathering up whatever they could carry. This area looked untouched by Devin's men or the Gorrani. But a group of looters were beating three others mercilessly for their satchels. Lienta and his watchmen slammed into them, knocking them all down, a few of them not rising after they passed.

Behind them, the sounds of fighting rose again, getting closer. The tent city wouldn't remain a refuge for long.

They burst from the haphazard array of tents at the outer wall, slowing, nearly everyone out of breath.

But instead of the gates Cory expected to see, the section had been hastily walled up with stone.

He didn't see any enforcers on the walls above.

"What happened to the gates?" Cory gasped. His lungs burned with exertion. He coughed and bent forward.

"Marcus destroyed them with the ley when we escaped after Tumbor collapsed. Dalton walled the breach up rather than replace the gates. Is it going to be a problem?"

Cory straightened, drawing in a steadying breath as he reached out with one hand. "It won't be a problem at all."

The entire gate tower disintegrated, rubble flying upward over a hundred feet into the air, illuminated by the fires of the city and the ley globes still burning along the wall. Cory's ears rang from the deafening explosion, its echoes muted. He watched the stone and debris cascade down before them with immense satisfaction and an almost overpowering weariness. Those with him flinched or ducked or cursed, all except Lienta and Sovaan.

They waited as the plume of dust he'd created was blown aside by the winds, expecting whatever remained of the armies outside to come pouring in. But there was no one waiting.

"They must have all converged on the main gates when they were breached," Lienta said.

Behind, fresh screams broke through the background fighting.

"They've reached the tent city." Lienta started forward. "Everyone, through the breach! We'll repeat what we did before—head directly out onto the plains, then circle around to the western side of the city. The Matriarch will let us in."

He herded everyone forward, up onto the mound of rock that had once been the walled-up gates, through the fifty-foot gaping hole in the outer wall's defenses. Cory paused once to glance back at the temple, the tent city already half overrun by Gorrani, the outer city burning in pockets, the Needle piercing the night sky above, limned in ley light.

Then he turned his back on it all and stepped out into the darkness of the plains.

Twenty-Three

"WE AREN'T GOING TO MAKE IT all the way to the Nexus in this barge," Grant said.

He gripped the railing before him with white-knuckled hands as the entire barge creaked and groaned and shook around them, as if buffeted by a strong gale. It was being hit with strong gusts, but it wasn't wind. The sail thrashed beneath the lashing currents of the ley, Kara concentrating hard to keep it under control. The Wolves in the compartment below with Allan were howling in protest, the voices nearly drowned out by the roar of the actual wind at this height and the thunderous ley geyser ahead.

But it wasn't the ley currents that threatened to tear the ship apart that would keep them from the Nexus. It would be the ley itself, when it reached a concentration high enough to consume the organic material of the barge.

"I'll get us as close as I can," Kara said. They were already over the districts surrounding Grass—Eld first, where Kara had seen Halliel's Park and the neighborhood where she'd grown up, and now Green. The streets were flooded with ley, the surviving buildings islands in rivers of white. The ley geyser spouted out of the shattered dome of the Nexus before them, surrounded by the sheared-off towers that had defined Grass. The jagged shards of the Amber Tower rose above the rest off to starboard, its tan-orange hue glowing with reflected ley light against the vivid blue sky of late dawn.

Grant leaned over the side, gazing at the streets below, then pushed back. "We're passing out of Green into Grass."

"You'd better warn Allan. When we get closer, we'll need to descend into the hull so that we're near Allan. In fact, if there's any spare rope around, we should lash ourselves together, along with our satchels. We aren't going to come down easy."

Grant stared at her. "Right."

He released his death grip on the railing and lurched his way to the hatch that led below deck. The barge dropped suddenly as he reached it, and Kara's stomach rolled queasily. He clutched at the hatch's side until she'd righted it, then descended, the Wolves' howls rising plaintively in the background.

Kara focused on the sail, eyes straight ahead at the massive plume of ley rising far above them. It grew as they drew nearer, until she had to crane her neck to see its top. The shuddering of the barge increased, and she began to lower it closer to the ground until they were hovering a bare ten feet above the river of ley beneath them on a direct course for the Nexus. Buildings ruined by the Shattering rose on both sides, windows gaping down at them, walls cracked or collapsed in sections. Once the height of luxury and power, the balconies and intricate stonework now looked desolate and worn.

The barge dipped again, Kara gritting her teeth to bring it back level. They were still too far from the Nexus. She didn't want to have to walk far once they went down to street level. She didn't know how long Allan could hold up against the force of this much ley. She didn't know if it would hold up at all. She'd never seen the ley so riled up, so violent, so beautiful.

She waited until the base of the ley filled her entire vision, to where spume from it rained down around her in globules and splatters, threatening to hit the ship. The buildings fell away, a ring of what had once been parks appearing on either side. She lifted the ship up over a ridge of debris from the broken towers and then began to bring it back down in a gentle glide.

At the last moment, before the hull hit the lake of ley that surrounded the inner towers, she turned her back on the geyser and sprinted for the hatchway. She stumbled on the steps as she shouted, "Get ready! We're coming down now!"

She found Allan and Grant at the base of the stairs, tethered together with rope. Grant threw her one end and whistled for the Wolves. They bounded close, their fear over the shuddering barge overriding their tendency to keep their distance. Kara tied the rope as quickly as she could, already sensing the ley brushing up against the bottom of the barge, then screamed, "Brace yourself!" as she grabbed hold of Allan and Grant. They hunched down into a crouch, Kara's face pressed into Allan's armpit, her eyes squeezed tight, the Wolves burrowing their noses between their chests. Grant howled, his chest vibrating with the haunting sound.

Then Kara let go of the ley.

The ship bucked and plummeted. She tensed for the sound of splintering wood as they crashed, but that never came. The ley was too intense, soundlessly annihilating the barge around them as it sank. Instead, they slammed into the stone paving of the park and rolled, Kara screaming as her exposed arm scraped across gravel and rock. But she didn't let go, Allan and Grant clutching her even tighter. One of the Wolves was wrenched away, its claws raking her thigh. It gave a sharp bark, cut off oddly as if severed with a blade.

They ground to a halt, Allan jerking out of her tenuous hold as the back of her head hit the ground. She moaned and brought her free arm up to her forehead, her other arm trapped beneath Grant. Opening her eyes, she found herself staring up into a solid wall of ley.

She jolted upright, then shrank back. They were surrounded by ley, a half sphere centered on Allan with a radius of barely twelve feet. Her free arm had landed a few feet from its edge, which moved as Allan began to rouse on the other side of Grant.

"Careful," she said in warning, her voice sounding odd in the confined space. "You're the only thing standing between us and the ley."

Allan stilled, taking in the small area of ground around him, littered with the metallic elements of the barge—nails, pulleys, joints. Grant sat up, still holding one of the Wolves under one arm. It struggled until he gave a short bark and growl, then he released it. The second Wolf scrambled to its feet and shook itself, padding forward to sniff at the ley.

"Where's the third Wolf?" Kara asked.

"I tried to hold onto him," Allan said, "but when we hit the ground . . ."

"He must have fallen free and gotten caught in the ley," Grant said. A simple statement, but it throbbed with grief. He huffed and stood, brushed himself off, rearranged the satchels slung over his shoulder, then glanced up. "How do we find our way to the Nexus? I can't see anything but ley."

"It's that way." Kara pointed. "I can sense it."

Allan stepped closer to her. "Lead the way."

She felt a tug on the rope tied around her waist.

"We should shorten the rope," Grant said, already retying his section.

Kara did the same without comment.

They walked forward tentatively, Kara in front, Allan in the center, Grant behind, the two Wolves to either side. Within a few steps, boulders emerged from the wall of ley, sections of what had once been one of the towers, the veins of a leaf patterning one side. Kara wondered if it had been part of the Flyers' Tower. They picked their way over it, then across the field of stone debris on the far side. The sphere shifted with Allan, smooth and silent. The ley ebbed and flowed around them, Kara tracing its currents as they moved forward. They'd been halted more than once by its swiftness while traveling the tunnels beneath Erenthrall, its strength too great for Allan to remain standing, but here the currents were weaker because the ley was spread out over such a wide area. But they'd have to be careful. They were approaching the source; she expected its strength would increase.

They reached a set of wide steps and ascended to the base of the tower, passing by the gaping mouth where there had once been a grand wooden door. The courtyard on the far side was littered with the desiccated remains of ley carts. The garden was a desolate series of stone paths wending around bare, sculpted beds, a few wrought-iron benches appearing out of place among all the stonework.

A wall forced them to sidetrack to an exit gate, then they crossed another street to another garden, a second tower, a courtyard with an empty fountain and a statue of a woman holding a child on her hip. Another wide street, and then they came up against the wall that surrounded the Nexus.

When they found the gate that opened onto one of the sets of stairs leading down into the circular depression where the crystal-domed building stood, Kara and Allan shared a look. The last time they'd been here, Hagger and his own Wolves had trapped them on the steps as they'd attempted to flee the quickening of the distortion. The Wolves would have killed them all if the distortion hadn't sealed them in a shard of reality where time had halted. Allan had gotten them out, using the same strange ability that kept the ley from them now.

They descended with Grant and his Wolves at their side. Over half-way down, they ran across a sword, Allan picking it up. "It's the one I drove through Hagger's chest." He tossed it to one side, next to a belt buckle and assorted metal buttons and a ring.

As they approached the building that housed the Nexus, Kara said, "Allan, the currents of the ley are stronger here."

"I can feel it. The sphere has shrunk as well."

Kara shot a glance toward its edge. He was right. It now had only a ten-foot radius. Her skin prickled as a wave of claustrophobia passed through her. "We need to be careful when we enter the building. The corridors may make it too strong to pass, like in the tunnels underground."

"I'll warn you if it gets that strong."

The doorway appeared, Kara hesitating at the entrance. But Allan said nothing, so she stepped inside, the sphere becoming even smaller. She could sense the ley geyser ahead as she followed the corridor, passing rooms and intersections, the flow of the ley shifting around them as the currents changed. Only toward the end, before they reached the central chamber, did Allan warn them to move quickly, to get past a particularly powerful corridor where the ley was swift. In that section, Grant and Kara were forced to hunch down, their tight bubble of protection shrinking further.

But as soon as they stepped out into the center of the Nexus, the strength lessened and they were able to stand upright. They could see nothing of the vastness of the interior dome, the ley blocking the view, but inside the sphere the floor was covered with shards of the shattered crystal dome, some of the blocks as large as Kara herself. The eddies here swirled around the geyser at the center, where ley shot out of the pit with tremendous force, enough to propel it hundreds of feet into the air. The floor trembled with its force, a subdued shudder Kara felt in her teeth. Trapped inside the dome, the roar was ten times louder than what they'd heard from outside, a hundred times louder than at the University.

"We need to get as close to the pit in the center as possible!" Kara shouted over the cacophony.

"I think I can hold the ley at bay! It's stronger than outside, but not as strong as some of the tunnels or corridors we've been in! Just don't fall in!"

Cautiously, they edged forward, making their way through the fallen crystals, climbing over them when necessary. The velocity of the current increased, rotating like a tornado, trying to drag them up into the geyser, but Kara kept pushing forward.

She pulled up short when the lip of the pit appeared, Allan bumping into her from behind. The force from the geyser was so strong it formed an indentation into the side of Allan's sphere.

"We're here," she said.

Allan leaned forward. "Now what?"

Kara shifted to one of the shards, sat down, and centered herself. She stared at what they could see of the geyser, not certain she could even delve into its depths, it was so strong. She might simply be carried away or burned out by it, as had happened to some of the Wielders caught unawares in the nodes before the Shattering. She'd manipulated the ley when it was this violent before, when repairing the distortion over Erenthrall, but she'd had the help of the Wielders at the Needle then.

"Now we find out if Marcus and Morrell have managed to fulfill their parts of the plan, because if they haven't, we've fought our way to the Nexus for nothing."

Kara braced herself and plunged her mind into the ley, then gasped as it seized her and attempted to spin her up into the geyser, away from the source of the ley that she'd sensed when her powers as a Wielder were first beginning to manifest, when Ischua had tested her in Halliel's Park so long ago. She fought back the memories of Ischua, of her father, who'd taken her there, as she dragged herself down into the pit. She had to keep to the side, the current farther in too strong. Even then, the deeper she moved into the channel she'd used to pierce the distortion over Erenthrall and heal it from the inside out, the harder it became. It would be impossible for her to get all the way to the source itself, not without help from Marcus and the secondary Nexus, but she didn't need to go that deep. Not yet. All she needed to do was get to the ley line that led to the Needle.

Crawling down the side of the pit, she bypassed the chamber where the Primes had once manipulated the crystals that had augmented the power of the ley before shunting it out into the city of Erenthrall. Beneath that, multiple tunnels branched off on all sides, the larger ones leading toward larger hubs like the Needle or even the Baronial nodes like the ones beneath each of the Three Sisters in the Northern Reaches, the smaller ones angling toward the district nodes here in

Erenthrall. She paused at each one long enough to verify it didn't connect to the Needle, then moved on.

When she found it, she gathered herself—not knowing how long it would take for Marcus to sense her, to react, if he was even there—and said, "I'm preparing to reach out to the Needle."

Movement, a Wolf's breath snuffling against her face, and a sharp command from Grant. Allan said, "We've got your back here."

She threw herself into the ley conduit to the Needle, letting the current take her. If Marcus and the other Wielders weren't there to support her, she didn't think she'd be able to return to her own body.

But, of course, if they weren't there, it wouldn't matter. The Three Sisters would quicken and destroy them all.

⌐

In the heart of the Needle, Marcus paced back and forth before the Nexus. The Wielders had cycled through holding the crystals in position and keeping the stream of ley that protected them from the attack on the Needle active in shifts, those coming off a shift collapsing into rough, fitful sleep, those going on clenching their jaws in grim determination. Even those who had sided with Iscivius and Irmona had fallen into line without protest. They could all hear the screaming and fighting in the city outside the tower. It came in waves, getting louder and closer, everyone inside the pit tensing in anticipation, then fading again, all through the night. They had no way to determine what time it was, since their only exit had to be kept submerged in ley, but he knew outside it must be at least midday. He was exhausted and hungry, but he couldn't sleep, not when he didn't know when Kara would show up. It had taken a combined argument from Artras, Dylan, and Jenner to convince him that he couldn't maintain constant vigil inside the ley, that he'd burn himself out. And even then, he'd only allowed them to spell him for a few hours at most.

Outside, the raucous fighting surged louder again, sharp and sudden. From their own vigil over Hernande, Artras, Cutter, and Marc lifted their heads.

"It sounds as if they're right outside the Needle," Artras said. "Perhaps even in the stellae garden. How can they even be fighting still? They've been at it all night."

Cutter rose, tested his bow, and shifted closer to the base of the stairs. "It's a large city, with many places to hide. If both Devin's men and the Gorrani have made it through the walls, it may take days before one side has rooted out all of its enemies."

"It's a bloodbath up there," Marc added.

No one responded, the pit settling back into the despondent, fretful silence that had persisted through most of the night.

Marcus halted his pacing, stepped toward Artras and Hernande. "Any change?"

"He's still unconscious, barely breathing. His heartbeat is exceptionally low. I don't know—"

She cut off as Marcus spun toward the Nexus. He heard her stand.

"What is it?" she asked.

"It's Kara. She's here."

The tension in the room ratcheted up as Marcus stepped forward to the pit. Everyone trapped here with them grew suddenly alert. Artras and Dylan shifted forward to his side. The Wielders holding the crystals grew alert. Those not on duty shook those slumbering awake. Everyone edged toward the pit.

Dylan cleared his throat, his voice still coming out ragged. "What do we do?"

Marcus stretched his hands out, reaching for the Nexus with his mind. "We send Kara our support. Get ready to reverse the direction of flow of the ley line from Erenthrall. We'll feed all other lines coming into the Needle into that. Everyone not currently supporting the Nexus, be prepared to step in if someone collapses or needs to drop out."

The Wielders began to spread out around the pit, but Marcus dove into its center, letting the ley swirl around his mind. He could sense Kara's presence as she inspected the crystals above, as she surveyed the ley lines that were currently active. They were receiving ley from the line that led to the Hollow and the northern lines, as well as the lines that shot out to the west and whatever was left of the Demesnes, but the lines leading east to Tumbor and Farrade were dead. The ley they were receiving was being funneled out to the southern lines, toward the Horn and the Gorrani Flats.

He waited until Kara had swept through the entire Nexus, taking stock. On the ley, he could sense her exhaustion, knew she could probably sense his own. When her presence settled before him, only a vague disturbance in the ley, he said, "Are you ready?"

"We're all ready," Dylan answered.

"I was speaking to Kara."

Then he realized: Kara couldn't hear him. They had no way to communicate. Every time they'd manipulated the ley before this, their physical bodies had been in the same room, but not now.

A ripple of frustration passed through Kara's presence. She hesitated . . . then shot back toward the line leading to Erenthrall. She didn't make it far—the velocity of the ley was too great—but her intention was clear.

"Kara needs us to reverse the flow now."

Dylan shouted at everyone to prepare, while Marcus reached for the crystals and centered himself on the flows. He didn't know how she'd let him know if anything else was needed, but they couldn't worry about that now.

"Reversing the flows . . . now!"

Seizing the power of the ley, he rotated the angles of the crystals above the pit, altering the refraction of the ley and shifting the currents in the pit below. For a moment, the ley was in flux, gouts of it shooting up from the pit into the chamber as it adjusted, but the new positions of the crystals held.

The ley swirled around him in chaos, then settled into its new directions. With a rush, the ley from the north and west redirected itself into the Erenthrall conduit. Marcus shouted in triumph as it caught Kara's presence up and swept her back toward the true Nexus. It may not have been done with the instinct or finesse Kara had with the ley, but it had worked.

Now all they had to do was hold it.

And pray that Morrell had been able to recreate the nodes in Tumbor.

"It's Captain Lienta!" someone on top of the wall shouted. "Open the gates!"

Cory huddled with Lienta, the Temerites, and the mentors and students from the University as the gates ground open far enough to let them all slip inside. They'd spent the night circling the Needle, heading far out into the plains to bypass any of the Gorrani or any of Devin's men, a maneuver that Lienta said Kara and the others had done when they'd escaped the Needle during the Kormanley takeover. They needn't have worried. The Gorrani and the others were focused on the attack on the Needle, the glow from the fires seen far out onto the plains on the low cloud cover overhead. But the clouds were breaking now, late morning sky and sunlight shining through.

Cory watched the surrounding ridge and the barren grasses to either side as they filtered through the gates, not relaxing until the heavy wooden doors had thudded closed behind them all. Exhaustion struck, like a physical blow. He staggered, one of Lienta's watchmen catching him. The man shouted, the students crowding around muttering cries of concern. Mirra was sobbing as she clutched his other arm, attempting to help hold him upright. He protested, tried to push them away, but his arms had no strength. His entire body trembled, and when he tried to stand upright, his knees gave out beneath him.

"Step back. Step back, I said! Give him room. Can't you see he's exhausted?" Cory was shocked to see Sovaan shoving through the crowd. The administrator halted before him, expression stern, as Mirra and the others fell back slightly. Lienta came up behind Sovaan.

"Lay him down on the ground," the Temerite captain ordered. As the watchman who'd caught Cory lowered him down gently, Lienta shouted, "Someone fetch a stretcher. And water and food!"

"I'm fine," Cory mumbled. Not even his voice had any strength.

Sovaan knelt beside him. "Like hells you are, boy. You've pushed yourself too hard, getting us out of that prison, then through the gates. All that after the punishment they'd put us through with that gas? It's a miracle you didn't collapse earlier." He gave Cory a cursory scan. "Are you hurt? I never even thought to ask."

"No. Just tired." He coughed, a harsh, hacking sound, and realized his entire chest still hurt from the aftereffects of the gas, but there wasn't anything anyone could do about that. He didn't think any of them would fully recover from that, unless Morrell could heal them.

Someone arrived with a stretcher and some water. Lienta handed it off to Sovaan, leaning over the mentor's shoulder as he helped Cory sit upright so he could drink. The water soothed his throat, cool against the residual burn damage. Sovaan pulled it back before he was done. "I'll give you more, but you have to drink slow. I don't want you vomiting it up. Then it's less than worthless."

Watchmen were setting the stretcher down next to Cory. As soon as he was finished drinking, they hoisted him up onto it, then lifted him. He tried to relax against the jostling as they followed Lienta through the Temerite section of the outer city to the embassy. Sovaan stayed beside him, his gaunt appearance making him statelier somehow. Or perhaps it was the weariness blurring Cory's eyes.

He started when someone grabbed his hand, swung his head to find Mirra on his other side. She twined her fingers through his and gave him a strained smile.

He must have nodded off briefly, for he found himself being settled onto the floor of a mercantile house that had obviously been repurposed as an embassy. The watchmen dispersed as Lienta gave out new orders and Sovaan called the students and Jerrain away. Mirra gave Cory's hand a squeeze, and he managed to smile in return.

Then he was left alone. He stared at the intricate details of the painted ceiling overhead, marred where sections had cracked or fallen away during the quakes. He could hear conversations going on all around him, reports on the fighting relayed from the wall and the edge of the chasm, orders and advice being exchanged. He heard Lienta's voice, and the Matriarch's, along with her assistant Janote. After a while, his eyes drifted shut, the voices fading into a soft murmur.

Until he heard someone mention the Three Sisters.

His eyes snapped open. "What was that?" he said, but no one was listening to him, and his voice was too weak, too cracked and ragged from the damage done by the gas for anyone to hear his words.

He rolled onto his side, realized they'd set him down beside a desk. He could see the wheels of the Matriarch's chair and the boots of at least five watchmen, huddled in discussion. He cursed. No wonder he'd been forgotten; no one could see him here. He reached for the desk, snagged its edge, and pulled himself upright.

Gathering his strength, he heaved himself onto his feet, leaning so heavily on the desk it shifted a few inches forward with a loud scrape.

Lienta and the men surrounding the Matriarch started, Janote reaching for his waist, to what Cory had no doubt was a concealed weapon. A few of the watchmen reached for blades as well, but Lienta stayed them with a hand.

"Cory, what are you doing here?"

Cory ignored the question. "What did you say about the Three Sisters?"

One of the watchmen hesitated, but both Lienta and the Matriarch nodded approval.

"One of the three is flashing."

"What do you mean flashing?"

"Flickering steadily. It's been pulsing at an increasing rate for weeks now, but this morning it changed. We aren't certain when—we've been focused on the activity at the Needle, plus there was cloud cover—but it's definitely flashing now."

Cory bowed his head, his exhaustion like the weight of a thousand pounds of stone on his back, but when he raised his head, he said, "Take me to the roof. I need to see it."

They abandoned the stretcher, two watchmen supporting him, an arm over a shoulder of each. Traversing the stairs was awkward, but eventually they made it to the roof.

The sounds of fighting rose through the columns of black smoke pouring out of the city on the far side of the chasm, but Cory's gaze shot toward the north, where the lights of the Three Sisters burned on the horizon above the purplish haze of the Steppe's mountains and the Reaches. Two of them were pulsing, at different rates, the one on the left significantly slower than the one on the right, but the third—

The third was definitely flashing, its light far more intense than the other two.

Cory sagged, his body dead weight, his mind recalling Dalton's vision.

"What's happening?" Lienta asked, although Cory suspected that he already knew.

"The distortion there is quickening."

"How long do we have?"

Cory shrugged. "At most, a few hours. Probably less than that."

"What about Kara? Can she stop it?"

Cory looked up to the scattering clouds above and the smear of the comet's white tail.

"I have no idea."

⤙⤚

Kara rode the surge of ley from the Needle all the way to Erenthrall. When she drew near the Nexus, she gathered herself, seizing the power of the ley and using it to create a shield against the raw chaotic power of the geyser. Moments before she shot into the well of the pit, she recognized that something there had changed, something subtle and fundamental, but she had no time to search and figure out what.

She launched from the tunnel across the roaring currents of the geyser, propelled almost immediately upward. Her presence shot from the shattered dome of the Nexus through the broken towers of Grass and into the midday sky. Pummeled on all sides, she retained her link to the ley line leading to the Needle, pulled up short, like a tether. She reached for the major lines connecting to the other nodes to the north—Ikanth, Severen, Dunmara—and those stretching East toward Temer and the coast. She snagged the line leading to the newly awakened node near the Hollow, even though it wasn't as strong, then added in the lesser lines that threaded throughout Erenthrall itself. With each connection, her presence steadied at the apex of the geyser. Each provided her an anchor, but she was still thrown about. The force from the geyser was too strong; only the strength provided by the power being fed her by Marcus at the Needle allowed her to maintain control.

But as she steadied, she sensed a disturbance. Something vibrated through the ley lines, buzzed through her body. She clamped her teeth together in an attempt to halt it, but it persisted, sinking into her bones. At her position atop the geyser, she swept herself around in a circle—

And spotted the flashing light of the distortion over the northern mountains.

She swore.

"What is it?"

Allan's voice, shockingly close, even though she knew he stood mere feet away.

"One of the distortions to the north, part of the Three Sisters, is quickening."

Now that she could see the source, she could feel it not only through the ley, but through the Tapestry as well. It sent out ripples in every direction, the Tapestry warping, too loose and unanchored to absorb the stress. Cory had told her the Tapestry had reacted when the distortion over Tumbor quickened, that he'd felt it as far away as the Hollow, that it was as if someone had snapped the Tapestry, like a matron would snap a rug to rid it of dust when cleaning. He'd said it had shaken the foundation of reality.

That had been before the nodes in Tumbor had been destroyed and the entire ley network south of Erenthrall had collapsed. What would the quickening of the Three Sisters do to the Tapestry now, when it had been loosened even further, when one of its fundamental anchors had been compromised?

"Dalton was right," she said, more to herself than the others.

"Right about what?" Allan asked. His hand gripped her shoulder.

"When the Three Sisters quicken, it will destroy us all."

Allan squeezed, his voice coming in closer, his breath hot against her neck. "Then stop it. You're the only one who can."

She wrenched her gaze away from the flickering lights of the distortions over the mountains and turned it toward the geyser beneath her. Ley sprouted around her in sheets, reaching its apex before falling away in arcs. Her tethers held, but they were only anchored to the north, east, and west.

She needed anchors to the south, or she'd never be able to stop the geyser.

"Let's hope Morrell managed to repair the nodes in Tumbor," she said, then reached for the dormant lines that led southward.

She cried out when she not only found the old lines, but freshly forged tunnels to hold new lines as well. "Morrell made it to Tumbor!"

Kara rocked backward as Allan grabbed both of her shoulders, practically shook her. "Morrell's alive? My daughter's alive?"

"I don't know if she's alive or not, but she made it to Tumbor. She must have repaired the node—I can't tell yet, the line to Tumbor is dead—but she did something more. There are new lines reaching to Tumbor and Farrade, tunnels that didn't exist before."

Allan sobbed, his hands flexing on her shoulders. "I knew she'd do it," he said in a cracked voice. "She's stronger than she looks."

"Yes," Grant's voice rumbled, "she is."

The tunnels were what Kara had felt when she arrived, a fundamental change to the layout of the Nexus in Erenthrall. Except that the new tunnels and the old weren't being flooded with ley. The system in Erenthrall had stabilized into a configuration without them.

"I need to alter the flow of the ley, somehow force it into the new channels."

Kara gathered the strength of the ley from the Needle and dove back down into the geyser, fighting its pressure the entire way. The deeper she went, the stronger the currents became. Her progress slowed and she fought harder, the ley blasting past her. She pulled on the tethers, tried to draw more strength from the ley feeding into Erenthrall from their sources. She reached, the currents she needed to adjust less than thirty feet away, but the power of the ley she controlled wasn't enough, even with the addition of the Needle.

She gathered her energy again, tugged hard on the tethers, and stretched.

She screamed in frustration, still twenty feet short.

"Something's wrong," Marcus said into the subdued silence of the Needle's pit. His voice echoed in the chamber, all eyes turning toward him.

"What?" Artras asked at his side. "What's wrong? Is it Kara? Is it the ley?"

Marcus shook his head, concentrating on the crystals on the Nexus they'd created, on the ley that surged through their node and out toward Erenthrall. He was tempted to travel down the line, as Kara did, but knew that he'd never reach the city. He wasn't strong enough to reach that far.

But he could feel something through the line, a subtle shift. No, not a shift, more like a . . . tug.

"It *is* Kara!" he shouted as realization struck. He spun, searching the crystals, their configuration, the faces of the Wielders. "She needs more power. What we've sent isn't enough."

"But we've sent her everything we've got!" Dylan protested. "The crystals have been positioned to maximize output. We can't reposition them without them threatening to shatter, not without the presence of a Prime, or without the help of the mages."

Marcus' gaze shot toward Hernande, but the mentor was still unconscious. "I know that!"

"Then what do you propose we do?" Artras asked.

"I don't kn—" Marcus' voice cut off as his eyes fell onto the thread of ley arching up toward the door and flooding through the Needle's first floor, keeping the Gorrani and Devin's men outside.

Dylan stepped forward, following Marcus' gaze. He spun back. "If you drop that thread, the Gorrani and the others will storm in here and kill us all."

"If you don't," Artras said on his other side, "and Dalton is right, then we all die anyway."

Marcus stared up at the ley-flooded entrance to the pit. The sounds of fighting sounded from outside. If anything, they'd escalated since they'd altered the flow of the ley, grown closer.

"Who's currently controlling that thread?" he asked.

Jenner stood. "I am."

Marcus turned. "When I say so, release the flow back into the Nexus here. I'll direct it to Erenthrall. It may not be much, but it might be enough." At Jenner's nod, he glanced around at everyone else—Cutter, Marc, Artras, Dylan, the rest of the Wielders present. "We need to hold the Nexus as long as we can, give Kara as much time as possible."

Cutter and Marc were already moving toward the stairs. Artras pulled out her knife and followed. A few of the Wielders grabbed what few weapons they had in the pit and joined them.

Marcus returned to the edge of the Nexus and stared down into the churning white ley, then raised his head, focusing on the crystals and the thread that protected them.

"Let it go, Jenner."

❦

Kara's scream cut off as a thin thread of new ley surged through the Needle's line. Momentarily stunned, she hastily seized it and wove it into the tethers, then dove into the center of the geyser with a half-disbelieving laugh. The vibration of the distortion to the north shivered into her joints as she grounded herself and then shunted the power of the tethers into a block, like a wall. The spiraling currents in the center of the geyser reacted, the flow disrupted, a portion of it funneling out into the new ley tunnels Morrell had constructed. Kara felt it surging toward Tumbor, toward Farrade, the line growing more and more tenuous the farther from Erenthrall it got, because it didn't have an anchor. She fed more and more ley into the lines, desperate for it to reach the node she hoped Morrell had rebuilt there. Once it reached the node—

She gasped as the line to Tumbor snapped, like a string suddenly pulled taut. The line to Farrade did the same an instant later. Without her aid, the lines strengthened as the chaotic eddies in the geyser shifted. Ley poured into the new lines, drawing from the geyser, as new lines sprang outward from Tumbor to Farrade, then spidering from both cities toward the Needle, toward the lands south and east and west. With each connection, the strength of the geyser lessened, the ley finding new outlets, new channels.

Kara retained her hold on the tethers until it had lessened enough she could begin stabilizing the chaos in the network throughout the city. Now that the pressure on the ley had been reduced, she could map out the lines easily. But the nodes and pathways within the city had been created for the Nexus, designed to be used with the array of crystals that had stood within its heart. Those crystals had been destroyed in the Shattering, and based on what Lecrucius and Iscivius had done at the Needle, they wouldn't be able to replicate them again easily.

If she had any hope of stabilizing the system, she'd have to rely on the old nodes, the original ones, like the one beneath Halliel's Park and in the Hollow. She'd have to create a new configuration, a blend of old and new.

Someone touched her shoulder. "I don't know what you did," Allan said, "but the ley is receding. It's lowered enough around us we can see the geyser. It's only half as high as before."

"I've shunted a good portion of the ley into the new lines to Tumbor and Farrade, but that was only part of the problem. Without the crystals here at the Nexus, the entire ley system in Erenthrall needs to be redesigned. I'm working on that now."

The Wolves suddenly broke into high-pitched howls. Kara flinched.

"What's happening?" she asked.

"Can no one hear that sound?" Grant muttered. His voice sounded pained, an underlying whine laced through the words.

Kara thought of the lines snapping into place and sucked in a sharp breath.

The quake jolted her from her seat on the edge of the crystal. Her body struck the floor hard, pain firing through her shoulder and into her chest, even though her consciousness was deep inside the geyser, her awareness spread through numerous lines shooting out from the Nexus. Allan shouted, "Kara!" and snatched at a flailing arm. He dragged her across the floor where she'd rolled, splinters of crystal biting into her skin, then pulled her up and held her to his chest. She wondered how close she'd come to falling into the ley, outside of Allan's sphere of protection, but it didn't matter. The entire city shook beneath them. Even deep in the ley, Kara heard stone cracking and crashing to the floor around them.

"Kara, if you can hear me, work fast!" Allan shouted over the rumble of the quake. "I'm not certain how much longer we can stay here!"

Kara didn't answer, dove back into the ley's configuration, sensing the lines, the nodes, the connections here and the lines that led outward toward the other cities. She'd never studied the ley structure before, not like she assumed the Primes had done before the Shattering. But she could feel all its individual parts.

It was like the stones in Halliel's Park, the ones Ischua had used to test her when she was a child. Or like the crystals in the new Nexus at the Needle. Shifting one stone or crystal altered the pattern of ley, altered the flows. Some configurations were good, but with a tiny adjustment, something better could be found.

All she had to do was find one that was stable, that would hold, without the need for supervision.

Taking in a deep, steadying breath, she exhaled slowly and mentally dug her toes into the sand, as she'd done for Ischua and her father so many years before. The quake faded into the background—Allan and Grant would protect her—until all that remained was the ley. She floated in it, at the center of the geyser, at the center of the Nexus.

Then she reached out and began manipulating the stones. She shunted the flow of the ley here, blocked off a conduit there. With each adjustment, the entire network shuddered and shifted, abandoned lines suddenly flooded, other lines flickering out. She shut off the node in Eld, used Halliel's Park instead, then reached for the node outside the city they'd discovered on their disastrous trek to Erenthrall last year. The system was intricate, each action having unintended consequences, but with each adjustment she learned a little more about how the nodes and lines interacted with each other. Turning off the node in Leeds caused the geyser to surge higher, the pressure too great, nearly sweeping Kara way. She swore and quickly added Leeds back into the network, focused on the nodes farther east. Adding a line from Hedge to Arrow caused the pressure to drop suddenly, Kara falling deep into the pit.

Someone shook both her and Allan, forcing her attention back to her body. "We have to go," Grant growled.

"Not yet! I'm nearly done!" Kara reached out frantically. She could sense the stability now, over half of the system already calmed.

"The entire building will come down on us!"

"She said wait," Allan said.

Grant grabbed Allan's shirt, dragged both him and Kara close. "We will all die."

"Then we die," Allan answered.

"She can't repair the ley if she's dead."

Something in the Nexus roared, an entire section of the ceiling falling in. Kara didn't see it, but she choked on the dust as it overwhelmed them.

Grant hauled them both to their feet. "Move!" he bellowed.

Allan hesitated, then hefted Kara into his arms as she screamed, "Wait!" But no one listened. In desperation, she slammed nodes on and off, blocked lines and released others, her connection to the ley growing more and more tenuous the farther Allan and Grant dragged her from the Nexus. She sensed perfection in the configuration, only a few adjustments away. With a ragged, feral cry, she stretched toward the last node and slammed it open as the network slipped out of her grasp.

She returned to her body with a wrench, moments before Grant, Allan, and the two Wolves ducked into the corridor leading away from the domed central room. She glanced back over Allan's shoulder, another portion of the ceiling caving in, the geyser gushing upward one last time before sinking down into the pit. The ley that had flooded the area had already receded into the ground.

They raced through the corridors, Allan and Grant shouting orders to each other as they ran. Kara thought about forcing Allan to put her down, but a stealthy lassitude had crept over her, like what she'd felt when she'd tried to heal the distortion over Erenthrall before it quickened after the Shattering. She barked a short laugh at the parallels between that moment and now: Allan carrying her exhausted body from the Nexus as they fled. Except this time the Wolves weren't hunting her. This time they were fleeing a quake, not a quickening.

And this time, she'd succeeded with what she'd set out to do.

"But is it in time?" she mumbled to herself.

They burst out of the darkened corridors into bright sunlight, everyone pausing, braced against the building as the ground continued to shake. Cracks appeared in the bowl surrounding the Nexus and shards of stone fell away from the remains of the towers on all sides. Grant pointed toward the stairs and shouted, "Up!"

They climbed, Allan's breath growing rough and harsh, coming in gasps as he slowed. Chunks of the bowl and parts of the steps broke free and rolled down the incline toward the Nexus below. They forged on, Allan staggering and collapsing to one side as they neared the top, hand clutched to his side. Kara crawled to him, caught his shoulder, and looked into his eyes, seeing his face twisted in pain.

"You don't need to carry me," she said. "I think I can walk."

They climbed to their feet, supporting each other, Grant already above, standing at the lip of the steps, the Wolves pacing around him impatiently. When they reached him, he asked, "Where do we go now?"

"Out of Erenthrall. To the top of the cliffs. I need to see the Three Sisters."

With the earth still shuddering beneath them, they headed south, toward the edge of Erenthrall.

Jenner was the first to die.

He was cut down by the Gorrani warriors that surged through the opening of the pit onto the stairs. He and Marc had held the outer corridor as long as possible, Cutter firing arrows from behind them over their shoulders. Marcus and most of the Wielders had remained in the pit. The corridor was too narrow for more than a few to be fighting at one time. Marcus knew that was the reason they were able to hold out as long as they did. But Marc and Jenner and Cutter and the rest had been pushed back, a foot at a time, until they'd reached the top of the stairs. Cutter had raced down them, past other Wielders going up, so he could fire at the Gorrani as they appeared from the far side of the pit.

Jenner fell before he'd reached the bottom, a vicious slice into his chest. He died without a sound, his body slipping from the stairs to fall to the stone ledge below. Another took his place, the screams and grunts and scrape of metal on metal echoing harshly throughout the chamber. Marcus watched from the edge of the pit, still monitoring the ley. A strange calm had descended over him, a blanket of acceptance.

When the Gorrani reached the halfway point, with three other Wielders cut down after Jenner, Marcus rushed forward. He kept his connection to the Nexus intact, but scrambled to the bodies beneath the stairs, snatched up one of the Gorrani's curved blades, and headed for the steps. Marc fought like a madman, thrusting and parrying and shoving the Gorrani back or over the side. He did it in total silence, only his expression enraged.

Marcus came up behind Artras, four body lengths behind Marc. He spun her around, startled by the murder in her eyes before she recognized him.

He pointed to the bottom of the stairs. "Go back down and make certain all of the Gorrani who fall are dead."

She nodded and started back down the steps. Marcus took her place.

He sensed a change in the ley a moment before a Gorrani sword sliced across Marc's neck. Blood gushed, but Marc drove his own blade through the Gorrani's chest before falling backward down the stairs, tripping up the desperate Wielders in front of Marcus. The Gorrani surged forward but were blocked by the tangled bodies. Marcus cursed as he was driven farther down the steps.

The reprieve was short-lived. Before Marcus and those few around him could rally, the Gorrani were on them.

He brought up the sword defensively, the motion awkward, uncertain. A Gorrani's blade smashed into his, numbing his entire arm. Marcus' breath came in grunting gasps, his entire body prickling with sweat, vibrating with a strange energy. The Gorrani screamed into his face, eyes wild—

And then the Gorrani's blade slashed across Marcus' chest.

Marcus stumbled backward, startled, but found no footing. He tumbled from the edge of the stairs.

He felt no pain from the wound until he landed on the stone ledge. Then the soothing blanket of calm that had enfolded him shredded, and he screamed as his entire chest burst into agony. Above him, the Gorrani streamed down the steps, the Wielder resistance collapsing. Marcus rolled onto his side, his clothes matted with his own blood, the searing pain cutting from his right shoulder down to the bottom of his rib cage on his left side. His chest felt hot, yet his entire body was shaking as if he were standing in the ice and snow of the northern wastes. He tried to crawl toward the pit, but his body was too heavy, his one arm too numb to function. With a groan, he rested his head against the stone and watched as the Gorrani poured out onto the ledge near the pit, cutting down the Wielders right and left. Cutter continued to fire arrows from the far side of the pit. Artras had retreated to Hernande's side, stood over him defensively alongside Dylan.

Something within the Nexus shifted again. The line to Tumbor. It had become active. Marcus grinned. "She did it." A laugh bubbled from his throat.

The Gorrani were halfway across the pit when the quake struck.

It threw half of them to the floor, a surge of ley erupting from the pit and catching a few of the Gorrani unaware as they struggled upright.

When the ley settled, Marcus realized the flow had calmed. Kara wasn't using all its power any longer.

With no time for subtlety, Marcus seized hold of the ley and sent it in a wall diagonally across the pit, cutting Artras, Hernande, Dylan, Cutter, and a few other Wielders off from the Gorrani. They stumbled back from it, shouting in anger and frustration in their own language.

Then, before he could reconsider, he shoved the wall forward, so that it would sweep across the Gorrani, up the stairs, and out through the corridors of the Needle into the stellae garden beyond.

A moment before it swept over him, he rolled onto his back and said, "For you, Kara."

Then he opened himself up to the ley and let it consume him.

Twenty-Four

RTRAS STRAIGHTENED in mute shock as the wall of ley that had cut them off from the Gorrani surged across the room and up the stairs, flowing out through the entrance into the Needle beyond. It left nothing of the Gorrani or the bodies behind except metal weapons, buckles, and jewelry.

"Gods," one of the surviving Wielders said. "What happened?"

Artras' gaze dropped to where she'd seen Marcus fall. "Marcus."

Cutter sprinted across the shuddering floor toward her. "He bought us a reprieve, nothing more. We have to get out of here before more of them arrive."

He reached toward Hernande, Dylan jerking out of his shock and reaching to help. They hauled him up and slung his arms over their shoulders, then began dragging him toward the steps. The other Wielders were already sprinting toward the entrance.

Artras rushed to the edge of the pit and reached for the ley. The ground still shook with the quakes, but the crystals remained steady in a stable configuration. The flows coming in from Erenthrall and the node near the Hollow were being funneled toward Tumbor and the connection to the south. She grunted in approval, then sped after Cutter and Dylan, heading up the stairs before them, her knife ready. "Kara has stabilized the ley," she said as she passed them.

The ground lurched, throwing them all against the wall to one side.

"It doesn't feel like it," Cutter muttered.

Artras didn't answer. The Wielders had already vacated the pit, but she still slowed as she reached the entrance. Another shudder sent a jagged crack racing across the pit's ceiling, a section of the stone ledge falling away below them. Dylan shouted, "Move, move, move!" and all four of them staggered into the outer corridor of the Needle as the ceiling gave way behind them. Artras raced ahead, slowing as she passed side corridors, wary of Gorrani, but there was no one within the Needle or in the stellae garden outside. She wasn't certain how far Marcus' wall of ley had reached, but she doubted it had maintained its integrity very long after his death.

The temple doors gaped open before them. None of the Wielders were in sight.

"Those gods-cursed cowards," she said, then turned to Cutter. "Where should we go from here? We have no idea where the Gorrani are. Or Devin's men."

Cutter glanced down at Hernande. "He's still unconscious."

"The bridge."

"What bridge?" Dylan demanded.

"He built a bridge over the chasm out of air," Artras said. "No one knows it's there except us, Lienta, and the Temerites, wherever they are."

"It's our best chance," Cutter said, "assuming it's still there."

They entered the temple, proceeding cautiously through hallways and rooms filled with corpses. Dylan gagged and coughed at the stench of blood and carnage; Artras automatically switched to breathing shallowly through her mouth, a technique she'd learned working in the slaughterhouses before becoming a Wielder. Dust rained down from the ceiling as the ground shook, debris falling in a few corridors. They heard shouts and the sounds of fighting, but all from a distance. Twice someone startled them by stepping around a corner, but after a wide-eyed stare, the intruder darted away. None of them were Gorrani; survivors, attempting to escape, like they were.

By the time they reached the doors leading to the outer city, the quakes had lessened, the earth settling down, the sharp jolts coming less and less often. The city was in chaos, people fleeing in the streets in small groups, headed toward the main gates, or cowering behind locked doors. Artras caught many furtive glances out of shuttered windows. Numerous buildings were on fire, the flames spreading, but they didn't pause to help anyone. Most ran from them before they were within twenty paces, skirting the dead that littered the streets. Artras,

Cutter, and Dylan kept to the base of the buildings, only cutting across the streets when necessary.

They found the chasm, raced along the partially built wall toward where Hernande had constructed his bridge. A few sections had broken free and dropped into the chasm due to the earthquakes, but cutting around these areas was simple. Almost no one remained in this section of the city.

When they neared the narrowest part of the chasm, Artras raced ahead and leaned over the wall, searching. "It's still here! I can see the stones marking its edge."

"Help us get him over the side," Cutter said as he came up behind her.

Artras tucked her knife away, then crawled out onto the invisible span as Dylan and Cutter heaved Hernande's body up onto the wall. Artras prayed Hernande wouldn't wake up now as she grabbed his shoulders and pulled him down onto the bridge. His arm slid over the side, dangling, but she heaved him farther out to give the others room to get over the wall.

Someone shouted from across the chasm, a warning, but Artras didn't look. "Lift his legs. I've got his arms."

With her walking backward, she and Cutter half-lifted, half-dragged Hernande across the bridge. The stones they'd used to delineate the bridge's edge were swept off on either side. Dylan followed behind, his expression one of stark terror as he kept close to Cutter.

By the time they reached the opposite end, a group of twelve Temerites was there to greet them, two of them hauling Hernande up and into the dead garden after helping Artras off the bridge. They kept a careful eye on Dylan until Artras assured them he was one of the Wielders.

As soon as they entered the half-collapsed building, the Temerites returning to their watch on the bridge, Artras collapsed onto a section of piled stone. She pressed a hand to her chest, her heart thundering, her entire body tingling with adrenaline. Someone rushed off to find a stretcher for Hernande, while Cutter and Dylan sank into seated positions beside her.

"Are you all right?" Dylan asked.

"I'll be fine," Artras said. "I just need to catch my breath."

That's how Lienta found them, with Cory and a slew of other Temerites behind him. He eyed them all, then asked, "Marcus? The
others?"

"We're all that's left," Artras answered. "Except for a few Wielders
who cut and ran." She faced Cory, who was kneeling at Hernande's side.
"We'd be dead, too, if it wasn't for Marcus. He used the ley to save us."

"What happened with the ley?" Lienta asked. The earth shuddered
again, a small aftershock. "Has it been repaired?"

"Yes, as far as I can tell. Kara stabilized it. Morrell must have succeeded as well. When we left, the ley was flowing toward Tumbor and
Farrade. There must be active nodes there now."

"Did Kara survive?"

Lienta asked the question, but Cory looked up. He looked exhausted,
gaunt and drained. Tears burned at the corners of Artras' eyes. "I'm
sorry, I don't know. I'm not strong enough to reach all the way to Erenthrall to find out."

Cory glanced away, then down toward Hernande. "What happened
to him?" he asked, his voice ragged.

Artras shifted down to Hernande's other side, reached out to touch
his face. "He used the Tapestry to construct a bridge over the chasm.
He said he needed to concentrate in order to do it. He's been in this
trance-like state ever since. Can you wake him?"

Cory hesitated, then shook his head. "I don't think it's being caused
by the Tapestry at all. I think it has something to do with what he did—
or what he was—before he came to Erenthrall and became a mentor."

Standing over them, Lienta said, "We should move him to the embassy. The Matriarch will have some of our healers look after him.
They should probably check all of you as well."

Watchmen moved forward and raised Hernande's stretcher. They
followed them to the embassy, Artras surprised to find the sunlight
fading as they made their way across the Temerite sector of the Needle.
The earth still trembled occasionally, but it had certainly settled since
the initial quake; she barely felt the tremors.

Inside the embassy, Lienta escorted them to their rooms, then departed to oversee the defense of their sector from whatever was happening in the rest of the Needle. Cory collapsed onto a pallet in
Hernande's room, the watchmen placing his mentor gently onto his
own bed. Artras settled into a nearby chair. Dylan and Cutter hovered

by the doorway. Two healers arrived and poked and prodded them all, looking into their eyes, testing their pulses, but in the end, they could only prescribe rest. They paid closer attention to Hernande, but not even smelling salts placed beneath his nose roused him.

Admitting defeat, the healers left.

Artras drifted to Hernande's side and stared down at his slack features, his beard scraggly and frayed.

"What are we going to do now?" Dylan said from the door.

"We wait," Artras answered.

"No, not about Hernande. I mean here at the Needle."

Cutter stirred. "We're at the mercy of the Temerites, here on their sufferance. Protected by them."

"And to think they traveled here from Erenthrall to find sanctuary with us," Artras said.

"What do you think they'll do? Once the fighting between the Gorrani and Devin dies out."

"I think they'll seize control of the Needle, take over the entire city."

Cutter said it flatly, without emotion. But Artras thought he was right.

"But what about the Nexus?" Dylan protested. "Who will oversee it?"

Artras turned. "No one. Didn't you see? After we escaped, the ceiling caved in. It will take years to clear out that stone."

"If the Nexus within is still even active."

"It is. We would have felt it if it wasn't. There would have been a resurgence of the quakes, if nothing else." She gazed off into the distance, in the direction of the node. She felt its pulse. "I don't think anyone needs to oversee this node anymore. Not that we have many Wielders left. I think Kara has rigged it so that no one needs to oversee it."

"Then where are we going to go?" Dylan asked.

She looked at him. "I think—I think I'm going to return to the Hollow. If they'll have me. It was quiet there. I can work with the node we discovered, or even help with the animals. I know a little something about butchering."

"We can't go anywhere right away," Cory said, startling them all. Artras had thought he'd fallen asleep.

He lifted his arm from where it covered his eyes. "We have to wait and see if Kara and Morrell and the others survived. If they did, they'll return here."

"And what if they didn't?" Cutter asked bluntly. "How long do we wait?"

Cory didn't respond, placing his arm back over his face.

Artras was too exhausted to even glare. "Right now, we all need to rest." She headed for the door, but paused by Cory's pallet. "Come find me if Hernande regains consciousness. Wake me if you have to."

Cory nodded.

She slid past Cutter and Dylan. "Come with me, Dylan. You can take Marcus' bed."

In her own room, she didn't even bother to change her clothes. She fell onto her pallet with a groan, considered rolling onto her side, but decided it was too much bother. Thoughts of Kara, Allan, Morrell, and the others swirled around in her head, but they weren't strong enough to ward off sleep.

Within minutes, she was snoring.

In the half-collapsed building where Hernande had performed the ritual that placed him into his trance, the soft light of a candle glowed. The watchmen set to keep an eye on what happened at the Needle and to guard against the bridge's discovery noticed it an hour after darkfall, when one of them took a break to piss. The candle was obscured by the rubble, placed at the edge of a cleared circle, a small rug laid out before it. Wax pooled around its base. Based on the amount, the watch-man guessed the candle had been burning for a day, maybe two, pro-tected in its little niche. Now, the wick was nothing more than a charred stub in the middle of a puddle of melted tallow, the flame barely visible.

He shifted around the small circle and knelt on the rug, then reached for the remains of the candle.

Before he could touch it, the tiny flame flickered, guttered and spat wax, and then died. A wisp of white smoke rose from a dull red ember in the charred wick, then faded.

Inside the Temerite embassy, Hernande sucked in a deep, rasping breath and opened his eyes.

"—wake him, Sovaan. He needs to rest."

"He's been resting for nearly fifteen hours now. I think that's enough. Besides, the Matriarch would like to speak with him—with all of us."

"If what you say he did is true, he may well be sleeping for days."

Cory listened to the two argue, but let the words flow over him. He knew they were talking about him, but he didn't care. His entire body ached, and he'd heard Sovaan and Hernande argue often enough that he could simply drift back to sleep without it disturbing him—

His eyes shot open and he bolted upright on his pallet. "Hernande! You're awake!"

Sovaan and Hernande stood in the hallway outside the open door, both with irritated expressions. Sovaan brightened and stepped into the room. "Good, you're awake! We need to get you washed up and presentable. The Matriarch wishes to see us all."

Cory ignored Sovaan and leaped from his pallet, grabbing Hernande in a rough hug. Hernande patted him on the back. He tried to speak, but his entire chest, throat, and head felt hot, prickly, and congested, the edges of his eyes burning.

After an indeterminate time, Hernande pushed him back. "I'm all right, Cory. Besides, this display of affection is unbecoming of a mentor."

"You aren't h—wait, what? What do you mean 'mentor'?"

Sovaan cleared his throat ostentatiously. "Yes, well, after Hernande woke, he, Jerrain, and I had a long discussion about what transpired inside the temple when the Kormanley seized control. It was agreed that you comported yourself in a manner befitting a mentor, not a graduate student. This is not the time or place for an official ceremony, but you are hereby unofficially granted the colors and privileges of a full-fledged mentor. You may discard your tans and don the duns of your status, not that any of us have been following the formalities of the colors since the Shattering. Jerrain wanted to be here, but he's still recuperating."

Cory spluttered. "But . . . isn't there supposed to be a hideously prolonged test? Practicums? An oral examination?"

"Under normal circumstances, yes. We feel the incarceration and the

method of our escape at your hands was a significant enough demonstration of what you've learned."

Hernande extended a hand, a gesture Cory knew from the gradua-
tion ceremonies indicated formal acceptance of the new title. "Congratulations."

Cory shook his hand. "Thank you. All of you."

Hernande leaned forward and stage whispered, "It was all Sovaan's
idea."

Sovaan waved a hand in dismissal. "It was a natural conclusion after
the . . . events at the temple."

Overwhelmed, Cory stood with mouth open for a long, awkward
moment, both mentors grinning, then decided to ignore the unexpected news and faced Hernande. "You aren't hurt? When did you
wake up?"

"Last night, apparently shortly after you and the others brought me
here. I tried to rouse you, but you were out cold. I went to find the
others instead. Sovaan told me what happened to you and the others
once you were captured. Lienta explained about what happened with
the Wielder's plan to take the Nexus and hold it after I went into my
trance state, except he didn't know what transpired in the Needle after
Marcus and the others broke away from him. We were waiting for Artras to fill in that gap. She's still asleep."

"Except now we've been summoned by the Matriarch," Sovaan said.
"We must wake her and the rest."

Before the argument he'd heard earlier could be repeated for Artras,
Cory said, "She wanted to know the moment you regained consciousness."

Artras was thrilled to see Hernande, although more restrained than
Cory. Like all of them, she appeared haggard and worn. Sovaan stood
back, agitated, as they laughed and cried over their recent experiences,
but finally broke in to remind them of the Matriarch's summons.

When they entered the main hall of the Temerite embassy, the
Matriarch was ensconced behind a large oak desk, Janote to her right
and a step behind her. The desktop was littered with papers, an ink-
well, a quill, and various personal effects. Behind her, the marble wall
of the mercantile was crazed with cracks. Lienta stood in front of the
desk, having just handed over a sheaf of papers. Dylan and Cutter
were off to one side. The room bustled with activity, watchmen seated

at desks on either side of the long hall between the pillars, runners scuttling to and fro. Late afternoon sunlight slanted through the windows. A low murmur of mixed conversation and rustling bodies filled the chamber.

"Ah, you've arrived," the Matriarch said when she saw them, setting the papers she held aside. Lienta faced them. "You slept well, I hope?"

"Well enough, Matriarch," Sovaan said for them all.

"I wish I could have given you more time to recuperate, but events are progressing at the Needle. I've received full reports from Lienta and his men, as well as more basic reports from some of the University students and mentors, as well as huntsman Cutter and Wielder Dylan, but I would like to hear your own accounts, if I may. It is obvious that there are certain key details missing."

Hernande stepped forward. "Forgive me, Matriarch, but before that, may I ask what you intend to do with all of us? And what you intend to do here, at the Needle?"

The Matriarch remained silent, her gaze fixed on Hernande, then she leaned forward, addressing them all. "At this moment, the Needle is in chaos. From what we can gather on this side of the chasm, Devin's men and the Gorrani continue to fight in the streets and in the temple. There is no clear victor, and no one appears to have seized control of a significant sector of the city, certainly not the temple or the Needle itself. In our estimation, neither force is now strong enough to lay claim to the city. Most of those who resided there before the attack have already fled. We have seen no sign of the Kormanley presence at all; the enforcer presence that held the city before appears to have been crushed completely. There are reports that Father Dalton is dead. There are reports that he has fled. In either case, they no longer appear to be a factor.

"So we will wait. We will give those who wish to flee a chance to escape, and we will allow Devin's men and the Gorrani the chance to kill each other off. Then, when the time is right, we will seize control of the Needle. We have been displaced from our home in Temer, with no assurances that any part of our nation even survives. It is obvious that Erenthrall is dangerous, no matter what Kara Tremain has managed to do there with the ley and the Nexus. It is also obvious that we cannot trust anyone else, only ourselves. We need a new home. I see no reason why it cannot be made here."

Her gaze landed on Artras. "But I need to know the state of the node here before that decision can be made final."

"You still have not answered my main question," Hernande interrupted. "What do you intend to do with all of us?"

"For the moment, I offer you sanctuary here, until you have recovered. It is the least I can do."

"And after we have recovered?"

"We shall decide at that time."

"I see." Hernande bowed his head and stepped back. Sovaan appeared agitated, Lienta discomfited, but neither spoke up.

"Now, tell us what happened within the node, Wielder Artras. And then we shall hear from you, Cory."

Artras hesitated, her eyes taut with the same unfocused anger Cory felt, but she recounted what had happened within the Needle, starting where she, Marcus, and the others had broken away from Lienta's watchmen and ending with the desperate hope that Hernande's bridge over the chasm still existed. It took longer than expected, with interruptions for clarification from the Matriarch, Lienta, and even Janote. Cory began his own story of the University students' capture, imprisonment, and escape with the sunlight fading from the windows, finishing well after night had fallen. The embassy chamber was now lit with torches and a few lanterns, one of which rested on a corner of the Matriarch's desk, its light spilling over her papers.

The room remained silent long after Cory and Artras finished, until the Matriarch stirred.

"We have much to discuss. Thank you for being so frank with us. Let us hope that your supposition that the ceiling of the Nexus at the Needle has buried it completely is correct. We will call on you again."

As everyone who remained began preparing to leave at the obvious dismissal, Cory stepped forward. "Matriarch. Kara and Allan, Morrell and Boskell, all of them—if they survived, they will return here. We should be here to greet them."

A pained yet compassionate expression flickered across the Matriarch's stern face. "I will take that into account when I make my decision."

Then they were ushered out by Lienta and the watchmen. Lienta muttered a few words of reassurance before closing the embassy's doors behind them.

"Well, that was . . . troubling," Sovaan said. "I would have thought they'd be more appreciative of what we've all done."

"We did nothing for the Temerites except offer them sanctuary here at the Needle, which ended up putting them directly into the path of the Kormanley, Gorrani, and Devin's dogs."

"We allowed them to take over a third of the city!" Sovaan protested, but Cory had stopped listening. Mention of the dogs had reminded him of Dalton's vision. He broke away from the others, pace picking up as he reached the stairs.

"Where are you going?" Artras called out after him.

"The roof!"

When he stumbled through the door onto the roof, he was panting. He immediately faced north and sought out the Three Sisters, two of the distortions still pulsing dully among the stars.

The third flashed.

The others followed more slowly, coming up behind him. No one said anything for a long moment, somber as they watched the distortion flicker. To the east, flames still roiled in a few buildings around the temple, but the fighting had died down. Watchmen lined the walls surrounding the Temerites, their torches lighting the battlements and the edge of the chasm below.

Artras finally muttered, "Is it going to quicken? Will it be another Erenthrall? Or Tumbor?"

"Dalton said it would destroy us all," Dylan said.

Hernande was chewing on the end of his beard. "What do you think, Cory?"

"I came up here after we escaped from the temple and watched it. I can't be certain, but I think . . . I think it isn't flashing as often as before."

"Then if it hasn't quickened already, perhaps Kara repaired the ley in time to stop it."

"There's little we can do about it from here, regardless," Artras said. "And it will quicken long before we manage to get there to stop it."

They all stood staring at the light in silence. Then they began drifting away, until only Artras, Hernande, and Cory were left.

Artras touched Cory's arm. "We'll wait for her, however long it takes. Here or at the Hollow."

Cory said nothing. She patted his arm, then shifted toward the door.

"Will you come down with us?" Hernande asked.

Cory drew in a steadying breath. "No. I think I'll stay here. The darkness, the quiet . . ."

"I'll be downstairs."

As soon as they were gone, Cory sat down on the hard stone of the roof and stared off into the night.

In the direction of Erenthrall.

~

In the end, the Matriarch agreed to let them stay. Within days, the Gorrani gathered their scattered forces and departed, headed northeast. Cory and Hernande watched from the walls as Lienta gathered the Temerite army in the courtyard below. They remained on the walls as the watchmen marched to the Needle's main gates and invaded the city. There was little resistance. Within half a day, Lienta had secured the temple and the watchmen were scouring the surrounding city, looking for remnants of the Kormanley and Devin's men. Patrols were set up on the walls, the main gates closed—someone had obviously opened them from the inside—and a heavy guard set upon the breach blasted into the southeastern wall by Cory himself. Temerite engineers were already working on patching that hole in their defenses.

Artras and Dylan occupied themselves by investigating the collapse of the ceiling at the node. As expected, the pit was inaccessible. More alarming was the fact that the black spire of the Needle itself had taken on a slight tilt, its southern edge sunk into the sands of the stellae garden by half a foot. Cory could make out that it was off true if he squinted. No one knew what it would mean for the node or the temple, but Artras and Dylan reported that the ley itself was functioning normally, unaided by any Wielders.

Once the students from the University had recovered—Jerrain's recovery would take another few weeks—Hernande, Sovaan, and Cory began their lessons again, using the half-collapsed manse where Hernande had created the bridge using the Tapestry. Mirra, Tara, Jasom, and the rest shrugged their imprisonment off much quicker than their mentors, although Cory did catch Jasom, the oldest, staring off into thin air with a troubled look once or twice. Within days, they were teasing each other and laughing, as students do. For the most part, they kept to the section of the city west of the chasm, none of them wishing to return to the temple, even though the Matriarch, Lienta, and most of the Temerites had shifted their activities to the central part of the city.

In the evenings, Cory would ascend to the rooftop of the mercantile and watch the horizon as the sun set, then stay long after dark. To the east, the auroral storms that had plagued the area around Tumbor dissipated. Hernande theorized they had arisen because of the slackness in the Tapestry, caused by the disruption of key ley lines. Now that the ley lines were restored—and the Tapestry with it; they could feel its tautness when working with the students—reality had been restored. He, Sovaan, and Jerrain spent long hours arguing exactly what the auroral lights were—a different kind of distortion? fluctuations in reality?—without reaching any firm conclusions.

To the north, the pulsing of the Three Sisters continued. Cory swore that the flickering had slowed, but it wasn't until the weakest of the three—the distortion over Dunmara, he thought—vanished that he felt certain. At that point, everyone began to relax, the tension draining from the Needle in an almost audible sigh.

Cory kept an eye on the remaining two distortions, regardless.

⟣⟢

Cory was working with Mirra and Jasom on creating illusions—both attempting to conceal a stone from sight by folding the Tapestry—when a scuffling sound caught Cory's attention. He glanced up to find Lienta standing in the doorway to the rubble-strewn room, the captain smiling.

"I've brought you some guests," he said, then stepped aside.

Kara emerged from the manse's inner shadows. She looked road-weary and worn, her face smudged, clothes stained and dusty, but she grinned as she said, "I made it back."

Cory didn't remember moving, but suddenly he was holding her tight, so tight she gasped that she couldn't breathe, and then he was kissing her and tears washed his face and he couldn't breathe, his chest constricted, his throat locked. Kara burst out in laughter, and then Allan and Morrell and Grant appeared behind her, Drayden and Okata hovering around in the shadows farther back. Everyone hugged or slapped hands to shoulders and talked all at once. Lienta must have sent someone to find Hernande and Artras and the rest, for they arrived as

well, the room full of exclamations of surprise and sobs and chuckles
and groans. A few watchmen arrived with wine and cups and cheese and
fruit.

It may have continued indefinitely, except Kara asked during a lull
in the noise, "Where's Marcus?"

The group ground down into sniffles and coughs and then silence.

"Marcus died protecting the node from the Gorrani." Artras
glanced around at the rest of them, cleared her throat self-consciously.
"He saved me, Dylan, Cutter, and Hernande. He sacrificed himself
for us."

"Marc, Jenner, and many of the other Wielders died fighting the
Gorrani as well," Dylan added.

In the awkward, grieving silence that followed, Morrell said, "Boskell, Sesali, and Hanter died for us in Tumbor."

For the first time, Cory took a close look at Allan's daughter. She
looked older, more confident, more certain of herself. A young woman
now, not the shy child they'd begun teaching earlier in the year.

Allan hugged her and kissed the top of her head. "Many people died
helping us, poppet. But they died so that we'd have a chance to repair
the ley. And you did it. You and Kara."

"And Marcus," Artras added.

"Is it truly fixed?" Hernande asked.

Everyone turned to face Kara, who refused to let go of Cory's hand.
Or perhaps he refused to let go of hers.

"Yes, I believe so. I monitored it as we fled Erenthrall, and it appears
stable."

"There haven't been any quakes for the last month," Hernande
added, "and the auroral lights have faded away. The last such storm was
spotted almost two weeks ago. We haven't seen anything since. With
all of that, and the slowing of the pulses of the distortions we can see,
I'd agree with you."

"You're assuming no one will disturb the nodes," Lienta said. "There
must be other Wielders out there who survived the Shattering, perhaps
even Primes."

"I don't think they'll be accessing the ley through the Nexus in
Erenthrall."

"Why not?"

Allan stirred. "The Gorrani there who were transformed by the auroral lights into snake-like creatures have seized the city. We only escaped because the ley had flooded the districts around Grass. They were already infiltrating those areas when we left. I didn't see anyone else, except the Tunnelers. They were headed north, out of the city."

"No one can access the ley here," Artras said. "Not directly. The ceiling over our own Nexus collapsed and sealed it off."

"And the Matriarch has no intention of allowing anyone to dig it back up again."

"Not in Tumbor either." Everyone turned toward Morrell, who straightened. "I used the auroral lights to repair the nodes, then created tunnels for the ley lines between the nodes. As many as I could. The aurora was wild, untamed. The power was immense and"—she swallowed—"exhilarating. Almost alive. I've never felt so much raw energy before. I thought, for a few hours, that I could do anything." Her voice caught and she glanced around at them all in mild embarrassment. But for a moment Cory caught a flicker of the raw, wild energy she described in her eyes. "It's gone now, though. I meant to repair the lands destroyed by the distortion in Tumbor, but I ran out of strength at the end. The earth there is still shattered. And I don't think, without the wildness of the aurora, that I'll be able to fix it."

"No one expects you to, poppet."

"But I want to. The land still hurts. It's still screaming. I can still hear it." She shuddered.

Hernande stroked his beard. "I can help, if it doesn't fade on its own. There are certain meditations I know of that may help."

"But that doesn't heal the land. I don't want to ignore it. I want to fix it."

Artras touched her arm. "Perhaps you can, in time. Right now, you've done enough. You need to rest. We all need to rest."

Lienta cleared his throat and stiffened. "Speaking of rest, I've been authorized by the Matriarch to offer you all refuge here at the Needle. She felt it necessary after all you've done to bring stability back to the plains."

"That's certainly a change from what we went through immediately after the attack on the Needle."

Lienta sighed, shoulders slumping as he met Artras' accusing glare.

"Yes, it is. Certain advisers argued against harboring you, considering all of you potential threats. I've spent a good part of the last month convincing her otherwise."

"Better to keep us close, so you can keep an eye on us?"

Lienta stilled, then looked at each of them in turn. "You must admit that you are all dangerous, for various reasons. Having you here would be in our best interests, not just for our safety, but for yours."

Kara's grip tightened painfully on Cory's fingers. "Are you going to force us to stay?"

"No. If you want to leave, you can leave. And you can return any time you wish. The Matriarch does not wish to make you prisoners."

The tension in the room abated, people returning to their drinks and conversations slowly, the tone more subdued. As if sensing this, Lienta motioned to the watchmen and discreetly exited.

Kara stared into her cup, until Cory interrupted wherever she'd gone in her mind with a tug on her hand. "Come with me."

Her brow furrowed, but she took a sip of the wine and set the cup aside.

He led her out through the rubble into the barren garden, to the edge of the chasm, the precipice where Hernande had created the bridge. They sat down on one of the low garden walls, away from the others. The sounds of the city washed over them, but it was muted and removed.

Cory wanted to talk about everything and nothing at the same time, but he let the silence stretch. He'd heard enough of what had happened to Kara, Allan, and Grant inside.

Eventually, Kara said into the quiet, "What are we going to do now?"

"We are going to go to the Hollow."

Kara faced him in surprise. "Are we now?"

"Yes." He stood, letting her hand go, and shifted to stare down into the chasm. "I've been thinking about it for the past month, in between worrying about whether you were alive or dead. We came here, to the Needle, with the idea that we could heal the ley and restore what was once great about Erenthrall, recreate it anew, but without the Baron and the Dogs and the Primes and all the rest. We've healed the ley, but I think in the process we destroyed any chance we had of recreating Erenthrall." He turned to Kara. "It's gone. The Amber Tower, Grass, the Nexus. The barge system, the flyers, the districts and mercantiles and parks. All of it. We can't rebuild it, not like it was. I'm not certain we should have even tried.

"But that doesn't matter. The world has changed, Kara. Something new should rise from the ashes, and we don't need to be the ones who will shape it. As Artras said to Morrell inside, we've done enough. We've survived enough.

"So let's return to the Hollow. Let the Matriarch take care of the Needle. Let the snake-like Gorrani have the ruins of Erenthrall. We had a life in the Hollow once. We should reclaim it. I know Sophia and the others would welcome us."

"What about the school? Don't you have students to teach?"

"I'm fairly certain I can convince Hernande and the others to move the school to the Hollow—"

"Sovaan? He'd move to the Hollow?"

"If we tell him we'll build a school there, one that he can oversee, perhaps."

"Perhaps."

Cory stepped toward her. "But it doesn't matter. Even if what remains of the University stays here at the Needle, I don't have to be a part of it."

Kara looked away. "I'd never ask you to give that up, Cory. Not after everything that's happened."

"You won't have to." He settled back down beside her. "And there's something for you at the Hollow as well. The node."

Kara perked up. "I could monitor the ley from there. And almost no one knows it exists."

"We don't have to make a decision right now. You and the others need to rest. We've got time."

"No. I mean, yes, we can't leave right now. Allan should spend time with his daughter. And we'll have to tell the others what we plan and give them a chance to decide. But I think . . . I think the Hollow is a good idea."

She grabbed his hand and leaned into him. He placed an arm over her shoulder and they sat and rocked gently back and forth, the low sounds of the others filtering out through the collapsed wall, the rest of the Needle bustling about them.

Kara opened the door to Marcus and Dierdre's room, but halted in the entryway. She stared around the chamber, at the table against one wall, the bed set to one side, the blankets rumpled. No one had touched the room since Devin's men and the Gorrani had attacked the temple, mostly because the Temerites had been focused on more important things inside the Needle and there hadn't been a shortage of rooms.

She wasn't certain why she'd come. Except, from what everyone said, Marcus had sacrificed himself in the end to save Artras, Hernande, and the others in the pit. He'd killed Dierdre and Irmona before that, when Tumbor collapsed. Both of those actions grated against what she knew of Marcus from before the Shattering. She'd loved him once, but he'd betrayed her for the Kormanley. Even after the White Cloaks had captured her and brought her here, even after he'd rebelled against Lecrucius to give her the opportunity to heal the distortion over Erenthrall, she'd had doubts about his motives. After all, with Lecrucius dead and Dalton subdued, he'd wielded more power within the Needle than ever before.

But that vision of him contradicted his actions after they'd seized control, especially in the weeks leading up to the disastrous attempt to heal Tumbor and what followed afterward. Who was Marcus, in the end? Was he Kormanley? Was he the Wielder she'd fallen in love with? Had he ever really loved her, or had it all been an illusion that Dierdre had shattered when she'd convinced him to become part of the Kormanley?

She didn't know. When Lienta had told her that his rooms had been left untouched, she'd thought maybe she'd find an answer here.

Heaving an exasperated sigh, she stepped into the room. As she moved about, fingers trailing along the table where a cutting board and knife had been set out, her sense of intrusion faded. Everything was coated with a faint layer of dust. A pitcher had fallen, probably during one of the quakes, its shards littering the floor. The room smelled dry and abandoned, even though there were a few pieces of clothing draped over the edge of a chair.

Then her eyes fell on the trunk shoved under the bed. She pulled it out, its metal corners scraping on the stone. It wasn't locked.

Inside, there were mostly clothes, but buried near the bottom were a few personal effects. A blue pendant that she recognized from when she and Marcus had lived together, before Dierdre. A fragile teacup. An old ring that had obviously belonged to Dierdre.

But tucked into one corner was a stone, blue-black, with swirls of white in it.

Her breath caught. "It can't be." She hesitated, then plucked it from the corner, rubbed her thumb across its smooth surface, her fingers tingling. "It's impossible."

But she knew this stone. She'd handed it to Ischua when she was twelve and he'd tested her in Halliel's Park, told him that it didn't belong. He'd given it back to her when she became a Wielder. She'd carried it with her through the years since, until the Shattering.

Marcus must have found it in her apartment after the Shattering. She'd never returned there, had assumed it was locked away within the distortion. It must have been, and yet somehow Marcus had retrieved it.

She suddenly recalled the shards they'd found already healed before they'd been captured and traded by the Tunnelers.

Marcus must have searched for her. It would be only natural to look in her apartment, where he'd found the stone. Dierdre wouldn't have had any idea of its significance, of its connection to her.

She closed her fingers around it and brought it to her chest, her eyes burning with tears.

Then she stood and walked from the room, leaving the door open behind her.

***

Six months later, Cory trudged through the snow that had managed to filter through the trees surrounding the Hollow, his breath puffing in the air before him, his body wrapped in layers of cloth and fur. The sounds of construction on the new school—one that would teach both the use of the Tapestry and how to be a Wielder—faded behind him, along with all the other industrious noises from the much-expanded village. Everyone had decided to follow Cory and Kara's lead, even Sovaan, abandoning the Needle with its temple and slightly tilted spire to the Temerites. Paul had grumbled, but Sophia had slapped the back of his head and then accepted them all with open arms. It had taken some time for a few of them to adjust, but now they'd settled into a routine, with regular sojourns to the Needle to trade.

But every now and then Cory felt the need to get away, especially after a particularly bad night of sleep, interrupted with nightmares where his lungs burned and he found himself trapped behind an invisible wall, unable to move or act as Father Dalton or Darius tortured Mirra or Jerrain or Hernande. The dreams didn't haunt him as often as they had immediately after escaping the Kormanley, but they still caught him at odd moments. Some of the others, particularly the students, suffered the same.

Last night's dream had been particularly bad. Most of the time he could force himself awake before the torture progressed too far. But last night, somehow, Dalton and Darius had managed to seize hold of Kara, and no matter how hard he struggled, how much he beat against the invisible wall, he could not break free. He couldn't even reach through the barrier and twist the Tapestry.

He emerged from the tree line onto a promontory of rock, his legs aching, his chest hurting from the cold. After a pause, he hiked the last few yards, brushed the few inches of snow off a large stone, and sat down so he could stare out over the expanse of forest and hills to the northeast. The plains were a sheet of white far to the east, dark storm clouds blotting out the horizon. But the mountains to the north were clear, the blue sky vibrant behind them.

Out of habit, he searched for the Three Sisters. Except there was only one now. The other two had slowly faded and died out, like all the other distortions they could see from the Hollow. Only the one remained—no longer flashing, but with a long, slow pulse that continued to slow as the months progressed. No more auroral storms plagued the plains either, although there were reports that some had been seen far north, beyond the mountains. No one had gone to verify their existence. The ley appeared . . . settled. No quakes. No new distortions. No ripples in reality. The Tapestry remained taut.

Cory let the chill wind gust over him, let the glitter of the snow in the sunlight being blown around soothe him. The silence worked away the tension in his muscles; the cold smoothed over the edges of the nightmare.

He heard someone approaching long before they reached him, footsteps crunching in the snow. He didn't need to turn to know it was Kara.

She hesitated at the edge of the forest, then shifted forward and settled beside him, her presence warm and welcome. She reached for his hand and their fingers twined together, strong and tight.

They sat and watched the horizon in silence, watched the pulse of the distortion to the north.

Until, with a tiny flash, it winked out.

Acknowledgments

This book would not have been possible without the trust and faith of my editor, Sheila Gilbert, and my agent, Joshua Bilmes. Thank them for working out the details and making it possible.

I must also thank everyone who believed in the series and bought the first two books. Without you readers, the story wouldn't have any true life. I hope this third novel lived up to your expectations.

And of course, there were tons of people behind the scenes who helped bring the book about, including everyone at DAW Books, who made the book better; my partner and family, who didn't kill me when I complained or struggled during the writing process; and my beta readers, who gave me invaluable feedback, such as "This sucks" and "That was cool." Without all of them, the book wouldn't be this good.

Now, to prepare for the next project! (I heard that groan.)